THE GREAT WEST WOOD

Philip Palmer

HELLBOOKS

PREVIOUS SF AND FANTASY BOOKS BY PHILIP PALMER

DEBATABLE SPACE (Orbit Books)

RED CLAW (Orbit Books)

VERSION 43 (Orbit Books)

HELL SHIP (Orbit Books)

ARTEMIS (Orbit Books)

MORPHO (New Con Press)

HELL ON EARTH (Hellbooks)

MURDER OF THE HEART (Hellbooks)

SOME GRATIFYING PRAISE FOR PHILIP'S SFF BOOKS

An original and propulsive mix of pagan magic and modern crime thriller.

> *M.R. Carey (author of 'The Girl With All the Gifts') after reading 'The Great West Wood'.*

'So crammed with startling ideas, scintillating prose, incredible aliens and plot twists that it evokes wonder and admiration'

> *Guardian review of 'Debatable Space'.*

One of the most funny and surprising sf novels of the last few years has to be Philip Palmer's *Version 43* (2010), in which a RoboCop-like cyborg (the titular "Version 43 ") is sent to a remote planet to investigate a crime... Bodies pile up in this mash-up of science fiction, detective and conspiracy thriller — with a lot of humor and a big-screen, hyperkinetic energy.

> *Washington Post, special feature on Version 43,*

I adore everything Philip writes, and am delighted to introduce you to his magical madness if you haven't experienced it before!

> *Lavie Tidhar. World Fantasy Award winning author, critic and editor*

Chapter 1

When night falls in Westwood it can be infuriating.

There's no rhyme nor reason to it, you see. No *pattern.* In Greenwich and in Lewisham and in Catford, and come to that, in Hampstead and in Hackney and in Shoreditch – in fact, in everywhere else in this land, and in all the other lands beyond my awareness - you can be sure that night follows day according to strict rules. Rules that are determined by the time of year, the planet's distance from the sun, and who knows what else. But not in Westwood.

The first dawn that lit up the streets of Westwood that day came early, at just past three am.

An hour or so later nightfall fell, just before the milk floats were dispatched (we still have milk floats in Westwood).

After which a second dawn lit the skies at about ten am.

And then at noon, just as Jack McBride is crossing the zebra crossing on Woody Hill, and at precisely the moment when his father George McBride cracks a spade on a human bone in the garden of the derelict house on Sylvan Way, the sky darkens and the sun sets.

The busy daytime high street is cast into darkness. Pedestrians blink in surprise. Shoppers find themselves lost in unlit shops. And on Woody Hill a teenage driver in an expensive Porsche fails to see the young lad on the middle of the zebra crossing and ploughs straight into him.

What the hell was that? the driver is thinking as his car bucks beneath him and he slams on the brakes and the vehicle screeches to a halt.

But of course he knows what he has done. He just hasn't realised it yet.

It is an appalling collision. The car is travelling at about forty mph when it hits Jack and I see Jack's body flying through the air and then I feel Jack's body crash down hard on to the tarmac and then it bounces and rolls and tumbles onto the pavement before it comes to a juddering halt.

'Jesus fucking Christ,' says George McBride at that precise same moment, as he throws down his spade and fumbles for the torch setting on his mobile phone.

Meanwhile, on Woody Hill, the young driver of the crumpled performance car that has stalled on the zig zag markings beyond the zebra crossing attempts to make his escape by means of a reverse doughnut manoeuvre.

No fucking way! I'm getting out of here! the driver thinks.

But he badly misjudges the manoeuvre and the car shoots backwards and goes off the road and on to the pavement. The car's rear end crashes into the shopfront of Grady's café, shattering the glass and startling the three customers inside, but barely perturbing Mrs Grady herself. With her usual presence of mind she turns the lights on and seizes a broom and sweeps up the broken glass and takes a fresh order of stewed tea with sugar. And she ignores the screaming of the young Asian boy, the driver I mean, Shakil is his name, who is now trapped inside his car behind a large inflated balloon known as an airbag that appeared from nowhere when he crashed for the second time.

Screams.

Pain.

Panic.

Fear!

An owl hoots. It is far away. In the park, perhaps? Yes. In the park. It is perched upon a bough of the old turkey oak next to Wilberforce.

I look closely at the owl as it perches there upon the branch, its big eyes staring.

Then I see a fox standing still as a statue next to the statue of William Wilberforce, its russet fur lit by the light of the full moon. Stars twinkle above this tranquil scene. It is a moment of calm in this green oasis where huge trees cast dark shadows on the night sky.

I savour it for a while then I leave the park.

I return to Woody Hill.

Shakil is unharmed, so far as I can tell, not bleeding at any rate. And I would guess he has suffered no significant injuries. But Jack is very badly hurt and unconscious and has been presumed dead by the several passers-by who are standing near his prone body. Though in fact he is not dead, his heart is slowly beating, so yes, he is alive. He is sprawled like a discarded sack on the pavement next to the hardware store. His head is almost nudging a bright red plastic bucket. His smashed torso is close to the clear plastic boxes that were neatly stacked that morning, as they are every morning, by Mr Amit Mohammed, the owner of the shop.

The streetlamps have switched themselves on by now. The looming shadows of onlookers are cast upon a scene of devastation. Jack's bloodied body is motionless. He breathes in short ugly bursts. In the sky above, the stars flicker like fireflies on a summer's night.

Jack is a good lad, I've known him since he was a toddler; no, tell a lie, since he was a baby. He is athletic, cheerful, he used to climb my trees when he was a lad, and he keeps his wits about him.

A few streets away his father George McBride is using his phone's torch to look at the object that shattered his spade so effortlessly.

It looks like a human body. Because it *is* a human body. Not a skeleton, more like a husk. A pupa. But this is no butterfly, it is a dead man, with skin dry-cured over the centuries to become a material with the texture of leather and the colour of dried shit. Not just any dead man, a murdered man. A murderer who was himself murdered long ago by the relatives and friends of some of those he had slain and raped and tortured.

I remember this man's death well. It unfolds before me as if it happened yesterday.

He was pursued by his enemies all the way from the West Country to his homeland, here, in Westwood. He hid for months in the wild forest then he was found and he was attacked and then chased. Chased through these wild woods with a spear in one side, his strength ebbing with every stride. Then when he faltered and fell, he was beaten and kicked and stabbed by all eleven of his assailants, five of them women, one a child of six. Stabbed until his body dripped with blood and the knives and swords had ripped his flesh apart. After which he was emasculated, with not only his cock but also his balls hewn off by a sharp dagger's blade. And after *that* a stone knife was embedded in each eye socket. He was a bad man, there is no doubt of that.

And now his long-dead corpse has been dug up again.

Hilary McBride is teaching Year 2. She's not meant to be teaching, she's just the teaching assistant. But Mr Grange is not well and the supply teacher hasn't turned up. One of the girls is taking Hilary's pulse as part of a doctor and nurse role play and Hilary is pretending to be very ill, whilst simultaneously teaching a maths lesson. The little girl, whose name is Sonibel, laughs. So Hilary laughs too. Hilary has no idea her only son is lying in a pool of blood just five thousand and six paces up the hill.

In Sylvan Way, George McBride is arguing the toss with his mate, Will, about the body that they have found. George is a paunchy middle-aged white man with less hair on his head than he would like, though he is still in pretty good shape for a man of his age.

'Let's just, you know,' George says to Will.

Will shuffles his feet. He looks again at the withered corpse they have excavated, and the sight makes him queasy.

'Let's just what?' Will says.

'Come on, Will, don't be daft, you know.' George is smiling, and he is hopping from foot to foot, as if he's your best mate coaxing you to go nicking sweets from the local shop.

George is a dandy by builder standards. Beneath his jacket he is wearing his trademark silver waistcoat with diamond pattern insets and he has dark moleskin trousers and wears a flat cap, which these days is fashionable again. He has an earring in one of his ears, the wrong ear according to his son Jack, it's the choice of ear that is code for saying he's gay, which he's not. But George was drunk when he had it done and he likes having this one touch of bling upon his flesh.

He is a good looking and sexually attractive man, so most women feel, though few men seem to understand how any woman could think that.

The two blokes are squaring off now.

'No I don't know. Fucking spit it out, George,' says Will.

There is a great deal of ritual male behaviour occurring now. Swaggering, swaying, standing too close to the other person in a macho and provoking fashion.

'Come on, Will! Don't be such an old woman. There might be valuables, like. To be found here,' says George, persuasively. 'Gold coins and the like. Let's take a shufti, shall we?'

'It's a fucking corpse, George! We have to phone the fucking cops. End of,' Will says.

'No need to take that fucking attitude,' says George.

'Is there fucking not?' Will says.

'No there fucking is not!' George says.

'I'm not a grave robber, George. I'm calling this in,' Will says.

George shades his smile to be a crafty smile.

'It's not grave robbing, my old mucker,' George says. 'It's treasure trove. Besides. Get real. You call the fucking Old Bill, and they see what's here, they'll tell you to fuck the fuck off. I mean, this is ancient news all this, ain't it?'

He has a point. The dead body is clearly not recent. This is never going to be an active murder investigation. The corpse is rock solid, shit-brown in colour as I have mentioned. And it has been mummified by centuries underground when it was immured in a peat bog that no longer exists, then buried under clay and concrete, then brought to the surface by a freak combination of events including a minor earthquake last year that would have brought this house down, if I hadn't been there to steady the soil.

Up the hill, Jack is conscious but immobile and deeply confused.

His thoughts are a jumble, a blur of emotions mixed with random memories flashing through his mind, as often happens at the moment of death or near-death. In the mess of random images I can see a memory of Shona. His sweet chubby older sister, smiling at something, maybe at him. Why is he thinking of Shona? He hates his sister Shona, I know this for a fact.

Jack is loaded into an ambulance on a stretcher. The paramedics have pumped him full of pain killers. He realises by now that he has been in an accident but he doesn't know his own name. His skull has been cracked and his spine has been splintered in three places but he doesn't know any of that yet. He is not in any pain though, which puzzles me. Perhaps he has suffered brain damage; or maybe it's just the shock?

On the pavement in Woody Hill the driver, Shakil, is blowing into a breathalyser bag. He is struggling to fill the bag.

I'm fucked, he thinks.

He looks appealingly at the copper who handed him the breathalyser. 'I can't do it, I ain't got no puff,' he says.

'Breathe into the bag, sir,' the copper says.

'I'm sorry. I'm sorry.' And Shakil sniffles and weeps. He hands shake. He looks like an emotionally devastated young man.

However I can tell that he is putting up a front for the sake of the onlookers. He is *pretending* to be scared and guilty and upset. In reality, he's just another callow young man who likes to drive too fast.

The ambulance pulls out into the road. Shakil watches it go. The copper who is breathalysing him checks the results. They are negative.

The cop's name is Sheila. Thick set, an amateur athlete, specialising in the long jump and discus, good at her job. I've met Sheila before, she's a local.

Sheila has already taken statements from witnesses and has this marked down as a failed hit and run. In other words, the driver *would* have driven off had he not bungled the reverse turn. Hard to prove that in court, though, she guesses. But it gives her good reason to dislike this selfish piece of shit she is dealing with.

'I'm a Muslim you, see, I would never drink and drive,' Shakil says to Sheila earnestly.

In the back of the ambulance, Jack McBride is starting to feel pain. Pain in his legs, and inside his head, and in his arms, and in his broken back. I assume it will soon get much worse for him.

I remember the day Jack was born.

It was a home birth, with two midwives present but no doctor. And Grandpa Maybe was there too, ah yes. A cheerful grinning presence, chatting to the midwives as if they were his own kin, and one of them had been born in Jamaica so perhaps she was. George had been sent out to the pub, taking little Shona with him, to calm his nerves, and to keep her safe.

I remember that Hilary's naked black skin was damp from the birthing pool which George had filled earlier that day. Two solid hours with a hosepipe it took to fill the bloody thing and all the while George was making sarcy little comments. Comments like, 'Never had shit like this in my day,' and 'What if it's a bloody seal?' So no wonder Hilary got fed up of him and told him to get out.

The fact of it is, George is a loudmouth and a lout, and his friends all say she's worth ten of him. And I'm sure that's true.

Even so he's good value, as far as I'm concerned. He's a rascal, a rogue, always up to no good. And I find that entertaining.

When George went to the pub Grandpa Maybe stayed behind and he helped with the birth and he was the first person to cradle the baby, baby Jack. Then he handed the tiny creature to Hilary who was exhausted by this point but still full of joy.

That was the day of Jack's birth.

This could very well be the day of Jack's death.

Hilary is still at school when she gets a call from the hospital: 'Mrs McBride I'm afraid we have some bad news,' a stranger's voice says.

A few minutes later George gets a call from Hilary. 'George, oh George. I can't even speak. I can't – can't – can't -'

A few minutes after that, Grandpa Maybe also gets a call from Hilary.

'Grandpa, please, pray for my boy.'

'Why should I pray for your boy, Hilary?'

Grandpa Maybe is a small man, with small hands, and very dark skin even for a black man. And he's always laughing at jokes no one has made, as if he has an invisible friend who is wisecracking to him.

His wife, Shona Mirabelle, Hilary's grandma, died many years ago. She was, everyone agrees, a charismatic and a generous woman; and Grandpa Maybe is one of the four men who might, just possibly might, have been the father of her child, baby Malcolm. The other three skedaddled when the news broke. And it was Grandpa Maybe who stepped up and raised the baby, Hilary's dad, as his own child. A single father, in the days when that was unusual.

He worked at Brixton market, did Grandpa Maybe, on the fruit and veg stall, and his real name is Bobby Fagon. He writes poetry and when Jack and Shona were small and he was babysitting them, he used to orate his poems out loud. Richly phrased lyrics of lamentation and of joy. I liked hearing those poems and when he was old enough to know it was rebellious, Jack used to love to talk in thick Jamaican slang with his old great-granddad. Hilary used to disapprove of this, but Jack loved being a rude bwoy, even though he was pale skinned and blond-haired; and most people in who met him in his first term at Big School didn't even realise he was, as they call it now, BAME.

Today Grandpa Maybe, who doesn't look a day older than he did when Jack was born, is writing a poem in his head when the phone rings and Hilary tells him that his blond-haired passes-for-white great-grandson has been in a terrible accident and is in the hospital.

He wastes few words: 'Which hospital? And what floor is the ward on?'

Then he puts on his best suit, instead of the rags he writes poetry in, and he gets a bus to the hospital, even though the wait at the bus stop is bound to be interminable. But he is not of the generation to order an Uber on his mobile phone, even if he had a mobile phone. He's a very old man now, is Grandpa Maybe; he'll be ninety next year, or maybe ninety-one, he hasn't kept very good track.

When he gets to the intensive care ward George and Hilary and Shona are in the waiting area and Hilary is all wept-out. Her skin is greyed with sorrow. George is tense and restless and he doesn't know what to say. He has changed out of his work clothes but he is still wearing a dapper dark jacket and a silver patterned waistcoat; smarter versions of the same fashion template.

Shona – that's Jack's sister, who has the same first name as her long deceased great-grandmother - is red-faced and keeps bursting into tears loudly, and improbably, as if she can't think of any other way to indicate grief.

'The boy, is he still alive?' Grandpa Maybe asks.

'Of course he's still alive!' Hilary shouts at him.

'Hush hush, sorry sorry,' murmurs Grandpa Maybe. He doesn't like being in hospitals, he thinks hospitals are places where you go to die, and he doesn't want to die.

Three rooms away, in an intensive care ward bed, after a short but agonising illness, Tom Finnegan, a legend in his lifetime in Westwood circles, slips out of this world.

A few moments later, and he is certified dead by one of the doctors.

At one time I had been fascinated by the adventures of this man. He was bold, and loquacious, he was an artist and a gifted travel writer, he had travelled the world in one-man sailing ships and on reckless safaris, and his tales of foreign lands had often enthralled me. So I feel I have to take a moment to observe and honour his death.

But then I get bored. For today my attention is elsewhere.
Here.
With the McBrides.

'I'll get some teas,' Grandpa Maybe tells them. 'Who wants teas? It's always good to have teas, at a time like this.' He's nearly fifty years older than the youngest of them and he has a walking stick and rheumy eyes. But no one blinks at the notion of sending him on such a mission in a hospital unfamiliar to him.

'There's a Costa's by reception,' George suggests, cheerfully.

'Teas,' says Grandpa Maybe. 'Teas will help.' But he knows they won't.

The hours pass. Hilary is holding in her pain. She has a big heart and it has been broken badly and she cannot speak for fear that her beloved boy will die and she will be left with just her rogue of a husband and her daughter, who she loves much less than she loves her son.

George is pacing up and down. He is restless; he doesn't know what to say, or what to do, and so he paces up and down, going nowhere.

Grandpa Maybe sits motionless, with no expression on his face. He can do that for long periods but it doesn't mean he is lacking in emotion. He is a man who does not easily break or yield but today he is close to despair.

Beside him is Jack's sister Shona and, surprisingly, even though her brother may be close to death, Shona is full of spite.

Not fair, Shona is thinking.

And she has a point. It really isn't fair.

For once upon a time Shona was the apple of her mother's eye. People who saw her as a baby always said things like: 'Bless her!' and 'What a darling!' With her pretty face and her light brown skin and the fact she was always gurgling with glee, she was the perfect infant.

Until Jack came along.

It was an easy birth, for Shona at least, sitting in the pub with her dad while the midwives did their work in the dining room at 44 Westwood Street. She still remembers those hours fondly. It was fun! His dad telling her dirty jokes. Letting her sip beer off his finger. The two of them playing on the slot machines. Then the good news came via his mobile phone, and he passed it on to her with a grin: 'Kiddo, you've got a baby brother, shall I buy more crisps?' And that evening Shona was introduced by her weary beaming mother to her baby brother, who to Shona's astonishment had freakishly white skin, as if Hilary had gone on a mad rampage and abducted some other mother's child.

He must be a changeling, Shona used to say to herself in later years. Her difficult and bratty teenage years. *That's the only explanation for it. He's a cuckoo. An interloper. He doesn't belong in our family. The real Jack must have been stolen by faeries!*

All through her teens Shona had hated Jack with every atom of her being. He was arrogant, he was rude, he mocked her weight, he taunted her for not having a boyfriend. And he even mocked her by just *being himself*. By being slim and cool and sexy when she wasn't any of those things.

All the girls loved him; none of the boys loved *her*.

And even back then, on the day of Jack's birth, at the tender age of five, Shona felt a burning resentment towards Jack. Because she knew she was no longer the favourite child; Jack was.

'You are the most beautiful baby in the world,' Hilary kept murmuring to Jack on his first day in the McBride house. And he had beamed at her smugly with his pudgy little baby face, and Shona had glowered.

All the aunties and uncles adored him, of course. He was funny, he was good looking, and when he was a bit older, he turned out to be a brilliant footballer. Good enough, many people said, to be a professional.

Not fair!

And then there was the Errol thing.

Shona is remembering the Errol thing now; I remember it too.

Errol had been the love of Shona's life from when she was nearly eighteen until she was twenty-one. She used to make out with him in his parents' house when his parents were out at the pub, and she didn't tell anyone about him for ages. Then one day she brought him home for dinner with her family and by the end of the night, Errol had fallen in love with her brother Jack.

She could see it happening. The teenage Jack was a remarkably beautiful boy. He had perfect skin, piercing blue eyes, a smiling face, and his football training gave him a V shaped torso and powerful arms.

And Errol, who was normally confident and full of attitude, that night became shy and awkward as Jack told stories of footballing prowess and his triumphs on the athletic track. Whenever Jack told a joke Errol laughed for ages. When Jack shrugged, and rolled his neck, Errol stared at Jack's big muscular arms and Jack's lovely soft bare throat and sighed.

Jack was only sixteen at the time, and Errol was in his twenties. So it was pervy, it was paedo, it was *vile*. Or at least, that's what Shona thought.

Errol wasn't even gay. He was a bloke's bloke, he had the hots for Beyoncé and Scarlet Johansson, she was going out with him for crying out loud! There was no way he was *gay*.

But somehow Jack had got to him. Just looking at that gorgeous, graceful boy gave Errol a visible erotic thrill. Like an electric charge reaching through space. Lighting up her lover's eyes, making him smile at her own brother the way he never smiled at her.

A few months later Errol ditched her for some slag from Clapham, but the pain of her boyfriend's unacted upon betrayal with her brother was the one thing that Shona could never forgive.

Her actual boyfriend had fancied her own fucking brother!

Jack was lazy too. That was another thing Shona hated about him.

He never did any homework; he was always at football practice, or hanging out with his mates. But somehow he got through GCSEs and now he was doing his A Levels; and he had managed to get an offer a place at Durham University to study history. He wasn't, it became clear, quite good enough to be a professional football player; that was *something*, Shona thought. But he did turn out to be clever enough to go to University.

And that was the deepest cut of all.

Shona you see had always thought *she* was the clever one. The swotty one. But somehow or other, exams never worked for her. She froze. Facts became strangers. So she left school with three E's and now she works the till at Budgen's five days a week. And her younger brother, the sporty one, the not at all clever one, had his future all mapped out.

Not fair.

Not fucking fair!

Now, after this terrible accident, the entire family are devastated by grief. But all poor Shona can think is:

What would have happened if that was me, in that hospital bed? Crippled and possibly dying?

Would anyone cry like this for me?

Next to her, Hilary is remembering the day she cradled her bloodied newborn baby boy in her arms. And how he bawled and she wept and she'd never been happier.

George is remembering Jack scoring that goal. *That* goal. The under-11's cup final, in Beckenham. The run down the line, beating two defenders with dazzling footwork, kicking the ball and bending it beautifully in mid-air, and in it goes! George remembers thinking that it was like watching David Beckham as a nipper. He remembers thinking, that's my boy! Such pride. So much pride.

Grandpa Maybe is remembering something else. It is a much older memory. He is remembering holding another man's baby in his arms and calling it his own.

But Shona – Shona just sits there like a stone. Festering with dark thoughts. Her fat arse is crammed into a narrow plastic chair in the hospital waiting area. She is consumed by guilt and self-loathing at not feeling the grief she feels she ought to be feeling. But no one, of course, notices.

Except for me and Grandpa Maybe.

And finally, the old man stirs into action. He stirs slowly, in truth; very slowly indeed. But even so, he does notice, and he does do what needs to be done:

'You need to let all that pain out, girl,' Grandpa Maybe tells Shona, in his thick Jamaican accent. And he puts his skinny arm around her. And he cradles her up against him, so that her head is nestling up against his face, just as he did when Shona was small.

And that opens up something inside her, and Shona gulps and chokes and then she weeps. For real this time.

And – to my astonishment - Shona finds herself filled to bursting with love for the brother she had always thought she'd hated.

Chapter 2

The urban village of Westwood sits upon a hill looking out across London. You can see the Shard from here. You can see St Paul's Cathedral, Tower 42, the Ferris Wheel, the Cheesegrater and the Walkie Talkie all silhouetted on the skyline and at night their red warning lights flash like burglar alarms.

Several days have passed since Jack's accident. The boarded-up shop window of Mrs Grady's café is the only remaining evidence of the terrible collision. The blood stains on the pavement have been steam-cleaned away; the broken glass from the smashed café window has been swept up and removed. There is talk of recalibrating the street lights so they are on all the time, 24/7 is the phrase that keeps being uttered, to avoid a similar catastrophe in future.

There are some strangers on the High Street today. Tourists we call them here, by which we mean, Londoners who do not know what Westwood is like. They are attracted by the gastro pubs, the many restaurants, the expensive shops selling odd bits and pieces that no one actually needs, but which always look lovely in the window. There are also plenty of locals around, including Clive from Crevasse Avenue, jogging briskly in tight shorts and a lycra top while holding his young daughter's hand. He is running with her to the bus stop where she can get her bus to school; strangely her slow measured pace is easily up to the challenge of matching his long loping strides.

And that's Carlos, a shabbily dressed London-born Latino who always has a parrot upon his shoulder; Marjory is the name of the parrot. It has a yellow breast, blue wings, a green crown and a white face, and it is a beautiful creature. Carlos is not a homeless man, though his clothes are ragged and his hygiene is poor. No, Carlos lives in a hostel which is about a quarter of a mile down Steep Hill, just beyond the twin precipices. His hostel is technically outside the bounds of Westwood but he counts as a local because he grew up here. And he saw and trapped and then trained the parrot after a dimensional portal opened up in the basement of the Saxon Arms and briefly allowed an influx of tropical animals of various kinds including anacondas, hyenas, cheetahs and a white Bengal tiger.

Meanwhile Pranavash Mohammed, that's the son of old Mr Mohammed, is helping a customer choose among an assortment of garden rakes stacked in the array of household items that is carefully arranged outside their shop.

'Try this one,' says Pranavash.

'Will it be strong enough? Our last one broke when I, ah, hit a wall with it,' the customer says.

'Trust me. This is the one for you,' says Pranavash.

In Fairyhill Road, just down from Woody Hill, a young female couple are setting out the tables for their new business venture, a teashop. You can't actually see it from Woody Hill but they have put a big sign up on the pavement there saying CREAM TEAS AND CAKES HERE!!! with an arrow pointing downwards. The greasy spoon next to the sign is busy as always. The pub two doors down on Woody Hill is rammed. But the teashop itself is empty. Camilla and Alice are the only ones there and they are the owners.

'Give it time,' says Alice and Camilla shrugs bitterly.

My guess is that these two ploughed their redundancy cheques from their previous proper jobs into this new venture. But they are new to Westwood so I can't discern what they are thinking. All I know is that Camilla is the tall posh one, with a fondness for scarves and bangles. And Alice is the shorter posh one, who also has a fondness for scarves and bangles.

A bell pings. Two boys walk in, still wearing school uniform. They look around at the décor, which is all very artfully designed, with empty wooden crates instead of tables, a Welsh dresser stacked with antique tea cups and cracked plates, and floral wallpaper that evokes Kew Gardens after a few rainy months. And the two boys stare at the two women wearing billowing skirts and hairbands and bangles and they scarper.

'Give it time,' says Alice.

'You already said that,' says Camilla.

The cakes do look nice but I feel discouraged by the funereal atmosphere and I leave the shop. I drift back up on to Woody Hill. Someone has dropped half a KFC chicken on the pavement and dogs on leads are being yanked away from it. A cyclist has fallen off his bike but he's not badly hurt and I don't know him and he doesn't interest me.

And look, that's a swallow up there! fast as the blink of an eye! And I follow it, flitting swiftly with it along the length of Woody Hill. I glide behind it as it crosses the Boulevard and flaps its way into the Memorial Gardens and then beyond, until it finds a perch on one of the two birch trees flanking the entrance to the park. And there I leave it.

I return my attention to the Boulevard, where the bus depot is located. I like watching buses. They form patterns when viewed from above. Battalions of red buses flow out on to the broad carriageway as if they are dancing. And I know what dancing is, so it's a good comparison.

A host of crows are perching in some of the trees. These are solitary creatures, by and large; except in Westwood, where they throng together cheerfully. These ones are hopping their way up and down the old Victorian steps in the Old Park. Another flock has gathered in clusters on branches on the trees along the terrace.

There are very many trees here, in Westwood. They stretch all the way along the Boulevard as far as the roundabout, like giant soldiers. Those trees are London planes mostly, tall and proud. And in the area behind the bus depot and to the east of the Memorial Gardens, the real parkland begins. Old Park and New Park and a little patch of ground between them that has never had a name. Here you can find ancient oaks and younger turkey oaks and beech trees and maples and poplars and silver birches and sycamores and firs and crab apples and limes and Turkish hazels and of course more of those ubiquitous London planes, which can survive even the smoggiest air by shedding their bark so the soot falls off them like loose skin.

The soot falls off. Like loose skin.

Every year this happens.

The Old Park is the richest haven for trees. For mile upon mile there is nothing but tree life and grass and lakes. It is arguably the biggest and the wildest park in all of London.

Once all Westwood was like this. In those days, in the very distant past, Westwood wasn't just a small London suburb. It was the heart of the greatest forest in Europe, greater even than the forests of Bavaria and Siberia, in a period when there was no channel separating England from the Continent. The Great West Wood some called it, in languages now forgotten. And it still survives. You just can't see it. You can only see the patches of the former West Wood that are scattered all around; the parks and the nature reserves and the wooded areas fenced in and celebrated for their biodiversity. But you can't see the ancient roots that lie deep below the soil, and have never withered and died.

And not far from the Boulevard, looming above a recent development of grey brick bungalows, is another clump of woodland. You can see it from the street if you look up when you exit the Saxon Arms. It is a patch of trees upon an old burial mound, and inside the mound are to be found the dry skeletons of one of the greatest armies that ever lost a battle to the Vikings.

And a long time before *that,* other warriors fought in these woods to create a pagan dynasty that was supposed to last a thousand years and which lasted, in fact, no more than a few hundred years. These were barbarians and their blood and the blood of their victims fed and nourished the soil when they fell.

The screams!

The pain!

The blood!

It was all so long ago, yet I can remember it as if it happened a few minutes ago.

And at that time there lived a murderer and an outlaw who became a king. A man who evaded capture for nearly twenty years after slaying every single member of the rival tribe whose patriarch had offended him.

He killed them all.

Hundreds of deaths. Hundreds.

So much blood.

When his enemies finally caught him they slew him, then castrated him, then they buried two knives in his eye sockets to ensure he stumbled blindly through his afterlife.

But he did not journey into the afterlife. Instead, he lay in ancient peat unseeingly. Until many thousands of years later a magical Westwood third dawn shone upon him and made his body quick again.

This man, whose name I cannot spell, and which you could not in any case say, has now escaped from the room in which he was trapped – the mortuary as it is called. He got up in the middle of the night, clad himself in a white gown, and calmly wandered out into the streets of Croydon.

Following his instincts, his memories of a world that long ago preceded the world he now finds himself in, the bog creature walked through the night-time streets until he found the plot of land where he had been murdered. Then it was a dark forest glade where light shimmered slowly down through a dense tree canopy. Where birds chittered unseen among the branches. Where foxes and badgers fought each night leaving fur and blood on the leaves to be illumined by the dawn light like dew. A time when all the squirrels were red and they flew from branch to branch. But all that has gone. Now an Iceland supermarket stands upon that spot, with two gastro pubs each side.

And as he stood there he remembered – and I remembered too - how he had run through dense woods with a spear in his side and a pack of angry killers at his heels, until finally he faltered and fell, and was caught.

Roars of rage from his enemies!

Boots kicking his body!

Fists punching his face!

A knife pierces his side!

A hammer strikes his skull!

And still he fights on!

He remembered how it all ended that day, after his pursuers had caught up with him, and after he had killed five of them with his bare hands. He remembered how his strength ebbed, and his spirit sank, when he knew he had finally lost. And finally a sword was plunged into his heart and his world turned to blackness.

And after that moment, the moment when he died, his memories blur like a dream that never ends.

Like a dream.

A dream that never ends.

The dream of a body preserved in a dry ocean of peat.

Until that third dawn's light shone upon his bones and the Bogman awoke.

And now he is back in Westwood, in the land where he once slew an entire tribe. In the land where once he had once been a handsome warrior with the strength of ten ordinary warriors. Now he is a naked shit-brown creature with the physique of a rotted corpse. And yet, despite his wasted body, he is more dangerous than ever.

And so that night, after leaving the site of the Iceland supermarket, the Bogman ran through nighttime Westwood. He ran along the Boulevard, he ran past the bus depot, past the petrol station, past the side entrance to Old Park, until he found a hiding place. A wilderness area known as Horniman Woods.

And there he hides, gathering his strength and learning about his new world.

This wood is another visible remnant of the Great West Wood. At one time it was the site of a branch railway. But then the railway line was abandoned and now it has been turned into a nature reserve and a site for strange pieces of art carved out of tree stumps.

I am enjoying myself, I decide. And that's because of the Bogman. Terrible though he is, wicked though he is, his rebirth is an extraordinary event; and there are few enough of those in my life these days.

The Bogman continues his journey through the woods; barefoot and naked now, having discarded his white gown.

He is exhilarated by the natural world around him, the taste and the tang of it.

He smells tree bark and it makes his spirit sing.

The soles of his feet are pricked by brambles and it excites him.

The scent of a distant bonfire is a source of delight for him.

I feel his joy.

I share his joy.

Ah, yes.

But then I am distracted by the scent of that distant bonfire; and by the crackle of burning twigs,

It is a good bonfire, well made. The flames are high, and the people who have built the bonfire are cooking potatoes upon it. I love that smell.

Now I am back.

I am drifting over this stretch of land which locals call Horniman Woods. I locate the Bogman again. He is running fast upon the old railway sleepers, his feet bouncing off the rotting wood. Not breathing yet breathless with excitement.

There are dog walkers nearby, in this woodland area. If he doesn't act soon, I realise, he will be seen.

And if he is seen, the Bogman will provoke a panic. Because his face and body are a truly awful sight. Withered brown skin and a featureless face and those staring unlidded eyes. The hands that flap as he runs have skeleton fingers. His body is marked with scars from decay and from the stabbings he received when he was slain. His groin is a hollow mess, where his genitals were hacked off. He has no teeth, so when he opens his mouth a black maw threatens.

A dog whines and the Bogman takes cover in instants. Shielded against a tree, his body blending with the colour of the bark to render him barely visible. He sniffs and he strains his ears. And finally a figure appears. An old man. Don is his name. He has a dog called Cecil, a Springer Spaniel, a lively breed, though Cecil is now very old and not at all lively. Don lives in the same street as the McBrides, I see him often walking his dog up and down the road. He is retired and has no family since his wife died, and his dog is his only solace. He wears a muddy jacket and has a flat cap upon his head, to conceal his bare scalp. 'Here boy,' he is saying, for the dog is off the leash and is relishing the outdoor world.

The Bogman growls and the dog hears it and flattens its ears and whimpers. It scurries onwards with its master.

The Bogman is safe. Or so he thinks. I can feel his relief; it is like the rain that breaks a muggy day.

He is intrigued. I can sense that. His observation of the man and his dog have given him new information about the world. And so he continues through the woods, at a walking pace now, and he sees a group of children playing on a tree branch. He studies them at length. Their parents come along and he watches them too A man wearing a thick overcoat and robust boots and a huge belly from eating and drinking too much. A woman with long grey hair, lean and with an upright posture, wearing fawn-coloured gloves on her hands. The Bogman looks and stares and wonders.

There is a pond in Horniman's Wood and that is where the Bogman goes. Does he remember the location of the water from all those millennia ago or can he simply sense it? I do not know.

When he reaches the pond the Bogman goes down on his knees and studies his own reflection in the flickering waters. He raises his hands and arms and he is clearly shocked at how wasted he is, how few muscles he has left.

He peers down at his wretched crotch and I can sense that causes him distress.

He does not speak but I guess that he is working out what has happened to him. Perhaps he is also wondering How? and Why? How did he come to be resurrected, and why would the fates have favoured him in such a way?

He does not know and nor do I.

He climbs a tree. I did not expect that. With fingers as hard as talons he clambers up the trunk of a turkey oak and flips his way up through the branches until he reaches the crown. Then he stands up on a branch on his two spindly legs and stares out at the view of London. His gaze is long and steady and his face is incapable of expression but it is reasonable to assume he is startled at what he sees. For there was no such place as London when he was alive. There were no huge buildings made of glass. No skyscrapers. No aeroplanes leaving contrails of white cloud in the air. No churches, no roads, no cars, just endless woodland and farmland and consecrated battle land.

His bark-like cheeks are damp. For a moment, I wonder if he is weeping; but then I realise it is raining, though only very slightly.

He clambers back down a little. He has heard something. Another dog walker is in the undergrowth. The Bogman follows the noise from the lower levels of the canopy, leaping from branch to branch adeptly. Eventually he sees a dog pissing on a tree. A sycamore tree. This tree has been pissed on many times, by many dogs, for nearly a century. The dog is a large one, jet black, a Rottweiler, and it is in magnificent condition. The Bogman inspects it from atop a branch where he crouches.

But the dog can sense him. It starts to bark. The Bogman stares curiously at it.

Then the dog attacks his tree, trying to clamber up it. No coward this beast; a fighter. The dog has no chance of climbing the tree of course but the Bogman is unhappy.

The greatest warrior of his age: bested by a dog. Oh I am cherishing this!

The Bogman starts to clamber up higher. But the brittle branch below him cracks and his skinny body tumbles to the ground.

He hits the ground like straw upon hay. But in a moment he is on his feet again. His eyes staring widely, his scrawny body offering no threat to this huge beast. And finally, the Bogman speaks. His words are strange, guttural, alien to me until long forgotten memories come drifting back and I remember that I know this language.

'Creature thou art mine,' says the Bogman and the dog clearly doesn't like that because in an instant it leaps through the air and tries to grab the Bogman's arm in its jaws.

The Bogman moves swiftly and the dog crashes to the ground beside him. The Bogman is angry. He waves his fist at the beast.

The dog leaps again and this time it succeeds in getting a firm grip with its teeth on the Bogman's wrist and its shakes its head angrily then it rips off his arm. It just splinters away, like a dry twig wrenched off a dead tree. The dog chews the Bogman's arm as easily as if it were tree bark; in other words not easily at all. So the creature spits it out and returns to its attack on the Bogman.

The Bogman is bereft, with only a stump where his arm used to be, shocked at his own fragility. But when the dog snarls a second time the Bogman moves.

The Bogman's resurrection has, I realise at that moment, done strange things to his body. There is strength in that one remaining puny arm. There is power in those skinny legs. And so he leaps, he grabs the dog with his remaining hand, he breaks its neck with a single twist then he smashes the beast against a tree until the head is a bloody pulp.

Then the Bogman picks up what is left of his other arm, which is not much. And he mourns for it.

We both hear an angry shout: 'Come here you stupid dog!'

Moments later the owner of the dog comes stumbling through the treeline. His face falls and his body sags as he witnesses the endgame of the Bogman's vicious assault – the broken bloodied corpse of his beloved dog, lying on the ground. The dog's owner is a grey-bearded man in a long black overcoat that has seen better days, and he is wearing a hat, and he is tall. And when he sees the Bogman standing there, drenched in blood, unrepentantly triumphant in victory, the man is enraged.

'You bastard,' the man shouts. 'You bloody bastard!'

The Bogman stares and does not move.

'What kind of monster are you! To do a thing like this!' the man shouts.

The Bogman stares and does not move.

The man takes a closer look at his dog's murderer. Naked, one armed, skinny; like a creature shaped from dry clay.

'You fucking freak!' says the man.

The Bogman stares and does not move.

The man has a walking stick in one hand, and a mobile phone in the other. He dials with one hand, all the while brandishing the stick as if it were a sword. The Bogman continues to stare calmly at him, not knowing of the dangers that can be created by a message sent by mobile phone. Armed cops, hunting dogs – all these could be set upon him if the man's message is not interrupted.

Then the call is put through: 'Police!' shouts the man into his phone. 'Tell them, there's a - '

The Bogman moves forward and throws a single punch at the man's head which connects softly, but even so, the man dies. It is remarkably swift.

Now that man and dog are dead, the Bogman strips off the dead man's clothes and sets them to one side, and then he digs a hole with his five fingers and buries both of the bodies.

Then he gets dressed. Long black coat, shirt and jumper and corduroy trousers. walking boots and the hat. Not a flat cap, a flamboyant hat with a brim. This dog walker was something of a dandy, it seems. A theatrical type, perhaps.

When the Bogman is fully clad he looks almost human. When he puts on the Fedora hat you can no longer see so clearly how withered and terrible his face is. The clothes hang loosely on him, but they do hang on him. The shoes are too big but from the outside, they look like shoes with flesh and blood feet inside, not mummified lumps of dead meat.

The Bogman is learning fast. To survive in this world of people, you have to look like people.

Then the Bogman tips back his head and howls like a wolf, his homage to the ancient pagan god of the woods.

I am the ancient pagan god of the woods; and I receive his homage with joy!

Chapter 3

I never sleep; but sometimes I lose interest in things. And the tiny events that happen each day in Westwood start to seem tiresome. And in the blink of an eye, assuming I had an eye, weeks or even months can pass.

And that's what happened after my encounter with the Bogman in the woods, when he howled like a wolf to express his fealty to the ancient god of the Great West Wood.

For a few moments I felt proud. Exhilarated. Exultant!

Then I became sad.

For it has been a long time since I was worshipped by any human. It has been a long time since any human even acknowledged my existence. And the having of that moment reminded me of how lonely I have become.

And so I disengaged from this world. I allowed my attention to lapse. And for a while I was nothing and nowhere.

Now I am back.

Quite a lot has happened in Westwood since I was last aware of it. Jack McBride has been discharged from hospital. He is wearing a metal contraption on his legs and a brace around his neck. He walks with a pair of crutches, but sometimes uses a wheelchair. My assessment is that he is recovering well.

The Bogman is still hiding in the woods. It took me a while to find him again, after my period of inattention, but find him I did. He kills squirrels for sport, since he does not need to eat them. Though he also does that, out of habit I assume, and the mess he leaves behind when his food spills out of the hole in his stomach is disgusting; albeit rich in nutrients for my soil.

A newcomer is moving into 42 Westwood Street, next door to the McBrides. This is a small quaint house with a beautifully maintained front garden; the back garden is even more impressive. The previous owner, Mary Runnymede, was a librarian and a keen gardener and although she has retired to a place by the sea in Ramsgate she still returns to Westwood every other weekend to prune the garden and throw away the weeds. She has retained a key to the back gate and does all her work at night. So if you didn't know better, you might think this house has a magic garden which prunes and weeds itself.

Once the removal men have gone the new owner of the house, a young man called St John Featherstone, takes stock of his new surroundings. He has bought furniture that is completely out of keeping with the rural feel of this lovely old cottage. A glass dining table. Art deco vases. A giant Chinese vase to keep large umbrellas in though all his umbrellas are small ones which get lost at the bottom of the vase. He possesses no books and he has had all the original oak bookshelves removed and replaced with paintings of animals, bought from a gallery in Dover Street.

I surmise that St John comes from solid middle class English stock, no doubt with bankers and hedge fund owners on both sides of the family. He is clearly used to affluence, and takes it for granted that he should own a house while still in his twenties.

When there is a knock on his front door on his first day in his new home St John is disconcerted. He opens it warily to see a plump black woman carrying a basket of blueberry muffins.

'I'm Hilary,' the black woman says.

It is Hilary McBride.

Hilary is still traumatised after her family's recent tragedy; but she is nice enough to bring gifts to a new neighbour despite everything.

'Thank you, I don't buy at the door,' St John tells her, trying to close the door on her. But she puts her foot in the way of it.

'These are a gift,' she says. 'I'm your next door neighbour.'

'Come in, come in,' he tells her, barely abashed. 'My name is St John.'

'Sinjun.'

'St John.'

'Very nice name.'

'Can I make you some tea?' St John asks.

'That would be - '

'I don't have a kettle,' St John says.

Hilary laughs. She seems at ease with this highly strung stranger, though I have noticed in the past that she is often tense with people she doesn't know.

'We can lend you a kettle,' Hilary says cheerfully. 'Teapot?'

'No.'

'Cups?'

He investigates the cupboards in his kitchen and returns. 'No. I'm very Marie Kondo.'

She has no idea who that is so she ignores the reference. 'We have lots of teapots,' she says. 'Give me five minutes.'

'I wouldn't want to put you to any trouble,' he says.

'No trouble at all. I hope you like it here,' she says, smiling.

'I'm pretty sure I will,' says St John. And he gives her a comradely glance. 'The area's really going up, isn't it?'

This I know is a reference to social class. For when middle class people like St John move in, the area moves 'up' and becomes better. But when working class people like Hilary and George stubbornly continue to live in an area that is becoming gentrified, it forces the area 'down'.

It is a very insulting comment in other words. But Hilary's smile doesn't falter.

She returns with a kettle and a teapot and mugs and makes him a cup of tea with a side helping of biscuits.

Up the road from this scene of domestic bliss, Don from number 58 is walking his dog Cecil. Cecil is half blind and wobbly on his back legs. Don retired several years ago from his job as a University lecturer and he always seems exhausted and fearful.

I have watched him for years and I always assumed he was just an ill-natured and anxious old man. But one day, out of curiosity, I followed him home and I could not believe the stench of mildew and entrails and hate which inhabits his house. He never opens his windows. The smell is almost tangible. I realised then that there were ghosts residing here. Number 58 Westwood Street is a haunted house.

And Don's ghosts are the worst kind. Invisible; inaudible; yet always angry. They are what is left when everything that is good about a person has been lost, corroded by time and the pain of dashed hopes, and all that remains is selfishness and spite.

No wonder Don is always so glum.

Cecil, however, is oblivious to it all; multiple mini-strokes have left this little spaniel oblivious to the supernatural.

And now, up the road from Don's house, at a safe distance from the spectral stench, on the day after Hilary met St John of the first time, a boy called Toby is floating.

Toby is eight years old and he is in Mrs Farley's class in Boscombe Primary School. The school is a two-storey building, sunk into the ground, made of simple prefabricated blocks with a pleasing façade, and a surprisingly large playground for a school that size. Jack and Shona both went to school here which is when I first started to pay attention to them. Shona was excluded for making witheringly sarcastic comments to the headteacher which I found highly diverting. And a few years later, Jack joined Reception and went on to excel on Sports Day every year by running faster and jumping higher than any other child that had ever attended Boscombe.

Hilary as you know is a teaching assistant here. But she is with Year 2, Mr Grange's class. The Hedgehogs they are called. Toby is in the Eagles class. The other classes are the Otters, the Voles and the Crows.

There are twenty-seven children in Eagles Class and they are all standing in the yard. This is the paved area outside the rear entrance to the building, where there is a hopscotch pitch and a basketball hoop secured to the wall. This is the area where the parents of the very young ones wait to receive their children at the end of the day. And here the Eagles children have been obliged to stand and wait for the last fifteen minutes for their lesson to begin.

Inside their classroom Claire Soames, the Eagles' teaching assistant, is in a state of panic. She is rather posh and is new to Westwood and has 'This never happened in my last school' written all over her young and pretty face.

The head, Mr Abioye, has been summoned to deal with the unfolding crisis, and he is expected to arrive soon. But until he gets there it's just Mrs Farley and Claire, who are standing upon the carpet of the Eagles classroom, and Toby, who is floating.

Not only is he floating, roughly fourteen feet in the air, Toby is currently trying and failing to flip himself around in order to stand upon the ceiling.

It's harder than it sounds.

'Look at this!' Toby is shouting, when he is almost but not quite upside down.

'Get down from there!' Claire shouts.

'Screaming doesn't help,' Mrs Farley tells her, severely.

Claire gives Mrs Farley a forlorn 'This never happened in my last school' look.

'Search his desk,' Mrs Farley says.

'What?' says Claire.

'Just do it,' Mrs Farley says.

'It's nice up here,' Toby shouts down to them.

'Yes, my dear,' Mrs Farley says. 'Don't leave footmarks on the ceiling, please.'

Claire starts searching Toby's desk. This is a bright red table with two plastic tray drawers for pens and notepads. Inside these plastic drawers Claire finds pens and several notepads.

'His bag,' says Mrs Farley.

Toby has managed to get himself on all fours on the ceiling, and is now walking like a dog. 'Look, look at me!' he shouts, though his voice is muffled because he is speaking into the ceiling tiles.

Claire has located Toby's bag. A quick search reveals that it contains a sandwich box with no sandwich and several empty chocolate wrappers. These wrappers are all that remains of two Yorkies, a KitKat, and an Orange Aero.

'There,' says Mrs Farley. 'The same as last time.'

'Are you saying, it's chocolate that makes him float?' Clare asks, accusingly.

'So it seems,' says Mrs Farley, sourly.

The door crashes open and Mike the caretaker backs in, pulling a blue gym mat along with him. He has a broad physique and tattoos on his arms which he has been encouraged to keep concealed during school hours. At the other end of the blue gym mat is Mr Abioye, the headteacher, dapper in a blue suit and a bright yellow tie. Mr Abioye was quite the athlete back in the day and is still considered to be a fine figure of a man. The two men drag the mat into the classroom and drop it on the floor. They are both breathless and bathed in the self-satisfaction of men who feel they are saving the day.

'Move those desks!' Mike says.

'We've already moved them,' says Mrs Farley, sharply.

There's a large space in the centre of the room, with the desks now wedged up against the wall. The bright blue gym mat is placed on this desk-less spot.

'If he falls from there to there,' says Mrs Farley, meaning, from the ceiling to the floor, 'he's going to break some bones. Regardless of the bloody gym mat.'

'You have a better idea?' says Mr Abioye in an irritable tone.

This never happened in my last school, says the panicky look in Claire's eyes.

All this is irrelevant, since Toby has now moved to the edge of the ceiling, and is nowhere near the space they have created among the desks. If he falls from where he is now he will hit the smart board which will doubtless explode and spray glass around the room.

'Toby, I want you to crawl to the middle of the ceiling, can you do that, lad?' says Mike.

'No,' Toby says.

'Do it please,' says Mike.

'No,' Toby says.

'It'll be safer,' says Mr Abioye. 'If you fall the gym mat will break your fall and you won't be hurt.'

'Or rather, your injuries will be minimised,' says Mrs Farley.

'I won't fall,' Toby says.

'Well you might,' says Mrs Farley.

'I won't.'

Mr Abioye is very tense by now. He looks like he wants to swear at this disobedient child but he doesn't dare do so.

'Is he always this badly behaved?' Mr Abioye asks Mrs Farley.

'He's not normally naughty at all,' Claire says.

'The last time it happened,' Mrs Farley says, 'it wore off in time.'

'You can't teach a class,' Mr Abioye says, 'with a child on the ceiling.'

'We should call the fire brigade,' Claire says, sternly.

'I did,' says Mr Abioye. 'I explained the situation. They refused to come.'

'Bastards!' says Claire.

Mrs Farley gives her a filthy look. You are not allowed to say 'bastards' in the Eagles classroom. Or indeed, in any of the animal-named classrooms.

'Try jumping,' Mike shouts upwards. 'Jump towards us, we'll catch you.'

'I like it up here!' Toby shouts.

Toby is still pretending to be a dog chasing a squirrel on the ceiling of the classroom. They can't see his face, just his back and his bum. But the floating shows no signs of wearing off.

'Push with your hands!' shouts Mike.

Toby pushes with his hands. That propels him away from the ceiling to a distance of about seven or eight inches. He is now floating in mid-air rather than wedged against the ceiling. But then, inch by inch, he starts floating upwards, until the ceiling once more blocks him.

'A boat hook,' Mr Abioye says, 'would do it. You know, one of those long sticks, with a hook at the end. A boat hook.'

They do not have a boat hook in any of the school's cupboards or storerooms. Primary schools do not stock boat hooks.

Mrs Farley's face explains all this in a way Mr Abioye finds galling.

'He's been eating chocolate,' Mrs Farley says to her head teacher. 'That's the root of the trouble.'

'Chocolate!' says Mr Abioye, angrily.

'That's what his mum said the last time,' Mrs Farley says: 'when he floated in school assembly. Chocolate is the issue. Chocolate makes him float. '

I recall the day when Toby floated off the floor in Assembly until he was higher than the highest gym bars. And when I delve into Mr Abioye's thoughts, I discover he is remembering the same event; with considerable anguish.

'So why did you let him eat chocolate?' Mr Abioye asks.

'I didn't. It was hidden in his bag,' Mrs Farley says.

'You didn't search the bag?' Mr Abioye says.

'*Claire* didn't search the bag,' Mrs Farley says.

'I didn't know I was meant to search the bag!' Claire says, close to tears.

'Toby come down, please,' says Mr Abioye.

'We need to start the class,' says Mrs Farley, who is by now extremely vexed.

'If he falls when there are kids in the room, he'll kill someone,' Mike the caretaker says. 'Health and Safety, thank you very much.'

'I'll take a PE class,' Mr Abioye says, 'in the playground.'

'Or I could fetch the meditation gongs,' Claire says.

In the end they do both. And by the end of the school day, at 4pm, Toby floats downwards and is caught by Mike the caretaker, who has been sitting there all day.

Toby's parents were summoned to the school several hours ago but they didn't turn up. They never do. So Toby's older brother, who is eleven, walks Toby home. It is only a short walk, across the road and five doors up, and legally there is no reason a boy of Toby's age shouldn't walk home alone. But this is one of the strictest of the school rules: no child under the age of 10 can leave school premises unless accompanied by an adult or an older sibling.

Liam is the older sibling.

'What the feck!' Liam says to his brother as they start the short walk home.

'Don't tell Mam,' Toby says.

'You think I talk to Mam about you, you daft dickhead,' Liam says. But he takes his brother's hand when they cross the road.

Liam is tall for his age. No one messes with Liam.

Toby however is small for his age and everyone messes with Toby. He is like a pet, endlessly teasable. There is no actual bullying at Boscombe Primary, and in fairness, the other kids are relatively nice to him, compared to how horrible they *could* be. But he's a weird kid and it's hard not to taunt and make fun of a weird kid when you are only eight years old. He has too many freckles and a frightened face. And the way he talks is odd; he either mutters his words or he shouts them.

When they get home Liam cooks them both tea then Toby retreats to his room. He will stay there until it is time to get up in the morning.

His parents don't get home from work till 9pm. Liam tells them nothing about the events of the day.

At the zebra crossing next to Westwood Junction Railway Station, a woman with a pram is waiting to cross the road. She is young and wears a dark hoodie with the hood up, and she wears chunky black shoes. She is wary, and instead of crossing the road she hovers near the kerb, glancing sceptically at the cars which have stopped, seemingly fearful they might have a change of heart and mow her down. Perhaps news of the crash on Woody Hill has reached her.

She is a light-skinned black woman, perhaps of mixed heritage, but I do not know her name. I wonder if she is visiting friends or family here.

Eventually the woman in the hoodie crosses the road, to the relief of the irritable drivers who have been kept waiting for ages.

Next to the zebra crossing at the other side of the road is a bed of shrubs and flowers planted by the Residents Association to brighten up the area. It does indeed brighten up the area. The colourful flowers break up the monotonous texture of pavement, road, pavement, road.

A cherry tree outside the newsagents is shedding its blossoms, like pink tears.

The horse chestnut trees further down the road are thick with budding candles and in a month or so these will ignite, to create a dazzling floral display.

I spot a blackbird, hopping on the pavement. It is a delightful tiny thing, with its jet-black foliage and bright yellow bill. It leaps then flaps upwards and lands on top of the advertising hoarding that bars the way to the railway track. It flaps again and scoots upwards and perches upon a branch of a tall sycamore tree. It flaps again and flies over the railway embankment.

I decide to follow it.

I soar my awareness over the hoarding and hover like a bird above the sloping wilderness. The coppiced trees cut back by Southern Rail are growing back now. Someone has been dumping garden waste - twigs and branches and an entire holly tree - and the land-wrack sits reproachfully on top of the undergrowth. There once were badgers living along here but no longer. But I have seen pipistrelle bats nesting under the railway bridge. Foxes often burrow their dens along here. I can see hoverflies and butterflies and slugs and snails and slowworms; and I also see a mountainous heap of dung, left by the great white Bengal tiger who joined us in Westwood at the same time as the anacondas, the cheetahs, the hyenas, and the parrot.

I wonder when the next train is due. Perhaps I will wait for it. I love to see the train's chunky caterpillar body hurtling upon metal rails, its cockpit like a pair of giant eyes staring. Once I hated the trains but I have become fond of them. They have become part of me, part of my Westwood.

I settle down to wait for a train to go by. And when a train passes, and vanishes into the tunnel, I wait for the next one. That occupies me for most of the day.

When I am bored of trains I go to 44 Westwood Street to see how Jack is getting on.

Jack is in his new bedroom, which is the middle room on the ground floor of the McBride house, which used to be the dog's bedroom before the dog died. It has now been equipped with an adjustable hospital bed and winch. Jack is lying on the bed, thinking hard and rapidly, though not coherently, about his current plight.

Some of Jack's thoughts get through to me, though much of what is in his mind is just a jumble of images and emotions. But one thought dominates:

I'm lucky. So fucking lucky, he is thinking.

That puzzles me; he has not been very lucky at all, in my opinion.

Now Jack is remembering running across a field with a bunch of other children. They are all wearing athletic kit; he is the fastest runner by far. I remember that day. It was a summer's day. School Sports Day.   No clouds in the sky. Jack's eyes glitter with joy. His body moves like a cat chasing its prey, fast and seemingly with no effort.

Then the memory vanishes and he experiences the car crash all over again. The sudden unexpected jolt. The flying through the air. The crashing to the ground. The no pain, followed by much pain. The waking up to find he cannot move his legs.

I explore his emotions, which are a blend of ugly things. Mostly regret. But a lot of anger too. He can no longer run fast of course, hence his poignant memory of running fast. And he is tormented by his memory of the crash. That seems logical too.

And through it all he has an inner monologue that is a babble of words, like a mad person ranting:

Yeah. Right. I've always been lucky. So fucking lucky. I'm young. I'm strong. I'm fit. I can endure this. Anyone else would've been totally fucked by it. Woudn't've coped at all. Nyah nyah. Lucky, see!

Then more remembered images.   The road; the zebra crossing, the ambulance, the hospital room.

Lucky!

Like fuck am I -

Fuck. Fuck fuck fuck fuck!

Ah.

Finally I understand what he is doing. He is trying to persuade himself not to sink into suicidal despair, even though he desperately wants to do so.

It's like soldiers who have their legs blown off yeah then climb mountains or run races with their artificial legs. Mental strength that's what counts. That's what I got in fucking bucketfuls, yeah!

I can feel his fear bubbling up inside him; he has a considerable amount of fear bubbling up inside him.

Mental strength. That's what I got see. Mental strength!

I cannot detect any mental strength in Jack; just fear and despair and rage.

It intoxicates me.

Fuck fuck. Mental fucking, fuck fuck.

I feel his pain too; it is as rich and vivid as a heroin rush.

I can't stand the fucking pain though. Pain is horrible. I don't sleep properly and when I wake up the fucking pain kicks in. Pain killers dull the pain a bit and they make me woozy and that helps but they never make it go away. The pain. The pain. Pain is for old people this is not fucking right. I just want it to go away. Just for a couple of hours every day. The pain. I never thought pain would hurt this much, yeah? Fuck!

I remember Jack through all the years in which I have known him, which is almost all of his life. Jack as a toddler, Jack as a boy, Jack as a teenager. Jack shoplifting from the local shop. Jack getting into fist fights, so many fist fights. Jack chatting up pretty girls. Jack fucking pretty girls.

It occurs to me that I did not enjoy being in Jack's mind when he fucked all those girls. But I'm enjoying it now; now that he cannot.

I'm strong though. Must remember that. Yeah yeah. Get fucking me. My upper body is strong. I can stand up in the shower by clutching on to the rails. That's how strong I am!

His eyes are closed, his fists are clenched, his body twitches on the bed, helplessly.

I hate having fucking carers. The way they – don't talk to me like – I'm not a fucking child! Except I am. I'm like a child. Someone had to wipe my arse, those first few weeks. How crap is that– no don't think about – no way I - I wish I was doing rehab. In a clinic somewhere, me and some ex-Paras and a couple of hard as fuck crippled SAS men, bulking up our abs and triceps and learning to walk again with legs that are shattered and broken and that hurt like buggery, but we don't care because we're warriors! That's where I should be, not here. Not in the fucking room where the dog used to have his basket. Not with – I hate this bed. I hate having carers. I hate that I can't tell the bastards apart. Two people come every day but I can't tell if it's the same two people. I used to be good at faces and facts but now - I listen to a song and I don't know if I've already listened to it and I can't remember the words. What's that about?

As I suspected, he has suffered a considerable degree of brain damage.

But fuck it, I'm so lucky. I really am. I got my family. I got my mum to look after me, she only works a few hours every day so even when she goes back to the school it won't be for long, and there's Shona. Daft bitch, and mouthy too, but she has to realise, it's her job to look after me now, innit. Ha. Daft bitch. She's my bitch right. But she don't know it - And there's dad, oh shit, he's no use, and there's Davey, I'd be lost without Davey, where the fuck is Davey, what? Davey is dead, when did my dog die? Did no one think to tell me when my dog died?

It happened four years ago. Hilary came downstairs and found Davey dead in his basket. The dog was twelve years old which is fairly old for dogs so it came as no surprise.

I can remember – no I can't.

I remember that first night in hospital. I felt so brave. I was fearless right. I was brave. Everyone expected me to cry when I found out I'd never walk again without a stick but that's nothing to me, nothing. To be honest I thought it would of been worst. Worse? Worser. I thought I'd never walk at all. Oh God I want to die.

Be braver, Jack, I think at him.

Don't be such a pitiful coward, I think at him.

But I'm wasting my time. He can't hear me.

I need to get up. I need to stretch my legs. But that means using the hoist. And that means ringing the bell so someone has to come along and they have to figure out how to use the hoist when the carers aren't here. I could I guess just roll out of bed but if that doesn't work and I fall on my face and can't get up again I'm going to look like a total twat.

I often spend time in Jack's mind; and when I do, I can see through his eyes. I can see what he sees when he gets up, and when he goes for walks, and when he sits in the garden and looks at the shrubs and flowers Hilary has skilfully planted and at the tall sycamore trees on the railway embankment that runs behind the house.

And I also see what Jack doesn't see.

It's weird, so fucking weird. Some days the colours go away. How is that possible? Red. Green. Purple. Yellow. Blue. Purple. Indigo. Violet. All the other ones. Puce? What colour is that? They all just go. That's normal, I guess, that's just the concussion kicking in. I assume, though I haven't told anyone about it.

In the park though, when they wheeled me around the park that first time, it was weird. The green grass was grey grass. The blue sky was grey sky. The flowers were all grey. Just different fucking shades of fucking grey. Grey!

You see, when he's depressed, when his spirits are at their lowest, Jack can't see colour.

Chapter 4

Kane's alarm rings, softly. It is midnight. He is immediately awake, and wary. He bounds out of bed. I watch him get dressed.

Kane is a TWOCer. This is the term for someone who steals cars. Taking Without Consent; it is an acronym that the police use for such crimes.

TWOC. I like that word.

Kane used to TWOC for fun. He would steal a car in Streatham and drive it up to Westwood and race it along the Boulevard, hitting speeds of more than a hundred miles an hour until the police came along. Then he would fuck off through the back streets of Sydenham and Penge and Beckenham and Bromley until he'd shaken off the bastards. He was arrested twice and went away from Westwood to some kind of youth detention centre. But he always came back. In those days, if you saw a burned out car in the car park by Tesco's, there was a good chance Kane had stolen it.

Fast and dangerous car chases down narrow suburban streets!

Sirens wailing!

Tyres screeching!

Abandoned cars burning up in alleyways; flames billowing in the night air!

Burned out cars; sad and soulless.

And at the end of it all, there's Kane walking home at the end of his night of motoring madness, not a care in the world. Grinning. Always grinning, sometimes skipping as he walks. Cheeky bastard!

That's how I came to know him. How he came to my attention. And ever since then, I have continued to notice Kane. Not every day, not every month even. But I am aware of him, and the mischief he gets up to.

Kane was a crew member back then. He grew up in London Heights, the big council estate, which was once a miracle of modern architecture they say and is now, so the inhabitants all agree, a shithole. Eighty per cent of the young men who live in London Heights are unemployed. The police use it for practising their surveillance skills, following random residents on the off chance they are connected to organised crime, and often they are. The waste ground at the back of London Heights is where the young men do their deals, divvying up drugs to the kids, who they call the shotters, who are then sent out to pubs and clubs to sell their wares. Police raids on London Heights usually fail because lookouts can see from the top towers of the Heights all the way across Westwood as far as Streatham.

Kane always said he wouldn't join a gang. He was a serious kid back then, in the days when he was at Big School. He'd seen what had happened to his dad. His dad was a tosser, so Kane always says. An idiot who threw his life away; so Kane always says. Kane's dad was a serial petty crook who spent half his life doing bird; and the other half of his life committing crimes that would result in him doing bird.

That wasn't much of a role model for a smart kid like Kane. When he was twelve years old Kane read a lot of books. He worked his way through the fiction shelves of the mobile library that came to the estate every Tuesday and Thursday. And he had an idea he wanted to go to University or become a professor, or something. He didn't know what, exactly, because no one in his mum and dad's families had ever gone to University, or anywhere good really. His mum had seven children by as many different men, and she loved all her kids, and she was a good mum, so Kane always said. Though he also acknowledged that she had crap taste in men.

Then one day Kane was told by a skinny nasty looking kid with terrible acne that he had to join the London Heights Crew. That's the name of the youngers crew who control this rabbit warren of an estate. And Kane said fuck off. And the crew member said you do as you are fucking well told or you'll fucking regret it. And Kane said no I mean it, just fuck the fuck off you dickless fucker.

And that's when the nasty-looking acne-faced lad put a knife to Kane's throat and threatened to rape his sister.

Kane loved his sister so it was an easy choice for him. He gave in and joined the London Heights Crew though in fact they raped his sister anyway. Her name was Caroline.

She was only fourteen, her rapists were twelve and thirteen, they were just kids. At one point she had to explain to them what they had to do, because they were getting so angry at their own incompetence she feared they would go berserk and kill her. I didn't watch it all, but I saw her the day afterwards crying her eyes out in the shower and when she was dried off and dressed up and ready to go out with her mates, I could see the light had gone out in her eyes. But she never told the cops, kids on that estate never do.

Kane could tell something had happened to his sister and he guessed what it probably was but he could never be sure.

'Are you okay Car?' he asked her.

'Course why wouldn't I be all right fuck off all right,' she said.

'No one's ever going hurt you trust me I'm gonna look after you, Car,' he said.

'Fuck off Kane. You're just a twat I don't need looking after grow up innit,' she said.

And that was that.

But later Kane found out for certain what had happened. He was told all about it by some of his so-called mates on the Crew. He learned that the word was out there; the word was everywhere. That Caroline Armstrong was a slag.

And that made Kane angry. Angry in every atom of his being. But what could he do?

That was the moment when Kane realised he wasn't going to look after anyone, not at his age, not ever. He just had to take it.

And Caroline knew she had to take it too. Because if she said anything worse would happen; to her, and to Kane too. And to give her credit, she loved her little brother and she didn't want him dead. So she took it and she said nothing.

They were just kids.

Just kids.

So Kane took it and he did what he had to do for a number of years and he was good at it. He went from shotter to younger in hardly any time, and he became a legend for his joyriding and car stealing skills.

The truth was, when he was in the London Heights crew, Kane was someone. He had status. He was looked up to by Man Dem. Which is the name they like to call themselves, this crew of teenage gangsters.

Man Dem.

Kane was looked up to by Man Dem because he knew cars. And in particular, he knew how to use a pair of relay boxes to hack the electronic signal from a car key inside a house in order to steal the car parked *outside* the house.

He was the king of the joyriders. The best car thief in all of South London.

But when he was seventeen, Kane said fuck off to it all. Fuck off to the crew, fuck off to London Heights. Just – fuck off.

So he stole a BMW and instead of burning it he sold it and he used the money to rent a flat in Forest Hill. Caroline had got herself a place in Bristol University by then. And when he asked her one day about what had happened back then, when they both lived in London Heights, she just laughed at him and she denied ever being raped. I mean like, no, fuck no, that never happened, what kind of slag you think I am?

And Kane took that as a good sign, a fresh start kind of thing. And he decided to make his own fresh start and he took a job in a garage. But six months later he was stealing cars again because it paid so well.

He can do it solo even though it needs two relay boxes working in tandem to steal a car. His trick for doing this is a clever one.

First, he attaches one box to the wall of a house with a nail or a metal bracket.

Then he rushes back to get the signal from the other box which he holds up near the car itself. The car key's signal travels through brick easily but you need to find the right position. And once you've found it, you can steal the code that lives in the Wi-Fi, whatever Wi-Fi is.

It works like a dream. Any car Kane wants, he can steal.

And so, after a year or so of doing this, Kane was making good money. He was saving some of it; the rest he spent on nights out and recreational drugs and holidays abroad. Usually Majorca, he loves Majorca. He kept well clear of London Heights, and he kept well clear of Man Dem. He even stopped visiting his own mother just to keep himself out of sight and out of mind. And it worked. The youngers all forgot about him and Kane is now minting it and he answers to no-one. Which is just the way he likes it.

Tonight Kane is stealing a car on Mildew Road.

That's why he set his alarm for midnight; that's the time he gets up to go to work.

Mildew Road is a long curving street with half-timbered houses built in the 1930s; all the houses are large and expensive and have their own driveways. There is a full moon. No one is about. Then a cyclist appears from around the corner wearing a face mask and with a rucksack on his back and no lights and no Hi-Vis, cycling fast and recklessly.

Kane.

Kane stops the bike expertly and swings himself off, just a few doors away from a tasty Porsche parked in one of those big driveways. He leans the bike against a wall and takes a white overall out of the rucksack, the kind the police use for scene of crime work. He gets dressed quickly until his face and body are covered in the white overall with a hood over his hair and he is wearing latex gloves. He now looks like an astronaut and he is forensically invisible. And when he walks into the driveway of the house with the Porsche, the security light comes on and his white suit lights up like a flame.

But no one sees him and he makes no noise.

He takes out the first relay box from his rucksack, and he walks up and down the front of the house holding the relay box in front of him, searching for the key chip signal. Most people leave their keys on a table in the hall, so it's not hard to get a positive fairly quickly. And when he gets the telltale beep, Kane tacks the relay box to the bit of the wall where the signal is strongest. Then he steps back to his rucksack and takes out the second relay box.

Invisibly, and undetectably even for me, the electronic signal travels through brick and air and via the two relay boxes and the car door pops open.

Kane then encodes a blank key chip with the code for this car so he can now drive this car anywhere; and so can its next owner. Then he opens up the boot. He puts his bike in there and closes it. He gets in the driving seat. He starts up the car with the encoded key.

The passenger door opens and a figure slips into the passenger seat. It is a man in a long black coat and a black Fedora hat.

'Just drive,' says the man with the hat.

Ah.

I didn't anticipate this.

It's the Bogman.

'Fuck you,' says Kane and pulls out a knife, and stabs the fucker in his arm, not to kill him just to scare him. Then Kane tries to get out of the car.

But the Bogman doesn't seem to mind being stabbed. He takes hold of Kane with a hand that is unbelievably strong, with fingers like skeleton bones. He takes the knife off Kane and he takes off his hat and then he plunges the knife into his own eye.

Kane takes a good look at the Bogman. A scrawny man with a face the colour of old mahogany with a six inch blade embedded in his eye socket, which doesn't seem to bother him in the least.

'Just drive, we're going to be friends,' says the Bogman.

And Kane takes a deep breath and puts the car into reverse. And he backs out of the driveway and in a few minutes he is speeding through Westwood.

'I need a mentor,' says the Bogman.

They are parked up now, in a cul de sac, lit by a streetlamp and the full moon.

'Who and what the fuck *are* you?' asks Kane.

The Bogman stares at Kane, with eerie blankness.

'A mentor. That's what I need. Is that the correct word?' the Bogman says.

'Fuck how should I know.' Kane says.

'Someone who mentors. Someone to teach me – about this world,' the Bogman says.

'You're fucking weird. Are those acid burns? Do you realise, you only have one eye?' Kane says, accusingly.

The Bogman has taken the knife out by now, and his left eye is an empty socket, and it looks awful.

'It will return,' the Bogman says.

'Your eyes can grow back?' says Kane.

'Yes.'

'You knew that when you stabbed yourself?' Kane says.

'I - ' For a moment the Bogman seems abashed. 'I assumed it.'

'Fucking wanker. You are something else you are. Something fucking else.'

Kane is a red-head, a white boy, a ball of energy. The Bogman looks at him through his one good eye with something approaching respect.

'I've been watching you,' the Bogman says.

'Have you?' Kane says.

'Stealing cars. You are very good at it.'

'You've been following me.'

'I have. I am good at hiding, believe it or not.'

'Not with a fucking hat like that you're not. You're lucky you didn't get your face kicked in as a fucking batty boy,' Kane says.

'I don't know that word,' the Bogman says.

'Well I ain't fucking teaching it to you.'

'In the day I hide my clothes. I hide in the woods, or I bury myself in the earth, in the Old Park. Where the dead men are,' the Bogman says.

'Jesus! There ain't no fucking dead men in Old Park,' Kane says.

'They wear hats and long coats and they do not move. I assume they are dead.'

'Those are statues. You fucking numpty,' Kane says.

'Ah. A new word. I have learned a new word,' the Bogman says.

'Numpty?'

'Statue.'

'You don't know what a statue is?'

'No.'

Kane stares at him for a few moments, baffled.   Then he averts his gaze. It's hard to look at the Bogman's face for too long, it does strange things to your sense of reality.

'It's like, a thing. Carved out of, like stone.   Are you fucking with me?' Kane says.

'No. I assumed – no. Now I understand. In my day, we did carve things out of stone. Small figures, often fat women, mother gods, yes, those were statues? We built too, stone circles made of – blocks of stone. But nothing as real as that which I see in the park. Nothing as lifelike as that. But that is where, near those 'statues', that is where I hide myself, in the mud and earth, and I listen. I listen to the birds and I listen to the foxes and I listen to all the dogs barking and I listen to the people talking. And that's how I learned to speak your language.'

'You're, what? An alien? A mutant?' Kane says.

'I am a human man,' the Bogman says.

'You ain't no human, you're Freddy Krueger.'

'I don't know a Freddy Krueger. What is a Freddy Krueger?'

'Long story. What I mean is, you're a freak.'

'Am I? It's true, people are afraid of me,' the Bogman says. 'They see me and they scream in terror, and sometimes I have to kill them and rip them to pieces with my hands, and then I bury the body parts.'

Kane stares, appalled.

'You're a murderer?' Kane says.

'A murderer is someone who kills people?' the Bogman says.

'Uh, yeah.'

'Then I am a murderer. But only to survive.'

Kane looks at the Bogman again; then he averts his eyes again. He is a boy, as I say, no more than a boy. And suddenly he is weeping salty tears and his entire body is shaking.

'Are you going to murder me too?' Kane says, weeping.

The Bogman gazes at this child, this pathetic child, with his coldest stare. 'That depends. Are you going to help me?'

Kane has nothing else he can say: 'Uh – yes.'

'Then no. I will not murder you.'

Kane is silent for a moment.

'So, like, what's a fucking mentor then?' Kane asks.

You have to admire him, this long dead savage who grew up in a world where a bow and arrow was cutting edge technology. He has adapted and he has learned. He has stolen clothes and money, he wears shoes, he has learned how to speak English, and also a smattering of Urdu. And he has walked the streets of Westwood and he knows the names of many of the people of Westwood, and he knows where the bad shit goes down. He knows where the brothel is, where the drugs can be bought, where the bad guys have their slaughters. He knows where the librarians (not the ones who work in the library, the other sort) hide their guns to rent out or sell to blaggers and bangers. All this, he knows.

He has learned what money is and how it can be used. He knows what mobile phones are and with Kane's guidance, he acquires one and is able to use one. Although his withered fingers find it hard to press the keys accurately so he relies a lot on Autocorrect.

He has come to terms with the bizarre rules of his own reincarnate state. The arm that was bitten off by a dog grew back remarkably quickly, and is now an almost perfect match for the other one. His skin will never look like human flesh but he has used the Fitness Trail in the New Park to bulk himself up, so that he no longer resembles a cadaver chewed by dogs. These days he has arms the size of a slender girl's arms, rather than fragile twigs that can be snapped off by a single dog bite. And his legs are stronger, and thicker, and his torso has muscles, not a six-pack maybe but still considerable core strength. And at night he runs naked around the park at a speed that would incur the envy of any professional athlete.

Over the weeks that follow his first meeting with Kane, his eye grows back too, as good as new. Or as at least, as good as the other one, since both eyes are thick brown blobs which swivel in their sockets, like dungballs moved by unseen ants. But with these two ugly eyes he can see in the dark, he can see long distances, and he can see ghosts. He knows that Westwood is the most haunted of all the London villages; but he ignores them all, all the ghouls and spectres and angry lost souls. He is alive now; he does not identify with the tribe of the dead.

'What is a shotter?' the Bogman had asked his newly appointed mentor that night, the night they first met. They were sitting in a small park near London Heights, with a statue of Prince Albert on horseback in its centre, surrounded by a children's playground with a slide and a climbing frame and swings.

'They are nothing, nobody. Foot soldiers,' said Kane. 'They sell the drugs, that's all they do, and then they give the money to someone else, to one of the youngers, who pass on most of it on to the Faces. That's where the real money is, higher up the chain.'

'Define real money,' the Bogman said.

'WTAF? Real money is lots of money. Shit loads. I dunno. Millions? How much does a drug dealer make? I don't deal drugs, not any more, I wouldn't know,' Kane said.

'The Mortons have real money?' said the Bogman.

The Mortons are the gang who control these drug dealers. They are the most powerful gang in South London since the Charlie Richardson gang.

'Duh. Yeah. Are you fucking thick or what? The Mortons rule the fucking roost,' Kane had said; and the Bogman absorbed his words carefully.

'Define roost,' the Bogman said.

Kane sighed exaggeratedly. His way of showing he was annoyed.

'Roost is where birds live. Yeah? Geddit? It's just a fucking phrase. It means – like - they're the top boys.'

The Bogman nodded.

'I understand top boys. I was once a top boy,' the Bogman said.

And then the Bogman tried to smile and it was like watching leather flirt.

'Don't go there, man,' said Kane, anxiously.

'Don't go where?'

'Don't go where you're thinking of going, don't go pissing on the Mortons' size fucking 10s, like.'

'The Mortons are dangerous?'

'Duh. Yes. They kill people.'

'I kill people.'

'Just don't – don't go there. If you want to make money, I'll show you. Come in with me. You can hold the relay box, we'll nick some cars. Up Chelsea way. If the Old Bill come for us, you scare them off, I leg it,' Kane said.

'Stealing cars.'

The Bogman considered the potential of such a potential new chapter in his life.

And Kane waited. Patiently at first. Then after a while, impatiently. But his impatience didn't speed things up so he just waited for a very long time for the Bogman to announce his decision.

'So it shall be,' the Bogman eventually said.

That was six weeks ago.

Now the Bogman is a TWOCer too.

Chapter 5

It's noon on Woody Hill and nothing much is happening.

I watch the people walking by; but there is nothing they do say that attracts or holds my attention. They are just people, walking by.

I am old.

I am so old I cannot even say how old I am.

I have seen many things in my long life and I am bored a lot of the time.

Two dogs snarl at each other on the pavement. One is a Airedale terrier, the other is a greyhound. Their minds are dull, their passions banal; for these are not wild creatures. All such toy beasts may fuck off so far as I am concerned; they are not deserving of my awareness.

A falcon flies over, flying so high it cannot be seen from the ground, and its mind is clear and hard. It sees everything. It forgets very little. When these birds espy their prey and when they swoop down in a soaring stoop from sky to ground and when they strike and shred some unwitting creature with their sharp talons it is exhilarating. But this bird has already hunted; so I do not bother to follow it in its flight.

I remember that day a few weeks ago when blood and violence came to Woody Hill.

The busy daytime high street is cast into darkness. Pedestrians blink in surprise. Shoppers find themselves lost in unlit shops. And on Woody Hill a teenage driver in an expensive Porsche fails to see the young lad on the middle of the zebra crossing and ploughs straight into him.

The McBride family are still dealing with this terrible tragedy. *They* are the unwitting creatures shredded by the talons of fate.

Is that a good metaphor?

I believe that it is. I believe I have a flair for metaphor and other forms of figurative language such as simile, metonymy and onomatopoeia. It is one of the many skills I have acquired over the last ten thousand years or so.

They are the unwitting creatures.

Shredded by the talons of fate.

I've known George McBride the longest of all the McBrides. He and his brother Mickey were born in Westwood and so were his parents and grandparents. Hilary was born in the Midlands and I only got to know her when she moved to Westwood with George.

But since that time I have followed her often. I was with Hilary when she got married. I was with her when George spent five years doing their house up in his usual slapdash fashion and never quite finishing anything. I was with her when both her children were born, one a home birth, the other in hospital. I was with her through her good times and her bad times.

And now her son Jack has been crippled and I'm with her through all of that. She's an unremarkable woman but she has a big heart and I like that about her.

When she was sixteen Hilary shocked her parents by leaving her family home in Birmingham and moving to Brixton to live with her Gran, Shona Mirabelle Walker, and her Grandpa Maybe, whose real name is Bobby Fagon. However, Bobby and Shona were no longer living together by then. Gran had another fancy man, well several to be honest. So Hilary would stay with Gran for one week, then she would stuff her clothes in a gym bag and stay with Grandpa Maybe for the second week.

Hilary rarely talks about those days but I have spent a good deal of time in her mind and I am familiar with her memories of that period.

They are dull memories by and large. They are memories of Hilary as a young woman watching telly and playing dominos with her granddad. They are memories of Hilary cooking dinner for her grandma Shona Mirabelle and listening to tales of Shona being in love with many people all at the same time and betraying most of them as well as stories of sex parties and acid trips and threesomes and all the things Hilary had never done herself.

And when her Grandma Shona died, Hilary moved in full-time with her granddad and they lived together very happily for seven years until she met George McBride when he was doing up Grandpa Maybe's house. And Hilary fell in love with him and soon after that she moved in with him, into a house in Westwood.

George is a rogue and a cheat and a liar. I've known him since he was a toddler having tantrums as a way of getting more toys. So I know for a fact that he's a rogue and a cheat and a liar. And when George met Hilary and brought her to Westwood, I saw the way he swept her off her feet with his bullshit and his jokes and his singing and his lively sex acts, and I wondered how long it would be before he broke her heart. .

But to my surprise, Hilary's heart remains unbroken. And even though George is a rogue and a cheat and a liar, she seems to be happy. She's clearly too good for him, even I can tell that, and I have a body made of soil and bark and fungus. But she was happy then and she's happy now; and they are still together.

I really don't know why.

In the Boulevard Bistro a couple are having lunch and it seems to me they are in love.

But they are strangers to the area so I cannot read their thoughts; I do not know their story and I never will.

I think more about Hilary. And her life story.

Hilary can barely remember now why she ran away from home, all those years ago. There was no real crisis. She was getting on all right with her dad and her mum. They were boring, of course, as most dads and mums are. Malcolm, her dad, was an accountant and in those days he worked for HMRC. Her mother Malaika was and is a doctor. There was a family plan that Hilary would train to be a doctor too, but she didn't fancy that. She wanted to be wild and crazy and so she fled to London and lived with her granddad and watched telly every night.

Nowadays Hilary speaks to her parents by phone every week and they see each other fairly often. But the London visits always take place in Brixton, in Grandpa Maybe's house. That's because Malaika, Hilary's mum, refuses point blank to come to Westwood after that time fifteen years ago when they came to stay and George quarrelled with everyone and little Shona sulked and Malcom insulted his adoptive father Grandpa Maybe by calling him a ridiculous and tiresome old man and then, when they all went for a walk in Old Park, it rained toads and Malaika had a screaming fit.

Malaika was so upset that she vowed never again to come to 'this bloody hellhole', and Malcolm agreed. And they have honoured that pledge ever since.

Hilary, despite her big-bellied, large-bosomed and cheerful appearance, is a shy and anxious woman. Crowds make her nervous. People shouting at her make her nervous. Police cars roaring past make her nervous. When she lived in Brixton one of her closest friends was shot dead by police, not for doing anything bad, just for selling a bit of weed and carrying a knife and hanging around with bad types who were gang connected. Montrose was his name, he was a poet, and a gentle soul. But the police chased him through the streets of Brixton even though he hadn't committed a criminal offence. And when he didn't stop running after being hailed, one of the coppers panicked and he was shot dead.

Maybe that's why Hilary is so anxious. She loved Montrose. If he hadn't been gay, flamboyantly so, she would have liked to marry him. He wrote poems for her and she has kept them all. She thought he would always be there for her; she even wanted him to be the best man at her wedding, though George would never have stood for that of course. But he *was* there at the wedding as a guest, and he wept when she made her vows, and she wept when she saw him weep. And when she made love to George that night, she thought about how cute Montrose had looked in his dapper suit and his black beret and his poetic goatee beard.

Then one day, just a few years later, he was dead.

But though she is shy, and is terrible company in large groups, and relies on George's banter and filthy jokes to get them through awkward dinner parties, Hilary is great with the kids in the school where she is a teaching assistant. All her children adore her. When she goes to Tesco's she's always being greeted and hugged by small lively persons who call her Mrs McBride. And who will never love anyone in the rest of their life as much as they love her at this moment in time.

She's the opposite of Jack, her son. Jack was born mellow and he has been dialling it down every day since then. At a teenager he was never anxious, never full of self-doubt. When Jack ran around Old Park, he was always at ease. Happy to be him. Good looking and fit and he ran so gracefully it was a joy to be pounded upon by his feet. Everything was easy for Jack.

But now the roles are reversed.

Jack is the anxious one these days. Full of fear. Tense. Paranoid. He panics when people come to visit him. He worries all night long instead of sleeping. And when he's particularly anxious, which is almost all the time, he sees the world in black and white.

And this is a terrible shame in my view because Westwood is a very brightly coloured place. The trees, the blossoms, the cars, the brightly painted facades, the red roofs, the multi-coloured clothes people wear, the different hair colours that you get these days. For those who have eyes to see, Westwood is a kaleidoscope of colour.

But Jack can't see any of that. For much of the time, his entire world is a black and white movie.

George is always at work, that's just the way George is. He's doing a roofing job in North London at the moment, and also renovating a house for a family in Clapham, and also selling stolen scaffolding poles to a crew in Rochester. He's a busy man, is George. He likes to multi-task, as he puts it, which is why his clients usually come to hate him. So George doesn't see a lot of Jack these days.

Poor fucking bastard, George sometimes thinks, when he does think about Jack. But that's not often.

Hilary drives Jack to the park every day, without fail. She pushes his wheelchair through the square of old Victorian statues including Disraeli and Wilberforce and Joseph Paxton and Mary Annakin and the Brontës, and then down to the lake. He can walk on his crutches, but so slowly it is exasperating, so they use the wheelchair for these 'walks'. She tells him the names of all the trees, but he isn't interested. She laughs every time she sees the green and yellow parakeets flying above them. But to him, the parakeets are not green or yellow they are just smudges of grey and he does not laugh.

Hilary always chats to the people she meets in the park. The dogwalkers, the joggers, the families out for a stroll, she talks to them all, even if they are total strangers. Every time she sees a dog she offers it a treat and exchanges the time of day with the owner, and introduces her son Jack. Jack sits silently in his wheelchair while Hilary babbles away. Hilary used to hate talking to strangers, she had no small talk. But now, when she's with Jack, she's a totally different person.

Sometimes she quizzes him about the people they have met. 'You remember those two sisters? Agnes and Matilda? I saw them in Tesco's today with a tall Indian man. Apparently he's their son in law. Bharat is his name. We had a little chat, he seemed nice.'

'Who are Agnes and Matilda?'

'You remember, the sisters. Grey haired, Scottish. They live together now. Agnes is a widow, Matilda never married. Agnes's daughter Emily is the one who is married to Bharat. He works in a hospital, he's an anaesthetist. Matilda and Agnes have a dog, a little Scottie dog. Called – oh what's its name?'

'No fucking idea, mum.'

'Jock. That's his name. After the dog in Lady and the Tramp. You used to love that movie, remember?'

'Whatevers.'

'Maybe we should get a dog. Dogs are good. Dogs give you an interest.'

'I don't want no fucking dog.'

Hilary is always smiling, always cheerful. But I'm beginning to think it's all an act. I think that she's only pretending to be happy, for Jack's sake.

Oh Hilary. I do like you.

A day has passed. The weekend is over and I go to Hilary's school to see her there. Hilary is tidying up her classroom. The books have got in a muddle and the children's coats have fallen on the floor so Hilary has to pick them up and put them back. All in all: not very interesting. Not in the least bit interesting.

I drift through the classrooms. I listen to the teachers talking. I look at the restless children. I listen to the thoughts of the teachers and teaching assistants, which are banal and repetitive. Nothing here speaks to me.

I go to Old Park. I see Don, walking his dog.

Everyone knows Don. Everyone says hello to Don, he's a familiar face, a friendly face.

I decide to follow him home. And when he gets home, the minute he is through the door, his ghosts start muttering silently to him. His hateful invisible inaudible ghosts who brand him with their pain and regret. And I can hear what they are saying, though he cannot.

I didn't do have you never why did you say the ungracious bitch I wish I had if only I could that never should have waste of fucking useless piece of I hate you I wish you had never been what the hell is wrong with you don't care about I wish I was dead no I wish you were don't you lay a finger on I don't love you I never did –

And so on. An eternity of selfish grumbling. Such is purgatory for these wretched souls.

I am used to Don enduring all this, stoically. But today he loses patience with the ghosts who are haunting him. He bangs his walking stick on his living room floor. And he squares off to the myriad entities whose spirits he can sense but cannot see or hear and he shouts at them.

'Will you,' he says, 'leave me,' he says, 'the bloody hell alone!'

But they do not.

Some time has passed. A day, a week, a century?

I lost interest in the world once again and once again a chunk of time has slipped past me, .

I delve back into the minds of some of the people I follow in Westwood, and I work out how much of their lives I have lost.

Ah. Just a few days, that's all. A few days have elapsed.

I go to see Hilary, it's a Saturday, she should be at home. But she's not. I reach out for her soul with the edges of my awareness; and I realise that she has gone next door to have tea with St John Featherstone.

And so I drift through the wall of number 44 and into the lounge of number 42 and I join them.

St John is a busy man, it seems; he works long hours and he normally doesn't get home till after midnight, so Hilary never sees him in the week. . But – I now discover, as her mind and her memories open up to me, like the petals of a flower touched by sunlight – every Saturday without fail Hilary bakes him a cake and makes him tea. She doesn't know why, she has just taken a fancy to him.

And so, while Jack sleeps, and George is either working or off down the boozer, Hilary chooses to spend her precious weekend hours looking after her posh and childlike next door neighbour.

Today, as the tea brews, St John shows her around his back garden, which has roses and climbing clematis and a cherry tree, nicely kept herbaceous borders, carefully pruned peonies and pansies and a fuchsia that has been coaxed to climb up the side wall. It is not only beautiful, it is immaculate. Carefully pruned, meticulously weeded. All in all the exemplar of a perfect cottage garden.

'This is amazing,' she says.

'I don't do much with it, to be honest,' he says, modestly.

He has no idea that a secret gardener has been at work again in the very early hours of Saturday morning.

In the tea shop in Fairyhill Road there is a customer. Two customers in fact, the two yuppies who have moved into a flat in the five storey house at the top of Westwood Street.

I wonder if this teashop will go bust soon. Alice and Camilla don't seem to have what it takes to run a business. And the kind of business they are running would be better suited to a Cotswold village than a busy urban area.

The teashop is brimming with scones and cakes and floral tablecloths but the two women have a desperate air. Alice is wearing a pinafore, which she thinks makes her look the part of jovial host. Camilla is dressed more severely in an all-black trouser suit.

'Um, can we see the menu?' one of the yuppies asks, the male one, looking around the small but deserted teashop rather sceptically.

'Yes, yes, yes of course,' says Camilla.

'The printer is broken,' says Alice, hastily.

'No you can't,' says Camilla.

'But we - ' Alice says.

'We can tell you what we have,' Camilla says. 'More or less.'

'Would you like lunch or tea?' asks Alice.

'Tea,' says the other yuppie, the female one, since it is clearly teatime.

'In that case, I'd recommend the cream tea with homemade jam,' says Alice.

'Perfect,' says the male yuppie.

'Lovely,' says the female yuppie. 'What flavour jam?'

'Strawberry,' Alice says, glowing in anticipation of their joy to come.

'I don't like strawberry,' the female yuppie says, tensely. 'I have an allergy.'

There is an awkward moment.

The awkward moment lingers and becomes even more awkward.

I pluck a memory from out of the dead air: and I discover that Alice had spent most of the previous day stewing and bottling this jam. Huge amounts of jam. Gallons and gallons of strawberry jam, all to her own recipe.

Alice looks bereft, like a child who has been told Christmas is cancelled this year.

Camilla meanwhile is glowering, clearly furious, both with the customers and with her half-soaked hippy dippy business partner.

And the yuppies are now visibly impatient. They are used to better service, rendered with a smile; and they don't like the aura of despair that is radiating from these two amateurish teashop owners.

But then Alice looks at the jar of homemade jam again and blinks with surprise, and then smiles. 'Tell a lie, it's damson.'

'My favourite,' the female yuppie says. smiling. And all of a sudden she is enjoying the vibe of this cosy little tea-room. 'Joseph, let's stay?'

'Why not?' Joseph says. He picks a table. 'Jane?' he says and she sits down.

I begin to drift away from this tedious scene. Then I pause.

It *was* strawberry jam. I could smell it, even through the glass. I am a nature god, of course I could smell the strawberry!

'Is that picture for sale?' Joseph asks.

Camilla looks at the picture on the wall. It is a landscape scene of an idyllic forest glade inhabited by strange looking children, in the style of Arthur Rackham.

Hmmm.

Strange.

I don't recall seeing it there before.

And yet I recall *everything*. Everything I have ever noticed since the dawn of time is as clear to me now as the morning dew on a warm day.

I am becoming interested. Something strange is happening here.

'It could be,' Camilla says cautiously.

'How much?' Jane asks.

Alice and Camilla exchange a look; neither of them has a clue.

'Twenty quid?' Alice says.

'Really? With the frame as well?' says Joseph, with a sly look on his face.

The frame is very old wood and the painting is highly accomplished. My guess is that this painting is valuable.

I realise that the two ladies are being diddled by someone who knows quite a lot about art.

This makes me happy. I love chicanery. I love it when pigeons swoop and steal the chips from a table in the café in the park before the diners realise what is happening. I love it when foxes tip the bins over and strew dustbin rubbish all over the road. I love it when George McBride cheats his customers by exaggerating how difficult a job is; or by smashing the tiles on the roof of a house with his heavy boots so he can subsequently suggest a new roof is needed.

Things are hotting up here.

Joseph is trying to keep the greed out of his eyes..

Jane is full of hope; she really loves this painting, for reasons she cannot explain.   Camilla and Alice are all at sea; they have no idea how much they should charge for this painting they didn't even know they had.

'Twenty-five with the frame,' says Camilla, eventually.

'Deal!' says Joseph. He notices that Alice has brought some Bakewell slices to their table. 'Ah I love these. My favourite, in fact.'

'On the house,' Alice says.

Then Alice takes the picture down from the wall.

But by the time she has turned around and handed the framed canvas to Joseph, the blank patch on the wall has been replaced by another picture, also a woodland scene, with even weirder looking children staring at a giant antlered stag.

At which point it occurs to me that this is the first such business ever to exist in Fairyhill Road.

And I realise: these two women have been *so* lucky.

I hover above Westwood and I look at the buses.

I go to the Saxon Arms. I see Shona there, sat at her usual table, lost in thought. She looks preoccupied. Anxious. Unhappy. I'm intrigued.

I delve into her thoughts and into her memories.

Ah.

Memories!

I have so *many* of them, you see. Sometimes I like to wallow in memories as if they were oceans. Not just my own memories but the memories of the various humans and animals whose lives and thoughts I follow now or have followed in the past.

I remember, vividly, a time when there were no houses in this area, and no cars, and humans hunted in my woods.

I remember the first humans who chopped down my forests and I remember how angry I was. And how powerless I felt.

And now I am remembering a younger Shona McBride in bed with a man twice her age. I am remembering how she felt, lying under the duvet, stark naked. Her sweat stale after half an hour of vigorous love-making.

The man lying next to her in the bed, the man who was twice her age, was her teacher, Mr Bradshaw. And although he seemed very old to her at the time, and his hair was starting to fall out in what is known as a male pattern way, he was slim and fit and athletic. Cycling was his passion, so he kept telling her. And he loved her and her soft skin and her beautiful body; he told her that too, often.

At the time Shona had believed she was horribly overweight and to be candid, she was. But he never told her *that*.

Mr Bradshaw was a music teacher and Shona played violin in the school orchestra. She loved music but she hated the violin and she hated the school orchestra. She only did music so she could learn to play the guitar but she wasn't allowed to. And she struggled to read music, the same way she struggled to read novels. There was some bit missing in her brain that meant the little notes just drifted away and she couldn't follow them. So a long time ago she had started memorising all the music the orchestra played and only pretended to be reading from the sheet music.

If she hears a piece of music once or twice Shona can usually recreate it in her head. It's a gift she has. But Mr Bradshaw had told her it's unprofessional to play without the music in front of you so she always did.

But one time he kept her behind after class practice to tell her off for not turning her sheet music pages at the right moments and one thing led to another. Shona was fifteen at the time, but she looked much older. Mr Bradshaw was twenty-nine.

The following night they met again and they had a few drinks and then he took her to a restaurant and they had dinner. It was only a pizza and pasta restaurant but he paid and she drank some wine and she felt grown up.

Then on her sixteenth birthday he took her out for what he called a very special meal. It wasn't actually the day of her birthday in fact, it was a week later. He made her bring along all her birthday cards and he read through each one, and she thought that was sweet. But looking back, he was clearly just making sure she really was sixteen. No longer jailbait in other words.

The posh meal they went for was in a hotel and at the end of the meal he told her he'd booked a room for them. And she was so flattered, she didn't notice it wasn't even a nice room. Just a bed to have sex upon, with walls stained with age. When they had done with all the fucking, he fell asleep and in the middle of the night she woke up and he wasn't there. He wasn't married but even so he'd gone back home. She snuck out, hoping he had paid the bill, and didn't get home till five in the morning.

And that was how their affair began. Before that night they had flirted and kissed and groped each other a little. But after that night, it was a full blown sexual relationship; her first.

'You've got such amazingly lovely skin,' he would say to her.

'Too much of it, I'm porky,' she would say to him, shyly.

'Soft, lovely, caramelly, lickable skin,' he would tell her and she would giggle.

I love chicanery.

I love liars.

I enjoy shameless acts of deception.

But I never much liked Benjamin Bradshaw. Don't ask me why.

Shona was doing her A Levels during all of this. She was planning to go to University. A world of possibility was ahead of her. But whenever she claimed she was going to the library to revise, she actually spent all her time with Benjamin, vigorously doing the human sex thing, the joining together of bodies while naked and shouting.

All this happened a long time ago. Six years four months twelve days ago, that was the day she broke up with him.

And now six years later Shona is remembering it all over again. With eyes full of bitterness and regret.

'What are you staring at?' Shona's friend Zara says to Shona.

'Him,' says Shona.

They are in the Saxon Arms. The oldest and most historic pub in Westwood. Shona is with Jo and Zara and Marielle, her three best friends.

Zara is the brainy one, the one who went to Oxford. She is a skinny white girl with long hair that looks lovely when it is brushed, though it usually isn't.

Jo is the cool one. He is wearing a jacket and a thin tie, he is thin and beautiful and soulful and looks like a young black David Bowie. Jo used to be Jo when he was a girl, and now post-surgery he is still Jo, rather than 'Joe'; which I suppose makes life easier when it comes to filling in forms.

And Marielle, she is the extrovert one, the one who always says: 'Why don't we.' She is a dark-haired edgy white girl, and always looks smart and sexy and spends a lot on her clothes. They are sitting at their favourite table in their favourite pub. So young, so fresh, yet already creatures of habit.

'Who?' Jo asks.

'Him,' Shona says.

They follow her gaze. They see a skinny middle aged man with receding hair wearing one of those cool jackets without lapels which on him doesn't look cool at all. It is him. He is back. Mr Bradshaw.

Shona stares at him, her former teacher. Her former lover.

She is remembering that final time. The time when it all went wrong.

'It's him. My music teacher,' explains Shona. 'The one who - '

The terrible and often-shared story comes flooding back to them all.

'The one who raped you?' asks Zara.

'He didn't - '

'As good as,' says Marielle.

'Fucking - ' says Jo.

'Perve, yeah,' says Marielle.

'Shall we – ' says Zara.

'I could take him,' says Jo.

'Jo you really couldn't and he didn't, like, yeah,' Shona says.

She continues to brood on her memories of that final time. The bust-up moment.

It was just a fun game, he'd told her. Kinky stuff, but nothing painful, or violent. Just role-playing Fifty Shades-y stuff. And Shona was well up for that. She loved to experiment – she was the first to dye her hair blue, after all, and also the first to watch Game of Thrones. She was game for anything!

So she wasn't shocked, she was amused, she even giggled, when he took the handcuffs out of his bag. His Soho bag he called it, he'd been shopping all day in the sex shops there.

'Fluffy handcuffs?' They were indeed pink. And very fluffy. And in her view, absurd.

'And eggs. I've got eggs,' he said, defensively.

'What, the ones you - '

'Yeah, those eggs, they - '

'I don't fancy - '

'You don't have to - '

'I'd rather - '

'What about this?' He produced another item from the bag. Not a dildo as she'd feared, or perhaps hoped, but a piece of cloth. He unwrapped it and awaited her applause. She realised that it was a blindfold.

A blindfold.

To go with the fluffy pink handcuffs.

She giggled again.

It was simple, he told her, matter of factly. All she had to do was take her clothes off. So she did.

Then he put the handcuffs on her.

Then he put the blindfold on her. And she felt chilly, and blind, and excited.

But after a while she got bored.

'What happens now?' she asked.

'Just wait.'

She waited. A long time.

'Yeah but what now?' she asked.

'Just be patient.'

'Not the eggs, I don't want the fucking - '

'I'm not going to - '

'You going to kiss me all over? Or touch me with a feather or something? My senses will be heightened, is that it? Like Daredevil? You know who Daredevil is?'

'Of course I - '

'Matt Murdoch,' she said.

'Is that his real name?'

'He has - '

'Shh.'

She was silent.

It was true, what'd she said to him. She couldn't see and that meant she could hear every sound more acutely than ever before. His breathing. The floorboards creaking. The traffic outside. Foxes squealing in the distance. Her own breathing. Her own heart, pit-patting. His breathing, even more laboured.

'You're not jerking off are - '

'Shh. Be silent.'

She was silent.

After a while a thought dawned on her. She became convinced he was taking photographs of her. On his phone.

And she was right. I could see it all, the whole scene. And there he was. Smiling a sly little smile. Taking pictures of her on his mobile phone, with no flash. No sound. Framing her image on his screen and capturing her image with a touch of his thumb on the white dot and then capturing her again. Each photograph a theft of her soul.

'What are you doing?' she asked, close to tears now.

'Just looking,' he lied.

'I've had enough now, ' said Shona.

'Shh,' he said.

'Just stop it,' she said.

'Be patient,' he said.

And that's when she started screaming.

She couldn't take the blindfold off because she was wearing handcuffs. So she wriggled and writhed and she felt trapped and afraid. And she kept screaming.

And eventually he took the cuffs off her.

'Was that good?' he asked.

But poor Shona was weeping, helpless, humiliated. She covered her upper body with her arms and her cheeks were damp with tears and snot dripped from her nose.

'Yeah it was great,' Shona said.

He beamed. Delighted.

'Your turn, what do you want to do?' he asked.

'I want to go home,' Shona sobbed.

That was six years ago. That was the last time she saw him, except for in lessons of course, in those final few weeks of summer term.

And now here he is again. Back in Westwood after six years living somewhere up North.

He is a nasty little man, so Shona believes. And I agree with her.

The girls at their table in the Saxon Arms stare across the room and take their measure of this man. They judge him, as only women can.

'He's waiting for someone, isn't he,' says Marielle.

'He's not on his own, that's for - ' says Zara.

'If he was on his own, he'd have a book or he'd be on his - ' says Jo.

' – sure,' says Zara.

'On his phone, texting, yeah, right,' says Jo.

Shona simply stares. She is very still. Waiting. Being patient. Knowing that she is about to find something out, though she doesn't know what.

Eventually Mr Bradshaw's girlfriend turns up. Wearing a black jacket, a scarf, with hair the colour of night. Spectacles, the big Specsavers kind, which make her look cute as well as brainy. Big black boots that reach up to her knees. A blue skirt the colour of her scarf. This is someone who takes a lot of time accessorising, and who always gets it right. Not a child, as Shona had been; she is a grown woman in her late twenties or early thirties.

Suddenly Shona is filled with rage. I realise she has seen something.

I look at the scene again. But I can't see what she has seen.

I delve into her mind. But her thoughts are an angry jumble of anger and pain and I can't work out what it is that she has seen.

'Shit,' says Shona eventually.

'What?' asks Marielle.

'She looks like me,' says Shona.

They all stare. So do I. They are all thinking about the same thing.

The Ross Syndrome.

It is a well-known phenomenon apparently, among humans who date other humans.

'No she doesn't,' Zara says. 'She's not a bit like you!'

'No, she's - ' Marielle starts to speak but then shuts up.

'Say it,' says Shona.

'Different looking,' says Marielle.

'Slimmer,' says Shona.

'I never said that.'

'She's fit,' says Jo.

'Older than you. She's got glasses. Not a bit - ' says Zara.

'Don't fuck about, bitches,' says Shona.

I can see it now; they can all see it too. The new woman doesn't look a bit like Shona except for one thing.

The colour of her skin.

It's a common colour. Not black, not white, the in-between colour. The light brown mixed-heritage colour. The colour of caramel, some say, though apparently you shouldn't say that any more.

'Most blokes have a type,' says Jo.

'He never raped me,' says Shona. 'I never said he did. And if he took photographs of me while I was naked, which I'm bloody sure he did, he never shared them. He never did that. He never - He just -'

She can't find the words; or rather she can find the words, but she can't say them. She can't tell her friends what she has just realised. She can share any secret with them; but not that one.

But I can hear her thoughts:

No he never raped me. And no, he never shared his pictures of me. He just looked at me. For ages. At my body. No, not at my body. I wouldn't mind that, we were lovers after all and I'm no fucking prude. But it wasn't my body he was in love with. And it wasn't me he was in love with.

It was my skin.

Her soft, lickable, gorgeously brown skin,

Shona feels sick.

'What a twat,' says Zara.

'Fuck he's seen you,' says Marielle.

'You sure you don't want me to go over and do him?' says Jo.

Shona raises a hand, smiling, waves at her ex-. Cool as a cucumber that's been in the fucking fridge, as her father George likes to say.

He sees her, and waves back.

'Are you okay, Shona?' Zara asks.

Shona is still smiling. 'No.'

The police are called to Westwood. A boy has gone missing; an eight year old boy. The uniformed sergeant, Sergeant Carter, is young, with freckles and fair hair, and he's new to this area. He is based in Streatham station, since the old Westwood nick on Incline Road is still infested with spiders and giant crabs after that incident last year. The PC who is with him is older, balding, and sullen; he's been here before in other words.

'So what happened? Sergeant Carter asks the head teacher, Mr Abioye, who appears to be as unflappable as ever. Though in reality, he is in a blind panic. 'You say missing, what does that mean? Was he in Assembly?'

'Well yes. And then – well yes,' Mr Abioye says.

'Well yes what? Was he abducted? Or did he just wander off?' Sergeant Carter asks.

'He wasn't abducted. He did just, um, wander off,' says Mr Abioye.

'Does he have a mobile phone?' Sergeant Carter asks.

'We don't allow mobile phones in lesson time,' says Mr Abioye.

'So when was he missed? Who realised it was gone?'

'His teacher, Mrs Farley. It was during break,' Mr Abioye says, sorrowfully. 'We just don't know what to do. The fire brigade came but they took one look and then, well, they bottled it.'

'What are you on about? How did he get out?' Sergeant Carter asks.

'Out?'

'Out of the school. You must lock the gates, surely. And no kid that age could climb that fence,' says Sergeant Carter.

Mr Abioye gives him a patronising look. I am aware that as a nipper, this headmaster could have *easily* climbed that fence.

'He was eating an Aero,' Mr Abioye says, eventually.

'An Aero?' says Sergeant Carter.

Mr Abioye points upwards. Sergeant Carter is confused. Eventually he follows Mr Abioye's pointing finger. He sees something in the sky.

'What am I looking at, sir?' Sergeant Carter says.

'His name is Toby. We don't know what to do,' says Mr Abioye.

'Whose name is Toby?' Sergeant Carter asks.

The PC coughs, courteously. Sergeant Carter looks sheepish. Stupid question: the missing boy is called Toby. It's on the incident report log. Toby O'Connell, missing person, call logged from Mike Simpson, the school caretaker.

Mr Abioye keeps pointing upwards. Sergeant Carter keeps peering upwards, but can't see anything. Then he takes out his phone and turns the camera on and looks at the sky through the screen, after adjusting it to 8 x magnification.

Now he can see.

Toby is up there in the sky, floating high above the school. He is floating about a hundred feet in the air, with arms outstretched like Superman. Though he isn't actually flying, he is just floating.

Sergeant Carter takes a picture of the scene, 'Fucking hell,' he mutters.

I can see Toby too, but up close now, for I have drifted up into the air and I am hovering near him. I see a flock of pigeons flying past. I see a swallow with its V shaped wings swoop right by him. He tries to catch it in his hands but he can't, and he giggles. Then the swallow is gone, in the blink of an eye.

Back on the ground, in the playground, Sergeant Carter is losing his temper. 'What is this, some kind of prank? Optical illusion? You know it's not safe to, er. Jesus! What if he falls and, er, fuck!'

But the PC with the bald head, whose name is Phil Richmond, is a veteran of these matters. Born and bred in Westwood. Fled to North London after one Westwood event too many; but has now moved back to be nearer his family. He knows what kind of things happen here, and he also knows that what happens in Westwood stays in Westwood.

'Put your pocketbook away, sarge,' says PC Richmond. 'And delete that bloody photo. This never happened.'

'What? What do you mean it never happened?' says Sergeant Carter, angrily. 'We have to do something. We have to get the poor boy down.'

'What poor boy? I see no poor boy?' says PC Richmond. 'Let's go sarge. We were never here. There is no missing boy.'

High above them - the school and the surrounding streets stretched out below him like a Playmobile village - hovers Toby. The floating boy.

Chapter 6

There are wild men in the woods this evening. Seven of them. Bearded and bare chested, and running amok among the trees at the far reaches of Old Park in the area beyond the fishing lake.

Mickey McBride is the leader of the wild men. His beard is unkempt and dusted with grey and he has the savage madly staring eyes of a city dweller who smokes a great deal of cannabis washed down with cheap Aldi wine.

'Halt.' The wild men stop at Mickey's barked instruction. And in a very orderly fashion they form a ring on the ground, lying down on their backs. Then they proceed to do sit ups at each other. The stench of naked male flesh is almost enough to drown out the aroma of tree bark and wildflowers and the fragrance of early Spring catkins.

Almost, but not quite.

'Up.' They spring to their feet, surprisingly lithe. Mickey is skinny and strong; most of the others are beer bellied and strong. But they are all strong. They sprint, they cycle, they box. They do all the things that in ancient times, the wild men of my woods never did.

'Primal scream!' roars Mickey. They let it rip and scream.

'And again!' roars Mickey.

They howl again.

'And again!'

They howl again.

The howling noise fills the woodland. A dogwalker with an Alsatian hurries his pace. His name is Matthew, this is his regular time for walking his dog but not his usual route. He is tall and sandy-headed and he must be single, because I never see the dog being walked by anyone else. It's a frisky beast, full of fun, who once knocked an old lady over by jumping up and licking her; but apologies were accepted and no harm was done.

It is evening by the clock which means it has gone 9pm but the sun has not set for a while so it is still daytime.

The sky is blue.

White clouds skitter across it.

The sun is a dazzling yellow colour like butter, melted.

The rows of mature cherry trees that guard the pathway into the wilder woodland area are budding, and the sweet gum trees further along bear their load of tiny gumballs like decorations upon a Christmas tree.

The great turkey oaks with their scarred barks are showing traces of greenery too, and a few tiny cherry shrubs are in full blossom.

And meanwhile, inside the secluded woodland area, Mickey has lit a spliff and is passing it around, and the rich forest air in the lungs of these wild men is slowly replaced by a dank cannabis fug.

'Fucking great,' says Mickey.

'What's this?' says one of the wild men, whose name is Al, and who works in advertising. He has been pacing around as he lets the weed take effect. And on the ground he has seen a shiny thing. He stoops to pick it up.

It's a watch. A man's watch. The kind which has small hands that point at numbers, not the digital kind.

'Not mine.'

'Nice watch.'

'Let me see.'

'Someone musta dropped it,' says Mickey. But Al is curious now. He follows the trail of crushed greenery in the patch of undergrowth near where the watch had fallen. Perhaps a sign of a struggle, he wonders. He keeps looking then stumbles on something potentially interesting and picks it up.

And he discovers it is the hand that the watch used to be attached to. You can see the tan line in the bare flesh. The stump of the hand is old and starting to go mouldy and it has clearly been chewed by animals.

When Al realises what he is holding he drops it like a hot stone.

The others crowd around and peer at the bit of mouldy flesh.

'Not real,' says Daniel, who is an accountant. 'Someone must have been filming here, some kind of horror movie, and they left a prosthetic hand behind. It happens.'

The smell of dead flesh tells a different story.

'There's been a fucking murrrder!' says Mickey, rolling his r's exaggeratedly, though I do not know why. His eyes light up with the thrill of the chase.

Now the wild men go to work. They kick away undergrowth with their feet. They follow their noses. They kneel down and with their bare hands they plough at soil that has recently being dug up and pressed back down again.

They uncover the body of the murdered man soon after. They carry on digging and the body of the dog that the man was with is also uncovered.

The man is oldish, tall, and mostly naked. He wears underpants and socks and nothing else. His skin is white and soiled with soil but his body is supple.

They pull the body out of the ground and try to give it mouth to mouth, which is crazy, because this man is long dead.

When no one is looking, Mickey picks up a wallet that has fallen in the ground, and slips it into his pocket.

'Who's got a mobile phone?' says Pierre, the least big-bellied of the big-bellied men. 'We should call the cops. This is serious.'

Accusing eyes stare at him. Mobiles are strictly forbidden at a Wild Man Gathering; that is one of Mickey's strict rules.

'Well. Hold on a moment, lads. Let's not do anything rash,' says Mickey.

George McBride is a man who likes to have several women on the go at any given time.

At the moment there's Helen, the widow in Tottenham who is having a new kitchen installed. And that's not all she's having installed; har har.

There's Penelope in Clapham who is a yummy mummy whose husband works all hours in the city and who has an au pair who takes the children round the park every afternoon. At which point George nips in to remind Penelope in the only way that counts that she is still young, sexually exciting, and able to pull a bit of rough.

And there's - well, the fact is, George has a rota that he refreshes on a regular basis.

Helen, the widow in Tottenham, is starting to take things seriously. She wants George to leave a spare toothbrush at her place and stay over sometimes. Surely he can manage that? George often stays away from home in fact, he does jobs in the Midlands and in Gillingham and occasionally even in Scotland and Wales. So it wouldn't attract any suspicion from Hilary if he took Helen up on the offer. But George is not a leaving a toothbrush behind kind of a guy. So he always finds an excuse.

Luckily Helen is the forgiving sort. Her husband died from a long and terrible illness after she had spent nearly ten years as a carer. Now, this is her 'her' time. So she drops occasional hints, but she never nags.

When you're ready, George, she often thinks. *I can wait. Whenever you're ready is fine by me.*

That will be never, Helen.

'Fact is, I never know what to say,' he tells her one afternoon, as the Spring air slowly dries the sweat upon their naked wrinkled bodies. They are lying together on the bed, both exhausted after a session of vigorous love-making. Helen's body is slightly older than his. She is in her early fifties, but still fit, still well shaped. With a shock of hair on her head that went silver when she was in her thirties. Like most widows she knows what she is doing when it comes to bedroom games and George appreciates that.

'To who?' she asks. She can tell something has been troubling him, and she likes that he feels able to confide.

'Well to the lad like,' George says. 'He's a good lad. We used to play knockabout in the field. God he was bloody brilliant. I went to see his football matches, almost every one. When he played tennis I was always there for the big matches. When he had the trial for the Arsenal youth team I was over the moon. Always had a smile for his old dad, did my kiddo. But these days, all he does is fucking mope.'

It's rare for George to open up in this way. Helen snuggles in tighter, and strokes his chest hairs with her fingertips, in little swirling patterns. His nipples are firm, from cold not passion, but it pleases her.

'Children are like that,' she says, sharing. 'I have two, I never see them. Well, Easter and Christmas, and my birthday of course. I sometimes think they like their mums in law more than they like me. Well I suppose I do have a sharp tongue but they should be used to that by now. They do call though, give them that, every week. One of them is in Edinburgh, one is in Bahrain. How old is your boy?'

'Just a lad. Seventeen. Eighteen this November. He was planning to travel the world,' says George.

'Well why doesn't he?' Helen asks.

George is lost in remembered pain. 'Well he can't.'

'Why can't he?'

'His legs. The thing about his legs, you know?'

'What thing about his legs? You never told me about his legs,' Helen says.

George thinks about it.

The fact is, his son is a cripple, and he is also clinically depressed. He stares at you like there will be no tomorrow and maybe there won't be, for him. Hilary keeps saying, we should take him to a therapist, he has mood swings, maybe he's getting suicidal. And George always scoffs at that. No lad of mine is going to be suicidal, so George says. Just give him time, let him work it out for himself. I mean, we put a roof over his bloody head, don't we? What more can we do?

But deep down George can't believe how the hell Jack can carry on carrying on the way he does. With injuries so terrible and life-changing.

George saw him in the bath once. Hilary was sponging Jack down, prior to cutting his toenails. And George could see that Jack's legs were withered, like sticks, like an old man's legs. This is a boy who used to have legs like tree trunks. Legs that could run him like the wind. He was a fit bastard and the girls loved him, and George had been proud of him. But now, well, what's the poor fucker going to do with what's left of his useless fucking life?

Or so George often asks himself.

'What's the thing about his legs, George?' Helen says, gently.

'Accident. Car accident, like,' George replies, brusquely.

'Oh I'm sorry, was he badly hurt?'

'You could say that.'

I know that George doesn't like having a cripple for a son. It irks him. It pisses him off. It embarrasses him. And it makes him squirm; it's a reminder of his own mortality and George has no time for *that*.

And what's more, George doesn't like what it is doing to Hilary. She's all Jack, Jack, Jack. Never wants a leg over. Never wants to get pissed on a Friday night down the pub, because Shona is always out and she doesn't want to leave Jack on his own. So they end up watching Netflix and going to bed at ten o'clock, after Hilary has tucked Jack up.

'He'll be all right though, won't he?' Helen asks.

George thinks about it.

'Not really, no,' George says. 'His spinal injuries, they're likely to get worse when he gets older. He has another operation on his right leg due, they'll put a plate in. He's in a lot of pain. Depressed most of the time. Poor bastard, he's totally fucked. It's a mystery to me why he don't, you know, top himself.'

His tone is casual and matter of fact. It's his familiar 'Sorry love, you're gonna need a new boiler but I think I can you a good price' tone, and Helen knows it well.

The air on their naked bodies gets colder. Helen gets quieter. She had a good marriage, she lost her husband to cancer, she currently struggles to stay close to her two lads, but she does care about them. And yes, she's having an affair with a married man, but so what? Surely she's allowed some fun, after all she's been through?

So all in all she's a decent sort, and also a realist. There are no stars in *her* eyes. But I can tell that at this particular moment she's appalled at George. Shocked and rather disgusted by his heartless words and his casual tone.

The mood between them changes. And George is smart enough to pick up on it. He can tell what she is thinking. He's not a stupid man, you have to give him that.

'I'd better be going,' George says.

Oh fuck, he thinks. *I've really fucked this.*

'You better had,' Helen says.

Bloody women, they're all so bloody - complicated. Why the fuck is that?

'I'm busy next week,' George says, casually. 'I'll send one of my lads to inspect the work. Shouldn't be long, another two weeks and you'll have a kitchen fit for Come Dine with Me, am I right, my lovely silver haired harlot?'

'Ha. I love it when you call me that. Yes, George. You are right, George.' Helen gets up and puts on a dressing gown. His clothes are piled up on the floor by the window. There are skid marks on his Y-fronts, which she can't help but notice. Helen feels nauseous but she is too much of a lady to let on how much she suddenly despises him.

'I'm going to have a bath. See yourself out, George?' Helen says.

'Course I will, my honey. See you week after next, all right?'

'Yes of course. That will be great.' And Helen smiles but I can tell she doesn't mean it.

'Sex bomb sex bomb you're my sex bomb,' he sings to her, grinning, and she grins back, and she does a little shimmy.

Encouraged, George stands up, his big dick swinging, beer belly sucked in, and he holds an imaginary microphone and gives it full welly: 'I'm your main target come and help me ignite!' he sings, rather beautifully, in a Welsh lilt.

I'll miss you, you daft fucking bitch, he thinks. *If only, eh?*

'Bye George.'

Don wakes up screaming. His hands claw at the air. His screaming turns to coughing, he has a bad chest. He staggers out of bed and spits in the sink. He has a piss and it goes everywhere, because that's what happens with old cocks. He can't be bothered to clean it up. He washes his face and when he looks in the mirror his face is ashen and his fingers are black, and rotted away.

Or so he thinks. To me his hands look normal but when I read his thoughts I can see the gangrene through his eyes, and I can see him gag and choke and vomit up a torrent of yellow puke and I can feel his horror as the floor of the bathroom becomes awash with streams of diarrhoea venting out of his bloodied arsehole.

He is not dreaming, he is awake, but he is hallucinating.

A roar of voices fill his ears. Incoherent, spirit crushing, desperate.

I listen hard but even I struggle to make sense of them because they are all screaming at once:

Mybabymylovertoosoonican'tgolikethisahdamnyoureyesthisisn owaytogoIwanttodieIhavediedwhyamInotdeadwhatisthisplaceinthe nameofthefathersavemeI'mfeelingbetternownonono

Hundreds of voices, filled with hysteria, spitting out phrases, appeals for help or last dying words, I can't tell which. And I wonder, if these are ghosts, why are there so many of them?

I ponder harder and dig into my memories.

And then it comes to me. I *do* know why. And I try to plant my knowledge in Don's mind but he can't hear me.

No one can ever hear me.

He gets up and goes downstairs to the kitchen and makes a cup of tea. He looks at his fingers, they are no longer black and withered, just cracked and stiff and painful. Like they always are these days. He pats his pyjama bottoms; they are intact, he doesn't have a bloodied arsehole, there is no trace of diarrhoea. He makes a cup of tea and puts a tot of brandy in it.

'If you've got something to say then bloody well say it,' says Don, to the air. He is comfortable talking to ghosts now. But the problem is, when they talk back he can't hear them.

'I won't bloody move, I'll tell you that. I've lived in this house for twenty years. My wife died in this house. But where is she, eh, you bastards? Is she with you or has she gone to a better place?'

No answer as always. Don is wide awake now. He walks through to his study, which is a corner of the living room where he has a desk and a computer.

Ah that's more like it.

I turn the computer on.

Don blinks when the screen flickers and comes on before he has touched it. But he assumes he didn't turn it off properly; that often happens. He sits down in front of the screen and logs in. He starts surfing the net.

He looks up Ghosts In Westwood. Obvious but wrong. He reads the story about the little girl who supposedly haunts the basement of the Saxon Arms. He discovers there is a decorated window in the basement of the Saxon Arms, even though there is no natural light, which is weird. And he reads about the chains on the walls of this basement of the Saxon Arms, and explores the various theories – that this was a torture chamber, or a haven for smugglers. All of this is fascinating. But it's missing the point.

Don hears a massed howl of pain and rage that rocks the house and I hear it too.

Don sighs. Defeated.

I decide: this is not my problem. If Don is driven mad by ghosts, that's too bad. And so I resolve to leave his house.

But I don't leave.

This is vexing me and I realise I need to do something about it.

So I take control of his computer and I write a word across his screen.

This is not easy for me, for I have never been taught to read or write, and I was born in an era where there were no humans on this planet, let alone computers. But I do my best. I write:

Pa;/lguw

I am astonished at myself! I made a word!

But the word is not the word I intended. My best is not a very good best. Don studies the word on his screen for a while, rather surprisingly taking in his stride the idea that a ghost is controlling his computer.

He frowns, in anagram solving mode now, and writes the word backwards:

Wugla/;P

Equally meaningless.

I attempt to try again, spelling the word correctly this time, but this time nothing happens. In all honesty, I have not got a clue about how to make this work. Hurricanes and wars I

know about, I have experienced many in my time. But QWERTYUIOP is a stretch too far for me.

But Don is digging in. He's not going to be defeated by this cryptic message from a ghost. He tries moving the letters around, trying to make a different word of the original word.

Pagu/lw;

Puwagl;/

And a few other equally ridiculous combinations. Finally he gives it up; this is getting him nowhere.

He goes back to the original word I typed:

Pa;/lguw

It occurs to him that the punctuation marks may just be mistypes, fat finger syndrome as the youngsters call it. He deletes them. That gives him:

Palguw

Then he does Spellcheck on the word on his screen. It comes up with a number of possible options about the word that might have been intended by whoever mystically typed it. But the first option is the correct answer:

Plague

Swiftly he Googles it: Plague. He finds the Wikipedia entry. In he goes.

And so Don reads about the Second Pandemic of medieval times. He reads about the Black Death in the 14th century, which may have killed as many as 60% of the entire world's population. From there he moves on and reads an account of the Great Plague of more recent times, just a few hundred years ago. And the moment he does the lights in his living room flash and the floorboard creaks, as I use my powers to hint that he is getting 'warmer'.

He reads on. In the years between 1665 and 1666, he learns, and I recall, the Great Plague devastated London, killing more than a hundred thousand people. A fifth of the entire population of the capital.

In cases where there was no treatment available 80% of those affected died a terrible death. Even with good medical treatment the mortality rate was high, in the region of 40%. But for most of the poor and the desperate of London at that time, medical treatment was nothing but a dream.

He continues to read, and I remember it as he reads. Those dark, terrible times.

Those were the days when fear stalked the streets of the country village of Westwood. Doctors were few and far between but when they did appear they wore masks that looked like bird beaks. Victims developed blistering swellings on their groins and all over their bodies and died in torment. And the dead were buried in improvised mass graves across London and its neighbouring villages. Huge mountains of meat that were dumped in trenches and covered over with layers of soil. In Aldgate, in Stepney, in Shoreditch, in Charterhouse Square, in Vinegar Alley in Walthamstow, in Cross Bones Graveyard in Southwark, and in Westwood. All this he reads about. And some of it I knew, but some is fresh to me.

The Westwood Plague Pit was small compared to some of the others. But the rats and their fleas did sweep through this area, causing terror and scores of lonely deaths. And at the end of it hundreds of corpses were hurled into a giant mass grave. And all who were buried there had died in agony, and none had been blessed by priests in their dying hours. And all are now angry souls, confined in their prison deep in the soil in a spot just south of the roundabout at Wildflower Meadow, close to the railway line.

In Georgian times this was blighted land, for people were afraid of the plague pits. But by the late Victorian period the old legends had been forgotten and rows of cottages were built to house the workers on the Westwood railway line.

Don's house is one of those cottages. Two storeys high with a cheeky pink rendering. A lovely little cottage, so all his neighbours say.

But beneath the many levels of the back garden, beneath the topsoil and beneath the layers of thick clay London soil, there dwell the angry ghosts of the 232 Plague Victims of Westwood.

I am tired of their rage, which has grown in the years since Don first moved here, until now it is a tidal wave of anger. I am tired of their haunting of innocent souls. I have given Don the hint he needs. The rest is up to him.

He does not disappoint me.

Don is in his 70s but he's a fit man and a strong man and a keen gardener. He also is a believer in the right tool for the job. And at dawn he is ready with his spade and his pick and mattock. The pick side of the pick and mattock is used to drive a hole in the soil, to open it up; the mattock side chops the earth into manageable chunks. And once the ground has been breached in this way, he can shovel the soil to the far end of the garden.

It is a massive task, well beyond the reach of a single man. But once he has carved out the first few squares of soil, I am able to help.

And so I shudder, I tremble, I clench my deepest reaches; and at the far end of his garden a deep sinkhole appears. Like a bullet hole in an ogre's brow.

Don is startled. He walks over to the sinkhole and he stares at it. He picks up a rock and drops it in, and waits for the sound of it hitting the bottom of the hole. He hears no sound. Then tentatively, he shovels up a spade full of soil and throws it into the sinkhole. It vanishes, deep into the earth.

Exhilarated, Don throws down another shovel-full of soil into this bottomless hole. And another. At first it is hard going. But after a while the soil becomes soft and motile – in other words, it moves of its own volition on to his shovel, he doesn't need to shovel it.

Eventually the living soil is able to circumvent the shovel entirely. Small columns of earth pick themselves up and march along the length of the garden like ants carrying giant leaves. Don stares at this, again taking it very much in his stride.

He goes to the kitchen and makes himself a cup of tea and when he returns he sits at his garden table and watches it all, by the light of the moon. As the soil moving increases in pace and volume, he cracks open a can of beer. And when the sun comes up he puts on his cap, so as not to burn his vulnerable bald head.

Don is three cans down by the time the sinkhole is sated, and the garden has been fully excavated. And he takes a long sip of beer and casts his eyes over the workings.

Well fuck me sideways, he thinks. And I can tell that for the first time in a long time, he is cheerful.

The hole in the middle of Don's garden is nine feet deep, and twenty feet long, and six feet wide. It reaches all the way across to the garden fences on each side and down to the very end. I have also caused a small sloping bank to be carved on the house side of the excavated hole with rough soil-steps moulded to allow Don to walk down.

The Westwood first dawn dawns. Time for Don to go to work. But he finishes his beer first. Then he has some breakfast. Then, still wearing his green wellies, he steps down the steps and into the sunken rectangle that has now replaced his entire back garden.

There are twigs lying on the soil, but they are not twigs. He picks several of them up and carefully cleans them with a cloth. They are in fact bones. A jawbone. A leg bone. Ribs. A skull. Fingers that have lost any connection with their hands hundreds of years ago.

Don can hear a soft sighing noise all around him. The noise of trapped ghosts who can finally feel the wind on their bones, as their skeleton-shards are warmed by the London sun. Job well done.

But Don has done his research. He has read books on ghosts and human remains and he knows how important it is that a soul should be laid to rest.

Next door meanwhile are nosing around.

'What are you up to there, Don?' asks Mr Merriman from the other side of the fence. He is an estate agent, and he is about to start some gardening. He peers over the fence, baffled at the vast hole in Don's garden which wasn't there the previous day. 'Is that a swimming pool by any chance?'

'Maybe,' says Don. 'Maybe not.'

Don has never been a great conversationalist.

Peering over the fence on the other side of the garden, Mrs Barclay is very anxious. 'Have you had planning permission for that, Mr Harwood? I wouldn't like to think it will undermine my foundations.'

Don's smile says it all.

'It's safe enough,' he says. 'Safe as houses.'

'What are those twigs over there?' she asks.

The bones of corpses once buried in a plague pit potentially still infected with traces of bubonic plague is the correct answer.

'Just twigs. This was woodland here once, you know . As far as the eye can see and beyond, this was part of the Great West Wood,' Don says.

She doesn't give a shit about any of that but she offers a friendly smile.

'Just so long as you don't undermine my foundations,' she says firmly.

'As if I would,' says Don.

Snooping neighbours are a major problem for the next phase of this job of works. So Don decides to wait until it is dark again to carry out the rest of his mission.

But first, he pops up the hill to the hardware store, the one run by Mr Mohammed and son, and he buys a dozen storm lanterns and a miner's helmet. They stock everything in that shop, he could have bought a caged canary as well if he'd been minded to. He also buys up the shop's entire stock of barbecue charcoal and instant lighting bags and Mr Mohammed and Pranavash help him load up the boot of his car with his haul.

'Have a good day, my friend,' Mr Mohammed says in friendly tones, though he does not and never will know Don's name. 'And enjoy your barbecue.'

'That I will.'

Once he's home, all tooled up, Don puts the telly on and takes a long nap and by the time the murderer in Midsomer County has been startlingly revealed, he is very well rested.

It's now pitch dark outside. Don puts on the miner's helmet and switches the lamp on, creating a powerful beam that emanates from his forehead. Then he carries out the storm lanterns and makes a little lattice with them all around the excavation site and lights them all.

The moon is full and the sky is dotted with blinking stars and Don's hollowed out garden is now as brightly lit as a gloomy art gallery.

Now that he's had a kip, Don is feeling more in the mood for manual labour. So he makes

numerous journeys back and forth inside the hole and up and down the steps that lead into the hole. And by the time he has finished he has dumped two dozen bags of barbecue coals and twenty-four instant lighting barbecue kits and very many old fashioned fire-lighters on to the dry bones that are strewn across the soil. Then he lights a match and carefully sets fire to the paper of one of the instant lighting barbecue packs that rests upon a heap of charcoal chunks.

And then, slowly, guided by the beam of his miner's helmet. Don trudges his way back to the end of the excavated hole and he steps carefully up the soil steps. And when he reaches the top he turns around to watch his handiwork.

It takes a while to catch, but before long a warm glow covers the 20 x 10 x 6 foot hole in the ground. Flames billow up as the paper bags holding the instant lighting barbecue packs catch fire and then the fire from the burning paper causes the charcoal pieces inside each bag to start burning. Meanwhile all around the excavated garden, firelighters snap and explode, creating fresh pillars of flame. Don feels the heat of it all as he sits back down at his garden table, sipping a mug of cocoa. At one point he nods off and when he wakes up the hole is merrily ablaze and the large black charcoal chunks are turning grey.

Then the bones ignite. Like firecrackers, popping and flaring in syncopated sequence. Desiccated bones steeped in plague toxins erupt into orange flames. Long-buried skeletons blaze furiously. Don recoils from the heat of blazing skulls and ribcages and arm bones and leg bones. And then the myriad sheets of flame conjoin and a single tower of flame leaps and stands up, as high as the house.

For a little while Don is worried the flames will spread and set his house on fire, but I do not allow that to happen.

The pillar of orange flame grows higher still.

It bucks like a typhoon but I hold it steady.

Then it climbs higher still. Until a hundred foot pillar of orange flame rests upon the hole in the back garden of Don Harwood, in 58 Westwood Street.

In the distance I can hear fire engines. All along the street, in living rooms and bedrooms, I hear mobile phones being switched on and people screaming: 'Emergency services please!'

'There's a fire!' 'Westwood is ablaze!'

Don goes to bed, job well done. And he sleeps on till second dawn.

When the fire officers arrive at the house they ring his front doorbell but he doesn't answer, so deeply is he asleep.

So a burly fireman uses a metal tool to smash down the side gate and then he and his team run towards the flames in full protective gear, trailing a hose pipe behind them.

But when they reach the back garden, the fire has ebbed and gone. There are no ashes here. No barbecued coals. No bones. No hole even. Instead, spanning the expanse of Don's large back garden, is a lake of glass, shimmering in the radiant light of the rising sun.

And at the centre of the lake of glass is a tree, also made of glass, with leaves made of diamonds and catkins made of dried human hearts, and flowers made of blood-red rubies each containing a single soul.

And when the east wind blows through Don's garden, the diamond leaves tinkle and ring out and the heartbeats of the catkins throb in sympathetic rhythm, and the red ruby souls softly sing.

Chapter 7

'It's a shithole,' says Kane.

The Bogman grunts.

Strangely, I still can't read this creature's thoughts even though he was born and raised in Westwood. Perhaps it is because he has been dead so long that he is not in any way 'human' or even truly alive. But no matter: his actions generally speak for him. The Bogman is pure evil.

Kane however is used to him by now. He's relaxed in the monster's company. And he takes the grunt as permission to keep on complaining.

'Piss on the stairs. Lifts never work bloody work!' Kane says. 'Windows don't open. And the bin area is - '

'Lifts?' asks the Bogman.

Kane sighs.

'I told you about lifts. Rooms that move. There was one in that shopping centre but we went up the escalator instead.'

'That's the place where I bought this hoodie,' says the Bogman.

He is wearing a black hoodie that proclaims on its chest: GAP.

'It suits you,' says Kane.

It does not suit him. But at least the hood of the hoodie covers the Bogman's scarred and misshapen head. And his gold-edged trainers and gold chain give him a touch of bling.

'Which flat was yours?' asks the Bogman.

Kane points.

'Third floor, Mandela Court. That one,' says Kane.

'And your mother still lives there?' says the Bogman.

'Yeah,' Kane says.

'You love her?' the Bogman asks.

'Sort of.'

'But you see her often though.'

'Not really.'

'My mother,' says the Bogman, 'was a witch. Is that the word?'

A rare personal revelation.

Kane pretends to take it in his stride.

'I don't know. Did she do witchy things?' Kane says.

'She cast spells. She cursed enemies. She fed me on the blood of wolves instead of milk from her teats to make me strong, and it made me strong,' the Bogman says.

Kane nods. He is using a deadpan face to hide his feelings, yet even so he is clearly shaken.

'Sounds like a witch. What happened to her?'

'They burned her. Made me watch. I was your age, more or less,' the Bogman says.

Kane is even more shaken by this.

'You took revenge?' Kane asks.

'Of course. I always do,' says the Bogman.

'Who killed her?' Kane asks.

'My father. My brothers. My sisters. My aunts. My two uncles. They hoped to appease the gods, but they did not.'

Nearby, in the central courtyard area, a married couple are bickering. A child is playing hide and seek with her daddy. A weeping willow weeps.

'So when you, ah, took revenge, you killed your entire family?' asks Kane.

The Bogman doesn't answer that.

Instead his tone becomes querulous, almost naggy: 'You should visit your mother. A boy should look after his mother. Protect her. As I did not.' The Bogman gives Kane a severe look. 'Visit her. Tell her you love her. Give her money.'

'I don't fucking want to,' Kane says.

There's an ugly pause.

Kane thinks: *Oh fuck.*

Kane thinks: *You pushed it too far you dickhead.*

Kane thinks: *Maybe the fucking freak will let this one slide?*

But the Bogman does not let it slide.

'Good point. Let's put it to the vote,' says the Bogman, in whiplash tones. 'Should you visit your dear old mum, who gave you birth, and endured your insolence and sloppiness for so many years, or should you not?' It is sarcasm as severe as a garotte.

'I'll visit her,' says Kane, hurriedly.

'Good.'

'I could do it now.'

'No. We have work to do,' says the Bogman.

Like the Bogman, Kane is also blinged up. His trainers cost nearly five hundred quid. He wears a Rolex watch which cost as much as a small car. He doesn't wear jewellery but he spent several thousand pounds on the tattoo he bears on his back and shoulders. It is a magnificent piece of art, a haunting scene of pagan worship involving trees and demons, inked by a master of the needle, to a design suggested by the Bogman.

Thanks to the Bogman's unique skills, Kane's car stealing business has expanded exponentially. He now has a crew working for him. He has relationships with some of the top dodgy car dealers in the UK, with deals negotiated by the Bogman which are all highly favourable to the sellers, namely, Kane and the Bogman. He has a bank account. He also has fifty grand hidden under the floorboards of his flat. He is saving for a deposit on a house.

Kane is going places and it makes him feel great.

The Bogman gets down to business.

'Where are they? These "shotters" of yours?' the Bogman asks.

Kane walks the Bogman through the estate to the waste ground behind London Heights where the drug deals are done. It is a patch of land the size of half a football pitch. It was once intended as the site of an additional set of apartment blocks, but it was left to decay, and is now a dumping ground for fly tippers. Old sofas, discarded Christmas trees, and burned out cars are among the detritus that litter the scene. Kane stands by a pile of tyres with no treads and looks around and whistles. Before long a few shabby kids appear, looking at him aggressively.

'Who you with?' asks a scrawny ten-year-old. His friends call him Tock, I don't know why.

This is familiar territory to Kane. He knows how to stand, how to hype himself. He gives the kid a withering 'fuck you' glare. His jacket is tightly fastened and bulges, so it's obvious he is carrying a gun with a shoulder holster beneath it. Tock pretends he isn't cowed but he is.

'I'm with me, I'm Kane, I used to be a younger here,' Kane says.

Tock eyes up Kane's trainers, clocks his Rolex, puts up a good stab of not being impressed. 'Fuck off bruv 'cos you ain't welcome.'

'Mind your manners, son, my boss deserves more respect than that,' says Kane sharply.

All the while the Bogman stands silently, his features shadowed by his hood. It is early morning for the third time that day and the sun's light is bright and dazzling.

'Nah, man, you gotta earn respect. For all I know, this ugly old fucktard be Five-O.'

Kane glances at the Bogman. 'Five-O means - '

'I know what Five-O means,' says the Bogman. His voice is warm, resonant. His voice in fact has more flesh on it than his desiccated body.

'Hey you scrongy uggz, your face be making my eyes splode, why doncha mong off,' says the boy called Tock again. He is only four foot something and in another context he would be a cute little kid.

'I want you to sell something for me,' says the Bogman to Tock. He nods at Kane. 'Then when you've sold it, I want you to give the money to him.'

Tock, the scrawny kid, stares at the Bogman warily. 'Are you stupid as well as thick as shit? I'm saying uh-uh, no way, I ain't dealing with you bruv.'

'You'll do as you are told, little boy,' says the Bogman calmly.

Tock flares up at that. 'Don't diss me, bruv, you can - '

'Don't call me bruv,' says the Bogman. 'Kane.'

Kane hands over a rock of coke in a clear plastic baggie to the child called Tock. They had found it in the Ferrari they stole last week, in the glove compartment. Clearly the car belonged to some major dealer or other. It's worth a packet but Kane is no longer connected, and so this is his idea, a way of monetising their lucky find with minimal risk.

'You giving me this?' Tock says, big-eyed.

'To sell. When you've sold it, ninety per cent comes to us,' says Kane.

'Can't help you, I ain't no shotter,' lies the scrawny kid.

'What's your name?' asks the Bogman.

'None of your fucking business.'

The Bogman tries to sound friendly. It's not in his range but give him credit for trying.

'Tell me your name, lad,' he says. 'You look like a nice kid. Maybe we could be friends.'

Stony sullen silence follows.

The Bogman resorts to his usual mode: intimidatory. Though his warm voice remains calm, and matter of fact. 'Or maybe not. Now I want you to tell me your name, and your address. Better still give me your phone and tell me your password and that way we will not only know who you are but who your friends and family are. I assume you have MUM on speed dial.'

The kid is still cocky. His two pals, both young kids with smart trainers and thousand yard stares, are hanging back from all this but they are definitely ready for action and both of them are holding flick knives loosely in one hand by their sides.

'You ain't getting nuttin' from me. We're protected we are.' And Tock nods at his pals, who nod back, and stare at the Bogman as if they know what they are doing.

'Kane,' says the Bogman.

Kane unzips his jacket and he takes out the gun. A Glock 17 pistol stolen from a police armed response vehicle that they had nicked when the feds were on a job.

Tock looks at it as if he's seen many guns before. And maybe he has. 'No need for that.'

Kane swivels and points the gun at the Bogman and fires the gun. Once, twice, three times, hitting him accurately in the torso. The Bogman's thin body is shaken by the bullet blows and gobbets of flesh and clothing fly from him with each impact. But he remains calm, and standing.

It takes a few moments for normal hearing to return.

'Blanks,' says the scrawny kid.

Kane swivels the gun again and fires at one of the tyres. One, two, three, four. Rubber flies. Bullet holes gape. Ten bullets are left in the gun. Then he swivels again and points the gun at the head of the scrawny kid.

'Just a one off,' says Kane. 'Sell this rock, we'll be back in a week. Don't cheat us. Now give me your phone.'

'Fuck off,' says Tock, the scrawny boy.

The Bogman steps forward. He pulls down his hood, fully revealing his terrible face, and his toothless empty mouth. He pats the scrawny kid on the head, and ruffles his hair.

'Come on. Spit it out. What's your name?' the Bogman asks.

'Pete.' Tock is just his nickname of course.

'Can't hear. Louder.'

'Pete.'

'You want to come and work for me, when you're older and your balls have dropped, Pete?' the Bogman asks.

Pete is staring goggle eyed at the monstrosity that is the Bogman's mutilated face.

'I ain't allowed to freelance. The Brothers don't like it.'

'Then don't tell them. Give my associate your phone.'

The scrawny kid hands his phone over. Kane flicks the screen.

'PIN,' says Kane.

'One two three four six,' says Tock.

Kane opens up the phone, scans the WhatsApp messages. Then he switches on Bluetooth and clones it to his own phone.

'Job done,' says Kane.

He hands the phone back to the scared looking kid. The kid looks at the Bogman. He nods, and touches his fist to his chest. His version of bowing the knee to one's liege.

'Good boy,' says the Bogman. He has the knack of absolute authority. Even without his horror of a face, he would command obedience.

'Nice one,' says Kane.

They get two grand for the crack cocaine. Just a one off.

But cars are still their primary game. They started small, stealing twenty or thirty performance cars a week by the tried and trusted relay box method. But then the Bogman decided they had to expand. After some research, which involved intimidating a number of car dealers by breaking into their houses at the dead of night, Kane discovered the favourite pub of a senior engineer at the BMW factory where key chips are encoded. And after a long conversation in a remote location with the Bogman, the senior engineer agreed to give them the software that will allow them to open almost any car.

Now they have staff, ten in all, all of them skilled in the art of car theft. Several of them are former estate agents with a passion for fast cars. One of them is a kid from Kane's estate who has just come out of jail. Kane is the manager of their car stealing business, the Bogman is the enforcer.

Anyone who tries to rip them off, answers to the Bogman.

Anyone who tries to cheat them on a deal, answers to the Bogman.

And any car owner who tracks his car down and tries to claim the vehicle back – well, that only happened once and it was unpleasant.

And so, within months of his resurrection, the Bogman has managed to establish himself as one of the most successful high-earning thieves in all of London. His is a class act without a doubt.

For the Bogman, it's not enough.

'Nice gaff, don't you think?' says the Bogman.

Kane looks at the gaff; which is a mansion with at least ten bedrooms and a pool and a running track.

'Yeah it's a nice gaff,' Kane says.

'Nice car too,' says the Bogman.

The car is a Lamborghini Aventador, custom made, and it is indeed a nice car.

I want that fucking motor, Kane is thinking. Though I don't need to read his thoughts to know that.

'Hard to flog, that's one of a kind that is,' Kane says nonchalantly.

'We aren't going to flog it,' says the Bogman.

They are in Bromley, one of the duller suburbs of London. Only a few scattered remnants of the Great West Wood remain on the surface; but my roots are still here, which allows me to easily follow their progress.

The Bogman is up to something. I don't know what but I am intrigued.

The house they are looking at is a gated Jacobean Manor House that was a school for many years and has now been restored by its millionaire owner.

'Besides, we can't get in,' says Kane defiantly. 'That house, that's a fortress that is. Look at the CCTV. Those gates. No way.'

Kane and the Bogman are not actually anywhere near this house. They are in a park, sitting on a bench, looking at a mobile phone image of the car and house as seen from above by an illegal drone. Kane operates it expertly with a joystick attached to his phone. The aerial robot soars above the house then swoops down and around the car. It's like being there.

'We don't have to get in. We just wait,' says the Bogman.

'I'm not fucking carjacking, man,' says Kane.

'Look into my eyes,' says the Bogman.

Kane looks into the Bogman's eyes. They are two deep brown pools of empty.

'We don't have to get in. We just wait. Let the car come to us.'

What kind of fucking lunatic are you? Kane thinks.

'No guns, though, I ain't carrying no gun,' Kane says. 'Give me that much yeah?'

The Bogman reaches in his coat and takes out a semi-automatic pistol.

'I said no! Fuck! I ain't carrying no fucking strap, man, if this all goes bollocks up that means serious time,' says Kane.

The Bogman stares at Kane, scornfully.

I never asked for this, thinks Kane. *I never fucking asked for it.*

He considers doing a runner but he doesn't dare.

He considers taking the gun and shooting the Bogman in the head with it and *then* doing a runner but he knows that won't work. For the Bogman cannot die.

His fear sits inside his chest like a parasite that will one day explode out of his body, like it did in that science fiction movie he loves so much.

Kane is the Bogman's bitch and there's nothing Kane can do about it.

The Bogman haunts Kane with another empty stare.

Then he holds the gun up by the barrel and Kane takes from him, reluctantly.

'I ain't merking no one,' says Kane, almost in tears by now.

'I do not require that of you,' says the Bogman.

'Whose fucking car is that?' asks Kane.

'It belongs to a man called Morton. His brothers called him Psycho.'

Time stops moving for Kane. Just for an instant it stops.

Or rather, it seems to stop. Then it carries on, inexorably.

'Oh fuck no,' says Kane.

'Oh fuck yes,' says the Bogman.

Kane's face resembles a painting I once saw: it was called The Scream.

'I said, didn't I say, I said don't do it. No gang wars. We don't want to mess with those bruvs. They are Faces. They roll heavy, they are fucking connected!' Kane says, in a shrill voice he can barely control.

The Bogman has reverted to wearing his Fedora hat, which he prefers to a hoodie. He takes off the hat. 'I am a Face,' he says. 'Look at my face.'

Kane can't bear to look at his face. 'I'm done, I'm not doing this no more, I'm getting the fuck out of here.'

'Conceal the gun, please, you're making an exhibition of yourself,' the Bogman says reprovingly.

The park is quiet, but there are dog walkers approaching, and a young man pushing a buggy. Kane puts the gun away. He looks at the screen.

He uses the joystick to lift up the drone, and he flies it away. The borough of Bromley is mapped out below him via the drone's viewfinder. He steers the drone and eventually it lands beside them by the bench, like a faithful hound.

'We need a crew,' Kane says later, as they wait in their car, outside the gated mansion. He is calmer now, calculating the angles. If he's going to do this shit, he wants there to be a chance he'll come out alive. 'Psycho Morton, he has minders. He drives in convoy. Everyone knows that . He is a bad bad boy. Two of us, one gun, won't cut it.'

The Bogman doesn't answer.

His silence does the job that it always does.

Kane is afraid.

He is afraid of dying.

He is afraid of *not* dying, of being captured and tortured by the Mortons.

He is afraid of failing in this crazy mission and incurring the Bogman's wrath; and

then being punished in some appalling way.

But he is also afraid of what might happen to him if he *succeeds*. If he survives the

job and goes on to become the evil sidekick of an evil gang boss; and hence never gets to have any kind of life of his own.

And the worst of it is, he is afraid about all of these possibilities all at the same time.

But then all his life Kane has been afraid. All of his life he has had no control about what he does and how he lives his life.

He is not just the Bogman's bitch. He is life's bitch.

'What's your game plan, bruv?' asks Kane.

'Just wait,' says the Bogman.

Just fucking wait, thinks Kane, scornfully.

The day before had been a washout; Psycho didn't leave the house at all. They stayed all night in the car and in the morning they were still there. Kane's anticipation of terror is proving to be worse than terror itself.

Just fucking wait.

Just fucking wait!

Kane feels wrecked and sleep deprived. But the Bogman of course does not sleep.

They have left the car by now and are standing on the pavement with a clear view of the gated mansion in Bromley, looking at the gates. Far enough away not to be seen by the cctv. The Bogman is still wearing his Fedora. Kane wears a baseball cap, turned the wrong way round.

Kane is thinking about his sister Caroline, who has just been offered a high paying job in Leeds. He hasn't seen her in ages. Last time he saw her she was so confident. She had so many friends. She seemed like a different person. And she didn't seem at all interested in what Kane was doing, but perhaps that's because he couldn't tell her anything about what he was doing. His entire life is illegal and if she knew he was working with a monster like the Bogman she would be appalled.

He misses her. He misses having her around, he misses bantering with her. He misses having her as a best mate. But he never calls her or messages her so it's his own fault they have lost touch.

'After this I mean. After we whack this psychopath. Assuming we get away with it. What next? Are we going to the mattresses or what?' Kane says.

'I have no idea what that means,' the Bogman says.

'Cause I ain't no wartime consigliere,' says Kane.

'I know what a consigliere is. You are not one of them. You are merely an assistant.'

'Well, thanks bruv.'

'Just wait,' says the Bogman.

They wait for three more hours. Kane nips off and gets a kebab. He pisses against a tree. He lights a spliff and tokes it and tries to get in the zone.

He rejoins the Bogman who hasn't moved by so much as an inch in all that time.

The gates of the mansion slide electronically open.

A car pulls out. An Audi. It is sluggish and its chassis hangs low, which suggests it is armour plated. Three men are inside, a driver and two passengers. The passengers are bodyguards. Death threats have recently been made against Psycho Morton by a North London Face. And so, as Kane observed earlier, he now travels in convoy, with bodyguards in cars in front and behind.

The Audi smoothly drives along the short driveway, followed by Psycho's Lamborghini followed by a Fiat at the rear.

Before the Audi can turn into the main road however the Bogman strides swiftly forward on to the driveway and blocks the exit with his body. The Audi slows and the driver sounds the horn, aggressively. The Bogman doesn't move. The Audi glides to a halt.

The Bogman still doesn't move. The Audi driver sounds his horn again.

Kane has moved closer to the house, but he stays on the pavement, mostly out of sight. He holds the semi-automatic pistol against his chest and under his hoodie. Not wanting to have it, or to use it.

The Audi driver sounds his horn again, then nudges forward, bumping his bumper into the Bogman's legs.

The Bogman stays put.

The two men in the back of the Audi get out. They are heavy set, almost comically so, suggesting they are wearing Kevlar vests under their shirts. They are clearly mercenaries, professional killers. They are both calm and deadly. They take it in turns to survey the scene, looking for backup that might indicate this is an ambush scenario. They spot Kane, a skinny white kid in a hoodie lurking, and they keep him in their sights.

One of them talks into his sleeve, alerting the other bodyguards in the Fiat to the potential danger. A nutter and a drug dealer. Could be messy, but nothing to worry about.

Then the two killers stroll over to the Bogman. He raises a hand and sticks up his thin middle finger, provokingly. His long black coat is old and muddy, his shoes are battered, his hat has seen better days. All in all he looks like a crazy homeless man.

One of the killers looks at Kane and does the two fingers at his eyes 'I'm looking at you' gesture to warn him to keep out of this. The other killer unbuttons his jacket for an easy draw. Their stance is confident.

'The end of the world is nigh!' screams the Bogman and they smile, getting a handle on this.

'Fuck off before I kick your arse!' says the killer with the unbuttoned jacket.

'The end of your world is nigh, cocksuckers,' says the Bogman in his usual warm, resonant tones.

The two killers pull out their handguns and there is a roar of gunfire.

The two merks fall to the ground. Kane is stunned. He can smell cordite. His ears are ringing. He has no idea what just happened. Slowly it dawns on him that he has the semi-automatic in his hands, and he is standing with his feet apart in the firing position, his heartbeat throbbing slowly. He just shot the two men dead. With astonishing accuracy considering the range. And swiftly too, drawing and firing four deadly shots in the blink of an eye.

A natural, in other words.

The Bogman turns in the driveway, looks at Kane, raises an arm, and then sticks up one thumb. A Roman salute to a worthy gladiator.

The Audi driver, who is trained in close protection driving strategies, slams his foot on the accelerator and the car bucks forward and hits the Bogman with a blow equivalent to being hit by a giant's fist.

The Bogman doesn't move. Not an inch. But the driveway beneath him cracks, as the kinetic energy of the car hitting him travels through his slight frame and into the ground. The Audi driver floors it again and as he does so the Fiat and the Lamborghini start reversing back through the gates.

The Bogman bends down, rolls himself under the car, then stands up, lifting the car easily above his head. Then he throws it. The car arcs up high, flying over the two other cars, and smashes against one of the stone pillars of the gateway; then drops heavily to the ground. The Fiat continues reversing, and crashes into the wrecked Audi. There is a screech of metal and a terrible crumpling noise, followed by screams.

The Lamborghini is now trapped between the Bogman in front and two wrecked cars behind. Behind the wheel is Psycho Morton. He considers the angles. It's clear he is wondering if he can scrape a route past the Bogman if he acts quickly enough and maybe he can.

But the cavalry are on their way. The two bodyguards from the rear-end Fiat scramble out of their car, and run past Psycho's car, blood on their faces but otherwise unhurt, carrying heavy duty machine pistols. The Bogman stays put. And Kane joins him, he still has twelve bullets in his gun, and he walks towards the bodyguards steadily, holding his gun sideways, which is a stupid way to hold a gun, but he does it anyway.

The bodyguards open fire but before the bullets can connect the Bogman grabs Kane and throws him to the ground. Then he carries on moving, more quickly than the eye can see, letting the bullets rip holes in his coat and body, and when he has traversed five yards in less time than it takes a hummingbird to consider flapping a wing, carnage ensues.

Blood gushes from arteries.

Heads fall off bodies.

Screams of pain are cut short by swift death.

The Bogman thrusts his hand into one man's stomach and pulls out his entrails. It is horrifying and even Kane, who is watching from the tarmac, and who has just killed two men, is shocked.

In seconds, both bodyguards are dead.

Then the Bogman walks over to the Lamborghini and taps on the windscreen. Psycho Morton sits inside, frozen. Keeping the door locked.

The Bogman raises his fist, prepared if he has to to punch his way into the car.

Psycho pops the lock. Then he gets out of the car. He is a barrel-chested shaven headed man with ugly scars on his head and face, the legacy of a brutal attack by a man with a machete.

'You are Mr Morton,' says the Bogman.

Psycho isn't remotely afraid, despite the horrors that have occurred. He looks at the Bogman and at the carnage he has perpetrated, as if querying an opponent who has been cheating at cards..

'Are you fucking mad or what? You fucking nutjob. I thought I was the fucking psycho. What is this, a fucking hit?' Psycho says, laughingly.

'No just a request,' the Bogman says.

Kane is back on his feet now, watching the encounter closely. He is taking deep breaths to fend off hysteria. In and out. In and out. Swaying back and forth on wobbly legs. Trying not to shit himself.

'Request away you cunt you'll get nothing from me,' says Psycho Morton.

'I'd like your car,' the Bogman says.

Psycho looks at his car. It is a very beautiful car. He looks at the Bogman. He looks at the dead men who are strewn upon his driveway, who were serious men, and who were swatted like flies. He hears the sound of police cars in the distance. He calculates the odds.

'How much?' asks Psycho Morton.

'What?' says the Bogman, startled.

'Seventy k, it's yours.' Psycho puts on his hard man, that is my final offer, face.

'You're not fucking *selling* it to me.' The Bogman's voice is no longer warm, no longer resonant. He is angry now.

'Apparently I am. Sixty k.'

'I want you to give it to me for nothing. That is why I arranged this terrifying display of violence,' says the Bogman.

'Yeah yeah, nice one pal, fifty k and that's my final word,' Psycho says.

Kane wants to laugh at this bewildering exchange but he doesn't dare.

The sirens are getting closer.

The getaway car they stole is two blocks away.

Without the Lamborghini, the Bogman has no chance of making an escape. Unless he kills the entire Bromley police force that is, which in theory he could do, but even he might find it a stretch.

'I want you to give it to me for nothing,' says the Bogman a second time.

But Psycho is grinning, shaking his head, don't pull my pecker mate suggests his body language.

'Tell you what, fifty k and I'll throw in the drinks cabinet as is. There's a drinks cabinet, see. You wouldn't think they'd fit it in, in a car that size, but they did, and it's a smooth drive, one careful previous owner, in other words, me. Fifty k, my final offer.'

'Pay the man,' says the Bogman to Kane.

'I don't have fifty grand!' says Kane.

'Write him an IOU. My credit is good. Is it not?'

'I think it is,' says Psycho shrewdly.

'Keys.'

Psycho hands over the keys.

'You'll be seeing me,' says the Bogman.

'To give me my money?' Psycho says.

'No. Well yes. But not just that. For your instructions. You work for me now. Your brothers will too,' says the Bogman.

'Dream on,' says Psycho, amused; and the Bogman kills him. With a single punch to the head which cracks the big man's shaven skull. Blood spurts out of Psycho's nostrils and his eyes glare with disappointment. Then he falls to the ground. Kane shudders.

'You drive,' says the Bogman, throwing him the keys.

A few moments later they are racing through Bromley, pursued by cops. They almost get away too, but in the end they have to crash the car and run for it.

Fucking hell, thinks Kane as he sprints wildly through the streets of Bromley, keeping two steps behind the swift loping strides of the Bogman.

Fuck-ing hell!

This has been the best day of his life.

Chapter 8

'Anything I can do for you?' Shona says sweetly to Jack.

Five months have passed since Jack's accident. He is still living in the middle room on the ground floor. The alternative is a chair lift and he has indicated he would rather hang himself than use one of those. His room is a decent size, and has no windows, which is good in his opinion, because it allows him to fester. The downside is that you can't get to the kitchen from the living room without passing through his bedroom.

Hilary has rigged up a curtain rail spanning the room to allow him a little bit of privacy. And George has promised to build a partition wall, which in fairness he is perfectly able to do, since he is a professional builder. But as Hilary says, if you hold your breath waiting for George to do a job, you will go bright red and choke to death.

Shona has her smiley pretty face on as she peeks through the curtain, en route to the kitchen. Jack is trying to watch a film on his laptop, it's La La Land, but he's not getting far because he is seeing the movie in black and white, which rather defeats the point of it.

Jack scowls at the interruption, and takes off his headphones.

'You what, slag?' He always calls his sister 'slag'; she seems to have got used to it.

'I said, is there anything I can do for you, my darling brother?' Shona says.

'No. Nothing. Fuck off. I'm fine.'

Shona smiles even more sweetly. 'Well, if you change your mind, if you want anything, anything at all, let me know.'

Jack's face turns a further shade of sullen.

'You can jerk me off if you like,' Jack says.

That doesn't faze her; nothing fazes her. She's a McBride after all.

'Well, it' s a lovely idea, but you're my brother, so it wouldn't be right,' Shona says.

'So when you said, "If you want anything, anything at all",' Jack says.

'Within reason.'

'Just fuck off. I'm fine. Go eat some cake, fatso.'

That stings; I can tell. But even so Shona continues to smile nicely. 'I don't mind you calling me fatso.'

'Yes you do,' Jack says.

'I used to mind, now I don't.'

'Lardass, porker, jelly belly, fatass,' Jack says.

'I love you, Jack,' Shona says.

'You're no fun any more.'

'I'm more fun now than I've ever been.'

'Who are you knobbing then?' Jack asks.

These two always talk to each other like this. It's a banter-battle that has lasted nearly a decade, ever since Jack was old enough to say 'cunt'.

'Don't be so vulgar, Jack,' Shona says.

'Still playing your music teacher's clarinet, har har,' Jack says.

'He doesn't play the clarinet,' Shona says.

'I meant, sucking his dick,' says Jack.

'I know what you meant. I saw him recently actually. He looks - '

'He looks what?'

'Fit,' says Shona.

Jack gives her a filthy look.

'You still want to fuck him?' Jack asks.

'I never wanted to fuck him, I was – coerced.'

'Oh fuck off, you were not, you filthy 'ho, you had a dripping wet fanny and you were gagging for it,' Jack says, nastily.

But Shona stays calm. 'No, that's not the case. There was an inherent power imbalance which made our liaison abusive and inappropriate.'

'You mean, you're a fat bint and no one else would fuck you,' Jack says.

'I really do love you, Jack. And can I say - '

'Don't say it.'

'I am SO sorry for you. What you're going through. It must be awful,' Shona says.

She's crossed a line: there's a long and terrible silence.

'Fuck off fuck off fuck off!' Jack shouts.

As he shouts he glares wildly. But not at her, but to the side of her. He is shouting at the doorframe.

Shona smiles back at him. Butter wouldn't melt in her mouth, as they say. Though why that should be a measure of innocence is beyond me.

'I mean it! You're a fat ugly cunt and I - '

She frowns, cutting off his rant. 'Why are you staring like that? Is there something wrong with your eyes?' Shona asks.

Jack is red with rage now. His entire body is locked rigid as if he wants to throw a punch at his sister but knows he mustn't.

'Jesus wept!' Jack shouts. 'No!' he shouts.

Then he says: 'But there is something wrong with my legs. And my hips. And my arms. And my head, I get headaches all the time, but my eyes, they're the one fucking bit of me that's - '

'No, you've got a squint or something. Hell-o! I'm over here, Jack.'

'I know, I know you are,' Jack says, feebly. Then he swivels his glare to where the sound of her voice came from; but she swiftly moves. So he's now staring at the wall.

'And now I'm over here,' Shona says.

Tricked. He's furious. He swivels his eyes again.

'Stop fucking moving, right,' Jack says.

He is trying hard to give her an intimidating stare, but his aim is way off. He is now looking daggers at a poster of Eminem.

'Are you blind, Jack? Is that one of your side effects?' Shona says.

She moves closer to him. Into his inner sanctum. His makeshift bedroom smells of masculinity and spunk. It's evident Jack that is not washing often enough. Though that is understandable, since he can't lie down in a bath, and taking a shower is a struggle for him.

'No of course I'm not fucking blind,' Jack says.

'How many fingers am I holding up?' Shona asks.

She holds up two fingers.

'Three,' Jack says.

'Wrong. How many fingers now?'

She is doing the offensive 'middle finger' gesture.

'None,' says Jack.

'Wrong. What colour top am I wearing?'

'Red.'

Shona looks as if she's been slapped; this is real now.

'Wrong, it's blue. Jesus, you really have gone blind. Are you having a stroke or something?' Shona asks.

'Do I look like I'm having a stroke?' Jack says.

'I don't know, what does someone having a stroke look like? Oh I'm sorry, you wouldn't know because *you can't see.*'

That one gets to him. Jack looks like he wants to cry but he doesn't.

She moves closer still. He can catch a whiff of her perfume now. Marc Jacobs from Boots, because she is going out later. And he turns his eyes towards the middle of the perfume cloud.

'I'm not having a stroke. This is – normal. It happens,' Jack says.

'What happens?' Shona says.

'This. What is happening now.'

And finally she sits on the bed. And she runs her hand through his hair, which is greasy. And she rests her hand gently on his arm, reassuringly. Like a mother stroking her child.

'Being blind?' Shona says.

'I'm not blind, Shona,' Jack says.

'Well yes you fucking are! Jesus! You can't see me, how is that not blind?'

'I can fucking see, don't fucking diss me, right,' Jack says.

She stands up. Sticks out her tongue at him, with a big sneery face on her.

'Oh yeah? So what am doing? Am I waving my arms or am I sticking my tongue out?'

'You're sticking your tongue out.'

'That was a lucky guess.'

Jack shrugs. Swallows a lot. Steeling himself. He wants to tell her the truth, he really does. So he does; but in a roundabout way.

'You see that trophy? Over there. Footballer of the Year. Go and pick it up and put it somewhere.'

'What?' Shona says.

'Footballer of the Year. Westwood League. Remember, I won it.'

'I know you won it.' It is on a shelf cluttered with empty Coke cans. His room really is a tip. She takes two paces to the side and picks it up.

'Where do you want me to put it?' Shona asks.

'Anywhere. You choose,' Jack says.

'Okay.'

She looks around, then eventually she puts it in the laundry basket, which is spilling over with dirty clothes.

'Laundry basket,' he tells her.

'What?' She's annoyed; she thought she'd hidden it well.

But then it occurs to her; this is not like a normal 'hiding things' game, since he has been looking at her all the time.

'Take it out of the laundry basket. Put it somewhere else,' Jack says.

'It's not that big of a room,' Shona says.

'You don't say "of a", that's an Americanism.'

'Yo, dude, what's this about?'

'Just put it somewhere.'

'Okay.'

She puts it on a shelf next to one of his tennis statuettes.

He can't see her; but he can see the football trophy as it moves and bobs its way across the room. Magically floating through the air, like the household objects and bits of armour in the final sequence of *Bedknobs and Broomsticks*.

'Nice one,' Jack says.

'What are you trying to prove?'

'You put it next to my tennis trophy. Good place, it should have been here all along. Put one hand on your head,' Jack says.

'Why?' Shona says.

'I said, put one hand on your hand.'

'I have.'

'Now ask me to guess which hand,' Jack says.

'Guess which hand.'

'Right hand,' Jack says.

'Correct,' Shona says.

'Yeah but I was just guessing. I can't actually - '

'Yeah but you got it right.'

Jack is exasperated.

'You're not getting it. Come here. Come here,' Jack says.

She doesn't move.

'I said, come here.'

She moves and stands close to him.

'I'm here,' Shona says.

'I'm going to grope your belly, okay?' Jack says.

'You're my fucking brother, paedo,' Shona says.

'Just – let me - '

He takes a grip of her belly flesh and squeezes it.

'You're hurting me,' Shona says.

'Don't be a baby. I just want to touch you. Feel your big fat belly.'

'Why?'

'Because I can't fucking see you, right!' Jack says.

'Finally! You admit it. But how come - '

'Jesus,' Jack says.

'What?' Shona says.

'Fuck.'

'What?'

'You've lost weight,' Jack says.

She's proud of this but she can't admit it. Because that would mean admitting she'd been ashamed of being fat before. 'A bit, yeah.'

'When the fuck did you lose weight?' Jack asks.

'I'm still pretty chubby though.'

'When the fuck did you lose weight, you stupid bitch? When did you lose that jelly from that belly?' Jack says.

'I don't know. Maybe – a month ago? No, three months ago. Or maybe more like five months. A couple of days after you got hit by a car - '

'Hit and crippled, don't pretty it up,' Jack says.

'I started losing weight. Don't know why. In fact, I think it was when I saw you in hospital. I went home and I lost a stone, overnight. Then when I saw you on crutches – I weighed the day after, and I'd lost another stone. Odd, really.'

The look of horror on his face is heart-breaking.

'Oh that's so wonderful. The more crippled I am, the slimmer and hotter you get,' Jack says.

'It's not like that, Jack,' Shona says.

'What is it fucking like?' Jack says.

'Don't be such a fucking baby.'

'I am not a fucking baby.'

'Then don't cry you fucking baby,' Shona says.

'I ain't crying you fucking slag,' Jack says.

He is crying, in fact.

'You dickbutt,' Jack says.

'Douchebag,' Shona says.

'Doggyknobber.'

'Bieber.'

'Shitgibbon.'

'Cockwaffle.'

Abruptly his sister-vision returns; he can see her.

'Blue. Your top is blue. Your jeans are blue, but a different shade of blue. It doesn't go, to be honest. Your hair is tied back. You are a hell of a lot slimmer, and it suits you. You look – quite nice really.'

Shona is silenced by this. Her brother's face is raw with emotion but she can tell that he is actually looking at her now, and actually seeing her, now.

'I'm not invisible to you anymore,' she says, redundantly.

'Yeah, I can see you and I can see colours too,' Jack says.

'You couldn't see colours before?' Shona says.

'No.'

'You can see things, but not people, and not colours?'

'No. It was just you. I could always see everyone else. In black and white, admittedly, but I could see them. Dad and Mum and Uncle Mickey and the doctors and people in the park, and in the pub just – not you. I stopped seeing colours and I stopped seeing you.'

'That's weird. Is there a word for that?' Shona asks.

'Yes.'

'What is the word for it then?'

'There is no fucking word for it you stupid hairy cunt!' Jack says.

She's miffed; he caught her out in a stupidness. These two keep a strict tally of such things.

'When did this happen? Is it a side-effect, I mean, of the accident? A brain injury or something?' Shona says.

'Nope.'

'What then?'

How can he explain, when he has absolutely no idea what is happening to him?

'It's just me. It depends on my mood, whether I see in black and white or not, or whether I see you, or not,' Jack says.

'In what way? What kind of mood?'

'Well like, if I hate myself and I think life is a waste of time and I want to kill myself, that kind of mood,' Jack says.

'Don't be a drama queen.'

'Sorry.'

The look on his face makes her want to weep too.

'Jesus. You're not being a drama queen,' Shona says, softly.

'I'm fine. I'm fine. Just sometimes. It gets – it gets – and I can't – and I want to – and the world is - and when that happens, the colours go away. Not metaphorically, they just go. Like a camera filter, blip, the colours go and the world is sepia.'

'And that other thing. What the fuck is that about? Why can't you see me, but you can see mum and bloody dad?' Shona says.

Jack has given this a lot of thought; but he has given very little thought to how to explain it.

'Because, it's, well. You know. I mean. It's what. Ever since. I've always. It's fucking obvious, innit, you stupid dickbrain!' Jack says.

'Not obvious to me,' Shona says.

'Because! Because! Because! You, yes, I do, them, no, I don't. You must know what I'm saying! Do I have to fucking spell it out?' Jack says.

'It would fucking help if you did you useless waste of space,' Shona says.

'Them, mum, dad, I don't, not since I was a toddler anyway, or maybe a bit, like everyone does with their mum and dad, but not so it hurts, not so much, as with you, because you, I do. I do. I do!'

'What the fuck are you on about?'

'I,' says Jack, and pauses.

'You, what?' Shona asks.

'El,' says Jack, like someone pissing out a kidney stone.

'Oh you are actually spelling it out, you really are a literal minded retard.'

'Oh.'

'We used to do this when you were a baby so you wouldn't know we were swearing.'

'Vee.'

'I know where this is going.'

'Ee. Why. Oh. You,' he concludes in a rush.

She gives him a look full of rage.

'No you fucking don't, you hate me, you've always hated me,' Shona says, angrily. 'You've always treated me like shit, you told me I was a fat cow, you told me I was fucking stupid, all my life you've - so you can't just don't turn around and say that now, don't you dare, don't you fucking dare I, L,O,V,E,U me, you arsewipe.' Shona is in tears and it makes her young and pretty face look old and blotched.

'Yeah, but,' says Jack.

He really is an idiot.

She's an idiot too. She wept for Jack in the hospital ward, when she was cradled in Grandpa Maybe's arm; and for a few minutes she was overwhelmed with her love for her little brother. He meant the world to her! She couldn't live without him!

But a few weeks later Jack called her 'fatso' and she went back to hating him. Because she was convinced that *he* hated *her*.

'When I said all that,' Jack says, 'I didn't mean it right. I was only kidding. Only ever kidding. It was just our game, our joke. I thought you knew that, like. My way of saying that – I - I think the fucking world of you. I fucking adore you.'

There is a terrible pause. And this is when I realise that all her adult life Shona has been a fool. And so has Jack.

The terrible pause continues.

Then Shona laughs uproariously. 'Of course I knew. I was just pulling your pecker, you twat. Not literally. Not your actual pecker, don't be daft. Course I know you love me. Course I love you too. I'm your big sister right, I love you to bits, oh what the fuck, let's go the pub and get wasted.'

'Yeah, cool, whatever,' says Jack.

The teashop in Fairyhill Road is thriving. But even so, there are tensions.

'I think we're in danger of diversifying too much,' Alice argues.

This is their 'them' time, the half hour before the shop opens. A large clock on the wall ticks down the time.

'Oh really? Is that what you think?' says Camilla, politely.

'Yes,' says Alice.

Oh for heaven's sake, says Camilla's face.

'Stretching ourselves too thin, I mean. What do you think?' Alice says.

I think you're a fucking idiot, suggests Camilla's face.

'What? What?' Alice is put out.

'We're doing well,' Camilla says firmly.

'I miss baking,' says Alice, sadly.

They brood on that for a bit. Alice is the baker; Camilla is the organiser. For years this project had been their dream and they had planned in detail how wonderful it would all be. But as it has turned out, neither of them are getting to use their special skills much.

And yet the customers keep coming.

'People love your cheery smile,' Camilla says.

'I don't have a cheery smile,' Alice says.

'That's why people come, in the hope of seeing your cheery smile.'

'What's that meant to mean?' Alice is enraged.

'I'm making fun of you,' says Camilla.

Alice looks like a sourpuss; that's the gag.

Alice wrestles with anger for a few moments then remembers she has a sense of humour.

'Fair enough,' she says, and attempts to crack a smile.

The fact is, Alice is a worrier.

She worries about the drains, and whether they might get blocked and cause a flood. She worries that the bank will foreclose on their business loan; though in fact they paid off the business loan a month ago. She worries that one day she will run out of things to worry about: and that day is getting close.

Ping.

The first customers of the day have arrived,

Alice and Camilla square up to the ordeal. A family. Mum and dad and three children, two of them teenagers. Locals, all of them. 'Are you open?' Dad asks. 'Cause the sign, you know.'

'Yes of course, do come in, so nice to see you,' Alice babbles. She beckons them in, as Camilla gets up and turns the CLOSED sign to OPEN.

'Okay, great,' Dad says.

But now that they are inside, the family can see that the counter is empty. Just a bare empty stretch of wood. There is also a table beside the counter which would be a good place to put cakes, but there are no cakes there either. No scones. No pastries. No biscuits. They stare at the blackboard behind the counter which features a clever caricature of Alice and Camilla, drawn by Alice, but has nothing else written on it.

'What do you actually serve?' Mum says, a little aggressively.

'Well what do you want?' Camilla says pleasantly.

'A fry up,' says the teenage girl.

'Bacon sandwich,' says the teenage boy.

'Coco pops,' says the toddler.

'Some sort of panini,' says Dad.

'I'd love some poached egg on fried bread and salty bacon and a hot cup of coffee,' says Mum, remembering her favourite meal as a child.

'Coming up,' says Alice, briskly. 'Now, do take a seat. We've got some comics for the kids, newspapers for the grown-ups.'

'I'd like,' says Dad, who is a fan of Sudoku puzzles.

'Ah yes,' says Alice, reaching under the counter and finding a book of Sudoku puzzles which she hands to him. Dad accepts the gift graciously, not batting an eye.

'I'd love a cup of tea from a big brown teapot,' says, Mum recalling a tea she had in childhood with her gran, which had been served up in a Doulton blue and white mug.

And it's there, waiting for her, on their table. A big brown teapot and a blue and white Doulton mug.

Dad and Mum and the three kids take their seats. On the table there's a Nick Fury comic for the boy; a Lucifer Morningstar graphic novel for the girl; a colouring book for the toddler, a Guardian for Mum, and a performance car magazine for Dad.

Another ping.

Three road workers enter, in their yellow vests, with large biceps. They blink. They clearly took a wrong turn, they wanted the greasy spoon.

'Take a seat,' says Camilla, as the smell of bacon sizzling on a hot pan smites them and lures them in.

They dither but Alice is standing at the door, blocking it, not letting them through. And Camilla is pouring big mugs of stewed tea from an urn and that does it for them. They sit down and are delighted to find that on the table there are three very old copies of The Sun, with the semi-naked centrefolds on page 3. The ones they don't publish anymore.

'Are those books for sale?' Mum asks Camilla as she is served her poached egg and bacon.

'Which books?' Camilla asks.

Camilla looks. There's a shelf on the wall opposite the family's table which features a selection of brightly coloured children's books, including the Just So stories and a complete collection of the Elinor M. Brent Dyer Chalet School books.

'Um, which one do you want?' Camilla asks.

'Can't remember, ' says Mum. 'I just remember, it's something to do with a magic carpet.'

Camilla walks over to the shelf and grabs the first book that comes to hand, which is E. Nesbit's *The Phoenix and the Carpet*. 'How about this one?'

'That's it!' Mum is thrilled. 'How much?'

'A pound?'

Dad is inspecting it. 'This is a first edition by the look of it,' he says, sceptically.

'One pound fifty?' Camilla says.

Alice arrives with the fry up and the bacon sandwich on a tray with two chocolate milk shakes.

'I didn't order this,' the teenage girl says stroppily.

'It's your favourite isn't it?' Camilla say sweetly.

'Well. Yes. I suppose it is.'

Ping.

Don can hear his other ghosts now. The burning of the plague pit extinguished hundreds of angry dead souls but there are still many spirits left in his house. These are the men and women and children who used to live in this house, or on this land, whose souls have lingered. Many of these 'ghosts' are not in any way real human spirits, they are just shadows and echoes. But some survive as disembodied entities, or as voices.

One voice in particular haunts Don. His wife Marie, who must always have been there. But only now with the absence of the plague-dead ghosts can he sense her presence. And feel her pale regret.

Don and Marie met and married at University in Loughborough. They were together for nearly fifty years. They were inseparable. Don was always a gentle soul, shy and self-effacing, and always diffident about putting his own needs first. Whereas Marie was a fiery tempest, a red-head till she the day she died. And she would always push him to be more pushy with his work colleagues, and even with his friends.

'Don't be so soft,' she'd say.

'You know more about it that *he* does,' she would say.

'You're your own worst enemy, you really are,' she would say; which he always took as a compliment. Which indeed it was.

They worked well together. They loved each other. But then she died. She died in this house nearly nine years ago, of an invasive cancer that hollowed her out in months. She had come home to die, once the writing was on the wall. And she died in the bed Don still sleeps in. And when Don speaks to her, Marie can hear him.

'I thought I'd dig up the front garden this weekend, love, what do you think?' Don says one morning.

A faint whisper comes from a universe away, not audible, in the sense that no recording device could detect it. But Don can taste and swallow and hence *hear* the word:

Yes.

Don smiles.

'Right you are then, love. I thought I'd plant some roses. I know how much you like roses. But not the red ones, I agree, that's too vulgar, some coral roses, I know you always liked coral roses. Remember, I had one as a buttonhole when we were married? Right, that's a plan, coral roses it is. How does that sound, Marie?'

A faint whisper from a universe away:

It sounds good, Don.

St John wakes up in the armchair in his living room. For a few moments he has no recollection of how he got home last night. But then it all comes flooding back to him. Not a crazy drunken night, as he'd initially assumed on waking. No, quite the opposite. He'd worked late at the office, trading with the New York office. Then he'd caught an Uber home. The driver had to wake him up and he didn't even manage to climb the stairs, he was so tired. He checks the time. Mid-afternoon. He must have slept right through.

On the glass dining table is a cake and a mug of cold tea on a coaster. There's a note from Hilary. It says: 'You're working too hard.'

St John knows it's true. He is working fourteen hour days as a matter of course, often sleeping in his office all week long then catching an Uber home on Fridays. He has no social life except from the Saturday afternoon visits from Hilary. And he slept through that this time.

When he checks his phone messages he discovers his parents recently got divorced.

'I really don't understand,' Hilary says to St John.

She made him some fresh tea when he went over to her house; he also took across the cake she had left him.

She is seriously wondering if he actually knows how to make a cup of tea for himself.

'Well it happens, you know,' St John says wisely. 'Couples drift apart.'

'Yes but they didn't tell you?'

Hilary gives him a look filled with horror. And it dawns on him how absolutely shit this is.

'Well, they did, of course they did, that was the email I got.' St John says.

'But not in person? What kind of – but then again, I can't talk.'

'Can't you?'

Hilary has become like a mum to St John over the last few months. It's a weird feeling, because his own mum is a high flying human rights lawyer who will almost certainly become a Dame one day. Whereas Hilary is, well, she's just Hilary.

But now Hilary is clearly in a candid mood; ready to unburden. St John manages to resist the urge to talk about himself instead. And he realises, with a degree of surprise, he actually does want to know more about her and her life.

'What do you mean? Were things hard with your parents too?' St John asks.

'Yes. No. Well. Hard to say.' A shadow crosses Hilary's face; not literally but he can see the pain on her dark features.

'Do you want to talk about it?' he asks eventually.

And she does.

She tells him about her dad Malcolm and the fact that he and her mother Malaika found it so hard to show their love for her. They weren't cruel, she explains; she never wanted for anything. But they were dull and never passionate and as a teenage girl it sucked the life out of her. And then she tells him of how she ran away from home at the age of sixteen, and came to Brixton, to 'find herself'. Which for a while she did.

'That's why I married George, I think,' she concedes. 'Because he's so different to my dad.'

'Why? Because he's not cold?' St John asks.

Yes, I guess so,' says Hilary. 'Because he's passionate. Because he says things, emotional things, things that most blokes can't say out loud.' She remembers; and she smiles. 'The first time I met George, he was in my granddad's bedroom with his shirt off, dancing to the radio. The Stranglers, that was the song. Walking on the beaches, looking at the peaches. Do you know that one? A bit smutty actually. And when he saw me he laughed and told me I was gorgeous and later on when we started going out, he was always telling me how much he loved me. Adored me. He told me I was the love of his life, in fact. '

Only to get into her knickers of course. Or at least, that's my take on the situation she has just described.

'And he's kind to me. He really is. George is kind. Passionate and kind,' Hilary says.

'And you love him.'

'Not really.'

St John is out of is depth. He's twenty-five, pushing twenty-six, barely adult. He is not competent to be giving marriage advice to a grown woman.

'George is a builder isn't he?' St John asks.

'Well yes. That's his van outside.'

St John mulls for a moment.

'I was thinking of having some work done in the kitchen,' St John says after a while. 'New units, and a new stove. One that heats things up faster.'

'That Aga is madness,' Hilary admits.

'Would George - '

Oh no. She's not going down that road again.

'He's much too busy, I can recommend some people,' Hilary says swiftly.

The cops have cordoned off the woodland at the top of the Old Park. An anonymous call the previous day had alerted them to the presence of a dead body in the woods, buried and covered over by leaves.

Mickey and the other wild men have kept well out of it except for Pierre, the one who wanted to call the cops when they first found the body. He's a male nurse in real life and he was feeling guilty at the way they just covered up the corpse again and legged it. Mickey had made a strong point at the time: 'We're all coked out of our fucking heads, lads, and half naked to boot, the last thing we need is the Old Bill up our fucking chuffs.' But even so, Pierre felt bad about it. Which is why, a few weeks after finding the body, he made the call.

Detective Inspector Callum MacAlister is leading the police murder team on the ground. MacAlister has set up a temporary incident room at the now disused Westwood Police station. He is a dour Scot who is well used to the vagaries of London life, but even he is horrified to find himself working in a building with mould on the walls, and windows which can't be opened because the glass has melted and fused with the stonework. Not to mention the strange creatures which some officers claim to have spotted scuttling across the floor, including a spider with teeth and a giant crab.

His bagman is Detective Sergeant Billy Armstrong, who has just been transferred from Dalton police station and who happens to be the older brother of Kane Armstrong. The same Kane Armstrong who is currently assisting the Bogman in his plan to take over all of organised crime in South London.

Billy and Kane have different fathers and hardly know each other; but they both bear the surname of their mother, Tanya, who still lives in London Heights.

The body in the woods has been identified. He is a man in his late middle age called Duncan Colthorpe. And MacAlister's murder squad already have a lead – Colthorpe's estimated date of death is Monday 12th March but his credit card has subsequently been used for purchases of electrical and white goods on the 17th and 28th of March . A cyber search has revealed that the IP address from which the online purchases were made belongs to a computer belonging to a man living in the Brixton area. An arrest warrant is swiftly granted. The dawn raid team prepare to do their worst.

The resident at that address is a businessman and self-proclaimed 'impresario', which means he books bands for pubs in return for free beer, by the name of Mickey McBride.

Oh Mickey, you idiot.

Just before the dawn raid at Mickey's gaff, at about 3am. Hilary McBride wakes up convinced that something is wrong.

She thinks back on her conversation with St John. That weird and childlike man who seems to earn more in a week than George earns in a year. She remembers how she unburdened herself to him, almost a stranger. Is that what's bothering her?

But no. There's something else. A sense of dread has enveloped her. She is sure that one of her children is in danger.

Suddenly she realises: it must be Shona. Shona is in danger! So Hilary tumbles out of bed, not in the least bit disturbing George, who is snoring. She doesn't even bother to put on a robe, she rushes out in her nightdress to Shona's bedroom and finds her deep asleep, strangely calm, snuffling faintly.

False alarm?

For a moment, Hilary considers the possibility that she is still dreaming.

She goes to the bathroom and stares the mirror and she sees her once smooth and lovely face is no longer smooth or lovely. She has dark bags under her eyes like a panda, her mouth is severe, her face is lined and her chin is strangely bumpy. She looks like an old woman, in short.

This proves to her she is *not* dreaming. For in her dreams, she has a face like Rihanna.

But the mystery remains: what was the premonition about then? If Shona is safe, who could be in danger?

Hilary makes the obvious deduction.

She leaves Shona and hurries down the stairs to Jack's room on the ground floor. She turns on the kitchen light and pushes back the curtain and peers inside.

What she sees doesn't make sense to her, so she turns on the main light. And then she screams.

Jack is covered in puke, sprawled on the bed. Unconscious.

Hilary rushes to the bed and puts a hand to his face. His skin is clammy and cold. She holds her cheek close to his mouth, but can't feel his breathing.

Hilary pounds his chest with her two hands in the way they always do in medical dramas to get the heart beating again. She counts carefully as she pumps then stops, and waits, then pumps again. She puts her fingers in his mouth to clear the airways. Then she CPRs his chest again.

Eventually Jack coughs and pukes and breathes. His spit and vomit spatters her nightdress, for which she will eternally be grateful. Then Hilary goes into the hall and phones for an ambulance.

Two hours later the door of Mickey's flat is smashed open and armed police pour in. DI MacAlister does the business, in his calm Edinburgh brogue: 'Michael McBride, you are under arrest for murder, you do not have to say anything but anything you do not say now which you later rely on in court may be used again you.'

The bedroom is crammed with cardboard boxes full of computers and laptops and fridges, delivered over the last few days by Amazon. And so Mickey is bang to rights as they used to say. Though apparently no longer.

'Oh fuck' says Mickey.

Jack in now is intensive care in the Westwood Hospital. A tube in his mouth, helping him to breathe. Tubes are connected to his veins, pumping in saline. He is alive but only just.

Shona is still at home, in 44 Westwood Street, having been hurriedly woken by her dad before he drove off with Hilary to the hospital. She is reading the note which Jack had left in his room. It must have fallen off the bed during the CPR. And Shona finds it, before anyone else sees it.

The note says:

'IT'S ALL SHONA'S FAULT IT'S BECAUSE OF HER I KILLED MYSELF. SHE'S A FAT NASTY BITCH. YOUR LOVING SON, JACK.

Shona sees it and doesn't believe it. Then she believes it. And she howls with rage.

And that is the night of the Great Storm of Westwood.

Chapter 9

Winds batter cars and houses at speeds of hundreds of miles an hour.

Trees shake and shudder.

Swards of grass ripple wildly like ocean waves.

Birds are plucked out of trees and tumble through the air.

And the sky is filled with blood. A dense haze of bird and squirrel and cat and dog blood as the wretched creatures are torn apart by hurricane-force winds ripping through the streets and parklands.

And so the Great Storm of Westwood rages.

In her bedroom Shona cannot sleep. I have never known her so despairing and full of self-hate. She truly believes that she has killed her own brother. That she, and only she, is to blame.

It's not true. Of course it's not true. Firstly, Jack is not dying. Secondly, she is not to blame.

Yet she firmly believes that she *is* to blame. That it's all her fault. And that's because of the stupid and cruel lies Jack wrote in his suicide note.

All this vexes me greatly.

How could he do such a thing?

How *dare* he?

I did not see Jack write the note. I did not see him take the pills. I was elsewhere. Distracted by the myriad events that occur every single moment in my domain.

But I was there in 44 Westwood Street that night, the night when Hilary couldn't sleep, and I was with Hilary when she stared at her son lying on the bed sheets with his face drenched in a stale pool of vomit.

And I thought to myself, casually: well, that's another death in Westwood. It happens. Such is life; such is death.

But later – later on, it all changed for me.

Later on, when Shona read the suicide note and I read the thoughts in her mind and I realised –

That I had been wrong.

That Jack didn't love his sister after all. He never loved her. All along, Jack hated Shona.

Otherwise – why? Why would he do such a thing?

And so I cursed him!

I cursed the treacherous young man who I have known since he was a boy. I cursed him for his betrayal of Shona and I cursed him for the pain he has brought to the McBride family and I cursed him for failing to be the heroic figure I always felt he could be.

Fuck you Jack. Fuck you.

Fuck you!!!

And at that moment, throughout Westwood, throughout the parks and in the streets, and in the alleys and the woodlands, my powerful winds begin to blow and gust and my sharp hailstones ripped into fox flesh and drew blood and birds cowered in branches that shuddered beneath them, and trees were uprooted and tumbled like skittles and cars skidded on the flooded roads and crashed into buildings or into other cars and everywhere you went in Westwood you could see the devastation caused by the storm to end all storms!

Elsewhere in South London mild breezes blew. The sun shone its soft light upon the world. It was, all in all, quite a nice day.

But in Westwood the skies were black and the thunder roared and the air was dank and red.

The Great Storm passed. As all storms pass.

And now I am angry with myself about what happened that day in Westwood. At what I did.

My wrath.

My thunder.

My biting winds.

What possessed me?

I am old. Time will pass, as it always does. Humans live so very briefly, and then they die. What does it matter? Why should I care?

But for a week after the Great Storm the skies in Westwood were grey with clouds and the breezes were bitterly cold and the soil was dry and cracked.

Hilary is being cheerful.

She visits Jack twice a day in the hospital most days and she is always cheerful.

'Fuck off, mum,' Jack says.

'Well thank you, my love,' she says, cheerfully. 'You can't believe what Brendan did in outdoor play yesterday. You remember Brendan?'

'I'm not interested mum.'

'I'll tell you anyway.'

'I just want to die,' Jack says.

'Me first!' Hilary says grinning. And even Jack has to laugh at that.

'You've no idea what it's like,' Jack says, self-pityingly.

'What's what like?' Hilary says, pretending not to understand.

'Being me! Being me. Being me!' Jack is ranting. His mood is foul. His skinny body aches. But he has no remorse for what he did.

'Then tell me. I'm your mother. I can share your pain,' Hilary says.

'Throw yourself under a bus, then you'll share my pain. Oh Christ, not again!'

Hilary looks across at the flowers she brought Jack, which have been carefully arranged in a vase by his bedside. And yes, it has happened again.

You see Hilary visits Jack twice a day without fail and each time she visits she brings flowers. Flowers from her garden, and sometimes flowers from St John's garden which he would happily give her if she asked, but she just takes them. Other times she brings flowers from the Small Park or from the florist's shop on the Boulevard. The flowers brighten the room up nicely for a while. A very short while. Then they die.

Today she brought a gorgeous spray of yellow and red roses and now the petals have fallen off and the flower heads are all dead. The leaves are dry and brown. The stems are brittle. The flowers reek of decay.

'Stop bringing flowers,' says Jack.

'They brighten the room,' says Hilary.

'They always die. Why do they always die?' Jack asks.

They always die because of *me.*

'I'm sorry mum,' Jack says very quietly. So quietly that Hilary barely hears him. When she does register what he has said, she starts to weep.

Two weeks after the Great Storm has ended, a week after Jack has returned home, Shona goes to the pub; and there she falls in love.

Her intention at the start of the evening is simply to get bladdered. She goes to the pub with her pals Jo and Marielle and Zara; and they are in close protection mode. They know their mate is suffering, That she is devastated at her brother's attempted suicide.

And so these three they have rallied round to support their friend.

Over the last few weeks, and very much to my surprise, Shona has behaved like a saint towards her selfish bastard of a brother. She has visited him in hospital; she has spoken tenderly to him; she hasn't reproached him even slightly; and she destroyed the note he left so that no one else will ever see it. She has astonished me, in fact, by her failure to seek or even desire her righteous vengeance.

And after she burned the note, and as she was burying the ashes in the back garden, she thought to herself: *He didn't mean it.*

She thought to herself: *He was depressed. When you're depressed, you can't see things straight. It warps your perceptions. You can't be held responsible.*

She thought to herself: *I know he didn't mean it. I know deep down he loves me. I know!*

And yet, as Shona sits there in the Saxon Arms with her three best pals, I sense that there is indeed an anger deep inside her. An anger she has suppressed so well she doesn't know it's there.

And so I explore. I delve. I sink deep into the labyrinth of her mind, like a heron plummeting into the waters of a lake in search of luscious prey; and there I see it. There I smell it. Her hidden rage.

Her hidden rage is darker than my wrath; the wrath that destroyed much of Westwood's parklands and caused hundreds and thousands of pounds worth of property damage.

But she refuses to give way to that anger. It seems, and this irks me greatly, that she loves her brother too much to hate him.

The pain is still there though. I know that; her friends know that too. She is off-kilter; not herself. As if the real Shona has been spirited away and replaced by a badly programmed replicant.

'How are you Shona, sweetheart?' Jo asks.

'I'M FINE THANK YOU FOR ASKING.' Shona says, brightly.

'What does your mother - ' Zara begins to say.

'HUSH THE BAND IS ABOUT TO START,' says Shona smiling.

The band is not in fact about to start. They sit in uncomfortable silence for ages.

But after a while the girls and Jo realise that silence is helping. Just being there is helping. The silence becomes a comfortable one. Every now and then one of them goes and gets a new round of alcoholic drinks but Shona sticks to fizzy water.

Finally, an hour later than advertised, the music night begins as a young black man sits on a stool and starts playing on a strange three stringed lute. Two slightly older brown musicians stand behind him, a woman and a man, poker-faced and sombre. And they accompany him by each beating together a set of metal cymbals or *qrakabs*.

I have heard this band before. I know its lutenist. I am *aware* of him and have been for some time. His name is Hamid and he was born in Morocco and he has been living in Westwood for nearly eighteenth months. And I know that the music his band plays is not Western music; nor is it popular music. It is religious music. Cult music, if you like; the litanies of a long-dead religious cult who once held sway across large parts of Africa.

As he plays his lute Hamid begins to sing. Or rather, he incants; it is like hearing a congregation of monks intoning a Gregorian chant in your local pub.

The rhythmic chattering of the *qrakabs* syncopates with the monotonous strumming of the lute strings and the three voices in harmony express their praise and reverence for a wide variety of spirits.

'Fucking hell,' says Zara. ' What is this shit? Is this garage? Is this your famous garage?'

Zara does not like garage, or house, or any music with a techno beat. She much prefers Dionne Warwick and Karen Carpenter.

'It's world music,' says Jo, knowledgeably; he listened to some world music at Glastonbury once.

But Zara won't let it go;. 'It's a fucking dirge.'

'I love it,' says Shona. The rhythms make her want to weep. This is not a song, it's an act of worship. The singer's voice is thin but effective; and he plays his lute as if it were a weeping guitar. The backing singers chant in eerie harmony creating a wall of sound as spiritual as a cathedral.

When the first song is over there is desultory applause. But the young black man takes it in good part. He puts down his lute, his *gimbri*, and picks up an electric guitar instead. One of the *qrakab* players, the woman, puts down her *qrakab* and sits behind the drum kit and bangs out a rhythm. The other *qrakab* player, the guy, lays down his metal castanets and picks up a bass guitar, and strums a riff to tune it. It doesn't take him long.

Without even looking at each other, the three-piece band segue into Johnny B Goode. The rest of the night is rockabilly and it goes down a storm.

But Shona is transfixed with her memories of the first song, the *derdeba*. A religious chant, and an evocation and celebration of the birth of the universe.

The next day, when everyone is at work, and with Jack at his physio class, Shona clambers up into the attic at 44 Westwood Street on a rickety metal ladder.

The attic in the McBride house is a crawl space and also a dumping ground. There are no floorboards so you have to clamber along the rafters until you reach the back of the attic where a series of precariously arranged planks provide the support for a miscellany of discarded toys, unfiled VAT receipts, broken hoovers, baby clothes, school art assignments, and all the childhood junk from Shona and Jack's rooms that Hilary couldn't bear to throw away..

Right at the back, in a dusty black case, is Shona's old violin. Untouched for years. Shona wriggles her way along the planks like a caterpillar. Then she picks up the violin case and tucks it under her armpit, and wriggles all the way back.

When she gets back down the ladder she is filthy with years of accrued dust and spiders' webs. She has to go out into the back garden to dust herself down and she keeps finding fossilised spiders in her clothes. In the end she strips to her underwear and washes her entire outfit in the washing machine on 60 degrees, then finds a big baggy T shirt to cover herself up while she explores her musical past.

The violin case is cracked with age and damp. The violin inside is dusty and warped. There are black pellets inside the body of the violin which indicate a mouse has been nesting there. It is out of tune of course so Shona cleans it and replaces the strings and retunes them. Then she draw the bow across the strings.

The violin makes an ugly sound; like a group of old white men grumbling.

Shona recoils at the noise she has just made.

She tries it again. Bowing a perfect F sharp. This time the tone resonates, her technique comes back. And she is able to sustain the note skilfully.

However the note she is playing reminds her of the time her physics teacher Mr Barraclough advised her that women scientists are few and far between and so she'd be better off training as a barista.

Shona is thinking: *This does not feel right. This is not for me.*

Shona is thinking: *This violin hates me because I am not worthy of it.*

Shona is thinking: *I cannot ever play beautiful music on this violin because it was skilfully crafted to play inspiring classical music written by the greatest musical geniuses of all time and I am just a gobby working class black girl.*

Shona tries a different tack. She picks up her violin again and turns it around, and she looks carefully at it.

Then she talks to it.

She reaches out to it, in words. She tries, absurd though it sounds, to befriend it.

'The fact of the matter is, my friend, that nasty old Devil, he went down to Georgia,' she says to her sulky mute instrument.

The violin says nothing.

'Down to Georgia, that's where he went, yes indeed,' she says.

The violin says nothing.

Undeterred, Shona says, more confidently now: 'And that old Devil, he was looking for a soul to steal, as the Devil often does. But truth to tell, the evil old bastard was in a bind because he was way behind, but even so he was willing to make a deal.'

And with that last phrase she tucks the violin under her chin and draws the bow across the strings:

Wah wah wahump.

A resonant riff like the lick of a deft cunnilingus; or so it feels to her.

Shona continues her tale: 'When he came upon this young man,' she croons, pitching it up now, half singing and half chanting, in a Mid-Western nasal tone, 'Sawing a fiddle and playing it hot, And the Devil jumped up on a hickory stump and he said boy, let me tell you what.'

Wah wah wahump.

Wah wah –

And her fingers take control and she plays a devilish lick. Her fingers leap up and down the fretboard. Her bow bucks and writhes. Her toes tap. Her body jigs. In short, she is lost to the music.

She plays first the devil's tune, as per the song. Fast and feverish and angry and demonic.

Then she segues into Johnny's riff, the tune that will be victorious when the tale is fully told. Electrifying, dazzlingly fast, virtuoso in her intonation and sound; picking up Charlie Daniels' melody and turning it into a cadenza of blistering energy and heart stopping inventiveness.

'Devil's in the house of the rising sun…!' she sings and her voice soars and darkens and deepens and she realises – she has never sung like *this* before.

'Chicken in a bread pan picking out dough,
Granny does your dog bite, no child, no…'

And her violin is possessed. It plays melodies that she has never heard before, that her fingers have improvised. It is as fast as a steam train, as soft as velvet, as irresistible as
teenage lust.

When gobbets of blood start to fly through the air Shona screams and drops the fiddle as it if is red hot. She stares at her hand which is a mess of cuts from her relentless fingering upon the nylon strings. It's years since she has played, she no longer has callouses, and so she has ripped through the flesh on every finger.

The carpet is stained with blood, and so is the violin. Shona sucks her fingers messily and before long her face and lips are also stained with blood.

And Shona howls with joy.

After five fallow years when she hadn't played the violin at all, she has just played better than ever before. Better by far than her violin tutor, that skinny lycra-clad sexually abusive mid-life-crisis piece of shit Mr Bradshaw ever did, or could. The soul of the violin was as one with *her* soul. The bow was her breath, the strings were her heart and liver and spleen, and the music spilled from the old violin with a joy like nothing she has ever known..

Neither the Devil nor that cocky young brat Johnny could have licked her in *this* fiddle contest.

And so Shona is in love. But not with Hamid, not with any boy, not with her family, not even with Jack.

Shona is in love with music.

Despite the best efforts of the Council clear up team, the Old Park is a dreadful mess in the wake of the Great Storm. Tree trunks have been blown over and are strewn upon the grass. The playground has been cordoned off and the broken remnants of the swings and the roundabout and the dinosaur see-saw are lying on the grass and the paths, along with the wreckage of the avenue of plane trees. Cherry blossoms sprawl like roadkill beside the shattered trunks of their splintered parent trees.

My rage on the day of the storm had been all-consuming.. The boating lake is now clogged with my leaves and branches. The fishing lake has lost its bordering hedges, and the water has been whipped with winds so severely that it is dark with the blood and viscera of carp and perch and gudgeons.

The Oldest Tree has weathered the storm but its sideways tilt has been exaggerated and it leans over at a sharp angle like a drunken man seeking to puke his guts onto the kerb.

Now that the storm has fully passed the dogwalkers and the kickabout footballers and the boules players have all returned, and are making the best of it. Tree surgeons have started carrying away the dead lumber in their trucks. It's predicted it will take a generation to return the Old Park to its normal tree cover.

But just as Shona in her bedroom in 44 Westwood Street begins to play her ditty about the devil's wager in the Southern state of Georgia, buds start to appear on the wrecked remnants of the trees of the Old Park.

Severed branches show unexpected signs of fresh growth.

Ugly tree stumps that have been snapped apart by winds start to sprout tiny tendrils of greenery

And in the Old Park, the Oldest Tree rapidly sprouts a new branch that in the course of a few hours becomes robust enough to plunge downwards and impale the turf, pushing its main trunk upright again.

It will take more than a generation for the trees in the Old Park and the New Park to grow back again by natural means. But I have decided I cannot wait that long.

And so, as Shona's bow draws out musical frenzies from strings that gouge blood from her fingertips, the trees and flowers and shrubs bud and blossom and grow.

By the morning the two Parks have been largely restored.

And in the course of the following weeks, the growth continues unabated . The railings that entrap Old Park are ripped out and tossed aside by fast growing shrubbery that is as fecund as a tumour.

Sycamore helicopters are caught up by the wind and spiral through the air and into suburban streets and gardens and land on garden soil and take root and grow. And by morning each seed has borne a shrub which has grown to a tree, which within a day is larger than the house whose garden it has commandeered.

By the end of that week, ten thousand new trees have grown in Westwood and the parks and streets and gardens are once more rich in greenery. And I am full of delight as every part of my Westwood body brims with vitality and life.

Shona: thank you for your gift.

Chapter 10

There is a great deal of sneezing these days in Westwood. Messy, explosive, green-mucusy sneezing.

All my fault. I cannot deny it. All those new trees are generating enormous quantities of pollen. Catkins bud and swell and fresh flowers bloom every few seconds and the wind catches up the pollen and swirls it like a painter mixing paints. Then sharp gusts of wind propel the pollen particles into the air.

It is Mother's Day. Tanya Armstrong is in the pub with her latest boyfriend Danny and some of her teenage and grown up children, and the three toddlers.

A stocky youth in a black bomber jacket enters the Wayfarer Arms. This is a pub just off Bicester Road, a few blocks from London Heights. The stocky youth in the black bomber jacket feels a surge of nostalgia as his gaze scans the pub. He drank his first pint in here. He puked his first puke outside of here, in the car park. He took coke in here, in the toilets, while his mum was chatting up the barman. This is a home from home for him.

The stocky youth's name is Billy Armstrong and Tanya is his mum.

But Billy an outsider now. All the drinkers in this pub hail from London Heights. It's a nice place to live in many respects, and the views are great. And not everyone living there is a thieving drug-dealing scrote. But many of them are.

Billy was once a part of this. As a cheeky ten-year old he went to work as a shotter, selling drugs in the waste ground behind London Heights. This is where Kane and the Bogman sold the rock of coke to another cheeky ten-year-old who is doing now what Billy did then.

THE GREAT WEST WOOD

But Billy chose a different path. He became a copper not a gangster.

'Hello mum,' he says as he approaches, and Tanya's eyes go moist.

'Sweetheart,' she says. 'Say hello to your brothers. This is Shane, Harry, and this little terror is Michael. Boys, this is your brother Billy.' Shane and Harry and Michael are toddlers; the oldest is six, and that's Shane.

'Half brother,' says Billy.

'You're an Armstrong, that's what counts,' says Tanya.

Billy sits, and places on the table his pint and a G & T for his mum.

'And this is Danny,' Tanya says.

Danny is a scaffolder by trade, wiry and astute. He susses Billy for Old Bill at a glance but it doesn't rock his world.

'Good to meet you, lad,' Danny says.

'Likewise,' says Billy.

'You missed Kane,' Tanya tells him.

'Kane?' Billy asks.

'Jeb's boy.'

'Ah yes,' says Billy. He remembers Jeb. He was one of the better dads he's known.

'He's doing well for himself now,' Tanya says. 'Kane I mean.'

'So I hear,' Billy says.

Billy is aware that his half-brother Kane Armstrong is a target nominal; a hard core criminal almost but not quite on a par with the Morton brothers. All of which is bad news for Billy and his promotion prospects. But as the saying goes, you can't choose your family.

'You should call him,' says Tanya. 'He could do with, you know. Someone to look out for him.' She is clearly worried about her gangster son and his (potentially terrible) future prospects.

'Does he give you money?' Billy asks.

'Course not,' Tanya lies.

Tanya doesn't love Kane as much as she does most of her other kids, but she has to admit, he is a good boy. He went a bit distant for a while, but now he's always popping in and dropping off wedges of cash for his old mum. She's never been so well off.

But she spends very little on herself. She saves, and supports her kids, and keeps Danny in fags and booze.

She pats Billy on the arm, fondly.

Tanya is thinking: *You're a good boy, Billy. But I wish you visited me more often, like your brother Kane does.*

Billy is thinking: *I hardly know you. You're like a total fucking stranger. And yet you're my mum. How the hell did that happen?*

'This is for you,' says Billy, and slips his mum an envelope of cash with a card inside.

You can't buy love, pal, Danny is thinking; but he knows not to say it out loud.

And then Billy is on his feet again, restless as a tiger.

'You're not leaving already?' Tanya asks.

'Things to do, people to see,' Billy says.

'Keep the money, stay longer,' Tanya says.

But Billy needs to get out of there. He doesn't like Danny. He doesn't like this pub. He doesn't like being the second main course, after his half-brother Kane has been and kissed his mum and thrown cash around.

'Keeping busy, lad?' Danny asks, not really caring.

'This and that. On a murder case at the moment,' Billy says.

'The body in the woods.'

'That's the one. Must dash. Bye mum, love you.'

'Love you too, Billy,' says Tanya.

Billy leaves and Tanya stares after him.

'Faites vos jeux, messieurs et mesdames, s'il vous plait,' says the croupier, who was born in Penge but has A Level French and a decent accent.

This used to be a cinema, long ago, in the days when Michael Caine was a young star. Then it became a bingo hall. After that for nearly ten years it was the British home of The Holy Rapture, an American evangelical group which believes the end of the world is nigh. Then they were evicted, overnight, after Kane paid some large bribes to the local council.

Now it's a casino.

We've never had a casino in Westwood before and I was not familiar with the concept, let along the rules. The gambling hall is in a palatial art deco style and on its pilasters there are plaster moulds of angels and animals, in groups of two, presided over by a man with a huge beard and a sulky-looking family. A sculptural retelling of the story of Noah. And inside the hall there are two roulette tables, two blackjack tables, two poker tables, and two craps tables. There are also bars upstairs as well as private rooms where pleasures of the flesh are celebrated then paid for. Waiters and waitresses circulate in tight leather clothes, taking orders on their mobile phones and arranging for VIP services for those who can afford the Bogman's exorbitant rates.

The Bogman calls the casino a 'palace of the flesh' in a way that implies such things were common in his culture. Back in the days when he was a king and the summer solstice was celebrated with acts of ritual murder and doctors were all magicians.

Kane is less interested in that side of the business, the brothel stuff. It's the casino he adores. He loves to walk around the tables, watching people, studying their tells, occasionally sitting down to enjoy a game of blackjack or throwing craps.

The music is in keeping with the architecture. It is music from the 1920s and 1930s – Fred Astaire, Glenn Miller, Nat King Cole, Al Bowlly, Louis Prima, Earl Himes, Cab Calloway, and the Chocolate Dandies among others. The floorshow usually consists of a troupe of energetic flappers or high-kicking can-can dancers. Occasionally Kane allows a fan dancer but by and large he doesn't like to have smutty stuff in the casino hall. He likes to keep it elegant.

In the nearby Old Park, shotters are doing deals, and punters are buying rocks or wraps with their rent money. And every night, needles and bongs are discarded, and pills are scattered where unwary children can pick them up and swallow them. There have never been street prostitutes in Westwood before but now there are hosts of park whores who ply their trade inside the Maze, or on the benches next to the children's playground in the shadow of the Oldest Tree.

It is vulgar and it offends me. Though in fairness having any humans at all in my woods offends me. But I force myself to endure it. One act of blind rage a millennium is sufficient, and now it is my role to be a watcher once more.

'We have guests,' Cynthia tells Kane.

Cynthia is the pit boss, and dresses in a smart black suit. She has a thin-boned prettiness that makes her look sweeter than she is, and her short black hair is streaked with purple. And though she is slim and feminine she has a weightlifter's thick thighs and broad shoulders. Kane is terrified of her but he tries not to show that.

Cynthia does a head nod thing to indicate where the guests are to be found - at the furthermost games tables.

Kane scans the scene and swiftly sees the group at the craps table. Gruff Morton, built like a docker, wearing a shiny old suit that can barely contain his beer belly. And Dave Morton, who is the CEO of Morton Enterprises, the legit side of the Morton crime empire, who is clad in an expensive powder-blue suit that is far too stylish for his craggy ugly looks.

And Daisy Morton, their niece.

Kane gives Daisy a long appraising stare.

Cynthia sees the way that Kane is looking at Daisy and doesn't like it.

From across the crowded casino, Daisy spots Kane looking at her and smiles. She is a redhead with freckles and a cheerful demeanour. She wears an atractive yellow and green floral frock and sensible shoes. Her thin silver necklace looks as if it was bought in a market stall, though in fact it's Cartier. You'd never guess that she was the only daughter of that evil psychopath, Psycho Morton.

This is how Kane and Daisy met:

After the brutal murder of Psycho Morton, and at the Bogman's insistence, Kane attended the funeral. It was a lavish affair; the funeral cortège formed a line of cars that blocked most of Streatham High Street for more than an hour and the service was held in the West Norwood Crematorium.

Kane put on a black suit and tie and joined the mourners, sidling past the massed ranks of blaggers and safecrackers and bent coppers to steal a seat at the back of the crem. And after enduring a long and tedious and hypocritical service in which very many people who had hated Psycho and had wanted him dead said how much they had loved him, and wished he were alive. Then when the service was done, the mourners walked in a queue past the coffin en route to the memorial gardens. And when Kane passed by the coffin, which was not an open coffin fortunately, considering the extent of Psycho's facial injuries, he left a note on the mahogany coffin lid in an envelope marked: FOR DAVE AND GRUFF MORTON.

The message was a handwritten note, dictated by the Bogman, written by Kane. It said: *We are ready to deal.*

And a few weeks later a deal was done. The Mortons agreed to give up control of all their criminal enterprises in Westwood and its environs including Streatham, South and West and Upper Norwood, Thornton Heath, and South Croydon to the Bogman; in return for not being brutally murdered as their brother Psycho had been.

And soon after that deal had been agreed in principle, Kane met Daisy Morton, Psycho's only daughter, at the final sit-down which was held to hammer out the details of the deal. The meeting took place in a Radisson Hotel near Heathrow, in a conference room with headed paper in front of each seat flanked with pencils bearing the hotel logo.

The moment Kane met Daisy sparks flew. It was an exemplar of the well-known saying 'love at first sight.' And that night, and every other night that week, their love was consummated in a Radisson hotel room, loudly and with passion.

And in the days, Daisy helped broker a business relationship in which the Mortons would become junior and passive partners in all of the Bogman's criminal ventures; which, Daisy had argued persuasively, was a win-win scenario for all concerned.

Kane now walks over to join Daisy Morton and her two uncles at the craps table, using the casual loping stride he perfected in his years selling drugs on street corners.

The boxman looks a bit like the singer Frank Sinatra as a young man, which is why Kane hired him. The base dealer and the stickman are all local girls, from London Heights. The speed of play is dazzling and the calls are sharp and precise: 'Snake eyes', 'Hard eight', 'Dos Equis,' 'Midnight'. Kane had no idea how to play craps when they first installed the table and he still has trouble following the rules and superstitions. But he's seen it played in the movies and to him it feels classy.

Kane waits as the Mortons play. Gruff rolls, craps out. And when the dice are handed on Kane feels able to speak:

'You have drinks right?' Kane says.

'We're being looked after,' says Gruff affably.

Kane had been surprised at how little bad feeling there was from the Mortons about the Bogman's murder of their brother. But the fact is, the Mortons had all hated Psycho. And at one point in the negotiations, Dave Morton frankly admitted that their older brother had become a liability and they were glad to be rid of him.

'Amazing place you have here,' says Dave Morton, still waiting for his turn with the dice, which have passed to Daisy.

'Wish me luck,' says Daisy and she cups two dice in her hand and blows on them then rolls.

She rolls a one and a two on a bet of Don't Pass and wins.

She bets again and rolls again.

Both dice fly true towards the back wall of the crap table and bounce.

She wins.

She rolls again. A seven. She loses and has to pass the dice.

'Give her the pot,' says Kane.

Everyone stares at him but he's the boss.

Daisy collects her winnings with a giggle.

'Is your dad around?' asks Dave.

'He's not my dad,' Kane says patiently. Old joke.

'We want to talk,' says Dave.

'I do the talking,' says Kane

'Takings are down,' says Dave.

'Takings are up,' Kane replies.

Dave is a well-dressed thug but he is still a thug. And Kane is getting nervous.

'We've revised our percentage. Takings are down on that,' says Dave.

'Are you fucking with me?' says Kane. To revise the deal now would be an act of war.

Dave gives Kane a thousand yard stare. Then it cracks. He grins. 'Course we are, son. You're doing great.'

Under the terms of the deal negotiated between Kane and Daisy, the Mortons get 30% of all the profits from drugs sold in this part of South London by Kane and the Bogman. They are making more now than when they had 100%. That's business for you.

'How about that,' says Gruff Morton, who is not smiling. 'Ha ha. Gotcha!'

'This place is doing well,' Dave says. His nose has been broken and reset so many times it is a miracle he can sneeze. But his teeth are brand new and Kane suspects he is using steroids to achieve his big-muscled look.

'It's off the table. Nothing to do with you,' Kane says.

'That's understood,' Dave says.

Daisy pats Kane on the arm. 'We need a private word.'

'Anything you have to say, you can say here,' Kane says, sharply.

'Just you and me. I have a deal to put to you,' Daisy says.

No new deal is possible. Kane knows that.

'Okay,' says Kane.

He takes Daisy upstairs to his office. He closes the door. He locks the door. She is grinning and soon she is naked. Her body is slim and freckled and when he is naked too they fuck on his couch.

Afterwards Daisy and Kane cuddle and plan their future.

The Bogman has installed microphones and cameras in all the casino's bedrooms. Not for carnal purposes, just because he likes to know what is going on.

And so he listens in to Daisy and Kane as they plan their future. He hears about how much Kane hates and resents the Bogman. He hears about how Kane plans to betray the Bogman and steal all the money they have saved and leave the old withered bastard to rot. And then Kane and Daisy will go away together and run a casino in the South of France, or in Jamaica.

But all this is what the Bogman has told Kane to say. Some weeks previously he instructed his protégé to pretend to be a traitor whenever he was with Daisy, in order to get access to the Morton family's secret strategies. It is a trick the Bogman often used in the old days to gain intel before a battle; he is the master of the alluring honeytrap. And in this instance, Kane is the honey.

However, I can read minds. So I know that Kane is not in fact pretending to be a traitor when he talks to Daisy in this way. I know that he is conspiring to *be* a traitor.

I know that Kane hates the Bogman more than he fears him. And I also know that he passionately doesn't want to be what he fears he has become.

A no-one.

A nothing.

The Bogman's bitch.

'Kiss me again. I love you, Kane,' Daisy says.

'I love you too, Daisy,' Kane says.

Then she weeps. Her freckled cheeks are damp with tears.

'We have to get away, we're better than this,' Daisy says.

'Yeah but I like the money,' Kane says.

'Money doesn't matter! Being together is all that matters!' Daisy says.

'Tell me about the Silk Road, Daisy. How does that work?' Kane says, pleadingly..

'Why? That doesn't matter!' Daisy says angrily.

'Just tell me,' Kane says.

Ah.

Yes. I see.

Kane is a clever boy; he knows that his every word is being recorded, and will be listened to by the Bogman. So he's playing a role.

Or rather, he is playing the role of someone who is playing a role.

But in reality he is in very much in love with this capricious, funny, damaged, emotionally unstable yet irresistible daughter of a gangster.

The Bogman listens in, smiling at Kane's lies.

Whereas I am amused at the Bogman's folly. The poor gullible fool!

Daisy tells Kane in detail all about the Mortons' Silk Road internet scams and how they operate and the Bogman listens intently, and memorises ever word.

Then Kane and Daisy kiss a bit more and they cuddle a bit more. But they don't make love again because Daisy starts to cry again.

'What's wrong, my love?' Kane says.

'Nothing. Nothing,' Daisy says.

'It's not nothing, tell me,' Kane says.

'You don't know what it was like for me. Having a monster for a father,' Daisy says.

'Hush hush, I do know, I understand, I'm here now,' Kane says.

Her face is damp with tears; her body trembles and shakes as the memories run through her.

'Stop it, stop it Daisy, you're frightening me!' Kane says after a while.

'I can't stop it,' Daisy says. 'This is how I was, ever night, after my dad beat me. And he beat me most nights. This is who I am.'

Her body continues to tremble and twitch. It is like watching a cow being shot with an electric prod in the abattoir. Her body convulses, again and again. Each shudder, a remembered blow.

If I had a heart, this would break my heart.

'No matter what happens, we'll always have each other,' says Kane.

'I know. I love you, Kane. Don't talk. Kiss me,' says Daisy.

He does; and then things get passionate.

Soon I get bored, and I leave.

A lightly clad prostitute is haggling with a potential male customer in the Flower Gardens. I recognise her; her name is Clara and she was at school with Shona McBride. I don't know the customer, he must be a tourist, not a Westwood local. He is middle aged and florid and rather unattractive, which perhaps explains why he needs to pay for sex.

A price is agreed. Clara wipes her lips and goes down on her knees. But I have no desire to watch and so I leave.

I remember that Clara used to be a gifted tennis player. Now she is one of Kane's whores.

Two teenagers are shooting up near the statue of William Wilberforce. The statue's face is blank and expressionless, for during the Great Storm the winds whipped away most of his facial features.

One of the boys has taken too much heroin into his veins and he starts to spasm and froth at the mouth and I expect he will die. But I'm not in the mood to witness the stages of his demise so I leave.

There is a dead body near the fishing lake. A man's dead body. The dead body is steeped in blood and it looks as if he has been stabbed. I don't know who did this or why and I don't really care.

I enter the lake and water embraces me and I hurtle forwards to keep pace with the arching slippery underwater flight of a swift speckled-skinned brown trout.

I return to the casino. Daisy and the other Mortons have gone. Kane is pacing through the casino hall, watching the action, sipping a glass of neat whisky filled almost to the brim. The Bogman joins him at the craps table.

'How much do we pay those cunts a month?' the Bogman asks.

He means the Mortons of course. His tone is a whiplash. Kane is suddenly full of fear.

Kane explains how much they pay the Mortons each month.

'Too much.'

This alarms Kane. He knows the Bogman and how restless he can get.

'You do know we can't move against them. They are too powerful,' Kane says.

His words are reasonable. The Bogman is not.

'Kill the two brothers first. We'll deal with the girl after that,' the Bogman says.

No! Kane thinks.

'We can't kill the two brothers,' Kane says.

'Find a way.'

Not my lovely girl! Kane thinks. *I'm sick of killing but if it's the price I have to pay I'll pay it. But not Daisy! Not her! She's my future!*

But Kane knows that defying the Bogman is impossible so his only option is to try and coax him out of his folly.

'There is no way. Trust me, the Mortons have security you wouldn't believe. Killing them would not be cost efficient,' Kane says, calmly.

'I don't care, we're doing it,' says the Bogman.

'But it can't be done!'

'It can. I'll do it.'

Kane gives it up. He clutches at one last thing.

'But not the girl. She has to live,' Kane says.

The Bogman chuckles. 'I know you like the girl. And perhaps, you even love her?'

Kane reins in a burst of powerful rage. It's painful but he does it.

'Hell, no, what, me? What makes you think shit like that?' Kane says.

The Bogman shrugs. I can't read his thoughts but even so I know he is remembering the recent intimacies between Kane and Daisy Morton that he has just witnessed.

'It's obvious, child,' says the Bogman. 'She has you snared. And no wonder. She's a tasty piece of flesh, I cannot deny it. And I commend you on your fucking of her, which was highly - ' He searches for the word. ' – expedient. However, we have to move on. Remember, there is no room for sentiment in business,' the Bogman says, in tones as cold as a day-old corpse.

He's testing the boy; I can tell.

What a bastard.

But then, he always was.

Kane is also remembering his recent intimacies with Daisy Morton. And steel enters his soul.

'No I won't stand for it bruv.' The Bogman hates to be called 'bruv'. Nice touch, Kane.

'And I'll tell you why, stickman,' says Kane. 'Because it's – bad business, yeah? She's the brains. She's the finance guy. She's the one with an MBA. We need Daisy Morton. She should be working for us, not for her fucking uncles. Capish?' Kane does a little swagger to finish off this tirade.

Despite his achievements, Kane is still just a child, barely nineteen. And he looks absurd in his posturing. But you can't deny he has courage.

The Bogman nods, approving. Not fooled, but approving.

'Then we kill her uncles and spare her. Will she mind?' the Bogman asks.

'She won't mind,' Kane says.

The Bogman puts a stack of chips on Pass and picks up two dice and rolls them. A two and a one. He loses.

'Stupid game,' he says, and he moves away to the roulette table.

The Bogman prefers this game. The rules are simple and the wheel is weighted so that the house never loses. Since he is the house that appeals to him.

'Faites vos jeux, mesdames et messieurs, s'il vous plait,' says the croupier.

The wheel is spun, the ball bounces. Kane gets a ping on his mobile phone and he answers it on automatic pilot. His eyes are still on the table, watching the gamblers, seeing how they are sweating and anticipating, putting their lives in the power of a little bouncing ball.

But then Kane checks his screen. He sees a text with a photo attached. He clicks on the photo. For a moment his heart stops.

He goes up to the Bogman and draws him away. They stand privately, below a plaster carving of two giraffes touching their necks together affectionately. Waitresses drift past them carrying trays of champagne. The Bogman looks the question. And Kane tells him what is going down:

'It's war.'

They go mob handed. Six youngers with guns, plus the Bogman's personal bodyguards who are Special Forces trained. Four trained soldiers, six very violent young men. Ten in all. But the Bogman is careful to leave behind in the casino enough trained bodyguards with military experience to protect the place, in case this is a ruse to lure them away.

As they motor across Westwood to London Heights, Kane has a stone for a heart.

Because of him, his mother Tanya is in dire peril. She could be murdered or raped, or both. And it's all his fault.

That was the message conveyed by the photograph Kane received on his phone in the casino. It was a photograph of Tanya, terrified, bound hand and foot, with a knife resting against her throat. And around a neck a placard bearing the caption: COME ALONE.

Of course, Kane does not come alone. He arrives with an entire army of killers, led by the Bogman. But he knows he has to play this carefully. So the six youngers and the four bodyguards and the Bogman have to stay outside the estate while Kane goes in.

Kane knows this estate like the back of his hand. He used to play cops and robbers here, when he was young enough to play with toy guns not real guns. He knows the best look out points. He knows how the sun will glint on binoculars from the viewing point on top of the Martello Block, and when he sees a glint of light on the top of the Martello Block he knows exactly what that is.

His assumption is that this is a negotiation not an ambush. Because Kane is no threat to anyone. He is the Bogman's silver tongue, no more. Even so he is wearing a stab vest and a rugby player's box beneath his clothing. He is carrying a gun and knows how to use it. And he is connected by Bluetooth to the Bogman and the bodyguards, waiting outside.

It is, Kane feels, all a bit Hollywood. And that gives him a buzz.

The estate is quiet, though not deserted. A small group of kids are playing kickabout in the central courtyard, using a wall as a goal.

Nice ball control, Kane thinks, as he tries to swallow his fear.

This isn't a high rise complex, the highest flat is three storeys. But there are a few walkways that lead from one low-rise to another. In some places, there are piss stains on the concrete. But there also pots with flowers and brightly coloured curtains and the softly stuccoed buildings have an almost Mediterranean feel.

'Crossing the walkway to Martello block now, over,' says Kane.

'Roger that,' says the Bogman.

But the Bogman isn't where he is supposed to be. He has entered London Heights from the rear, from the waste ground area. He has free-climbed a sheer concrete wall in order to appear on a third storey terrace. He too can see the glint of light from the top of the Martello Block. He climbs another wall; and now he is crawling, not walking, on the roof of the Pevsner Block. Shimmying his way along swiftly and smoothly. The concrete is rough and cuts into his skin but he has no sense of pain, and no skin to speak of. So it doesn't hurt him.

The Bogman knows that Kane is wrong. This is an ambush not a negotiation. He knows this because he has done this kind of thing before, but with the roles reversed.

He knows there is a strong risk that Kane will be killed by the Mortons today, but that doesn't perturb the Bogman. People die; that is the way of it. Only he will live forever.

Kane is now on the landing outside the front door of his mother's flat. His body offers a perfect target if there were a sniper on the balcony opposite, but there isn't.

The Bogman is on the roof of that building opposite, his mud-coloured head almost impossible to perceive however hard you look. He is keeping his eyes trained on all the parts of the London Heights complex. He has identified several watchers but all of them are young kids who do not carry rifles.

'Going in,' says Kane.

'Take care,' says the Bogman.

Kane takes out his key but then finds that the door of his mother's flat is open.

'Shit, the door is open,' Kane says.

'Should it not be open?' says the Bogman.

'Not on this estate. My mum would never - '

'Withdraw, I'll come with backup,' says the Bogman.

'She said come alone,' Kane says.

Kane pushes the door open and goes in.

Watching him from a distance, the Bogman smiles as best he can with his lipless lips.

Then the Bogman scurries along to the edge of the roof and climbs down the wall, again using his peat-stained fingers as adhesive pads.

Inside the flat, Kane draws his gun and his body instinctively mimics the body language of every cop show he has ever watched. He is listening acutely for sounds, but he can hear none. And as he checks each room, he does the dialogue in his head.

Hallway – clear.

Living room - clear.

Kitchen – clear.

There is a back balcony as well as a front balcony, accessible via the kitchen. Kane doesn't think to look there. If he had, he would have seen that the small patio area is occupied by a plethora of plant pots and two of the Morton brothers' heavies, leaning with their backs against the wall. Shaven-headed killers who were both thrown out of the army during basic training for excessive violence. Both are juiced up with PCP. Both carry guns. But Kane knows nothing of this.

THE GREAT WEST WOOD

A skittering figure leaps from a balcony opposite and down into the courtyard and runs across the football pitch marked out on the poured-rubber ground surface. The kids playing ball see a blur but the Bogman is naked now and his unclothed body is so thin and spindly that few would confuse it with an actual person. He is like a Giacometti sculpture shaped out of dry brittle clay. And he runs as fast as a breeze.

Kane steps into his mother's bedroom and his gun scans the room. There is a wardrobe which is closed and he stands beside it, and reaches out with one arm and pulls the door open. No one comes out. He tilts his head and peers inside – could there be someone hiding in there? He just can't tell.

He wrestles with the dilemma – how to find out if there is a gunman hiding inside the wardrobe?

Sweat is trickling down his face and his gun hand is trembling badly. Kane is scared. He is close to shitting himself. But there's a part of his mind that stays calm.

'Come out with your hands up,' he says loudly, and no one comes out.

'Last warning,' he says then he gives it up and fires six bullets into the wardrobe. The bullets fly through the wood and into the wall behind and into the flat next door, rocketing through into the neighbours' bedroom and passing through their bedroom wall. It's a miracle that no one is killed by his reckless shots but they are not.

Then Kane opens the wardrobe doors fully and rummages inside. Dresses, jackets, jumpers, he pulls them all out and tumbles them on the floor. Some have gaping holes in their fabric and smell of gunpowder. But there is no one there. The wardrobe is empty.

And now, finally, Kane can turn his full attention to the figure on the bed.

It is his mother. She is wearing joggers, as she always does around the house, and a T shirt advertising a metal band she saw at a gig when she was younger. The T shirt is black but if you look closely you can see it is soaked in blood. A red line stretches across her neck and there is a pool of more blood on the pillow beneath her yellow hair. Her face is waxy and her eyes are closed.

'Mum' says Kane.

No answer.

Kane tucks the gun in the waistband of his jeans, putting the safety on first, then he takes his mother's neck pulse.

He can feel a pulse.

'Thank fuck,' he says.

Then the two guys who were hiding on the back balcony step inside the bedroom and leap forward and grab his arms.

Out in the courtyard, the Bogman bides his time. Every now and then he calls through a sitrep on his Bluetooth to his bodyguards and youngers. So far he can see no trace of an ambush party. But that doesn't mean there isn't one.

The kids playing football are like all kids, they are observant. They have spotted a shadow that keeps moving from place to place. They assume it's something weird. So they ignore it.

The Bogman is the shadow and now he is motionless. He is trying to hear what is going on in Kane's mother's apartment but it's too far away. So he bides his time a while longer.

This is not the first time he has infiltrated the scene of a major ambush. But back then, he was mortal and slow and killable. Now, he is enjoying himself.

Inside the flat, Kane is fighting like a wild animal, bucking and kicking and almost wrestling free of the grips of Morton's two heavies. But they are big men, and strong, and one of them worked for a while as a psychiatric nurse, and finally they subdue him.

Kane finds himself pinned to the ground, face pressed against the carpet. His arms are cuffed behind his back. He is pulled up on to his feet. 'We need to talk,' he says calmly.

'Kane I'm so sorry,' says his mother.

Kane turns and looks. He is shocked at what he sees. He cannot speak. His mother stares at him with eyes full of pain and regret but they are also eyes full of life and vitality. Her throat has been cut, she is drenched in blood. And yet, impossibly, she is alive and brimming with energy. How can that be?

He puts it all together.

Fake blood.

Fake knife gash across her throat.

She has been made up to make her look pale and waxy like a corpse.

He can see it clearly now. The scene setting; the deception. The trap salted by a boy's love for his mother.

I am not surprised. I knew this was going to happen. I watched Tanya accept the devil's bargain from Gruff Morton earlier that evening. And it's true, I could have warned Kane. I could have saved him from this. But I chose not to.

If I had a heart.

But I don't.

'I had no choice,' says Tanya, weeping so badly her words are slurred. 'They gave me no choice. Oh my baby my baby my baby.'

Kane has a snappy response in mind but his mouth won't function and his brain won't move.

'We can do a deal,' he says eventually to his captors.

'You won't hurt him, will you?' says Tanya.

'Not a word of this to anyone, love,' says one of the heavies, gently. His shaven head has a sandy tinge. He has big freckles on his face and looks like a rugby player. His warm sorrowful tone alerts Kane to a terrifying reality: this guy was Tanya's boyfriend once. Or maybe more than once.

'Of course we won't,' says the other heavy.

Kane is marched out of the flat. Out on to the front balcony where he has a clear view of the courtyard where the kids are playing.

'Oi,' shouts one of the heavies down to them. 'Fuck off.'

The kids carry on playing football.

'I said, fuck off!'

Kids like that are not easily scared.

The crew-cutted guy who once had a fling with Tanya takes out a gun, a Sig Sauer.   He screws a silencer on to it though that this is mainly for effect, they don't really make much difference.   Then he assumes a double handed wide legged stance and aims.

A dark haired white kid shoots at goal. It is saved. The ball is thrown back into play. A cheeky black kid traps the ball then boots it hard above his opponents' heads.

When the ball is in mid-air the guy with the gun fires and scores a direct hit. The ball is penetrated by the bullet and it squeals and it spirals towards the ground and lands, flat as a pancake.

'Now fuck off!' screams the other heavy.

Give them credit, the kids don't panic and run, they just quietly walk away. They retreat into their flats and they bolt their front doors and they put their tellies on and they watch Netflix, loudly.

'Now what?' Kane asks.

They throw him off the balcony.

The Bogman watches it all.

He is still just a shadow against a wall near the front entrance of a ground floor flat. Close enough to hear the impact, close enough to hear Kane's stifled scream of pain, close enough to hear his subsequent laboured breathing.

The Bogman murmurs into his Bluetooth: 'Let the battle commence.'

One of his bodyguards, Clive, gives the signal to his people: 'We're going in.'

These four bodyguards have previously fought in the small war in Afghanistan and they are seasoned in the ways of urban combat. Weapons are drawn. Hand signals are made. A count is counted. Then they move swiftly together, towards the entrance of the estate, prior to separating out and seeking cover. Letting the six youngers behind make their own way into the battle space.

Or at least, that is their intention.

Instead the six child bangers who used to work for the Mortons and now work for the Bogman but who, it seems, are only too happy to work for the Mortons again, wait until there is clear ground between them and the four scary ex-soldiers. Then they raise their machine pistols and begin firing.

They are kids but their aim is good. Even so it takes five minutes before the last of the ex-special services guys falls to the ground. By this time all six of the youngers have been shot too. The oldest of them is thirteen; the only one of them to survive is just ten. But their job is done.

Kane's breathing is getting worse. The Bogman takes a chance and breaks cover. He runs across to Kane, and when he reaches his body, he looks up at the two killers on the balcony, daring them to shoot at him.

They shoot at him and he dodges their bullets like a wind that can bend around corners and then he pulls out his own gun and fires back. He misses but they scramble out of sight and the Bogman kneels down beside Kane.

'Ambush,' Kane informs him.

The Bogman laughs. Late to the party, as always.

Into his Bluetooth he murmurs: 'Where the fuck are you?'

Twelve front doors open. The twelve doors of the twelve inward-facing ground floor flats. And now twelve warriors stand in the doorways, relics of another age, wearing black and

grey armour trimmed with red fabric and grey masks. These samurai warriors have trained in the art of kendo in a dojo in Camberwell for many years. Their skills were honed in tai chi retreats and a sword-fighting camp in Japan. They look magnificent and they know it.

On the first floor level six other men carrying Mac-10 sub machine guns step out of a maintenance room and spread out across the balcony and open fire.

The Bogman yells in exhilaration and dodges every bullet; but a second round of bullets catches him and his body dances like a puppet tugged on a string. Then the samurai swordsmen run at him and the fight begins.

Kane tries to watch it, propping himself up on one elbow, but his vision is swimming and it is too fast. He hears the roar of guns. He hears screams. Then he blinks and by the time he has refocused his eyes it is all over.

That's how fast it is, in a real swordfight.

There are dead bodies all around but no trace of the Bogman. Three of the samurai warriors are still standing though one is spurting blood from his arm stump and surely has not long to live. These three survivors are using their remaining reserves to hack at a body on the ground.

Kane can't tell what is happening; but I can. The Bogman has been cut up into small pieces.

I can also hear the sound of sirens as police cars and ambulances race to the scene. Someone must have tipped them off. Someone who had seen the gangster army waiting outside the estate perhaps.

Kane is close enough to hear one of the dying warriors swearing in a posh English accent, lamenting the fact he has been hacked down in his prime. Shocked and humiliated that no one told him that this would be a suicide mission.

The Bogman had been shot repeatedly by the Morton gang's gunmen, but as always the bullets passed right through his body with no ill effects. He is immortal after all, with a withered body held together by sheer force of will. So bullets cannot harm him.

But the swords are a different matter entirely. The Bogman has been hacked into so many pieces that even he can't carry on fighting. His dry skinny body has been chopped into scraps of leather.

And as for Kane, he now lies sprawled on the ground, his head in a pool of blood, not breathing, not moving. Apparently dead.

I can hear his breathing though, faint as a whisper in a church nave.

Clever boy.

Then a woman walks into the courtyard. A shy-looking pretty young woman dressed in jeans and a cream top; it seems she's taken the trouble to change her outfit since she appeared at the casino.

It's Daisy Morton.

Daisy surveys the scene. The killers nod at her, acknowledging her authority. She walks over to Kane.

'Is he dead?' Daisy asks.

'Yes,' says one of the hired killers.

'Get up Kane,' Daisy says.

A beat later and Kane rolls over and gets up on to his feet. He is in pain, clearly. But the fall was from a balcony only three floors high and Kane is like a cat. He is fine.

'Do you approve?' Daisy asks, looking at the diced up pieces of the Bogman, barely hiding the arrogance of her smile.

'You had to do it,' he reassures her. 'I'm glad you did it. He was a bastard, he coerced me into doing everything I did, and you have set me free. And now, sweetheart, it's you and me. Because I love you. I really do love you. And you love me.'

Daisy raises a hand and one of her killers puts a Sig Sauer pistol in it.

'No I don't,' she says, and shoots Kane in the chest.

Kane falls to the ground. He groans for a while and then his breathing abruptly stops. Daisy kneels and takes his neck pulse with a finger. Nothing. She stands.

A moment later and the neck pulse starts up again; Kane can do that. He can control his breathing and stop his pulse for minutes at a time. The result of many years of goju-ryu training in the church hall in Forest Hill, and a deep immersion in the kung fu movie genre. He and Daisy used to watch old Jet Li movies together after sex; it was their bond.

And as he lies there, his body sprawled on the hard ground of the courtyard of London Heights, his heart slowly pumping blood out of his chest wound, Kane is remembering how he and Daisy used to love watching samurai movies together. She introduced Kane to the Inagaki trilogy and he'd loved it. And she used to marvel at it. The power of a samurai warrior with a sword!

It is then that that Kane realises how long this has all been planned, and how skilfully he has been duped by a lying Morton.

A terrible sadness envelops him as he lies there; feigning death.

I watch as the surviving gunmen bag the remnants of the Bogman. Each part will be cremated separately and the separate ashes will then be buried separately.

The gunmen depart with two dozen bin bags just minutes before the cops arrive.

But they missed a bit.

Just a tiny scrap of flesh, close to the deflated football. Like the gristly parson's nose from a cooked chicken. A scrap of desiccated flesh no larger than an egg. Once, this was the Bogman's heart.

And it is still throbbing. Pulsing.

A tiny red artery flickers like a car's brake light.

A shred, a morsel, a relic of the Bogman is still alive.

Chapter 11

It is not my way to interfere in the affairs of the men and the women who live in my domain.

And yet I cannot deny that sometimes I do. I meddle. I interfere.

I change things.

I know full well that the Bogman is an evil man and I have seen many of the many terrible things he has done. In his youth he was a killer for hire. In his maturity he was a bloodthirsty warrior king. And in his resurrected days he was a murderous gangster who defiled the streets and parks of Westwood with gunfights and muggings and whores.

And now, despite his appalling injuries, he still lives. His heart still beats. He still has the potential to rise again.

If I chose, I could prevent that from ever happening; I could put a stop to all his future evils right now. I have numerous means at my disposal. Bitter driving winds, icy cold, hailstorms. All these are ways in which I could pummel his husk of a heart and extinguish the last remnant of his despicable life.

However, and although he has done terrible things, I cannot deny that this creature from the past has brought me considerable entertainment. His cruelty. His rages. His many murders. It has been one hell of a show.

So for now, I decide, I will let his heart endure. And if a stray dog picks it up and chews it up and shits it out, transforming this once great king into a steaming turd – so be it. Whatever will be will be.

The truth is, I am growing bored of all this. I don't care if Kane lives or dies and I don't care if evil stalks the streets of Westwood. I don't care because it is not in my nature to care. I am what I am. I am the capricious kind of god.

I move my attention elsewhere.

Shona is playing sets with Hamid now. She is the girl singer in a Moroccan rockabilly pub band, a slick covers combo which occasionally plays obscure and monotonous gnawa classics.

Hamid still does his classic Billy Fury and Gene Vincent numbers but now they have Shona to mix it up with some Brenda Lee and Mama Cass Elliott and Dusty Springfield and Mavis Staples songs. Her showstopper is a hommage to Tina Turner's version of a Creedence Clearwater Revival classic, a slow slow SLOW take on the opening bars of Proud Mary which evolves into a blistering hell for leather climax.

Rolling.

Rolling yeah.

Rolling on the river.

I am there at every set. You can't see me, Shona. You don't know I'm there. But I'm there.

You are a sweet young woman with a shy smile but when you are on stage you are someone else, and you take me somewhere else. In your black jeans and your plain black T shirt, and with your faltering smile and your bashful manner, you really don't look like much at first when the intro starts. As you awkwardly await your cue.

But when you hit the spot and start to sing your voice is rich and full, like young love.

And when you rock you have so much energy and your voice is exhilarated and raunchy. And when you hit the high notes you stay there and stay there and stay there until it seems the air will crack before you do.

Rolling on the river!

In the teashop, Camilla and Alice have taken on staff. A young man, Miguel, from Spain, and a woman in her fifties, called Dulcimer. Which is a strange name, but apparently her parents were musical.

Business is booming and they are making more money from the sale of first edition second hand books than from the cakes. But the cakes are the best in Westwood and that's saying something.

'It's too good to be true,' Alice tells Camilla one day.

'Get a grip, Alice. Count your blessings, thank heaven for clouds with silver linings, and don't look a gift horse in the mouth,' Camilla says.

Camilla has always had a firm grasp of clichés; and she also knows that sometimes that's what people need to hear.

The two women share a smile, lovingly, as if it were a child.

For years they dreamed this dream. And now that it has happened, it is even better than everything they dreamed of.

Meanwhile St John is working longer hours than ever at his investment banking firm in Canary Wharf. One time he works through the night on an important deal and in the morning the ambulance is called because it is believed he is having a heart attack. He is rushed to A & E and a doctor takes one look at him and puts a paper bag over his head and encourages him to 'Breathe!'

He explains later to Hilary: 'Panic attack.'

'Panic attack?' Hilary says.

'I get them from time to time.'

'You need to quit that job,' she tells him. 'It's going to kill you.'

But next day he is up at five am and in the office by 6.30 and he doesn't get home till midnight.

Don is with his wife, walking his dog.

Cecil is now very old indeed. He is wobbly on his back feet. He doesn't see so well. He doesn't hear so well. When Don feeds him, he has to tap him on the head to get his attention, so he knows there is food in the bowl. Don has stopped giving him the packet dog food; for a while he gave him cheap cuts of beef but the vet said that was bad for his liver, so now Cecil eats dog biscuits and cooked chicken thighs from the supermarket.

But twice a day Don and Cecil go round the park and now Marie comes too. Not her body, for she is dead, not her ghost, for she is without a physical presence; just her voice. Her faint whisper of a voice that seems to come from a universe away.

'Ah look at the kids playing in the school yard,' mutters Don, as he steps out of the house.

Lovely, says a faint voice, from a universe away.

They walk up the road and turn into a narrow alleyway.

'The mess on this alley. Cigarette stubs, look at 'em!' Don says.

That's the teaching assistants, that is, Marie informs him. *Sneaking a sly fag at breaktime. They can't do it in the school, not even outside, so they come here.*

'Well they should put a stop to it.'

They work hard those girls, Don, give 'em that.

'You were always much kinder than me, Marie.'

Still am, you grumpy old fool.

Don laughs at that, out loud. He misses being called a grumpy old fool by Marie.

At the end of the alleyway they turn right, and walk up Steeper Hill. Don stops talking because he is so breathless but Marie chatters away.

Those windows need cleaning.

Keep up, Don, you're like an old bloody man.

Oh, isn't she the woman who used to look quite pretty?

Anyone who sees Don, and almost everyone in Westwood sees him, for watching Don trudging up the hills and around the park is a spectator sport in these parts, would assume he's just a senile old fool talking to himself. Sometimes he gestures, and often he laughs out loud. And when he walks he is clearly under the illusion he is walking next to someone else, though it's as plain as the nose on your face that it's just him and his dog.

But Don is not a senile old fool. Marie really is there. I can feel her, I can hear her. I recognise her sharp tones, her no-nonsense attitude. Marie always wore the trousers in that family, as they say. And now she is back Don has had to smarten up his act. New shoes, a new jacket. He's done the front garden as he promised and put up those shelves in the study he always said he would put up. He cleans the oven every week and he's a dab hand at ironing, with a bit of gentle guidance: *Don't forget the yoke, you always forget the yoke, that's why you look like such a tramp.*

'Yes, Marie.'

Once Steeper Hill has been surmounted, Don and Marie and Cecil cross the Boulevard and enter the Old Park. They admire the new growth there. The tall poplars that once again encircle the Maze. The freshly grown turkey oaks which are already as high as a house. The avenue of cherry trees that now greets you when you walk past the lake, weeping white blossoms on the path. The patch of woodland which thanks to my recent fecundity has in just a few months grown into an imposing forest that covers much of the hillside.

'Was that there before?' Don wonders, as he looks at this green and vibrant forest that soars upwards to the clouds.

Course it wasn't, you daft bugger.

'What's that about then? Climate change or summat?'

Look. A magpie.

'I see it,' Don says.

Cheeky bugger.

'I love magpies.'

So do I.

There are signs everywhere saying 'Do not feed the birds' but Don likes to feed the birds. So he takes out his Tupperware box of bird food from his bum bag and scatters it and the magpie eyes him imperiously. The Tupperware box has been filled with Don's own blend: a mix of wild bird seed, energy balls, and coconut shells, with several handfuls of live worms harvested from Don's front garden. He throws a handful at the magpie which flutters away then hops warily back and pecks. Within moments a flock of pigeons has appeared and they startle the magpie away, and start scrabbling for the sprinkled food for themselves, flapping around Don and landing on him, surrounding him like applause. All around him feathers are flapping and beaks are pecking.

Then a Canada Goose lurches into the throng, soaring up off the lake and plummeting through the air, before smashing aside the smaller birds to steal some coconut shells. The magpie meanwhile flies away, proud as ever. Unwilling to be part of a mob of less beautiful birds. The magpie carries a worm in its mouth and as it flies it swallows the worm which survives for two or three minutes in the magpie's gut before the severed pieces finally expire; and another life is lost in Westwood.

'This is Father Glackin.'

Father Glackin is a kindly looking man who like many priests of the Catholic Church practices abstinence in principle. He likes a drink, in other words, and a fag too. And as a young seminarian he took care to sample widely all the pleasures of the flesh that would soon be denied him. As a way of stocking up no doubt on fond memories to savour in his later years.

Father Glackin has a mellow mind, full of humour and self-mockery, but I can tell he is anxious.

'And you'll know what you're doing then, I take it?' says Mrs O'Connell, rather confrontationally he feels. They are sitting in the O'Connell front room, furnished by DFS, with some fat and cheerful Toby Jugs on the mantelpiece which are clearly worthless family heirlooms of indefinable sentimental value.

'Well I've done the course,' he says. 'But I don't claim to be an expert in such matters.'

'That would be the exorcism course,' says Mr O'Connell, to clarify matters.

'It would indeed,' says Father Glackin.

'The Vatican course.'

'None other.'

'Then you'll certainly know what to do,' says Mrs O'Connell.

Father Glackin sighs.

Victor O'Connell, Toby's dad, works in IT, which is something to do with computers I gather. But his own da was a construction worker and his grandfather was a navvy on the railways. And Victor likes to say he graduated from the school of hard knocks. His wife Maeve is a hard-looking woman who was once considered something of a catch.

Once caught, she could not be thrown back, as Victor discovered.

Marie is what the younger humans call a keeper. A devoted and devout woman who would kill her husband, she says, if he ever so much looks at another woman. In fact Victor often looks at other women, and he does so very intensely. But he's scared of his wife so he has never acted on those desires.

It was Maeve's idea to call the priest in; Victor was reluctant. He has seen too many horror films. He knows how these things always end. But Maeve is an unstoppable force.

'In the eventuality,' Father Glackin says patiently, 'that there is clear evidence of demonic possession in this child, I am indeed possessed of the lore and expertise to um, expel those spirits. But let's not rush ahead of ourselves eh?' Father Glackin eyes the O'Connells shrewdly, then gives Toby a beneficent smile. 'This young lad looks the picture of health, I see no overt signs of malignant possession, you've not shown me proof of frothing or convulsing, and so far as I can see, his head is pointing in very much the same direction as the front parts of his body.'

That was Father Glackin's little joke but no one sees the humour in it.

'He's cursed,' says Mrs O'Connell savagely.

'Excluded from school for God knows how many times, suspended, barred,' says Mr O'Connell. 'Banished!'

Toby had received a formal warning for floating above the school playground earlier in the year. And more recently he was spotted floating even higher, over the railings and as far as the next street. Which was a clear breach of school rules and a health and safety catastrophe. So Mr Abioye has had no choice but to exclude him indefinitely.

'For doing what?' Father Glackin asks, expecting something from the usual drop down list of childhood misdemeanours: smoking, wanking, stealing, bullying, telling lies.

'I wasn't doing any harm,' says Toby.

'Floating,' says Mrs O'Connell.

Father Glackin raises an eyebrow: Ah.

'Floating?' says Father Glackin.

'That's what I said, Father, floating.'

'Floating in air?'

'Well he'd hardly be excluded for floating on the water in the swimming pool now would he, Father Glackin?' says Mrs O'Connell.

'Floating is indeed a sign,' says Father Glackin.

'So what can you do?' asks Mrs O'Connell.

'I can pray,' says Father Glackin. 'I have liturgies I can recite. And I can, of course, sprinkle the child with Holy Water, with which I am plentifully supplied.'

'Well do it then. All of that,' says Mrs O'Connell.

'You'll need to leave me alone, with the boy,' says Father Glackin.

The O'Connells withdraw, leaving Father Glackin alone with the child, ready to confront the devil.

Toby smiles at him shyly. 'I'm a really bad boy, aren't I?'

Father Glackin feels a pang.

The O'Connells are in the kitchen, waiting. Victor tries to think of something appropriate to say but nothing occurs to him. Maeve makes a pot of tea and gives Victor a plate of biscuits. The tea is strong and piping hot and the biscuits are chocolate Hob Nobs. From their front room they hear a low cadenced murmuring as Father Glackin recites his set texts in Latin. Victor wonders if the holy water will leave mildew marks on the carpet. If it does, there will be hell to pay from Maeve.

The whole process takes an hour and when it's done Father Glackin bids them farewell.

The O'Connells join their son in the front room, where Toby is standing on top of a damp patch in the new carpet. The O'Connells pretend not to notice.

'Oh my darling boy,' says Mrs O'Connell. 'This is a burden lifted.'

Mr O'Connell has learned his lines thoroughly, and delivers them like a hostage on YouTube. 'I'm not a man given to showing his emotions, lad,' he says, 'but you have to know I love you very much. You are the apple of my bloody eye. Come here and hug your old dad, you scamp!'

Toby remains standing on his damp patch, and he is wary. 'Am I cured then?'

'So the priest has assured us.' Though in fact he did no such thing.

'So I can go back to school?' asks Toby.

'If they'll take you, yes,' says Mr O'Connell.

'Sure they'll take him, they have to,' Mrs O'Connell insists. 'He has special needs. He's an exorcised penitent, they don't come more special than that.'

'And you're not angry with me any more?' says Toby. He has one of those faces that shows his emotions rawly and without concealment, like a silent movie actor. He is close to tears now.

'Not one bit,' says Mrs O'Connell.

'Not a jot,' says Mr O'Connell.

'You're our darling boy,' says Mrs O'Connell.

'And we love you,' says Mr O'Connell boldly.

Mr O'Connell is on a roll now. He has never said those words before and now he has said them, he can't stop saying them: 'Yes I bloody love you, boy, you're a marvel, I love you, I really do,' he says.

'Will you take a biscuit?' Mrs O'Connell asks craftily.

Toby is a like a mouse trapped between two cats, his eyes darting one way, then the other. Fear written all over him, but hope slowly dawning.

'Am I allowed?' Toby asks.

'Your soul has been cleansed; what harm can a HobNob do?' his mother says, soothingly.

Toby takes the biscuit carefully. He bites a little piece off it. He savours the crispness of the biscuit. The chocolate coating melts in his mouth. It is delicious. He takes a bigger bite and it isn't snatched off him. Victory is in sight! He swallows the whole biscuit and feels a heady chocolate rush.

Mr O'Connell beams at him. Mrs O'Connell nips to the kitchen and returns with a carving knife and walks behind her son, hiding the knife behind her back. Toby is the picture of innocence. Smiling; clearly hoping for more. Mrs O'Connell dips to her knees and carefully swings the carving knife under his feet.

The knife passes through the air beneath Toby's feet. Toby appears to be standing on the damp carpet, but in fact he is floating. No more than a centimetre in the air. But floating nonetheless.

'Ah shite,' says Mrs O'Connell and stands up and Toby turns and sees the knife and his feet bump back down on to the carpet.

'Sorry Mam.'

'So you should be,' says Mrs O'Connell, and puts the knife down. Then she clenches her fist, and she has big hands for a woman, and she draws her elbow back, and she punches her son in the face.

She hits his nose expertly and it squishes and cracks. Blood gushes out of both his nostrils. Toby stands defenceless, hands by his side, awaiting the next blow.

Mrs O'Connell takes a step back, so her left leg is leading, then she swings the right leg forward in a perfect punt; for in her day she had been a star of the woman's rugby team in her Irish school.

It's a perfect drop kick; her heel strikes Toby in the jaw; and he goes rolling over.

Toby lies still and tries to stop breathing, so they will think he is dead. But his parents are wise to all his tricks and he is clearly still alive, and huffing quite loudly. Then his father Mr O'Connell pick him up by his shirt collar and dangles him in mid-air, as blood continues to seep from the boy's nose.

'What are we going to do with you, laddie?' Mr O'Connell says, and swings his arm back, then throws his son at the mantelpiece as if he were a baseball.

Eight-year-old Toby flies through the air and hits the mantelpiece and bounces off and lands back on the carpet and rolls over. Mrs O'Connell pulls him upright and cradles him from behind, her arms tucked under his shoulders to leave his middle exposed.

Mr O'Connell rolls up his sleeves. He doesn't want to get blood on them.

'It's for your own good, son,' he says.

Toby sniffles. 'I know it is, daddy.'

'We have to drive those devils out of you,' says Mrs O'Connell.

'I know you do, I know you do! Hit me daddy, drive those devils out!' Toby shouts.

Mr O'Connell delivers a short jab to his son's ribs, and follows it up with a one two combination, also to the body. Then a few left jabs to the face and finally he delivers the uppercut that knocks Toby unconscious.

Then Victor picks his son up and carries him into the kitchen and lies him down on the kitchen tiles. Mr O'Connell finds a cushion from the living room to rest under Toby's head, to keep him comfortable. His breathing is loud and raspy though the nosebleed has stopped. But from the shape of his rib cage, some of his ribs got broken in the ruckus.

'The poor wean,' says Mrs O'Connell.

'What have we done to deserve this?' says Mr O'Connell bitterly.

It's not as bad as it seems. This lad has healing powers, and both the O'Connells are aware of this. That is one of the things that made the O'Connells so certain their son was inhabited by a demonic spirit.

By morning Toby is right as rain and his mam gives him a quick bath to get the blood off his face. His broken ribs have healed and his bruises have faded and so have the thick yellow stripes on his upper body. By lunchtime, he'll be fit and undamaged again.

But as he gets out of the bath, Toby's mood is glum. Irredeemably dark. In short, he is the most miserable and sour-faced kid you have ever seen.

'No chocolate,' Mrs O'Connell reminds him, as she rubs her son dry.

'Of course not, Ma,' Toby says.

'You know what chocolate does,' Mrs O'Connell says.

'Of course I do, Ma,' Toby says.

Chocolate is one of the few things that makes Toby happy. And when he is happy, well, that's when the devil comes upon him and he floats.

Chapter 12

Everyone is being nice to Jack and it is making him feel ill.

Part of the being nice is everyone pretending he didn't do what he did do. When he came round in hospital - that was back in late Spring, before the casino was built - his mother cheerfully informed him that he must have got his pills mixed up. And even though he kept telling her he wanted to die, she kept smiling and pretending everything was all right.

And all the doctors and counsellors who spoke to him were careful never to use the words 'suicide' or 'attempted suicide'. They just lectured him about positive thinking and how to handle anxiety and how good it was to be alive.

Then Shona came to see him in hospital and she was lovely and she didn't once criticise him or tease him. And even when he was sulky and mournful she was still a ray of sunshine. Happy and friendly; not a bit like the cranky annoying sister he'd known all his life.

Even his dad was being nice to him. Taking an interest. Sitting by his bedside, telling him the football results and how well or badly Arsenal were doing as if Jack still gave a shit. Telling Jack funny stories about the current building job he has on and how the owners of the house are a pair of useless wankers who have no idea he's hiked the price up by 30% for no justifiable reason. Although when Jack complains about the pain he is in, and starts babbling about how terrible he feels about the distress he's caused to everyone, and how he wants to make amends, George's interest tends to waver and he makes his excuses and scarpers to the pub.

During all his time in hospital Jack felt he was being treated like an heroic invalid; rather than the useless sack of shit he actually is.

He wanted to be punished! Instead, he has been forgiven.

Finally, after getting the all clear from the doctors, Jack was allowed back home. And the first thing he did when he got home was to search his room for the suicide note he had left for everyone to see. And he couldn't find it anywhere.

This made Jack very confused. He kept asking himself: Where has it gone? And did my mum find the note? If so, why hasn't she mentioned it? Why hasn't she told me off for writing such rubbish? And did Shona see it? And if so, why is she being so annoyingly fucking nice to me?

Jack knows that he should not have written that note. He knows it was a cruel and stupid thing to do. It was, he tells himself, a moment of madness. Just like taking the pills was a moment of madness.

But does that mean Jack is repentant? Or is he just feeling sorry for himself?

I decide that I am not willing to forgive Jack the way everyone else seems to have done. He has wronged his family and he has made me lose my temper in a way I have not done for many years.

Every day Jack is in pain and that makes me glad.

It's been a hard time for Hilary but she bears it well.

As well as worrying about Jack, and looking after Jack, and working with all her kids at the school some of whom are very troubled indeed, and offering her friendship and affection and practical support to the boy next door who can't even make a cup of tea, Hilary has to deal with the fact that Uncle Mickey has been evicted from his flat, after being arrested for theft. The theft of credit cards and cash belonging to the guy who was murdered in the park.

When Hilary first found out what her brother-in-law had done she was appalled. Stealing from a corpse? How could anyone sink that low?

Shona also thought it was disgusting and said so, very loudly. Jack didn't know about it for ages, because he was in hospital; but when he was told about it, he was shocked and scornful.

George however took it all in his stride. He's used to his older brother's ducking and diving. And in fairness, George himself is no paragon of virtue; he's made a career out of cheating his customers and padding his bills.

George and Hilary had some bad and loud arguments when Mickey had to move in, after his eviction. 'Bloody waste of space' was one of Hilary's milder comments.

For a few weeks Mickey slept in Jack's downstairs room when Jack was in the hospital and then at the rehab clinic. Then. when Jack came home Mickey slept in Jack's original upstairs bedroom for a few weeks. But George has got in the habit of using that room as his snore room; for he is a prodigious snorer after a few pints. So after a few very awkward weeks, George managed to put Mickey up in one of the houses he is renovating, in Brixton.

But when the owners move back in, or when they put the house up for sale, Mickey is going to have to find somewhere else to live.

Today Jack is in a café talking to the young man who crippled him: Shakil.

Shakil was prosecuted for dangerous driving after the accident on Woody Hill. But he was acquitted in court because the stipendiary magistrate had been born in Westwood, and knew at first hand how disorientating it can be when the sun sets in the middle of the morning.

So Shakil kept his licence. But in the months since the accident, guilt has been plaguing Shakil. He knows he acted appallingly in trying to drive away from the scene of his crime. And he knows that only his own incompetence saved him from being a hit and run driver; in which case, he would without a doubt have received a custodial sentence.

And to his credit, Shakil is ashamed of himself. He is ashamed of being the kind of person he discovered he actually is. Selfish and arrogant and amoral. A spoiled rich kid in other words.

And so over the last few months Shakil has been coming to Westwood often. Walking the streets. Sitting in the cafés. Staring at the scene of his crime – the zebra crossing where he ran over Jack.

Shakil has visited Westwood so often that he is now no longer a tourist. Which means I can see into his heart. I can read his thoughts. I know he is about to start university in a few months. I know he has a place at Southampton to do a BSc in Business Entrepreneurship. I know that his father runs a successful knitwear company and the plan is that Shakil will take over the family business in due course, so this degree will be an excellent stepping stone.

I know that Shakil would actually prefer to be a DJ, but he's not very good at it. He'd also like to be a rap star, but he's not very good at that either. His fallback is to be a vet and no one knows if he would be any good at that. But if that's his dream, he's doing the wrong degree.

Shakil and Jack are about the same age. They are both good-looking boys, and gifted with the kind of charm that breaks hearts.

And today Jack has agreed to meet the person who crippled him; so that Shakil can in some way make amends.

'So we're good?' says Shakil, after the two of them have talked for a long while.

They are in the café up the road from the zebra crossing; they serve good cappuccino here. Shak has drunk two large mugs of it.

Shakil waits, anxiously, for Jack's response.

Is he forgiven, or not? That is the question which is burning in this young man's soul.

Jack likes the power this gives him: the power to forgive or to not forgive. So he shrugs, matter of factly. Hiding the pain he is in with practised ease. When he replies, his tone is casual, matter of fact: 'Yeah yeah yeah we've done all - '

' – done all that, been there, I know, but I just wanted, like - '

'These things happen right.'

'They happen yeah.'

'I mean it's not like you were speeding or shit,' says Jack.

Shakil makes a big meaningless theatrical gesture with both hands. 'Hell no,' Shak says.

'Or drink - '

'- driving. I mean I wouldn't, I just wouldn't!'

In fact Shakil had been extremely pissed the night *before* the accident. He drove from Finchley Road to his parents' house in Hampstead so plastered he didn't remember making the journey.

And the following day he had been badly hungover but he decided to drive to Brighton for a piss up with his Brighton mates. And because he was still buzzing from the craziness of the night before, he took a detour through Westwood to see how fast he could go on the Boulevard Run. This is a little spur off the main carriageway that has four lanes and no traffic cameras, and is always quiet because it doesn't lead anywhere. It's where all the boy racers go to drive fast and furiously like their favourite characters in the movie *Fast & Furious*.

In other words, Shak had been driving far too fast while making a mobile phone call to discuss which pub he was meeting his mates at on his way to a high speed drag race on a public road whilst incapacitated by a massive hangover. But no, he wasn't drunk.

'Accidents, like, yeah,' says Jack.

'Shit man, I can't believe it You're so brave,' says Shak.

'I'm really not,' says Jack.

'You really are, man. You're my hero. It's been what, five months,' says Shak.

'More,' says Jack.

'And here you are, getting around, getting on buses,' says Shak.

Jack shrugs; one of the bodily movements he can make that doesn't hurt.

'Upper body strength does it, I can walk faster on my crutches that most people can, you know, like - '

'Run?' suggests Shak.

'Run, that's right.'

'Respect man.'

After his failed suicide attempt, Jack made the decision to become a noble cripple. The alternative was being a whiny self-pitying cripple and that wasn't working for him.

So noble he is. These days, as I have noticed, he never complains. He's always quick to hop up and hobble into the kitchen to make a cup of tea for his mum when she gets back from school. He puts his own clothes away, rather than leaving them on the floor. He's even offered to do some gardening, though in fact it's impossible for Jack to pick up weeds without falling over.

But he doesn't use a wheelchair ever now. He can take a shit on his own. He belongs to a hospital support group where he offers solidarity and friendship to other young men who have suffered life-changing injuries. He is even talking of going to university in a few years' time, and plans to re-sit his second year of sixth form so he can do his A Levels, which he couldn't take last summer because of his injuries.

'So, what you doing?' Jack asks Shak.

'Uni. About to,' says Shak.

'Cool,' says Jack .

'Guess so,' says Shak.

'Where?' asks Jack.

'Southampton.'

'Cool.'

'You know Southampton.'

'No.'

'Me neither. It's a good course.' Shakil talks at length about the degree in business entrepreneurship which he doesn't want to do and then he talks about his love of rap.

'What do you think of KanYe?' says Shak.

'Don't go there,' says Jack.

'There's a Welsh band I love, Goldie Looking Chain. They're really like, out there,' Shak says.

'Guns don't kill people rappers do,' Jack says.

'Them's the one!' says Shak.

'Ask any politician they'll tell you it's true,' says Jack.

'Lush mun,' says Shak.

'Classic.'

They share a laugh. The café is quiet, it's an independent Italian place which specialises in paninis and has amusing signs on the walls saying things like You Don't Have to Be Mad to Work Here But It Helps and As You Slide Down the Banisters of Life May the Splinters Never Point The Wrong Way.

'So are we done?' Jack asks.

'Are we what?' Shak says.

'Sorry didn't mean to, that came out - '

'I don't know, are we? I mean, it's for you to tell me like, if we're done, isn't it?' Shak says.

There's a difficult pause.

Jack is wrestling with his emotions; he doesn't in fact know what they are and neither do I.

'I don't know, what is it we're doing?' Jack says.

'I wanted to, you know.'

Just like Jack, Shakil hasn't the words, or even the concepts, to express what he is feeling.

'You manned up. You came to see me, face to face,' says Jack.

'That's what I did yeah,' Shak says.

'Like the movie, where the guy meets the Jap who tortured him in World War Two.'

Shak looks alarmed at the parallel.

'Colin Firth?' asks Shak.

'That's the one,' says Jack.

'But I didn't torture you.'

'You know what I mean.'

Shakil keeps looking at Jack, thinking of questions. Not having the guts to ask them.

He asks one: 'Do you drink?' Shak says.

'What?' Jack says.

'Drink? Booze like?'

Shakil recently decided he is an alcoholic and has given up drink entirely. His parents, tee-total both, are delighted.

'Not any more, the meds. Painkillers,' says Jack.

'You take painkillers?' Shak says.

'Like air.' Jack does a gasp gasp gasp mime . 'I got a regime like.'

'And that makes the pain go away. Kills the pain like.'

'Painkillers don't do that,' Jack says.

'They don't?'

'They just - ' Jack fumbles for the words . 'They redefine the pain. They make it gettable through. But there's still pain.'

'You in pain now?' Shak asks.

'I wasn't, but now you made me think of it, I am.' Jack makes an 'I'm in agony' face and Shakil shudders.

Jack hides a smile.

'Shit. What can I do?' Shakil asks, anguished.

'I don't know, what can you do?' Jack says.

'To help,' Shak says.

'You offering me money?'

A straw, to clutch.

'Money would help?' Shak asks.

Jack thinks about it. 'Probably not, the NHS is better than private for something like this.'

'I could, you know, pay for you to go on holiday,' Shak says.

'You loaded then?' Jack asks.

'My dad is.'

'Where would I go on holiday?' Jack says. 'And how? And I mean, shit man, what you doing, what's all this about money? We were chatting, like, chatting man, and here you are, with the money shit. What is it, guilt money?'

Yes says Shakil's desperate face.

'I don't actually have the money myself, but I could ask for it, guilt money sounds terrible,' says Shak.

Jack hides a smile.

Shak feels and looks like shit.

And all this pleases me. I'm enjoying Jack's subtle cruelty towards the boy who crippled him; it has a degree of finesse.

'Don't sweat it. We're cool,' Jack says.

In fact, I realise that I'm starting to warm to Jack once again. He has been significantly less whiny and gutless and self-pitying of late and I approve of that.

'You sure?' Shak says.

'I wouldn't say it otherwise,' Jack says.

'Yeah.'

Their coffees are cold. Jack has nowhere to go. It's a Saturday and his best mates are playing football and then they'll go to the pub and get pissed and talk about the match. Not his scene.

'You like football, Shak?' Jack asks.

'Follow it a bit. Spurs maybe? No I'm bullshitting I haven't seen them play in years. No not really,' Shak says.

'Music though,' Jack says.

'Yeah.'

'I love music.'

'Me too.'

'My sister's in a band,' Jack says.

'Is she?' Shak says.

'Yeah.'

'Cool.'

There's a long and random silence.

Eventually Shak figures out that Jack is asking him out. Not in a gay way, in a boys' night out kind of way.

And that's when I realise: Jack needs a friend.

In the High Street a Fiat is trying to park in front of the Iceland supermarket and is messing it up badly. The driver is a middle aged man who seems to have no spatial awareness. He is a menace in fact. His wife is already in Iceland buying the groceries. A red bus gets stuck behind him and the driver sounds his horn.

The wife emerges from Iceland and gets in the car. It's still not properly parked but it doesn't matter any more The car lurches out into traffic.

More horns sound.

The red bus shudders back into action and slowly crawls along Woody Hill.

Don is walking Cecil.

Is your hip bothering you? Mark asks.

'Always,' Don mutters. But he still manages to walk at a good lick.

A wren on the branch of a sycamore tree is singing its faint bubbling song, its feathers shaking as if caught in a hairdryer's blast.

Then it leaps and falls and with a single flap it turns the fall into a landing, and it hops upon the grass, cheekily.

Martin is walking his dog Alexander around the Old Park for the last time ever. He is sixty nine years old and in his youth he drove motorbikes down country lanes and ran up and down mountains. Now his knees are fucked and his bike was written off the last time he crashed it. But he loves to walk around Old Park. He knows all the dog walkers, and all their dogs. He knows all the trees, their names and their quirks. He knows which flowers flower first in spring and which trees shed the most leaves in autumn. He has walked in this park on cold winter mornings when the ice turned the grass into a slippery death-trap and he has seen thirty-one springs and summers in this park and thirty autumns and winter.

But Martin's wife wants to move to St Alban's to be near the kids and grandkids. Martin loves his kids and grandkids but he loves the Old Park more. If it was up to him, he wouldn't move. He'd make the bloody kids and grandkids come to *them*.

It is not up to him. Martin's wife has made the decision. The furniture van is booked and they are ready to move house in the morning. It is no doubt the right decision but once Martin is no longer walking in the park, I will miss him.

Not for long though. I never miss anyone for long.

And that's Hilda over there. With her wide-legged stance and her startled eyes. Hilda is the oldest dog walker in the park. She is rickety on her feet and uses a stick to balance herself. Her hair was grey then it went so wispy it's now just a memory of grey. Her face is as wrinkled as an oak tree's bark and she has had bypass surgery four times. Her dog is a little pooch, a fluffy Pomeranian called Aida. Hilda's big fear is that when she dies her dog will be left alone, or will have to be sent to Battersea Dog's Home. Her favourite conversational gambit is to ask a total stranger if they will look after Aida when she is dead, and she usually doesn't give up till she gets yes for an answer.

In fact Aida is Hilda's fifteenth dog. She has been walking this park since the Park was first fenced off and walked the lands here before that. She remembers when the sculpture park was first built, in the 1850s, when Westwood was becoming popular as a neighbouring district to Crystal Palace. She remembers when there was a ski slope close to the sycamore tree where the wren leapt off a branch earlier today. She remembers the Tandem Shed, which rented out bikes to park-goers but went out of business earlier this century.

Hilda is nearly two hundred and fourteen years old and no one really knows the secret of her longevity. She attributes it to her love of opera and the fact she drinks a glass of sherry every day before her supper, but apparently that's medical nonsense. Yet the fact remains, she is the oldest person in Westwood by far. When she dies, I will miss her.

But not for long.

Chapter 13

Hamid is sleeping. He often falls asleep after sex. It's quite adorable, Shona feels. He's a vigorous lover so no wonder he gets sleepy. In fairness, he always kisses her lots first, after they have both climaxed. And he says nice things to her. And he always asks her if it was good for her, before he nods off. Though he never says 'I love you' because that's not his way.

He doesn't snore, exactly, but he does make odd snuffly noises. She always has to wrap him up in a sheet to make sure he doesn't get cold as he sleeps. She likes to sneak some light kisses in while he snores away. Gentle butterfly kisses on his taut black skin. Hamid is a man of few words, but his body is eloquent, and so are his guitar and lute. He often has a dreamy look, because he likes to remember the songs he loves. And he plays them in his head when he goes shopping, or when he's eating.

Shona gets up and puts on his dressing gown, which is actually a kaftan from Morocco. She pads into his kitchen hoping in vain as always to find some teabags or digestive biscuits. All he drinks is undrinkable coffee sweetened with huge amounts of sugar. His kitchen is a shelf and a two ring cooker and it's in the same space as his living room and dining room. Vinyl albums are carefully stacked on shelves and upon themselves. They are organised by musical genre, though not alphabetically. He has crap speakers in this place and can't afford better ones so he always listens through headphones. But if Shona brings her own wireless headphones they can listen to the same song at the same time, and that's sweet.

Hamid's musical taste is eclectic and by and large it's too weird for Shona. But she does know the difference between gnawa and chaâbi music now and loves both musical traditions, though only in short bursts.

Still hungry, and now restless, Shona returns to the bedroom and picks up Hamid's guitar and strums it. She wonders if the noise will wake him but she doesn't care. She knows all the chords but has no fluency in chord changes. It's a simpler instrument than a violin which has no frets; but because she spent so many years practising on the violin those movements are instinctive for her.

However the guitar has always been her favourite instrument. And she would love to be able to play it well.

She strums a G then an F minor chord and it's not too bad. Then she improvises some notes to bridge them. She remembers the rhythms of an Othmane Mouline song Hamid had once played to her. And she copies the riff, a serpent eating its tail as each iteration returns to its starting point note and repeats.

She makes the riff funkier. Or maybe poppier. Whatever. She embellishes the riff into a developing melody She adds more chords.

'La la la la,' she sings. 'La la la la la la.'

Hamid is awake, she realises, watching her. Amused. Or maybe impressed? She can't tell. She loves his dark mystical look. She loves the way he can stare without blinking for ages, if he's interested in something.

'La la la la la la,' she sings.

'You need lyrics,' he tells her, softly.

Fuck off she thinks but she doesn't say it.

She finds from somewhere a middle eight elaboration for the song that takes it in a whole other direction. But again she is lost for words: 'La la la! La la la la! Lalalala la!'

She strums a finale, with a final chord that surprises even her.

'It's good, did you write that?' Hamid asks.

'Write what?' Shona says.

'The song. The one you just sang.'

'Not a song, just doodling.'

She wonders if he is taking the piss.

He wonders how she can not know how fucking good that was.

'I'll record it,' he says. 'So that, you know, you don't forget it.'

'No need,' Shona says. 'I'll remember it.'

He thinks back and plays in his head the song she just made up. He re-listens to the chord changes, the fast connecting riffs, the mood, the soul of it, the jarring discords that impossibly resolve in the final bar. It feels like a song that has existed since the dawn of time. And yet she just impro'd it while coming down from an hour of great sex.

He realises that this girl he randomly met is not just a great fuck. She's a musical genius.

Some men would take a realisation like that badly. But Hamid is a philosopher as much as he is a musician. He feels humbled by her talent; and he actually likes being humbled. It makes him feel more alive.

Unusual for a man, in my experience; but admirable.

Hamid stands up now. He is naked, and she allows herself the guilty pleasure of looking him up and down. His taut body. His smooth skin.

'La la la la,' Hamid sings, hitting her melody perfectly, but mocking her choice of words.

'Don't make fun.' She puts down the guitar. 'Sorry.'

He is still naked; she can't help noticing that. He has one of those bodies that does things to a girl's decorum.

'Why are you sorry?' Hamid says.

She gives him a 'duh' look. 'Because I can't play the fucking guitar?'

He considers that, carefully. He is a careful man. A devout man, too, despite his love of sex. When he sings and plays gnawa, he really means it. It is his homage to the gods. But he also loves rockabilly; and treats that too like an act of worship.

'You can play a bit,' he says. 'Not skilfully but you can play.'

Fuck off her face tells him.

'And you can write songs,' says Hamid.

And Hamid cannot.

He is a virtuoso on the guitar and the lute, and also on the keyboards. But he only ever plays covers and traditional music. He can improvise a lick; he can find variations on a theme; but he cannot conjure up new melodies. But until this moment he had never felt that to be a lack, a shortcoming.

Now a tiny pang of jealousy touches his soul. But mainly what he feels is respect.

He can tell though that she is misreading his caution as spite. That was not his intent. 'I mean it. You can write songs. You have that flicker of flame in you. Exhilarating flicker, exalted flame. You are a songwriter. And that is what you should do. From now on Shona, you will sing all the songs, and you will lead the band and I will play for you.'

And he smiles, very gently, and bows his head; as if yielding to her an imaginary crown.

She realises he is serious and she does not know what to say.

'Come here,' she says eventually, her body aroused, and not just with desire.

Don is wandering around Sainsbury's looking at his list. But he can't read his own handwriting, and he'd forgotten to write down half the things he needs anyway. He dithers.

Toilet Duck, says a voice from a universe away, the voice of his dead wife Marie.

Don glances around; no one near.

'Are you sure, love? I thought we had some?' Don says out loud and a young couple with matching shocks of yellow hair turn into the aisle and see him talking to himself, and dart away into another aisle to avoid him.

We have bleach for scouring the bath but Toilet Duck is for the toilet and we're out, Marie's voice says, authoritatively.

Don dithers. He knows where it is, he really does, but he does tend to lose his bearings these days. These supermarkets, they really are confusing places.

Marie takes pity on him.

Head for the pharmacy and then go straight on. You can get crackers while you're passing Aisle 4, says the voice of the ghost of Marie Harwood. *To go with that nice cheese you bought.*

'Right you are, love,' says Don, out loud,

'Remanded on bail,' says the chief magistrate, a silver-haired woman with thick black-framed glasses and an all-black outfit, making her resemble, in Mickey's opinion, one of the crows in the Old Park.

'Objection,' says Mickey rising to his feet.

'You can't object,' his duty solicitor tells hm, wearily, though he's well past the point of no return with Mickey.

'I've pleaded guilty, Your Honour,' Mickey informs the Crow, then he looks to the other two magistrates for some signs of clemency. The Scottish male magistrate withers him with a scornful glance. The South London female magistrate with the ash-blonde hair gives him an equally scornful glance. 'What more can a man do?' Mickey says, rhetorically. 'I've thrown myself upon your mercy, so sentence me now and be done with it. I'll do my bird. No sweat. Don't do the crime if you can't do the time, I always say.'

'You always say many things, Mr McBride,' the Crow says severely. 'Perhaps if you had said fewer things we might have - '

The duty solicitor glances up. Is this going to be an expression of prejudice, he wonders briefly? Grounds for calling a mistrial due to the magistrate's admittedly well-founded bias against the incorrigible and shameless Mickey and his courtroom ramblings?

But the Crow doesn't elaborate. And the duty solicitor looks down again, at his notes. He is not in fact doing a Sudoku on the piece of paper he is writing on but it does look a bit that way.

'I did it, I'm guilty, send me to jail,' Mickey says.

'This is an either-way offence,' the Crow says. 'Which we have resolved will be heard by the Crown Court where you are welcome to enter your plea of guilty.'

'No fucking way,' Mickey says.

Another severe look.

'No fucking way, Your Honour,' Mickey says, meekly.

'Please remove your client, next case,' says the Crow.

The duty solicitor puts a none too gentle hand on Mickey's elbow and steers him out of court.

'Well you fucked that up,' Mickey tells the duty solicitor a few minutes later.

Then Mickey does a little bantamweight warming up dance in the corridor outside the court room. Jabbing and ducking and and weaving circles around the duty solicitor, to prove a point. In a fist fight, lawyer against villain, Mickey would win.

But it doesn't work that way. That's not how British justice works.

'We presented our case, we have to abide by the court's decision,' the duty solicitor says stiffly.

Mickey has been charged with theft, the theft of the wallet of Duncan Colthorpe, the man killed by the Bogman. It's one of those offences which can be tried either-way, in other words, either in the magistrate's court or in the Crown Court. And either way, Mickey knows he is looking at jail time. It's not his first offence: in the past he has been convicted of drink driving, driving a car without insurance, stealing one pound coins from the trolleys in the trolley park in Asda, and numerous drug related offences. He has usually managed to get off with conditional discharges and community service orders. But this time, Mickey is going down and he knows it.

But in the magistrate's court the maximum jail term is six months for this offence. At Crown Court the maximum is a chilling seven years.

Six months is a hotel stay. Mickey has already worked out how he can run a pyramid buying scheme from his cell and he knows he will quickly make new pals there. He's that kind of guy.

Seven years, even with remission, is serious time. That would make Mickey a criminal.

And Mickey does not want to be a criminal . He wants to be a free spirit, a Wild Man of the Woods. He wants to duck and dive and say Fuck You to the Man.

But in fairness, Mickey accepts he was a total fucking idiot to steal that wallet. It was an impulse theft.

Lawyer and villain part company. Mickey is met in the lobby by his brother George. 'Could have gone worse,' says George cheerfully.

Mickey is inconsolable. 'How?'

'Well you got bail, didn't you?' George has already agreed to put up a surety for his brother and bail was not challenged by the prosecution.

'Well that's no fucking use unless I flee the country which I can't because, like well. You just know that won't fucking work,' says Mickey.

'You could come and live with us again,' George suggests. 'We can chuck Shona out of her room this time. She's got a bloke now, it's a waste her staying with us. Then you'll be like, with us.'

'What good will that do?'

George sighs. His older brother is not only a waste of space, he is thick as shit.

'Where you're living now, yeah? The house I loaned you?' George says.

'Yeah?' Mickey says.

'It's in Brixton right?' says George.

'I know it's in Brixton.'

'And everyone knows Brixton.'

'Well of course they do, it's Brixton,' Mickey says. 'It's on the Tube. It's famous. They have a carnival every year, the Brixton Splash. They have Electric Avenue. It's Brixton, man.'

'It's in the A to Z,' George puts out. 'Like every other place in London, it's in the London fucking A to fucking Z.'

'Ah,' Mickey says.

Finally, Mickey gets it.

Westwood you see, is the only district in London which is *not* in the London A to Z. What's more, there are no traffic wardens here, and no speed restrictions. If you don't bother paying Council Tax no one will ever track you down. And the police station has been abandoned ever since it was cursed, and is now only used for special operations, such as when the Murder Squad used it to investigate the killing in the woods.

Uniformed police from neighbouring areas are of course able to enter Westwood when there's a call out, as they did when Toby floated, and when Colthorpe's body was found. But half the time they get lost and go back again. Unless it's rape or murder, you can commit almost any crime you want in Westwood with a very strong chance of getting away with it.

So if Mickey lives in Westwood, he can skip bail and it's odds-on that no one will be any the wiser.

'What about your surety?' Mickey asks, generously he feels.

George looks scurrilous. A small reach for him.

'Well like, it's flexible payments plus my car as collateral, but that's a junk heap. So - '

'I have to be tagged,' Mickey says.

'No problem,' says George. 'I have a mate who knows how to take those things off. And the signals don't work anyway. Not in Westwood.'

'You know what you're asking?' Mickey says, sourly, and arguably ungratefully.

'Look Mickey, you don't want to go to jail. Fucking jail! You'll come out a fucking recidivist with a loose arsehole. No brother of mine should have to do that,' George says.

'But if I skip bail - '

'Yeah I know. You can't ever leave Westwood. Not for the rest of your life,' George says.

Mickey thinks about it.

'Will I have my own bathroom?' Mickey asks.

'Fuck off. You can piss out of the window, like the rest of us.'

That night Jack takes Shakil to see his sister sing. The band is playing at the Saxon Arms, the oldest pub in Westwood. The one with the haunted basement which used to be a dungeon.

It's Shona's band now, by unanimous agreement of everyone else in the band. And she has chosen a completely new repertoire. She starts off by singing a classic Toni Braxton song, Unbreak My Heart.

Her voice is rich and soulful.

Hamid's gentle guitar licks are astonishing, caressing her lyrics.

The bass and drums syncopate and slowly rock the rhythms.

Jack is stunned. Awed at his sister's talent. But he tries to play it cool.

'Love this,' Shakil says.

'Don't know it,' Jack says.

'Whatever happened to - '

'Shhh.'

Unbreak My Heart is a low contralto ballad of lost love and desolation. Shona sings it beautifully. Don't leave me in all this pain. Don't leave me out in the rain.

Unbreak my heart.

The pub is packed and there is total silence when Shona sings. Normally punters keep buying pints and conversations continue to flow when a band is playing. But for this song, for Shona, there is complete focus.

Hamid continues to make his guitar sob with despair, cherishing the melody line.

Shona closes her eyes and sways as the music soars around her.

And even when she is not singing all eyes are on Shona. The audience see Shona singing the song. They feel Shona feeling the song. They hear Shona longing for her lover to return and put the pieces of her heart together.

Tears pour down Jack's cheeks and for a fearful moment he wonders if Shak will see how distressed he is, and wonder why. What could possibly cause him to feel such all-consuming grief? But then he realises there are tears pouring down Shakil's cheeks as well.

Jack takes hold of Shakil's hand and squeezes it and Shak acknowledges the gesture with a tiny shudder.

When the song finishes there is total silence. Eventually the total silence becomes a statement and Hamid takes the hint and repeats the lyrical melody line slowly and with reverb three times. Then the song begins all over again and Shona's heart is unbroken all over again.

When the show is over Shak sips his Coke and melted ice. 'I'm in love,' he growls.

'With my sister?' Jack taunts.

'No with that fucking guitarist. Have you seen his eyes? He's fucking gorgeous,' Shak says.

Jack blinks. He gets it. He isn't surprised, he just gets it. He smiles.

'He's Moroccan,' Jack says. 'From Marrakech. You should hear his gnawa.'

'What the fuck is gnawa?' says Shak.

'Moroccan, like, music. Like they play in Morocco.'

'Cool.'

The lights have come up. Shona and Hamid and the band are at the bar and eleven different blokes are trying to buy her a gin and tonic, and she is saying yes to all of them. Hamid is quiet, moody, sipping a mineral water. He glances around the pub and sees Shakil, who is a handsome devil, and for a moment his eyes linger.

'Shall we go over?' Shak says.

'What?' Jack says.

'Meet the band, meet your sister,' says Shak.

Jack scowls and the room turns black and white again and he can no longer see Shona. Just the three gin and tonic glasses she is holding which bob in the air as if by magic.

'No?' says Shak, reading his mood.

'Not here, not now. Not yet,' says Jack.

How can Jack introduce his new best friend to his sister when he can't even fucking see her?

'You must be close, you two,' says Shak.

'Not really. She hates me,' Jack says.

'Why?'

Because he tried to kill himself and then tried to pin the blame for it on her.

'Because she's a girl, you know what girls are like,' Jack says.

'Not sure I do.' Shak allows a smile to slowly spread. 'Not sure I ever will.'

'Walk me home, will you?' Jack says.

It takes a while. Jack is a slow walker, with his two shattered hips and the plates in his knees, and he relies heavily upon his walking stick as a third leg. Sometimes they have to stop for Jack to take a breather. And when that happens, Shak cradles Jack in his arms till the shooting pains go away.

After they have left the pub, Shona wonders who the Asian boy is and wonders why Jack never brings him home. She wonders if Jack is gay. If he is, she will be thrilled, but somehow she doesn't think he has any sexual desires at all these days. She wonders why he keeps mocking her by turning up to watch her sets, as a living reminder of how much he hurt her and humiliated her by leaving that note.

She wonders whether her heart will ever unbreak.

Chapter 14

'It's all about the vibrato,' Mr Bradshaw explains, holding Rayowa's shoulders lightly with his palms to encourage her to relax in her bowing.

Rayowa smiles at him shyly. She's a sweet girl. Pretty too. Her dad is from Nigeria, her mum is from Devon, and they have just moved to Westwood.

'Now try it again,' Mr Bradshaw says.

She runs the bow along the nylon string, trying to conjure up the right note. Something resembling C natural emerges.

'How is that, sir?' Rayowa asks.

'Call me Benjamin. I prefer to be called Benjamin,' Mr Bradshaw says.

That's daring. Rayowa is only fifteen but she is already feeling grown up.

'How's that, Benjamin?' Rayowa asks.

'Give it time,' Mr Bradshaw says. 'Feel the note, in your heart. That's the trick to it.'

She pulls the bow across the string a second time. D sharp.

Her hair is so close he can almost breathe it. She smells of soap not perfume, as school children generally do, and Mr Bradshaw likes that.

Dawn is rising over South London. It is a yellow dawn streaked with orange. A Van Gogh dawn. Warmth spreads across the land. Owls retreat to nests. Shrubs and plants and trees are awakened by the aroma of sunshine. Robins, blackbirds, wrens and song thrushes sing a celebratory chorus as the day is born.

But on the streets of Westwood, it is already midday.

Jack is WhatsApping Shakil.

'How's the packing going?' Jack asks.

It's finally time. Shak is going to Southampton to take up his University place.

'Nightmare. I keep finding little wrapped up presents in my suitcases. They're so fucking clingy, man. They bought me saucepans. Who the fuck wants saucepans!' Shak says.

'Well you might want, no, you're right, who the fuck wants saucepans,' Jack says.

'I mean, will it all even fit in the car.'

'Will it?'

'Well I guess we'll take the people carrier, so I guess so.'

Jack doesn't mind that Shak's family is stinking rich. Except sometimes, he does a bit.

'It sounds great, all that seaside air,' Jack says.

'When are you coming to visit?' Shak says.

'Ah you won't want - '

'First weekend is freshers stuff, drinking games, all that shit.'

'Not then then,' Jack says.

'Well maybe then, I don't drink,' Shak says.

'You don't want me there on - '

'It's this Saturday, are you free?' Shak says.

'I could get the train, I suppose,' Jack says.

'There's room in the car. It's a big car. I could do with the company,' Shak says.

Shak is looking at Jack's face on his phone screen, trying to read his expression. Wishing they could be in the same room, so he could hug his best friend first, and *then* ask him.

'Don't be daft. I'll be a spare wheel,' says Jack.

'Company like, I might get lonely,' says Shak.

Jack lets his phone hand drop, so all Shak can see is wardrobe and carpet.

'Let me think about it,' Jack says.

'That's a yes then,' says Shak.

Normal face-timing is resumed. The boys stare at each other. Jack looks earnest.

'I'm hard work in a car,' Jack says. 'Toilet stops every twenty, thirty minutes. I get stiff so I make, well, weird noises.'

'It's not far. We can do toilet stops,' says Shak.

'Your mum and dad will think it's really strange,' says Jack.

'I've told them you're my boyfriend, they're cool about it,' Shak says.

'Oh fuck off,' says Jack.

'Well I did.'

'You really did that?' Jack says.

'I really did that,' Shak says.

'And they're cool?'

'Of course they're cool. They're cool people, mum and dad.'

'But I'm not your boyfriend,' Jack says.

'Well I know that but they don't so mission accomplished,' says Shak.

'But what if they find out I'm not actually your boyfriend? What if they – in fact, do they know that - '

'No,' Shak says.

'They don't know that you – that you - '

That you crippled me, is what Jack means.

'Hell no. Why would I tell them that?' Shak says.

Shak's face is grim. Guilt does that.

'Of course, it might look fucked up, if they knew,' Jack says.

'That's why I haven't fucking told 'em,' Shak says.

'Fair enough. How long will I stay with you?' Jack says.

And it's that easy.

I'm surprised at this development; and also amused.

'Well there's a spare room. My dad bought a house see. I told him to leave one room, like, spare,' Shak says.

'I can't live in your spare room when you go off to University classes. I mean, Jesus!' Jack says.

'Why not?' Shak says.

'I don't know why not I just can't.'

'There's fuck all space at your house, you keep telling me that. With your Uncle Bloody Mickey lurking all over the place like Julian Fucking Assange,' Shak says.

'He's not so bad.'

'You said he was a cunt.'

'Well yeah.'

'So what about it? Are you moving in with me?' Shak says.

Jack is tempted. But he knows he can't say yes to this idea. It's one of those things that people just don't do.

'Yes.'

St John is at his desk in a tall office tower in Canary Wharf and he has done a terrible thing. I do not understand what terrible thing he has done but I heard his mental screams of distress from all the way across London and I have crossed the river to be with him.

I do not like Canary Wharf. It is all concrete and glass and though my roots are buried here, they are buried beneath miles of pavement and road and car park. The trees here are all ornamental, there is no wildness. Even the kestrels and the hawks which love the City of London find bleak pickings here.

That day St John leaves his office early and his face is pale and he is carrying a cardboard box. I assume things have gone badly at work but because I do not understand what he actually does it's hard for me to guess what might have gone wrong. He dumps the box of his personal possessions in a bin then goes in a pub but the atmosphere there is so desolate he leaves again. He catches a Docklands Light Railway train until he can change to the Overground and once he is on the Overground I am on firmer soil myself.

When he gets home he goes into his living room and looks around and he sees for the first time what a terrible and soulless room it is. Then he picks up his phone and he calls his dad and blurts out all the terrible things that are troubling him and that's how I discover he has been sacked. The phrase 'billion pound losses' is uttered and I know that is a large amount. I wonder if he will be evicted from his home.

After the call is over, he sits in his chair like a car crash victim and I wonder if he will be all right.

It is early evening. I drift through the living room wall of St John's house into the house next door, 44 Westwood Street, and then I drift up the stairs.

Shona's bedroom used to be the box room. It was called the box room because it used to be full of boxes, and because it's the size of a box. Her dad painted it once when Shona was a toddler, maybe seven or eight, and she remembers him doing it. It hasn't been painted since. But still, it's a room, and it's hers.

Shona had refused point blank to move out when the plan for Uncle Mickey to move in permanently was proposed. So after a lot of shouting and guilt-tripping ('Prison will kill your Uncle Mickey, he's not a young man you know!') Shona had moved out of her bedroom into the box room. George now sleeps every night in Jack's old bedroom upstairs, since Hilary can no longer endure his snoring. Jack remains downstairs in the middle room that has been converted into a bedroom, so he doesn't have to climb the stairs. And Uncle Mickey is sleeping in Shona's room surrounded by pictures of boy bands and movie stars that she put up when she was a teenager and couldn't be bothered to take down. Blink 182 and Rihanna occupy pride of place. But Mickey doesn't care, he'll sleep anywhere.

Mickey's electronic tag has been shattered, his bail has been revoked, and Mickey is now officially a fugitive.

Shona spends a lot of time in Hamid's new place. He's in a loft apartment now which someone loaned to him. People always loan things to Hamid, he's one of those people. The loft apartment is airy and light and they have great sex there but Shona needs to know she has a home to go to, a bed she doesn't share. So three or four nights a week she's in the box room.

She has a keyboard in the box room, which she props up against the wall when she is putting her clothes on. George has drilled some holes in the ceiling and put hooks there so her dresses and coats can hang down above her bed. If she sits up abruptly at night she gets a face full of summer dresses. But it gives her a bit more space and she uses one of those long sticks with a hook which shopkeepers use to pull down their awnings to get her clothes down when she needs them.

Shona is reading her mother's poems.

These are not poems written by her mother, they are poems which Shona found when she was clearing out the box room. There was an old desk in there which hadn't been used in twenty years and it was too big to get through the door so Shona sawed it into pieces and dumped the planks over the fence by the railway line.

But before she got rid of the desk, Shona found in one of the drawers a folder full of typed sheets of paper with a title page saying: **Songs of Montrose.**

They weren't songs of course, they were poems. But the title gave Shona the idea. Up until

now she has been writing melodies to lyrics written by Hamid and they are all terrible.

You are the rose in my garden
I dream of you each day and night
I'm falling falling falling falling falling falling falling falling
Falling for

'Crap,' Shona had said.
Hamid had flinched.
'How about this?' Hamid had offered:

My angel madonna whore
You make me sore
You are such a goer
My darling darling ooh ooh madonna whore

'Ick,' Shona had said. 'I am not singing *that*.'
And then there was:

South London Blues
I got that, yeah,
Motherloving
South London Blues

Camberwell and Brixton
Gotta get some licks in
On the road to Peckham
Gotta get some sex man
Those goddamned South London

'No. Fucking. Way!' Shona had said.

All shite.

Ideally Shona should have written her own lyrics of course. But she found it incredibly hard. She had spent a couple of days reading the lyrics of Amy Winehouse and marvelled at them, their wit, and maturity, and their easy flow. She read song lyrics by Radiohead, by Gnarls Barkley and thought they were great. Rag N' Bone Man, yes, it all works. Even Adele's lyrics aren't bad. The Beatles' lyrics, sometimes idiotic, but always perfect for the tune. How did they do that?

And as for Bernie Taupin, well!

Shona knew she needed her own Bernie Taupin. And she did think of asking Jack to help, but then she thought twice, because he is barely literate. Hamid was a sucker for clichés and English isn't his first language anyway. And Shona's own lyrics are like boots filled with lead trying to dance the foxtrot.

And then she found these poems.

Whoever Montrose was, however Mum knew him, it's clear from the poems that he was a gay black man living in Brixton in exciting times, back in the 1990s. The poems were all about the moments, the experiences, the texture of the time. The food, the music, the culture, the street slang. The cops beating up black men. The black men beating up black men. Gun crimes, yardies, puff, reggae, rap, Diana Ross and Gill Scott-Heron playing at the Brixton Academy, street fights, riots, Electric Avenue. White women falling in love with black men and white men falling for black women and children being born and teenagers finding their own true selves and love and hate and jealousy and rage and all the emotions of the world crammed in there in taut, vivid, lines of conversational prose that somehow had a poetic pulse and rhythm.

Shona is trying out some chords. She finds a rhythm. Creates a riff.

She sings; inventing a melody to accompany the lyrics on the page in front of her.

She sings with a voice that is richer and darker and deeper in timbre than ever before. A voice which allows her to run along the scales from low to high notes in unexpected ways. The words and the music are indissoluble, one could not exist without the other.

Twenty-five years after being shot to death by racist London cops, Montrose the Poet's voice speaks again; but now he sings.

Tanya is using a hand sanitizer outside the hospital ward to cleanse her hands. She rubs and rubs and rubs until the sanitiser is empty and her fingers reek of disinfectant. And finally she goes in to see her little boy.

Kane is in a coma still. He does not dream, he does not think. He is in a vegetative state and sooner or later the doctors will have to pull the plug. But no one has told Tanya that yet.

Uncle Mickey is in his bedroom, Shona's old bedroom, with headphones on. He is smoking a spliff, and watching a movie on his laptop. I won't say what else he is doing, but I can see that there are naked people having sex upon his computer screen.

Jack is trying to climb the stairs. But despite several attempts, he can't manage it.

So he leans his stick against the wall and he goes down on to his hands and knees in a series of awkward phases. Then he crawls slowly towards the staircase, and he drags himself up a step at a time, like a centipede, but with only two legs. He has no idea how he will get back down but he feels he has to do this.

The rest of the house is empty. George is at work. Hilary is at work. And Shona is in the box room singing songs which he could hear from downstairs. Muffled by her door, but still extraordinary. And now he wants to get closer. He wants to hear the songs properly. He wants to beg for her forgiveness.

But he can't get up the fucking stairs.

In London Heights the footballing kids are back and one of them dribbles past two defenders and scores a goal by kicking the ball at a wall with goal posts painted on it.

'Goal!' the goal scorer shouts.

There is much hugging and other displays of affection as the goal scorer is mobbed.

And during his victory lap the kid sees a scrap of gristle on the ground and he steers clear of it. He has seen it before. They have all seen it before. And they have tried to throw it away but touching it does strange things to a boy. It causes nightmares, and panic attacks. The local dogs give it a wide berth. It is a piece of dead meat that visibly throbs.

The Bogman's heart still lives.

Chapter 15

I watch the Bogman's heart throb for a while. I watch the child footballers play. I look across at the view of London from London Heights. I look at the clouds and their evolving random shapes. Then I drift back to 44 Westwood Street to find that Jack has finally reached the top of the stairs.

He is breathless and his body aches but he can hear his sister singing far more clearly now. A rich contralto with a soprano's range. Like Amy Winehouse and Whitney Houston conjoined in a single voice.

Fuck, he thinks. How does she do it? Where did that fucking *voice* come from?

He doesn't know the song. But it's wonderful. Raw aching emotion in a Jamaican patois mixed with South London argot about being shivved, being broke, getting your heart broken, loving your lover, resenting your parents, getting beaten the shit out of, running with a gang, running from the feds, dealing coke, smoking puff; just everyday life for a young black man back then.

Being alive!

It is magical.

And also, true. So very full of trueness, that it breaks Jack's heart.

Jack listens for a long time then he wonders how he will get back down the stairs again, without Shona realising he has been listening to her.

A few hours after Tanya has been to see him, after she wept silently, full of guilt at what she had done to him, a thought stirs in Kane Armstrong's mind. Because he is not dead, not quite, not yet. But the thought cannot cohere.

His body is wasted from his months in intensive care. His complexion is paler than death.. He has bedsores that have to be treated twice a day. His heart needs mechanical help to beat. His lungs need mechanical help to breathe. In any other period in history he would be long dead but these people have managed to keep him alive even though he is, by all objective criteria, worthless.

But still, something remains. A whispered memory of who he once used to be. And for a moment, that whispered memory becomes almost a thought.

The thought is a word. A word rich in emotion. A word that pains him and perhaps it's the pain that is keeping him alive.

The word is: *Daisy.*

'Look Auntie Tanya!'

A three year old child is dressed as Cinderella. This is one of the children Tanya looks after. Not *her* children, these are children who belong to several posh families from the big houses overlooking the playground. Tanya is paid to be the childminder to these kids, usually seven or eight of them at any given time. It is one of the ways she pays her bills. But she loves all these children as her own.

'Do you like it, Auntie Tanya?' The Cinderella girl twirls, showing off her glamour.

'Course I do, darling,' Tanya says.

But she's not looking.

Mr Mohammed is selling one of his storage boxes at the front of his shop. His customers are Mike and Helen Dingwall, the couple from the house in 288 Westwood Street; the ones who have scaffolding outside their house. They have had their kitchen renovated and their bedroom extended and now they want boxes to store all the stuff they don't need, but can't bear to get rid of.

It takes a while for Mr Mohammed to locate what they want because the boxes are stacked carefully according to size. And to find the boxes they have indicated he has to take them all down and take the small ones out of the big ones and put the loose lids on the ones he is selling and finally he has a sale.

'Great,' they say.

'You're very welcome,' says Mr Mohammed, smiling.

Always friendly, Mr Mohammed. Always busy.

Beep beep beep. That is the noise made by the pedestrian crossing. It makes that noise so that blind people know when to cross.

Buses are hurtling out of the bus depot, one two three four. I love the rush of red.

'Fuck you you fucking bitch you - ' Some guy, some random guy in the street, shouting at his girlfriend down the phone. He is holding it in front of him and shouting like she is ten streets away. I don't know this man but I've seen him before. He doesn't interest me.

The crows flock like black cloaks then they land upon a tree branch, and flap down to the ground in ones and twos. They are lively and restless. They caw and trill at each other but by and large the sounds have very limited meanings. Yes. No. Come. Go. Beware. Mine. Yours. I defy you. I give in. Mate with me? Like you. Dislike you. Fuck off. That's about the limit of their vocabulary.

But they have other ways, these crows, of communicating, and sharing memories, and even philosophical ideas. Ways that even I struggle to understand.

What are they up to? I wonder. What are they thinking?

A caravan pulls into the caravan park, towed by a large Volvo car. Three children and mum and dad are inside, they have come from Wales. They even speak Welsh, a language I love, which reminds me of – well, other languages, other times.

The car pulling the caravan drives slowly down the deserted driveway. Then as it passes a stand of trees, dozens more mobile homes suddenly become apparent. Like Red Indians who have been waiting in hiding in order to ambush the cowboys in an old Western movie.

You'd never know this place existed, this caravan park. It's tucked away behind the White House, a beautiful white stucco mansion, where John Fletcher, the sculptor who designed the Victorian Gardens in the Old Park, used to live. An ugly man, with a face like a statue carved by a butcher, so his friends always said. But good natured to a fault. His parties were – ah yes!

A class of children, not yet teenagers, sit at their desks in Westwood High. They are bored by what their teacher is talking about. They have yet to learn that ideas can be exciting.

The teacher is talking about medieval history and the three field system.

I remember it well.

In the school gym it's PE time. The kids are practising gymnastics, doing handstands, or taking turns to leap on and off a wooden horse.

One of them, a skinny girl, does a cartwheel and I am impressed.

The music room. I wait outside it as a violin plays badly and then it stops.

I think about what that means.

It is a music lesson but the violin has stopped playing.

Why?

I think I know why.

I look at the door, which is locked. Doors in schools are never locked.

I enter the room but not by breaking the lock. I simply flow, and my flow flows into the door, and whirls around inside the grain of the wood, which is seasoned oak, and then I flow a bit more and I am inside the room.

Oh Mr Bradshaw, what *are* you doing with that girl?

Out of the school now, across the road, up the hill, towards one of the trendiest pubs in this area, the Glade Arms. It has a pub garden, a large one, overlooked by oak trees, old ones. Very old indeed. The stories they could tell, if they could only talk.

In the back part of the gardens I see a robin and a chaffinch eating from the same bird table.

In Horniman Woods again. Smelling bark and wildflowers which are scattered along the steep banks of tanglewood and thorns flanking the old disused railway track. The tunnel is boarded up now and graffiti has been painted over the wooden boards. Names of teenage gangs. Slogans about peace and justice and Palestine. Hearts pierced with arrows. I remember how the train used to roar through that tunnel, sounding its whistle.

I go to Old Park. The cherry blossoms on the avenue of trees that guard the way to the densely wooded area where Colthorpe was murdered last year have budded, and are about to bloom.

Soon, in a few days, they will erupt into flower. And the blossoms will blaze with pink beauty. And people will take photographs of them and feel spiritually enriched. And then, a few weeks later, the cherry blossoms will fall from the tree and get blown away, and then they will be gone.

And then, a year later, new buds will bud.

'What the *fuck* are you doing there, Jack?' asks Shona. She has emerged from the box room to discover that her brother is half way down the stairs, head first, crawling down.

'Nothing,' he mutters into the stair carpet.

Damn! He almost got away with it.

Uncle Mickey has finished his porno film and is desperate for a pint.

But first, he lights another spliff.

Traffic has ground to a halt on Woody Hill because of the road works.

'I've got my own bag,' says Don Harwood to Megan, the check out lady at Sainsbury's, and she gives him a friendly smile.

Fuck off he's mine, bitch, a voice says, and Don can hear it, but Megan cannot.

Hilary is putting away one of George's suits in their bedroom, which hasn't been decorated for nearly fifteen years and that really bothers her; but that's George for you. Then, in the top pocket of the jacket, she finds a piece of paper that has magically survived the dry cleaning process. She unfurls it. It is a receipt for building work done, with a handwritten message scrawled upon it. The message says: 'All my love you sexy man, Veronica.' Hilary blinks.

She puts the note back where she found it and puts the suit away. She tries to remember the last time George wore this suit. He would have taken it when he went to Glasgow, perhaps? When he was bidding for a contract to renovate a house up there last month?

Later Hilary cleans Uncle Mickey's bedroom, since he has just gone out daydrinking. And as well as the tissues in the wastebin she finds a drum under the bed. A little tambour drum, the kind you can hold in your hand and tap. A drum? What's that about? She remembers all the wild man nonsense. That has something to do with drumming, doesn't it?

She tests the tensile strength of the drum by prodding it. Then she taps a rhythm on it with her finger. Then she finds a nail scissors and punches some holes in it. Then she replaces it under the bed.

She wonders if later, perhaps tonight, over dinner, she will ask George about the note from Veronica from Glasgow.

That night Hilary makes beef and ale pie for George and Shona and Jack and Mickey. Mickey adds the aroma of beer every time he breathes out,. Jack has carpet burns on his face. Shona isn't hungry anyway so she makes herself a salad.

And when the meal is over and Mickey and Shona and Jack have gone up to bed, Hilary has a chance to say something to George about this Veronica woman he's clearly been shagging. But she doesn't.

The day after the evening when Hilary failed to confront George about his womanising, another storm grows up in the Old Park. But this is a gentle storm not a hurricane. Soft warm breezes shake the trees and ruffle the hair of dogwalkers. Shrubs tremble. Leaves shiver. Then the wind grows brisker, and gumballs from the sweet gum trees that have fallen on to the ground are swept aloft and hover in the air like balls in a bingo machine. And soon the air turns pink as the cherry blossoms on the smaller shrubs near the Maze are blown off their branches and become a hovering haze. And the waters of the lakes ripple. And pollen is swept from the flowers and the flowering trees and forms a shimmering fecund fog.

Don is walking with Cecil and he is alarmed at the way the sky turns the colour of pale blood from all the flying cherry blossoms. And he sees something sinister in the way the gusts of wind come from all directions including up and down, rather than from the east or west or south or north, as is traditional.

He walks into one gust of wind and it shakes his body as if he were a dentist's drill and Cecil barks and yaps and cowers down, afraid of being swept away by the wind..

The pollen cloud arches and swirls and forms into patterns in the sky as if it is a murmuration of starlings.

Then whoosh!

The pollen cloud moves.

It soars across the sky, momentarily eclipsing the sun. Little tendrils of pollen are falling off and landing on the ground like soft hail. But more pollen is being captured all the time by more winds and it is swept upwards and becomes part of the great pollen cloud. The pollen cloud then sweeps over the meadow, and up over the tall forest canopies, and over the terraces and into the Victorian Sculpture Park.

The dark life-giving cloud hovers above the wind-scarred statues of Gladstone and Disraeli. And then it moves and soars over the female authors and Mary Annakin. Then it moves on out of the Old Park entirely, across the Boulevard, till it is above the streets of Westwood. And although it is still daytime the sky abruptly darkens.

Before long the swirling pollen cloud has reached Westwood Street and there it hovers above one of the houses. Number 44. The house where Jack is packing for his trip to Southampton. It is taking him a while and the pain from his legs is making him weep. He knows it will be a long slow trip because of all the toilet stops, and by the time he gets there, after a bumpy journey in a Chelsea tractor, Jack is going to be a total mess. He knows that. And he doesn't care.

He feels the room darken but he doesn't know why. He turns the light on.

The pollen cloud that hovers above Jack's house is touched with magic. My magic. I have given it healing powers.

And if I were to swirl the pollen cloud downwards; and if I were to creep balls of pollen through the open windows of Jack's room; and if I were to wrap his body in pollen and force pollen down his mouth and make him choke with pollen and fill his gut with pollen and contaminate his body with pollen so excessively that for months to come he will piss pollen and shit pollen - then, I know, my magic will work its magic upon him and Jack will be healed. Then he will be, as the humans like to say, as right as rain.

I'm tempted. Not because I care about Jack, because I don't; but because it would be something to do. Some days I just want something to do.

I imagine it, how it would be. Jack would be Jack again. He would run and swim and have sex, and every day his body would remind him that he is a fit, athletic and gorgeous breaker of women's hearts. I could change his life. I could so easily change his life.

But why should I? What has this boy Jack ever done for me?

I move the pollen cloud onwards. It sweeps away from 44 Westwood Street, scouring the sky, moving westwards across Westwood. I know that just a few miles away, outside the bounds of Westwood but still within the range of my deep buried roots, is the South London Intensive Care Unit, where Kane lies in a coma. I could save him if I chose. I could propel particles of pollen through the partially open window; and waft them into the ICU room; and billow them over his face. I could push the pollen particles into his mouth, past the breathing tube, and crawl them down his throat and swim them down into his gut and slip them through the thin membranes of his veins and then into his arteries and then into his heart. And there, the magic pollen would heal the terrible damage caused by the bullet Daisy shot him with.

I can do that. I can bring Kane back to life.

Maybe later.

For now, the pollen cloud still billows above the streets of Westwood. And even the locals are disconcerted at the way daylight slips away and dark storm clouds appear. But these aren't storm clouds, it is my pollen swarm. It is a living organism that is propagating itself and expanding in mid-air. And those birds which rashly try to fly through it find their lungs are choked and they can't breathe or fly and so they plummet downwards like the bombs in the Second World War that are silent until they hit their target. And when the birds connect with the ground, hitting it with incredible speed, they die messily.

Then moments later they are reborn.

On it swirls, the pollen cloud.

Over the church spire of Saint Peregrine, then onwards, it flies; till it is above Prospect Avenue. Then the cloud takes a right turn in the air above Desolation Road, close to London Heights, and soon I will reach my destination.

The pollen cloud pauses and builds in mass. It is a single black cloud hanging like fate above this low rise council estate.

The pollen swarm is now so heavy and so densely packed that the air below it is being crushed. So that the kids playing football suddenly find their ball is stuck in mid-air in invisible treacle. And their heads and bodies are heavier by far than they used to be. And they are moving as if they are a slow motion replay on a television football match.

The heavy air gets heavier and pushes down on them. Their knees buckle, and they are bent over double. They try to stagger away in that position, like old men in a comedy sketch. But the pressure gets greater and they are forced to fall down on to their hands and knees. And then they have to crawl slowly along, desperately searching for normal air.

A dog barks and howls at the heavy air that is hurting its body until suddenly its spine is split and its ribs are crushed. It dies before it can emit a last howl of dismay.

The children however manage to escape safe and sound, rolling out of the mass of heavy air to find that they are as light as children again.   I observe this but I do not care.

For the truth is I never care. Not really, not truly. I am a curious creature and sometimes I take a liking to people and sometimes I even help them out. But deep down I am amoral, like most gods.

And when I am bored then sometimes I will rage, and sometimes I will meddle; and sometimes I will do nothing.

Today I will meddle.

The pollen cloud descends, blackening London Heights. It encircles the scrap of tainted meat that has lain upon this concrete playground for nearly eight months now. Sniffed at by dogs, rained upon, hailed upon, booted around, attacked by bacteria, and chewed on by flies which subsequently died in agony. It is dead flesh but it is also a heart and it still beats, after all this time.

A shard of the pollen cloud hits it like a spear and the heart glows and then the pollen shard glows too.

At first just a few pollen particles light up, like motes of dust in a sunbeam. Then the glow grows and a tendril of light emerges, reaching up from the ground into the air. Then the tendril of light becomes thicker, it becomes a stream of light. Then the stream becomes thicker still; and before long an illuminated giant pollen creature has been created that stretches its body all the way from the ground up to the tip of the pollen cloud.

Then the pollen cloud catches alight and it burns, forming a giant sword-shaped flame with its hilt uppermost, dazzling the atmosphere.

And before long, sparks of burning air tip out of the sky and rain as hot hail upon the courtyard of London Heights Estate.

And the heart on the ground remains impaled by the tip of the pollen sword and as the pollen sword burns it glows brighter.

Then the heart starts to beat and its scraps of flesh turns pink and they grow, and they grow. And the pollen sword melts away and becomes sparks flickering in the air.

Soon the dead pulsing heart has become a live pulsing heart.

Then the heart swells and spreads and slowly becomes a torso.

And the torso grows limbs. And the limbs sprout a head. And the head develops eyes and a mouth and teeth and a tongue and ears.

When the pollen has vanished entirely a naked man lies face up upon the poured-rubber surface of the courtyard of London Heights. His skin is dark brown in colour, peat-stained still, but without the scars created by his murder and mutilation. And with flesh that is featureless and soft, not like cracked leather. And when the body opens its eyes they are made of white jelly and the irises are blue and they glitter with life.

He is hairless and unnaturally smooth, this resurrected Bogman, with no wrinkles and no markings on his body at all, not even folds in his flesh. But he has a cock and balls now, and plenty of both. And nipples, and fingernails, and teeth. And his bald head is shiny with sweat as he tries to pump blood around his body; a body that has not pumped blood for thousands of years.

And his body is young again.

A shower of rain falls, and dampens his soft brown body and eventually, the Bogman slowly gets to his feet and looks around.

I already regret what I have done but it is done now.

The Bogman is back.

Westwood, beware.

Chapter 16

When the school bell rings at 3.30pm, Father Glackin is waiting in the courtyard to collect Toby.

'Afternoon Father Glackin,' Hilary says, as she emerges from the adjoining classroom. The Father has been coming to the school for many years to liaise with the School Counsellor, Mrs Penny. There are a lot of Catholic children in the school and the Father is a diligent and caring priest who does a great deal to support the troubled children in his parish. He also has a degree in psychology, so he's not all mumbo-jumbo as you might think. If he hadn't been a parish priest, he might have been a School Counsellor himself.

He's a friendly face and Hilary is glad to see him.

'How's that rogue of a husband of yours?' he asks cheerfully.

Hilary's face falls. George did the plumbing in the Catholic Church Hall a few years back. It is still very much the will of God whether the water from the taps comes out hot or cold.

'Up to all sorts,' Hilary says.

'You look troubled,' Father Glackin says.

That's true enough. Her son is a cripple; her husband is having affairs; her daughter is dating a musician.

'I'm not Catholic, I don't go in for confession,' she says, cagily.

Her response was swift; but he can read her like a book.

'But if you did, what would you confess?' asks Father Glackin.

And Hilary smiles, and picks the one trouble that troubles her most. 'That one day I'll swing for that bastard.'

'Ah I'll make a note of that. For when you need a character witness in court,' says Father Glackin.

'I was just jesting, Father,' Hilary says.

'And so was I,' Father Glackin says.

He smiles. The classroom door opens and the Eagles pour out, calmly, one at a time, and are greeted by dads and mums and grandparents.

Father Glackin spots Toby.

'Ah there you are my boy,' says Father Glackin.

Toby looks at him. Eight years old but with eyes as weary and defeated as the thief on the cross next to Christ; the one who had just watched that evil piece of shit Barabbas walk away to freedom.

'Father Glackin,' Toby says.

'I'm here to pick you up, you remember?' Father Glackin says.

Toby doesn't.

'Ah now do I need a form to fill in?' Father Glackin looks around helplessly.

'You need a password,' Hilary says. It's not her class but rules are rules.

'Horniman,' says Toby.

'His mother told me Horniman,' Father Glackin says.

Hilary shrugs; whatever.

Liam is waiting impatiently for his brother. 'You coming, tadpole?' he asks. Toby looks at him like a boy for whom death would be a relief.

'Change of plan, he's coming with me,' lies Father Glackin. 'Your parents asked me to, ah, collect him.'

'Like I give a shit.'

Liam is gone and it's just Toby and the Father now. 'Let's go, take your hands out of your pockets,' Father Glackin says. Toby obeys and shuffles after the priest. Hilary watches them go. Mrs Farley joins her. She takes on board what has happened; it's fine by her.

'I am so bloody knackered,' says Mrs Farley. 'Why do we do this to ourselves, eh?'

'It's four pm soon,' Hilary says. 'Wine o'clock for teachers and TAs.'

They share a cheeky smile.

Not a joke.

Father Glackin doesn't intend to hold the little boy's hand but they are walking side by side and his hand is big and comforting, and Toby reaches out and catches hold of it. The touch of the boy's small fingers in Father Glackin's big hand gives the priest a pang. No sex is one thing, you get used to that; but not having a child?

'This way lad,' says Father Glackin, turning left not right.

'Yes sir,' Toby says.

'You don't need to call me sir, Toby,' Father Glackin says.

'No sir,' Toby says.

Toby is placid and calm. Father Glackin has the feeling that if he asked the boy to jump in front of a bus, he would.

'Do you want to know where you're going, Toby?' Father Glackin asks.

'No sir.'

They reach the end of the road and wait at the crossing opposite the Protestant church.

'Have you been inside there?' Father Glackin asks.

'Yes sir.'

'Don't call me sir. When?'

'Christmas sir. Nativity play, sir.'

Father Glackin has a good working relationship with Ned Wallis, the C of E priest at Saint Peregrine's. Which used to be Saint Mary's, but was renamed after the patron saint of people suffering from cancer and AIDS and other serious illnesses, at Ned's insistence.

To get to the Catholic church you have to cross the Pelican crossing that spans Treacherous Hill, the steepest hill in Westwood. This road also has a devilish rake so that even when you walk *across* it, it is like climbing a small mountain. The Green Man flashes and they step on to the crossing. Father Glackin tries to pace himself, breathing slowly through his nose and out of his mouth. But he still has to bend half over to manage the camber and by the time he reaches the opposite pavement his heart is pounding and he is breathless.

'Are you dying, sir?' Toby asks.

'Not yet,' Father Glackin wheezes.

They walk past Saint Peregrine's with its tall spire and two streets later they approach a red brick building dating from the 1930s marked CATHOLIC CHURCH OF OUR LADY OF THE ROSARY.

'Have you been here before, Toby?' Father Glackin asks.

'Where?' Toby asks.

'Here,' Father Glackin says.

Father Glackin points. Toby looks. He clearly has taken no notice of his whereabouts until now.

'I'm hungry sir,' Toby says.

'We'll make you some toast,' Father Glackin says.

'But no jam.'

'Why not?'

Toby gives him a severe look.

'Because I like jam,' Toby says.

Father Glackin's heart sinks. He opens the front door and lead the boy in.

'Take a seat, son,' Father Glackin says.

This is the room the Father reserves for meetings and private conferences. The church itself is through the double doors but in honesty it is not much more than a small chapel.

Sarah Lemaitre is waiting for him, reading a Kindle. She glances up when he enters.

'Ah. Good. Thank you for being here, Sarah,' Father Glackin says.

'Any time, Father,' says Sarah Lemaitre.

Father Glackin checks his watch. He is feeling nervous. He takes his phone out and checks his messages, his emails and texts and WhatsApps. In case there is an angry message from the O'Connells, demanding the return of their son. But he has done his homework. He knows the O'Connells both like to work late. Or rather they like to go to the pub at 5pm and stay there late. He knows they are careless parents, latchkey parents, who rely on ten-year-old Liam to handle the childcare for Toby. And he also knows that as a priest and a man of good character, he has a good chance of being believed by the authorities regardless of what bullshit he comes up with to explain why he has picked up Toby from school without parental permission. Provided of course that is he is not foolish enough to be alone in a room with Toby without a witness; in which case tongues will wag. But even so he is nervous.

Technically, of course, this is kidnap. But it is kinder, Father Glackin feels, to call it borrowing.

'This is Toby?' says Sarah gently. She is naturally a very nice woman but she also know how to switch it on.

'Yes miss,' says Toby.

'Call me Sarah,' says Sarah.

'Yes miss.'

'Sit down Toby.'

'I thought I'd made a cup of tea and some toast,' says Father Glackin, to give the two of them some space. 'No jam. But maybe some biscuits?'

'No biscuits,' says Toby, disapprovingly.

Glackin feels rebuked.

'Just toast then, for the lad. Will you have a tea, Sarah?' Father Glackin asks.

'You know I will, Father,' Sarah says.

Father Glackin goes through to the kitchen area, and Sarah is left alone with the little boy.

'Do you know who I am, Toby?' Sarah asks.

'You're the lady who is in this house,' Toby says.

'I work with Father Glackin. We help each other. I'm a social worker, he said you might want someone to be your friend,' Sarah says.

Toby considers that.

'No thank you,' Toby says.

'Fair enough. Do you have any friends?'

'No miss.'

'Will you roll your sleeves up, Toby?'

Toby rolls his sleeves up. His arms are thin and pale and unmarked by bruises.

'Thank you Toby, now roll them down again,' Sarah says.

'Yes miss,' says Toby.

He rolls his sleeves back down and continues watching her with wary eyes.

Sarah raises a fist angrily and Toby flinches.

Sarah lowers her fist.

That one usually works, as an indicator of domestic abuse.

'Sorry, there was a fly,' she lies.

'No there wasn't,' he says, disapprovingly.

He is looking at her as if she is a predator. He seems frightened of her. Sarah has seen it all before but even so she is disconcerted and unhappy.

Father Glackin returns with tea and toast. He's brought some chocolate biscuits and he takes one and eats it.

Toby eats his toast. He doesn't drink his tea.

'Toby's a good lad, aren't you, Toby?' Father Glackin says to Sarah, just to keep the conversation moving.

Toby eats his toast and says nothing.

'He has a flinch reflex,' Sarah murmurs.

Father Glackin is not surprised; far from it.

'The neighbours have – told me things,' Father Glackin says. 'They've heard noises. The saw the family in the garden one time, when - '

'You told me that,' Sarah says.

'No one wants to be a grass but sometimes you have to speak out.'

'More toast,' says Toby. Father Glackin gets up and goes into the kitchen to make some more.

There is a long silence. Sarah is watching the boy, assessing him. Toby is watching her, assessing her.

'What does a social worker do?' Toby asks.

'We help people. Especially children,' Sarah says.

'Will you help *me* then? How will you help me? Will you take me into care?' Toby asks.

'Do you want to be taken into care?' Sarah asks.

'I don't know what care is.'

'Are your parents hurting you, Toby?' Sarah asks, gently.

Father Glackin is by the door, holding a plate of toast. He pauses. Letting the moment have space.

'What will happen if I say they are?' asks Toby.

'That's not the point. All you have to do is tell us the truth,' says Sarah.

'What will happen if I tell you the truth? Toby says.

'Then I can help you,' Sarah says, simply.

Toby stares. He says nothing. Father Glackin puts down the toast on the table.

'Come here, lad,' Father Glackin says.

Toby stares. He doesn't move.

'Stand up,' Father Glackin says.

Toby stands up.

Father Glackin opens his arms. 'Come here.'

Toby walks towards him holding both his palms spread out in front of his face: a protective stance.

'Put your hands down, lad,' Father Glackin says.

The hands stay up.

'Put the hands down, no need to be afraid, 'Father Glackin reassures him.

Toby puts his hand down by his side. He stares at Father Glackin with a face that has forgotten how to smile. It is heart-breaking.

Father Glackin swiftly cocks his right arm, moves his left shoulder forward with practised pugilistic skill so he can corkscrew his body round, then launches a savage right cross to Toby's face.

It connects powerfully and Toby's nose explodes and Toby falls to the ground. But he does not scream or whimper, or make any kind of noise.

'Jesus fucking Christ,' says Sarah.

The blasphemy stands uncommented upon.

'Get up, lad,' says Father Glackin.

'Have you gone totally fucking mad?' Sarah shouts.

Sarah stands up and moves swiftly. She puts herself in front of the big priest as a human shield. She's a small woman, bird-like, but fearless.

'If you want to hit someone, hit me, you piece of shit!' Sarah says.

'Come now, I would never do that, Sarah. Look at the boy,' says Father Glackin.

Sarah is still in confrontational mode. Fists clenched. Daring him to bring it fucking on! She's half his size but in a fight she might well win, because she's a terrier.

'I said, look at the boy,' Father Glackin says.

Sarah turns and looks at the boy.

He is standing up, face expressionless, his nose is bent to one side, and is clearly broken. Blood trickles down his cheek where the Father's ring caught him.

'How's your nose, lad? 'asks Father Glackin.

'It hurts,' Toby says.

They both stare at him.

A few moments elapse. And everything changes.

There is no longer a raw cut on Toby's cheek. His nose is no longer bent.

'How's your nose, lad?' asks Father Glackin.

'It's fine,' Toby says.

'You broke it.' Sarah whispers.

'It healed,' Toby says.

'Not possible,' Sarah says.

'Miracles happen, get over yourself, Sarah,' Father Glackin says.

'Please don't hit me again,' says Toby.

That one wounds Father Glackin badly.

'I won't. Not again,' says Father Glackin. 'Never again. No one will hit you ever again. That's what your parents do to you, isn't it?'

Toby isn't sure what to do so he tells the truth.

'Yes.'

'And you heal afterwards so no one can tell you've been hurt.'

'Yes.'

'Your mother beat you with a broomstick once, didn't she, in the back garden. And she broke your arm and you lay there screaming. And your neighbour saw and called the cops. But by the time they came your arm wasn't broken and you had no bruises. Do you remember that, Toby?' says Father Glackin.

'Yes.'

'What's going on here, Edward?' Sarah asks Father Glackin.

'It's a Westwood thing. The boy heals. It's magic. It's Westwood. It happens,' Father Glackin says.

'Yes but why the fuck do HIS PARENTS BEAT HIM UP?' Sarah asks, furiously.

'Toby can you answer that?' Father Glackin says.

He doesn't want to.

'Answer it, please,' says Father Glackin.

'I'm a bad child. I'm evil,' says Toby.

'Why are you evil?' Father Glackin asks.

'I do evil things,' Toby says.

'What kind of evil things?' Sarah asks.

Toby is silent.

Father Glackin takes a Yorkie bar out of his coat pocket. Every kid loves a Yorkie bar. He feels it; it hasn't melted in his coat, it is still firm. Solid chocolate chunks: no nonsense.

'Show Sarah what you can do,' Father Glackin says, and he hands Toby the Yorkie bar.

Chapter 17

Dawn in Westwood is on time for once.

Jack is packed and ready. He has showered, washed his hair, and done his exercises as best he can. He is sitting on the sofa in the mindless manner of people who are waiting to be given a lift.

His phone buzzes. His lift is here. It is 6am, Shakil's dad likes an early start, he likes to get ahead of the crowd. He has been explaining to everyone for days that it's A3 all the way to Southampton, as if they should care. Shak has prepared a playlist which he and Jack can both listen to on their wireless headphones. Rap, metal, and 70s funk, a toxically good combination.

Road trip!

Jack hobbles to the front door and opens it. He braces himself on his stick, then grabs his wheelie case and lifts it outside. Then he steps one foot at a time over the step and then brings the stick across, and once he has got his balance, he picks up the case again. He has it down to an art now. His upper body strength is formidable. And he is still lean and ripped. Girls in bars take one look at him and get horny and think, phwoah, he's hot!

And then they see him walk, after which passions cool.

Jack stands on the pavement in the early morning light, and he sees a large people carrier turn the corner and drive towards him with no driver at the wheel. Just like the magic double-decker bus in Harry Potter.

Jack's smile falters. And it wasn't much of a smile to begin with.

The people carrier pulls up. Shakil's dad Mr Khan gets out of the front passenger seat and hurries over to grab Jack's case. He is a thin man with spectacles and is wearing a cardigan over moleskin trousers and he is very rich, after selling a large proportion of his shares in his knitwear company, which he still runs. The cardigan looks like an own brand design, and is rather stylish if you're an old person, in Jack's view.

'You must be Jack,' Mr Khan says effusively. Mrs Khan joins them on the kerb. 'I'm Jacinta,' she says, offering a hand.

'Ghulam,' says Mr Khan, offering his own hand.

'Bright and early, eh,' says Shak's voice. And Jack turns his body and opens himself up for a hug, guessing where Shak might be on the pavement but guessing slightly wrong. But Shakil doesn't notice and Jack finds himself being embraced.

'We've heard so - '

' – so much about you. Shall I put that stick, in, ah?'

'Yes,' says Jack.

Ghulam has the boot open and slips Jack's case in, then the stick. Jack is thinking: *There's room to put my entire bedroom in that bloody boot.* Which is not true but it is indeed a very large vehicle.

'I'm taking the first leg, then we'll share the back seat, eh?' says Shakil's voice, which keeps moving around in a really annoying fashion.

'Yeah whatever,' says Jack.

'I hear you boys have a "Playlist",' says Jacinta.

'Yeah yeah,' says Jack.

'We can croon along to Perry Como while you listen to Motörhead, eh?' says Ghulam cheerily.

Jack doesn't know who Perry Como is and Motörhead are just a one hit wonder in his opinion. But Jack gives him marks for trying.

'Well,' says Jacinta, patting Jack's arm and looking at him fondly.

Jack knows what she is thinking. She is thinking wedding bells, the first gay wedding in the family. In short, she is enjoying a vision of her and her husband basking in the pride of being completely metropolitan and cool with it all.

Except Jack isn't gay and he isn't Shakil's lover. And in fact Shakil doesn't have a lover. He has gay intent in abundance, which is why he came out to his family, but has not yet achieved consummation. Which he is very sheepish about.

Jack goes in the back with Mr Khan and Mrs Khan goes in the front with Shakil and gives a running commentary on how bad Shakil's route is: 'If only you'd got on to the A3 at Wimbledon, Shak, it's a much faster approach.' And 'Oh! You missed the short cut!'

Jack and Mr Khan have not much in common and Jack doesn't like talking in cars anyway. But to get things started, he gives a full breakdown of the current Arsenal team under the Spanish guy, Arteta, rating each player in detail. But then he is lost for words when Ghulam asks why he doesn't support a South London team like Millwall or the Palace. And he has no comeback when Ghulam berates the fact that the Arsenal stadium is now named after a right wing Middle Eastern regime.

'Yeah well, it is what it is, like,' Jack says.

'Well, you know much more about it than I do,' says Ghulam smoothly.

Shakil drives like a madman. A gifted madman, admittedly; his road control is excellent and his anticipation is superb. But his eyes constantly misread 20mph for 60mph and he loves to accelerate towards junctions then brake just in time. In this car, he can get away with it.

Jack finds all this alarming enough in itself; but it is all doubly stressful because Jack still can't actually see Shakil. He can only see the steering wheel that appears to be moving itself, and the roads they rapidly veer into. It is terrifying.

To allay his terror Jack closes his eyes. But that's even worse, his stomach lurches and he feels like vomiting.

'Feel free to listen to music,' Ghulam says. So Jack puts on his wireless headphones. Ghulam immediately takes out his phone and starts sending emails. Jack clicks Shuffle.

The first song is Ace of Spades.

Oh fuck, he thinks: What are the odds on that?

With his eyes closed, and heavy metal playing, the drive is like an acid trip.

When he finally opens his eyes the car has stopped and it is empty. He blinks. He sees the Khans waiting for him outside the car, and he shuffles along to the edge of the seat. He opens the door.

Ghulam is waiting with his cane, ready to hand it to him. Jack swings one foot out, pauses. Braces himself on the car door. Takes a calm breath. Swings the other foot out. Lifts himself up with the legs, smoothly, keeping his back straight. He slides effortlessly into an upright position and takes the cane and rests some weight on it. Then he tries to move but his feet aren't responding properly because of car stiffness so he waits. Everyone else waits. No one shows a tremor of impatience. Shakil is still invisible, Jack wonders where he is standing.

Eventually Jack is able to swing his feet into motion and once he starts walking he is fine. His car door is slammed behind him. He hears the beep of the car alarm. He is aiming at the service station, it's Fleet, he knows it well.

'Smooth drive, eh,' says the thin air.

'You drive like a fucking lunatic,' says Jack cheerily.

Shakil laughs. Or rather the air laughs. Jack focuses on walking. One step, another step, using the cane as a bridge between steps.

Shakil stops laughing. He has just remembered that he crippled Jack when he drove into him while driving far too fast across a zebra crossing.

Nice one Shakil, you total twat; that's the thought that is running through Shakil's mind.

'It's okay,' Jack murmurs. Catching Shak's sudden pang of guilt even though he cannot see him.

'What's okay?' Shak says.

'Doesn't matter. I need a piss,' Jack says.

Jack takes a while to reach the disabled toilet inside the service station. And it takes him a while longer to sit on the toilet and do his business. And he has to use the sink to brace himself when he stands up again and for a moment he wonders if the sink will break, but it doesn't.

Jack shuffles out of the toilet leaning on his stick and Jacinta is waiting for him patiently.

'The boys are upstairs,' she says.

'Thanks, mum,' says Jack, out of habit, and could kill himself for it.

But Jacinta doesn't notice.

Or at least, she pretends she doesn't notice.

They get the escalator to the first floor and Jack discovers he has a sausage bap from Harry Ramsden waiting for him. Another sausage bap floats in mid-air and bits of it are vanishing.

Jack thinks: *This is going to be a long drive.*

Chapter 18

There was a time when the Great West Wood stretched all the way across Europe, reaching as far as the majestic Black Forest in Germany, covering most of France and all of Belgium and the Netherlands, and extending as far north as Denmark. It was one of the largest of the many great forests of the world; and I was its god.

And in later years, when the landbridge between Britain and Europe was swept away by floods, tens of thousands of years ago, the remains of the Great West Wood still spanned this entire island, from the east coast of England to the western reaches of Cornwall and all the way up to Snowdonia.

Thus, although my focus is in Westwood, I still have roots across much of England and Wales. And so I can follow Jack on his journey from London all of the way to the house where he and Shakil will be living, close to the University of Southampton Halls of Residence.

There are lots of trees in the street where they live; which means there is a substratum in which I dwell, where fossilized tree roots from a time before mankind was born are interwoven with the fresh roots of the street trees. So if I want to, I can stay and watch Jack settle into his new life.

But I am losing interest now in Jack and his traumas; and I return to Westwood.

He is an arrogant man, I can tell that at a glance. Thick set, with an angular head, and a nose that can smell a chance to cause trouble a mile off. He is wearing a suit, which is unusual in a local café like this one. And he is looking around at the paintings and bookshelves and the Meissen vases in the teashop with a predatory air. Dulcimer comes to his table.

'What can I get you, sir?' Dulcimer asks.

'Do I order at the table then?' He seems aggrieved at the quality and promptness of the service.

'If you like. What would you like, sir?' Dulcimer asks.

He considers that carefully.

'Is there a menu?' the man asks.

'Never has been in all the time I've worked there,' she says.

He shakes his head despairingly. Then he makes an impossible request, just to wind her up:

'I'll tell you what I'd like. I'd like a sirloin steak, rare, washed down with a glass of 2015

Chateau Lafitte Rothschild.'

Dulcimer take the order without blinking. Unaware that this particular wine is £700 a bottle.

He obviously can't wait till she passes the order on and gets a bollocking.

'Is that a problem?' he taunts her.

'Shouldn't be,' Dulcimer says.

'You're licensed then?' the man asks.

'Sorry?' Dulcimer says.

'To serve alcohol?'

'Yes we are,' Dulcimer says, firmly.

Miguel brings a glass of Chateau Lafite Rothschild to the table, well decanted.

'Would sir like to try?' Miguel asks.

'What's this?' the man asks.

'It's your wine, sir,' says Miguel.

The man sniffs the wine. He sips the wine. He gulps the wine. An expression of bliss spreads across his face. 'Very nice.'

'Your steak will be with you in just a moment, sir, 'says Dulcimer.

When the food comes it is the best meal he has ever eaten.

St John Featherstone is woken up by a banging at the door. It is 12.30 in the afternoon, so it's late to still be in bed. But most days these days St John sleeps.

He ignores the banging, and drifts fitfully back to sleep.

When he does wake up and goes downstairs he discovers the glass table is gone. The ornaments and art deco vases have also gone. The TV is gone. The awful animal paintings are gone. A card dropped on the floor says: BAILIFFS APPOINTED BY THE COURT HAVE CALLED AT THESE PREMISES. WE HAVE EFFECTED ENTRY AND REMOVED YOUR PROPERTY FOR NON PAYMENT OF BILLS.

St John wants to weep but instead he goes out into the garden. As always it is beautifully tended. He hasn't paid the mortgage for three months so it's just a matter of time before he gets evicted. But he decides to savour the moment.

'Do you need any help?' Hilary calls out to him over the garden fence.

'You saw what happened then?' St John says.

She gives him a warm and non-judgemental smile over the garden fence. He appreciates that.

'Poor boy,' Hilary says.

'My own fault,' St John says.

Hilary eyes the fence. It is five feet tall and she is five five, arguably in both directions. But she gives it a try; she vaults the fence.

St John looks at her in awe.

'You need a job,' she tell him, only slightly breathless.

He beckons, and she sits down at his garden table, which the bailiffs didn't take. He sits opposite her. He is calmed by her calmness, even though he knows he ought to be bricking it.

'I know, but I can't get one,' St John says. 'I'm overqualified and under-skilled and my references are terrible. And I'm in debt.'

'How much debt?' Hilary asks.

'One point two,' St John says.

'What's that in real money?' Hilary asks.

'One point two billion. Those are my trading losses.'

Hilary is floored by that.

'What about your mortgage arrears, though? That's what I meant,' Hilary says.

St John doesn't like to think about it. He doesn't like to think about how much money he used to squander when he was earning big-time. The holidays with the lads in five star resorts. The lap dancing clubs after work. The hundred quid bottles of champagne. The huge tips to waitresses at overpriced restaurants where he was always too drunk to enjoy the food. Oh, and all that Colombian marching powder, the devil's dandruff as some people call it, which he didn't even like taking.

'Three grand and rising. And that's the least of it,' St John says.

'I wish I could tide you over,' says Hilary kindly.

'Why would you do that?' St John says, startled.

'But I can't. Not that kind of money.'

'I guess I could go and live with mummy and daddy.'

'But they don't live together any more,' Hilary reminds him.

'Good point.'

'Let's go out for tea,' Hilary says. 'My treat.'

Hilary and St John walk up the hill. He's not used to it and the steepness knackers him, and he goes very red at one point.

'We'll try the new tea shop,' Hilary says.

At the top of Westwood Street they turn right on to Woody Hill. Then they turn right again and down into Fairyhill Road, to the new teashop. Hilary has been meaning to go there for some time.

Camilla greets them. She seems taller and more confident than before. Her trouser suit is maroon today; a bold choice but it works, in my opinion. The afternoon rush has passed. It's been another good day. 'What would you like?' Camilla asks.

'What have you got?' Hilary asks, looking around, and seeing no menus, and no blackboard.

'Anything you want, you can have,' Camilla says.

'I'd like to be happy,' St John says bitterly. 'I'd like to be not broke, not lonely, and not such a pain in the bloody arse.'

'Coming up,' says Alice.

'And maybe some tea and scones?' Camilla says.

The Bogman has disappointed me.

Many millennia ago he was murdered brutally and returned to this earth in an unforgiving mood. Within hours he had slain his first innocent and his vicious gang war with the Mortons was a source of great entertainment to me.

Now he has been murdered again and resurrected, again. But this time round his mood is sombre and mellow; though I cannot read his actual thoughts. But I do know he has had several opportunities to commit murder or pillage and failed to take them.

Soon after he was reborn, he broke into one of the flats at London Heights and stole some clothes - trainers and a cap and a T shirt and jeans. And on his way out he was stopped by a gang of youngers in the courtyard and taunted by them. One of them threatened him with a knife, and maligned his integrity, his manhood, and the sexual morals of his mother. The Bogman could easily have killed the sharp-tongued vicious little kid and eaten his entrails as an example to the others. But instead, he chose to walk away, following by mocking cries.

From there he returned to the woodlands where he retrieved his secret stashes. Clothes, money, credit cards, a pay as you go mobile phone with enough credits for a year, and several guns. All buried near a tree in case of precisely this eventuality. He re-hid all but one of the guns and used the money to rent a room in a bed and breakfast in Penge.

And there he now resides. Living a solitary life. Watching the TV news. Fondling his new sexual organs, which despite their impressive dimensions do not work properly. And reading books he has bought from the independent bookshop by the roundabout.

The Bogman learned to read English during his previous incarnation as a gang boss, but his reading then consisted of newspapers, crime reports, and profit and loss accounts for his casino. When he reads his first novel in his tiny Penge bedsit it comes as a revelation to him.

Now he reads crime novels and literary novels avidly all day long. He also reads history books. He even reads books on philosophy.

His room is small and he has no storage space so once he has read them he gives all the books to a charity shop. But he remembers pretty well every word of every book he reads. That was one of the secrets of the Bogman's success in the days before he was the Bogman: a remarkably retentive memory and a quick mind.

After a few weeks of living in the bedsit, the Bogman bought a suit and went to the Casino in Westwood. And there he wagered some money on the placement of the ball on the roulette table and lost it all. He knew that he would; he used to be the House so he knows the odds. But he was just trying it out.

Some of the croupiers thought he looked familiar, but with his smooth brown skin and bald head he does not very closely resemble the exploded bombsite that once was his face.

Another time he went back to London Heights and talked to some of the shotters. He gave them money for drugs but did not take the drugs, but instead he asked for information. He asked about Kane Armstrong and learned that Kane is a 'fucking vegetable' now, and resides at the South London Intensive Care Unit. The Bogman then asked the young drug dealers which bus he could catch to go there and was given fairly good directions.

Before he was able to leave however he was stopped by some youngers who saw him as a threat, and stabbed him in the chest and legs. This vexed him so he seized the blades and hurled them away. But he did not exact vengeance. No one was hurt. No one died.

As I say, disappointing.

What has happened to the malignant monster that once he was?

Kane meanwhile is declining. Soon his life support will be switched off and that will be the end of him.

I wish I had healed Kane and not the Bogman. He might have been more fun.

I wonder what is going on in that strange pagan's head.

Today he is walking through Westwood, and I follow him. He walks on the pavement along the route of the South Circular for nearly half an hour. He walks past the Salt Lake Park and the Salt Lake Primary School. And then he walks on as far as the Aldi which adjoins the site of an ancient burial site. This is a fenced off area which consists of a grassy mound which years ago was excavated, and its contents moved to the Westwood Museum. Hardly anyone ever visits this museum, but it does have an exceptional collection of Bronze Age and Stone Age artefacts.

The Bogman is clearly fascinated by the burial mound, and he paces in long loops around the mound of grass. I assume he is remembering how it used to be. Then he glances up at the sun to get his compass bearings. And he catches a bus back to Westwood and goes into the hardware store and buys a shovel.

He returns in the early evening with the shovel and paces out a distance from the edge of the mound to a point due southwest. This involves clambering into someone's garden and out the other side until finally the Bogman finds the spot he is looking for, in a back alley. The alley is paved so the Bogman dances upon the concrete slabs with heavy feet and a pounding rhythm. Leaping high like an Irish dancer then crashing down hard until the concrete cracks, and he is able to rip the concrete layer away with his bare hands. Then he begins to dig.

He digs and digs, building a mountain of earth at the end of the alleyway then he takes all his clothes off and folds them neatly and clambers into the hole. Once there, he continues digging with his bare hands, thrusting his dark peaty body through the clay soil until he has vanished from sight. And only the worms erupting out of the soil above betray how powerfully he is tunnelling.

When he emerges he is clutching a mud-coated object which he carefully sets down. Then he puts his clothes back on and gets the bus home, still caked in mud, still carrying the muddy object. Once home he rinses the muddy object under the tap in the bath then scrubs it with soap and a J cloth until it gleams gold.

It is his crown.

That is when I realise that the mound he has just excavated must have been the burial site of the king who stole it from him.

But once he has retrieved his crown, and cleaned it, the Bogman no longer knows what to do with it. He puts it on his only shelf, on top of a pile of crime thrillers. It is a gold crown inlaid with rubies and he killed nearly a thousand men in order to win it. But that was a long time ago, and in all honesty, the craftsmanship is by modern standards rather crude.

That night the Bogman goes for a pizza in Westwood. More for the company than the food, because he has no sense of taste and cannot digest what he eats. Afterwards he goes for a walk and pukes the contents of his stomach up against a wall.

And then he notices that the building he has just vomited on houses a club playing late night music.

The Bogman has no real penchant for music. But he does vividly remember the fanfare of horns and cacophony of drums on the day of his coronation.

He decides to go in to listen. There is a £5 entry fee which he pays in cash. The doorman puts a stamp on his hand but it does not work, his skin is too shiny, more like plastic than skin. So the doorman nods him in. The Bogman no longer wears a cap or a hat, and his bald head makes him look like the villainous Lex Luthor in the TV show about a super-powered alien; except that he is brown not white. He takes a table near the front and buys a bottle of red wine to drink alone. It will not make him drunk and when he pisses it away his urine will be claret red and thirteen per cent proof; but the habit of drinking booze soothes him.

The warm up act is an Irish band. One man plays a bodhrán, the singer has a beard, and there is a great deal of diddly-diddly. The Bogman is not impressed.

Then a skinny black man walks on stage carrying a lute. He sits and plays an ancient tune, a religious lament. An evocation and a conjuration of spirits. The Bogman is moved. If he were able to weep, he would have wept.

Then the black man is joined by two musicians of South Asian heritage and a mixed race girl singer. The black man sings Race with the Devil, an old Gene Vincent song, and the band rocks, and the woman harmonises beautifully.

Then it's her turn to have a solo song. She looks at the audience, with a look that is full of soul; and in a moment, they are all her willing slaves.

'This is one I wrote myself,' she says. 'Well, the music, not the words. God bless you, Montrose.' And she sings.

It is a ballad about being a young man in a world which hates you; but you don't care because you are full of beans and life makes you laugh and all the boys that you fuck in bedrooms and in the back rooms of gay bars love you for just long enough.

'Just long enough' is the refrain.

It is not a very apt song lyric for a woman by any means, but she carries it off without bothering to change the pronouns. Some of the lines are oblique and weird. Evocative snippets of street slang. But somehow they make sense. And the melody is like nothing the Bogman has ever heard before.

The singer is Shona.

The Bogman is in love.

Chapter 19

When the landbridge between England and Europe was finally flooded and this land in which I was born became a paltry spit of an island, a part of me died.

Most of me died, in fact. My body was ripped from me; my limbs were severed; all that remained was a ragged scrap of my former grandeur.

The pain I felt then was an agony beyond the comprehension of any mere human. It was a pain that has never ebbed or eased.

I was mighty once.

Now I am not.

Three men in Hi-Vis vests are walking through Old Park marking trees with a large X.

This is not the first time this has happened. People like to 'manage' woodland and every now and then some busybodies will decide that the trees in my parks are too old or diseased and have to be cut down before they are blown down by winds. This vexes me and one time I was so annoyed I set fire to most of Old Park and almost destroyed the Victorian Sculpture Park as an expression of my feelings on the matter. The fire cleansed the old growth and carefully danced around the Bhutan Pine (the tallest tree in the park) and the Oldest Tree (the oldest tree in the world, not just in the Park).

The point being, I do not want outsiders 'managing' my woods. I can do it perfectly well myself.

But there is something particularly ominous about these Xs. The men who are marking out the trees are busy and officious and I am not able to read their thoughts, because they are not denizens of Westwood. So I listen to the gossip on the streets and I read all the stupid little notices which are put up on lampposts, in order to gather further information about what is going on. And before long I discover a worrying fact.

A new development is being planned and it looks very likely to go ahead.

New developments are like plagues; they come and go with tedious regularity. A few years back there was a plan to build a replica of the Great Pyramid of Giza in the woodland below the Sculpture Park, as a hommage to the old Crystal Palace and its Egyptian artefacts. The Pyramid was intended as a museum and a civic centre and a shopping mall. Though the locals cynically suspected that the shops and gyms would eclipse in scope all the socially useful areas. But that was not the point; it would have been an eyesore, and building it would have entailed cutting down hundreds of my trees.

And so when the first clod of earth was broken by a yellow digger a sinkhole opened in the ground. And the digger plummeted down the hole and was never seen again, though luckily the driver escaped before his vehicle tumbled down the hole. And the development was abandoned.

But now there's a new plan. Social housing and office blocks will be built on a strip of land adjoining the park, but the major road to support it all will occupy land currently within the park's bounds. It is to be a 'redefined boundary' which means scores of trees will be chopped down and the Old Park will shrink, and be bordered by a busy main road.

Sixty trees have already been marked with Xs which are death sentences. And so I sigh wearily; and a wind springs up and knocks off caps and hats and billows up ladies' skirts turning them into upside-down parachutes, and scatters picnics so that the air is alive with flying sandwiches and potato crisps; and the workmen who are attacking my trees are blown off their feet like skittles.

Twenty-two of the trees marked with an X are plane trees which have the ability to shed their bark. The rest are oak trees and ashes and birches and a handful of conifers, all of which do not have the ability to shed their barks.

So I compel the plane trees to shed their bark in a single slough, and the Xs crumble into powder, and bare white wood shines.

Then squirrels go to work on the other trees, biting and clawing and mauling at the trunks of the ashes and the birches. And the deer – we have a small community of deer in Old Park who are rarely glimpsed but they are there – rub their horns furiously against the barks of the conifers and the oaks. And within a few hours, all the Xs have vanished.

But the next day the men in Hi-Vis are back. And they re-mark with Xs all the trees whose barks had been shredded.

And then they mark out a long stretch of woodland which is to be obliterated. Planning permission has now been granted. Local protests have sprung up but they are being ignored. In a few weeks' time the trees will be cut down and in their stead an ugly road will be created.

Later that day, the squirrels and the deer rip off the Xs once again. But the death sentences remain.

St John opens another envelope.

It reads: 'This is to confirm your mortgage has been cleared as a good will gesture.'

He blinks and smiles. Then he opens another envelope.

It reads: 'Please find enclosed a payslip for your UltraBank bonus payment for the last two years; we apologise this has not been processed sooner.'

He shrugs. Well well. How unexpected! Then he opens another envelope.

It is a Reader's Digest Grand Prize scratch card. He scratches it, and discovers he has won their Grand Prize. He smiles.

After a while he becomes tired of good news and goes out the back garden. He notices with some surprise that the garden has become unkempt and there are weeds. There are black patches on the leaves of the rose bushes. The clematis is overrun with ivy. And I realise that his secret gardener has finally given up her secret gardening. Either she has died or perhaps, or so I hope, she has finally got herself a life.

St John stares with dismay at the plethora of weeds and it occurs to him; this is his garden, he should do something about it.

Hilary is in her back garden reading.

'Do you know anything about gardening?' he calls over to her.

'Just a bit,' Hilary says.

'And how is Toby?' Mr Abioye asks.

Mrs Farley is cautious.

'As well as can be expected,' Mrs Farley says.

Toby O'Connell has been placed on the Vulnerable Child register after social workers intervened following allegations of domestic abuse. But the case is pending, and Toby is still living at home with his parents. Every day Mrs Farley inspects the boy in case he has bruises or scars on his body but she has found no evidence as yet. This is completely against school regulations and the law of course, but Mr Abioye has taken a personal interest in this case. And he is terrified that one of the children over whom he has a duty of care will end up being murdered by his parents.

'Is he smiling?' Mr Abioye asks.

'He pretends to smile,' says Mrs Farley.

'Floating?'

'Not that I've seen.'

'Why the hell don't they just take him into care,' snaps Mr Abioye.

Mrs Farley says nothing.

Sometimes nothing is the best thing to say.

The fact is, Sarah Lemaitre and Father Glackin did their best to have young Toby taken into care. But the case was considered to lack 'substance' and removal 'was not felt to be in the best interests of the child'. So Toby still lives with his mum and dad; and they still beat him and deny him chocolate.

Father Glackin has explained some but not all of the truth to Mr Abioye. And now the burden rests heavily upon the shoulders of the head teacher of Boscombe Primary. A child in his care is being beaten up daily, but because he heals so quickly, no one can prove it.

During school break Mr Abioye walks around the playground, watching the children play. Toby is alone, no one talks to him. He is not a part of the football game, he is not chatting to his mates. Rarely has Mr Abioye seen so solitary or so mournful a child.

Mr Abioye himself has always been the gregarious type. A natural socialiser. The leader of the pack. When he was a boy, he was both an athlete and a dreamboat. All the girls in his school loved him, because he was so calm and good-looking. And all the guys were in awe of his football playing skill and sprinting prowess and they admired him and wanted to be like him. He was exceptionally popular, in other words, despite being a black boy in an almost all-white Kent village. His dad was the local solicitor and was much admired by all, which helped too. Everyone liked the Abioyes, in those parts.

Later, when he was a grown man, at University, surrounded by radical friends full of anger and attitude, he was asked about his experiences of racism as a boy; and Abioye always had to make up stories. Lies, basically, about how he was subject to racist abuse and crass banter. But in fact, though he knew about racism in theory, and though he had heard stories of other black boys and girls being bullied, in his youth no one was ever racist to *him.*

It took Egbo Abioye a long time to realise that his experience of growing up in Britain was not *everyone's* experience.

He also realised, looking back on it all, that he had been an arrogant and self-regarding young man who honestly believed that if everyone loved *him,* the world must be a decent place.

Then one day, while doing A levels, Egbo told his history teacher he was thinking of applying to Oxford, and the brief look of disdain he glimpsed on the teacher's face changed his life for ever.

Egbo did go to Oxford. He achieved a First in History after a dazzling viva, in the mid 1980s. He went on to do a Masters in post-colonial studies before doing his PGCE.

In short, he proved the look of disdain wrong though he never saw that teacher ever again. But the lesson had been learned.

When Egbo Abioye moved from his home in North London to Westwood with his wife Heather and his father Samuel, he was quick to realise that Westwood is not like any other place in London. Unlike many incomers, who remain blind to the ways of Westwood, Egbo saw it all. He very quickly realised that there are hills in Westwood which run uphill in both directions. He was also very much aware of the randomness of nightfall, which often happens two or three times in the same day, and he did not manage to 'unsee' it, as many incomers do. He knew all about the anacondas, and the howler monkeys, and the cheetahs, and the white Bengal tiger that lives along the railway embankment. And, to be honest, he was thrilled to be living in a place that in many ways was even wilder than the wilds of Africa.

And yet, in Westwood, as in every other place in the world, some children grow up unhappy and there's nothing you can do about it.

Egbo's father has cooked them all dinner this evening.

Samuel Abioye lives in a granny flat in the top floor of the Abioye house in Westwood. It is fully self-contained; he has his own bathroom and his own toilet, and he can if he wants to live happily up there without ever bothering to come downstairs.

But Samuel, like his son, is a gregarious man. For many years he was a solicitor in that small village in Kent and he retired at the age of sixty-eight to enjoy his retirement with his beloved wife. A year later she was dead of cancer and he had suffered a nervous breakdown, after a botched attempt to ease her passing with morphine, which resulted in a confrontation with the CPS that caused him considerable distress.

The Abioyes never talk about those dark months and Samuel remains a cheerful and chatty man. But he no longer speaks to any of his old friends, because they know too much of what happened. And his wife's family have chosen not to forgive him.

All ancient history. Samuel is cooking Bolognese, his speciality; and the ragù is bubbling away. Heather and Egbo are on the sofa, cuddling, as they like to do. Egbo is still a fine figure of a man despite his grey hairs and creaky knees; while she is by all accounts an admirable woman who works as a pediatric nurse, and often saves the lives of babies and small children. It is a warm and happy home; which for me is both tedious and irritating. But I have a feeling something will happen here, and so I linger awhile.

Dinner goes well. Everyone talks and the wine flows. I am bored. So very bored.

It is nearly midnight and Egbo is in his bedroom making love to his wife Heather. Despite their age they are virile and agile and they both end up extremely satisfied, physically and emotionally.

I do not watch.

I have noticed there is a spider's web on the top of the wall in the bedroom, in which a spider waits like an eight-legged nemesis. Bad housekeeping on Heather's part but good for me.

Three flies have been caught and eaten by the time the interminable fucking has concluded and the two Abioyes fall asleep.

That night Egbo Abioye is woken by a dream. He gets out of bed and makes his way downstairs. He is restless so he decides to go for a run, even though it is still dark out. His gym stuff lives in a backpack in what is laughingly called the 'garage' though it has never housed a car. So he pads into the garage in his pyjamas and bare feet and strips naked. He puts on a black tracksuit and a black bobble hat without a bobble and black Nike trainers. He puts over this a yellow Hi-Vis sash, so cars can see him when he jogs through the streets of Westwood.

It is magic hour: that long strange hour that exists in Westwood between three am and three oh five am.

And so there are two moons in the sky and the multi-coloured stars flash brightly and the constellations bear no resemblance to the usual constellations. It is a time between times, when the unreal and the real coexist. Egbo knows this time well from his dreams but he had no idea it really existed. But in Westwood it does.

He runs fast through deserted streets. There are no cars, only antelope, and high-pronking spingboks. The smell of the savannah is in his nostrils, and lions and lionesses and wildebeest and hyenas and zebras stalk the streets of Westwood.

He runs until he turns a corner and almost falls down a crevasse so he retraces his steps and immediately finds himself outside the house where Toby O'Connell lives.

Toby's house is lit by twin moonbeams, and as Egbo watches a figure steps out of an upper storey window and floats upwards. It is a boy in pyjamas, floating high in the sky. It is Toby.

Toby flies up higher, lit by the silver light of those two moons, until he can no longer be seen. Before long he is so high the sun burns his face and makes him screw up his eyes. Then it ignites his pyjamas and Toby becomes a ball of flame and he falls downwards. His body hurtles like a meteor towards the pavement upon which he will, in just a few moments, land with a terrible crash and be killed.

But a man is standing in exactly the right place, directly below the flight path of the fireball boy. It is Mr Abioye. He waits and waits and when the fireball crashes towards the pavement he is there, and he catches the fireball in his strong arms, and his limbs catch fire but it does not hurt him.

And the fires are quelled by a swift soft breeze and Toby rests in his arms, his pyjamas and flesh unscathed, staring up at Mr Abioye.

The boy has been saved. Toby smiles. And Mr Abioye carries the boy home with him in his arms, through the moons-lit streets, until magic hour ends and there is only one moon in the sky and the smell of the savannah has gone.

'Where am I going?' Toby asks.

'Home. With me. You will be my child,' says Mr Abioye.

In the morning it becomes obvious that was all just a dream and Mr Abioye feels a bit stupid. But when he goes for a shower he finds his tracksuit abandoned in the corner of the bathroom, and the sleeves are singed. So maybe some of it *was* true.

Mr Abioye is late for work but he goes straight to his office and calls Toby's parents at their place of work, which is an office block near Borough Market. He summons them to an emergency pastoral care meeting at the school and tells them Toby has been excluded again, and that he has to leave the school, and to leave Westwood too, by order of the police.

It is a very alarming message and naturally it gets the urgent attention of the O'Connnells.

In the playground Toby is playing football with his schoolmates. He is a natural. He kicks the ball high in the air above the defenders; then he leaps after it, and jumps over them. A twenty foot high leap. Then he lands yards away from the goal and kicks the ball and hits the goal, which is painted on a wall, and scores.

'Goal!' shout the other children and no one seems to think he has been cheating.

Mr and Mrs O'Connell arrive two hours later and are confronted by the headteacher in his office in a strange and angry mood. His hands are badly burned, and he holds them palms uppermost in front of himself, in obvious agony, his wounds weeping pus. But his face does not betray any emotion.

'Make your son happy, or you'll answer to me,' Mr Abioye orders them in his very best voice of command. And the O'Connells dissolve into tears.

'How? says Mr O'Connell. 'The devil is in the boy!'

'We do our best, but he's a monster!' says Mrs O'Connell.

'No matter how hard we beat the little bastard, his bones always mend!' says Mr O'Connell.

'It's not natural,' weeps Mrs O'Connell.

And Mr Abioye laughs.

And then his gaze becomes intense and terrifying and he does not blink or move so much as an inch as he stares at the two O'Connells.

And the stench of animal shit fills the room, and the O'Connells start to choke and splutter.

And magic is in the air; but it is not my magic. It is Abioye magic.

And that is when I realise that the distant ancestors of this South London headteacher worshipped other gods. Wild gods, strange gods, gods who once were far more powerful than I am now. Gods who live still, for those who have the power to believe.

Mr Abioye speaks. And his voice is as dark as doom.

'No you are wrong, Mr and Mrs O'Connell. The devil is not in the boy,' says Mr Abioye. And he laughs again and it is a most terrifying laugh: 'The devil is in me!'

And Mr Abioye opens his mouth wide, baring his sharp ivory teeth and his dark red bifurcated flicking tongue. Then he opens his mouth wider still; until it is the size of a hippopotamus's gaping maw. And then he takes a deep breath, and he sucks in air, and the wind from his sucking breath sweeps the O'Connells up and they fly off their chairs and into his mouth, Mr O'Connell first, followed by his wailing wife.

Then once they are in his mouth he eats them, both of them, crunching their bones because that's the best bit, and then gulping them down, shoes and hair and teeth and all. And when they have been digested he burps a sour burp and he feels nauseous. But the deed has been done.

Later the police arrive at the O'Connell home following an anonymous tip and find a typed and unsigned note saying that they have left for Ireland. As a result, Toby and Liam will have to be taken into care. Father Glackin arrives to supervise their fostering, together with the very nice social worker, Sarah Lemaitre.

Sarah decides that Toby will continue attending Westwood Primary. And Mr Abioye announces that he can live there too. For Mr Abioye has built a bedroom in the stock room that used to be a classroom that belonged to the Otters, who are now in the new and more spacious annexe. And Sarah inspects the room and approves Mr Abioye's plan, even though it is against best practice and the law. But Mr Abioye can be a persuasive man. 'The system failed this little boy,' he says, 'so we are not putting him back into the system.'

I know how this story ends; for you see sometimes, though not always, I can remember the future.

And so I know that Toby grows to manhood here, living in this little room, going to classes in the days until he finishes primary school, then going for dinner with Mr Abioye and his wife and father every evening, before returning home to the school to sleep.

And when he goes to big school, he continues this system. He goes to the Westwood Secondary School in the days, and spends his evenings and weekends with the Abioyes or with his friends, and returns to his bedroom in his old primary school to sleep. The school catering staff provide him with meals; his pals often come to visit him in the school premises and they are able to play kickabout in the school gym.

And when Mr Abioye retires at the age of sixty-six, Toby continues to live in the school, looked after by the school staff and having meals and family outings and holidays with the Abioyes. Toby is still living at his primary school while he takes his O Levels and then his A Levels at Westwood Secondary School. He doesn't move out until he goes to University; by which time he is a confident young man well able to make his way in the world.

And every morning throughout his Big School years, his teenage years, Toby would climb up on to the roof of the school via a long metal ladder. And once up there, looking out across Westwood, he would eat an entire chocolate bar, usually an Aero, which is all he ever ate for breakfast. Then, as the chocolate rush kicked in, and happiness blossomed inside him, he would gently float upwards until he was hovering high above the school, a tiny dot in the sky.

And from there Toby would float across Westwood Street, drifting through air above the alleyway where the TAs go for a cheeky fag each break time, and up over the sheer cliff face of Steeper Hill. And he carried on floating on air until he was over the busy Boulevard where he liked to count the buses which milled below him. Until finally he drifted back down to earth in the Sculpture Park.

He then would enjoy a very pleasant walk across the width of Old Park and out of the side entrance that leads to Dubious Avenue, cutting through a Council estate to arrive at the back gate of his secondary school.

And every day as he walked his walk through Old Park, the trees waved their leaves at him and the shrubbery hummed soft melodies that only he could hear and the birds flocked in the air making beautiful shapes with their murmurations - usually hearts or circles or stars or diamonds - to celebrate his existence.

And when no one was looking, Toby would float up high to the tree canopy of the most densely forested area and there he would steal blue-green blackbird eggs from the nests, never more than one or two from a single nest, which he ate raw. The birds sometimes protested at this but I quelled them, and I coaxed them; until they agreed to consider Toby's thefts to be their gift to him.

And so in this fashion, each day for nearly ten years, I greeted Toby on his walk to school, and I surrendered him my bounty.

Chapter 20

When Shona and her pals talk, they tend to babble.

'You know what it's like when you're - ' says Shona.

'Course we do,' says Zara.

' - that age - ' says Shona.

'Yeah I know, I know, it's like - ' says Jo.

'It's like yesterday for me, not so much for you old bitches!' Mariella says.

Marielle grins; proud that she can really dish it out.

The other girls scowl. But it's all play-acting, no one really means it.

If I could smile, which I can't, I would. These youngsters are delightful.

'Who you calling bitch, bitch!' says Jo, in tones of fury.

Shona rolls her eyes. Zara makes a face. Marielle looks smug. The babble continues:

'Don't call me a - ' says Shona.

'Oh come on Mari, you're only six months younger than me. How comes that that makes you - ' says Zara.

' – bitch, bitch!'

'- younger than me!'

'Six months is a lot, I'm the baby of this group!' says Marielle.

'No you're not, I am!' shouts Jo, in righteous rage. For as far as he is concerned he is fresh-minted, just two years old.

'And you *are* a big baby! no, not really,' says Zara, feebly.

Zara is not so good at banter; she takes things to heart too much.

'I do feel sorry for her, though' Zara continues, in more serious tones. 'She's so young. Fifteen is so very – young.'

They nod. The group mood darkens.

Jo offers up a secret, a secret which in fact they all knew: 'When I was fifteen I knew, I just knew, that I was in the - '

' – wrong body, yeah that must have - ' says Shona.

'It was, yeah,' says Jo.

'When I was fifteen - ' Zara says wistfully but no one is listening to her.

'When I was fifteen I - ' Shona starts to say but Marielle interrupts:

' – you thought were in love with that vicious twat, is that what -'

' – was reading comics all the time,' mutters Zara.

' – you were going to say?' Marielle says.

'It wasn't love, no, I just felt more grown up,' Shona says.

'And I've never been happier hey don't look at me like that, the Fantastic Four were on a roll,' Zara says softly, unheeded.

'But you didn't fuck him,' says Marielle to Shona, referring to her teenage relationship with Mr Bradshaw: 'Till you were legal.'

'No, that's true,' says Shona.

Shona and her pals are in the Saxon Arms at their favourite table. The Girls Table they used to call it but not since Jo transitioned. Now it's the Usual Table. Jo has grown a moustache and he is wearing a T-shirt to show off his hairy arms. Shona is in jeans and her Minorca T-shirt with a lizard on it that her family bought for her on holiday in Minorca. Marielle is over-dressed as always in an expensive black bomber jacket and black lipstick that makes her look like Rosa in Brooklyn-99. Zara is wearing a blue dress she bought in Top Shop but which she doesn't think suits her, but Shona thinks it does, and Marielle thinks it doesn't, and Jo is undecided between those two opinions.

'And he did that thing - ' Zara remembers.

'With the birthday cards,' Shona confirms.

'Creepy,' says Marielle.

'Perve,' says Zara.

'It was my choice, I knew what I was doing,' says Shona.

'Did you?' asks Jo.

'No,' says Shona.

'What are we going to do, are we really going to get him sacked?' asks Marielle.

'If we can, yeah, but how?' says Shona.

They are stumped.

Shona, Marielle, Zara and Jo are planning how to destroy Benjamin Bradshaw.

A week ago Marielle had spotted Bradshaw in the pub where she works part time being very gropy and intimate with a very young mixed race woman. Not the previous mixed-race woman, a different one, a much younger one. Extensive research, namely asking the other barmaid, revealed that the girl's name is Rayowa Hassan and she is a fifteen year old pupil at Malham High, where Bradshaw now teaches.

The older girlfriend has clearly been ditched, and Bradshaw has reverted to seducing impressionable schoolgirls. Just as he did to Shona all those years ago.

'I don't know if I want to, I really don't,' says Shona.

'All we're going to do is - ' says Jo but doesn't finish the sentence.

'She does love him,' says Marielle 'She really does. So is it fair to - '

'She doesn't love him,' says Zara.

'I don't,' Shona says.

'We're not talking about you, we're talking about her!' says Zara.

'Ah. Sorry,' says Shona.

'Even if she does, he's still a – can I say that word?' Jo says.

'Depends on the word,' Marielle says.

'Arsehole,' says Jo.

Marielle is the one with detective genes. She waited outside Bradshaw's new school until she spotted Rayowa. Then she followed Rayowa home and knocked on her door and asked to speak to her in private. And Rayowa had burst into tears and admitted everything and said that it was true love. And that when she was old enough Benjamin was going to marry her and she was going to have his babies.

Not likely, admittedly. But it's clear that Rayowa is not being abused or coerced, she has genuinely fallen for him.

'Does it matter though?' asks Shona. 'She may say she loves him, but how do you know if she really does?'

'Yeah true. She's just a kid. She's too young to know what she really thinks about anything,' says Zara.

'Oh don't be so patronising!' says Shona.

'When I was fifteen I was convinced I would be Mrs Liam Payne,' says Marielle.

'I wanted to knob Alicia Keyes,' Jo says. 'But I couldn't, not then.'

'And not now either,' Shona says, brutally. ''Cos she's like, outta your league?'

'The fact is,' says Marielle, 'you can't break an omelette.'

'Huh?' says Zara.

'What does that even mean?' says Shona.

'You can't *make* an omelette, *make* an omelette, without breaking eggs,' says Zara. And seeing the blank faces all around her she adds: 'It's a metaphor.'

Their moral dilemma is: Is it acceptable to get Bradshaw sacked, if the price is breaking a young girl's heart?

'He's not breaking the law,' Zara argues.

'We don't know that,' says Shona.

'What law?' says Mariella.

'The age of consent law,' says Zara.

'There's an age of consent?' says Marielle.

'Let's just let it go,' says Shona. 'It hurts too much to think about. And besides, it's not our problem.'

'True,' says Zara.

'Nailed it,' says Marielle.

'Don't you want to hurt him?' asks Jo, and the question makes Shona feel like shit.

'No,' says Shona.

Then she thinks about Rayowa. A posh girl by the sound of it; her dad works in the City and her mum comes from a wealthy family who own land in the West Country. But still, a girl. With no barriers, no way of holding back. A child, not an adult.

That was me once, Shona thinks. *Rayowa is the new Shona. Oh my God.*

I remember how Shona wept with sorrow for days and days after the breakup with Mr Bradshaw. And all her sorrow caused her to binge-eat for solace; and the binge-eating made her get fat; and the getting fat made her even sadder. And then she failed her GCSEs; and that made it all even worse..

I had no idea, Shona thinks. *I was so young. I thought I knew everything but I knew nothing! The bastard. What he took from me. He took –*

She can't put into words what he took from her but she knows she'll never get it back .

'No,' says Shona, 'I don't want to hurt him. But I will.'

All it takes is a single phone call.

Jo makes the call, deepening his voice and trying to give it a Northern accent, without much success. And when he fails to get through to the head teacher of Malham High he leaves a message with her secretary instead. Then once the call has been made they forget all about it.

The rest plays out like a TV movie. The head launches an internal investigation. A CCTV camera in the music room has recorded all the beats of a recent sordid encounter between Rayowa and Mr Bradshaw, during what was meant to be a music lesson. Within hours Benjamin Bradshaw has cleared his desk.

Rayowa's parents are never informed. Rayowa herself is offered counselling, which she declines. The police should have been notified, so Bradshaw could be placed on the sex offenders' register, but they weren't. That was Bradshaw's deal with the school's headteacher for going quietly.

I watch Bradshaw as he cycles away from the school, a violin case hooked over his shoulder as he pedals off into the distance. Well, to Anerley anyway.

And I listen to his mind too, as he cycles swiftly and recklessly through traffic. He is seething with rage. He has no idea who has done this to him. But his thoughts are angry and murderous, and shockingly graphic. Whoever did this to him he will find them and he will – and there the ugly images take over.

But as he reaches home and gets off his bicycle, and wheels it into his front garden, an idea strikes him. He realises, he *does* know who did this to him. A woman scorned did this to him. And he knows her name and where she lives and he starts planning how he is going to punish her.

And at that moment I feel a pang of dark familiar pleasure.

For finally, after months of tedium, after all those months of watching the Bogman develop a soul, and observing the teashop thrive despite all odds, and enduring St John's run of impossibly good luck, and seeing the reliably miserable Shona find happiness with her sexy lover, and knowing that even poor crippled Jack has a friend he can rely upon – I find myself exulting at the thought that something terrible is about to happen in Westwood.

While I wait for Benjamin Bradshaw to enact his plan of revenge against Shona, life goes on in Westwood.

The Bogman is building a home in Horniman Woods.

It is a home made of wood, a shed really. He tore down an oak tree with his bare hands and shaped the planks with a saw. This wood is old and robust but he uses soft pine planks for the floorboards. There are windows without glass and there is no furniture yet, just a bare floor. But it is a home.

It takes him a week to build and it's an impressive piece of craftsmanship. The shed has a thatched roof and a huge front door, large enough that he could bring his cattle and sheep indoors in winter, if he had cattle and sheep. There are two floors linked by an interior staircase hewn out of tree stumps and polished to a shine and all the wood has been treated with a paste made of herbs and tree bark and seasoned in the sun, so that it will not warp. In the middle of the ground floor there is a trap door and beneath the trap door is a tunnel that has been hewn out and propped up with old railway sleepers and which allows the Bogman to enter and leave his home undetected, if he chooses.

The stench of the treated wood does not bother the Bogman for he has no sense of smell. But even so, once he has completed his home he continues to spend his nights outdoors, sprawled on high tree branches. He does not sleep but at night he allows his thoughts to slow down and become close to nothing. It is his way of relaxing; and when he gets like this I can start to hear his thoughts and feel his emotions. And so I know that when dawn comes the memories start to swamp him and he re-experiences the key moments of his short life again, and again. And every time he does that, he remembers more and more about the people he murdered and tortured; and he mourns for them.

The fact is, the Bogman has gone soft. He has lost his killer edge. He is haunted – and this really does piss me off - by regrets.

When he builds himself a bed and moves into the shed at night, then steals a duvet and pillow on which to lie, I despair of him entirely. A warrior should sleep on hard soil, his hand close to his sword. A fucking duvet! What is wrong with him!

The Bogman is sad and he is lonely, I know that. I am aware of that.

But I consider him to be pathetic so I leave him in his wooden home and move on.

Don and Megan from the supermarket are on their first date; and I decide to tag along.

They go to the poshest restaurant in Westwood, the Boulevard Bistro. It's lively and popular but also very loud and the waiter talks in a whisper in a strange accent so they can't understand what is on the Specials menu. And they end up ordering food they don't actually want so the meal is a disaster. But afterwards he walks her home and he kisses her goodnight.

I'm happy for you, says Marie as Don walks back up the hill to Westwood Street, after walking Megan home.

'Are you love?'

She seems nice. You're good together. I really want you to be happy.

'Marie love,' Don is choked with emotion. 'It's not that I don't love you but - '

But she's alive and I'm dead, says Marie gently.

'That's right.'

And she's full of life and full-bodied and sensual and she's a hell of a lot more fun than I ever was.

'Yes. Well I suppose she is. Thank you. Thank you, love. I knew you'd understand,' says Don, deeply moved.

Well yes I do. I do understand.

'It means the world to me. To have your – blessing like.'

You're welcome. I'm sure you'll both be very happy.

'Oh I think so too. I've never been happier!'

Don goes up to bed with a skip in his step. He is already making plans to see Megan again.

The ghost of Marie bides her time. She is too canny to say anything to Don yet; it's too soon. But she has no secrets from me. I know that she has no intention of letting that old bitch steal her beloved husband's heart. He's worth two of her! That ugly whore Megan is dirt common, and badly educated, she doesn't even have a degree! She's a bloody check out woman at the supermarket for pity's sake!

If he'd fallen for a teacher, or a businesswoman, then maybe, just maybe, Marie would have moved on and let it go. But she's not going to let him throw his life away on this mutton dressed as lamb harlot.

No bloody way!

I like Marie. She knows how to hate; I admire that.

And so does Ben Bradshaw. What a bastard that man is.

As I think about it, about what he is about to do, my oak trees creak. My aspens shiver. My wild grasses tremble on a breezeless day.

I am laughing!

Shona is weeping. Sobbing her poor heart out. The poor silly little bitch.

My oak trees creak. My aspens shiver.

Far away from Shona and her grief, close to my western boundaries, Jack is out with Shakil and his mates in the Weatherspoon's nearest to Southampton Uni, chatting about his failed dream of being a footballing star.

'I could have been a contender,' Jack says.

'You could have gone professional?' Shak's mate asks.

'Arsenal wanted me. The youth team,' says Jack.

'Well why didn't you?' says Shak's other mate.

Jack can't quite remember, but I do. He was too lazy, he kept missing training sessions.

'I wanted to go to Uni first. Stretch my intellect, before I joined the Premier League like. But then - ' He gestures at his broken limbs.

There's a moment of pathos then Shak calls him out.

'Bullshit,' says Shakil. 'You just didn't make the cut, you useless tosser.'

Jack pretends to look offended; then he grins. True!

There's a group laugh at Jack's expense. Jack takes it on the chin, smiling.

Jack is having a great time. Everyone here likes him. 'Shak and Jack' have become a legendary team. And Shak's gay friends are generous and funny and spiteful but only in a hilarious way – there's no malice in it.

Jack loves being the only straight guy in a world of gay men. And he loves being the only non-student in a world full of students. No one ever questions what he's doing there. No one makes fun of the fact he walks with a stick and has to go to the toilet four or five times every hour. He's just 'Jack'. Or 'Shak's Jack'.

And that's when he gets the call from Shona. Seven calls in fact, but he ignores the first six. Before finally, sheepishly, pressing the green phone icon.

I am with him as he listens to her; and I am with her too, as she spills out her pain in a series of incoherent vowels.

'What?' Jack is saying. 'What's that, love?'

She sobs.

And as she sobs, the barks of my ancient oak trees creak and rip open, baring savage smiling gashes.

My acorns pop like pricked balloons. Sap oozes out on to my leaves, lasciviously, Sycamore helicopters soar upwards into the clouds, with blades sharp enough to shred avian

flesh.

And I listen, as Jack hobbles out of the pub and stands in the street where it's quieter.

'What the hell is up, hon?' he asks.

But still, all he can hear is sobbing and snorting down the line.

'What is it?' Jack says.

More sobbing.

'Is it mum? Is she dead?' It doesn't occur to him it could be dad. He couldn't imagine her being that emotional if dad had died.

'It's Hamid,' she eventually manages to say.

'Your boyfriend Hamid?'

'How many Hamids do you know?'

'Sorry, sorry. What is it? Has he dumped you?'

'Yes. Sort of. It's complicated,' Shona says.

'I'll call you back. Give me ten minutes.'

Jack calls an Uber and when he gets to his room, he video WhatsApps Shona, so he can see her puffy face and red eyes.

'Tell me everything,' he says. And they talk and talk, till the early hours of the morning.

It was all Shona's fault; that's the way she told it to Jack. Things were going so well with her and Hamid. And it might have carried on that way forever, if she hadn't fucked it up.

All of which is true. She made an enemy of a dangerous man; and that is a stupid thing to do.

But a clever man too. At first I thought Mr Bradshaw was going to be just another stalker. Planning murder or a campaign of harassment or an acid attack. Which would have been horrible and awful; and hence, enjoyable for me.

But no, he's smarter than that. He knows how to put a knife in a woman's heart without leaving fingerprints, or using a knife.

Three nights ago Shona and Hamid had played a gig and gone back to his place and she fell asleep next to him and when she woke he was fast asleep next to her.

She got dressed and kissed him goodbye and left in the dawn light and walked back to 44 Westwood Street. So she wasn't there when the armed police kicked down the door of Hamid's loft apartment and stormed in with guns pointing accusingly and faces hidden behind masks.

Hamid hadn't woken up properly from his dream when the noises started, and his body reacted instinctively and by the time the armed police reached his bedroom he had thrown himself out of the bedroom window and hopped from windowsill to windowsill down the face of the five storey building until he reached the ground floor. He was naked and it was night and the armed police outside the house didn't see him when he started to run; he was past them in moments, sprinting effortlessly.

Then the searchlights came on and the dogs were released and by the time the cops caught up with him, Hamid had been mauled and his arm was trapped in an Alsatian's mouth and his face was full of rage.

Hamid's injuries were treated at the hospital but he was kept in cuffs throughout. And at the insistence of the Counter-Terrorism Commander he was conveyed to Paddington Green police station the following day.

It was two days before Shona found out her boyfriend had been arrested. For all that time she assumed he'd just walked out on her. It was in his blood, she knew that; Hamid was a wanderer. His family were Tuaregs, they had lived in the desert, a tent their only home, for many millennia. The Tuaregs are born warriors, they are masters of guerrilla warfare; and Hamid grew up hearing all these tales of his forefathers and knew it was his heritage. To wander, and to fight.

For six years he had wandered all across Europe. He had busked in Paris and Rome and Florence, he had slept in trains and on beaches and railways stations. He has been in London for less than a year, the longest he has stayed in any European capital.

And now he is in a small prison cell with painful dog-bite injuries being accused of planning a major terrorist attack in Docklands.

At the end of the fourth day he is released and he phones Shona. And George McBride picks him up in his builder's van at the Paddington Green nick . George is a dab hand at bailing people out of jail and he takes this in his stride. Shona however is fearful.

'I don't really know you,' she tells Hamid later, in the bedroom of his loft apartment; its front door badly patched up by George.

Hamid has a tendency to be morose and reserved; not always, but sometimes. But today he has surrendered fully to his darker side. His face is a mask. His heart is in a cage. He is sitting close to her yet it feels as if he is a million miles away.

'I don't know what you're talking about,' he says stiffly. 'I'm innocent. I am not a terrorist. That is why they let me go.'

'You're on bail,' Shona says.

'I'm not on bail, I'm on their Watch List. There's a difference.'

Three days of interrogation failed to get Hamid to confess. His computer was impounded, his flat was searched, but no traces of radical propaganda were found on his computer, and no traces of explosives were found in his flat.

'What did you do?' Shona asks.

'I did nothing,' Hamid says.

'You must have done something. You're a Muslim aren't you?'

Hamid's mask stiffens; sensing and resenting her suspicions.

'I'm a pacifist Muslim,' Hamid says.

'You must have done something.'

'Stop saying that, Shona. I did nothing.'

She offers to stay the night but Hamid declines.

The next day he is gone. He sends her a text message explaining that he is returning to Marrakech, to be with his family. She knows he will never return.

'I didn't believe him,' the tearful Shona tells Jack.

'Did you say you didn't believe him?'

'No. But he knew.'

'Well maybe it's all true,' says Jack, and Shona gets angry with him for a while.

'Well I don't really know him,' Jack admits.

'Hamid is not capable of hurting anyone. All he cares about is music. And me. He cares about me. He never said so but I know he loved me.'

Did he really? She isn't sure but she has to tell herself that.

'It was all a fit up, he was framed, that's why the cops arrested him, someone framed him,' Shona says.

'Not likely, hon,' Jack says.

'It's what happened,' Shona insists. 'I know it. I know it for a fact.'

The day after Hamid left the country for good Shona received a photograph of her boyfriend leaving Paddington Green station, accompanied by Shona and George, taken by someone with a mobile phone camera on the other side of the street.

The text bore the caption: FUCKING SNITCH.

It took Shona a couple of hours to realise who sent the message. Then she went to the Gipsy Bell, the band's regular venue, and asked the manager if anyone had been around asking for her. He was evasive but eventually he admitted he'd had a visit from an official with the Border Force, who claimed he was investigating Hamid. The pub manager had promptly given the investigator Hamid's home address.

'It's our country,' the manager explained to Shona. 'People shouldn't take the piss.'

'Fair point,' said Shona; vowing that she will never play in that venue again. 'What was his name, this official?'

'I forget,' the manager had said.

'Did he leave a card?'

'No.'

'What did he look like?'

The pub manager hesitated, then gave her quite a comprehensive description.

Skinny. Fit. Very fit in fact. Balding, slightly. Wearing a tweed jacket, with patches on the elbows.

That description perfectly fitted a man Shona knows.

'And did he have a warrant card, this man? Did he show ID?'

The manager thought about it. 'No.'

Shona has of course realised that it was her former lover and former teacher Benjamin Bradshaw who fitted up her boyfriend. But she doesn't know the details.

But I do. I know it all. I saw it all unfold, step by delicious step.

And now here he is, Benjamin Bradshaw, her nemesis, reading the newspaper report of Hamid's detention and subsequent release. He learns that an 'African man' has been assisting police with their enquires. And he smiles. He is the cat that stole the cream, and blamed it on the cat next door.

And then he calls a mate, an ex-teacher turned copper, and asks for further details. He learns that Hamid Bennani has left the country voluntarily, almost certainly to avoid deportation proceedings. It is very unlikely his visa will ever be approved by the authorities again so in effect, he has been banished from this country forever.

'How do you know this guy?' Benjamin's copper pal asks.

Benjamin keeps it casual. Mate to mate. 'Ah well, he's been hanging out with some of my pupils, see. A real creep. I was thinking of calling the Prevent Hotline and reporting him. Someone obviously beat me to it.'

'Well, good call,' says Benjamin's copper pal. 'He was a little piece of shit, according to the Counter-Terrorism boys. Stood mute, showed no respect. Right fucking attitude. He's on our radar now, so you won't be seeing him again. Not ever.'

Benjamin doesn't admit to his copper pal that he is the person who made the anonymous call about Hamid Bennani, alleging he was part of a South London terror network with plans to explode a car bomb in Canary Wharf. Benjamin had done his research thoroughly. Well, you'd expect nothing less, considering he is a teacher. He'd re-read the 'Prevent' Duty Guidance for Schools issued by the government to all teachers to train them in how to spot radicalised children. And he'd already done a WRAP day as part of his school duties – that's a 'Workshop to Raise Awareness of Prevent'. So he knew the buzz words, the buttons to press.

So Benjamin had called the Prevent Hotline and he had made his allegations against Hamid, claiming he was planning a terror atrocity. He even named a number of Muslim boys, former pupils of his at Westwood High, who (he claimed) had attended a mosque where the imam was a radical Muslim who was outspoken in protest against the Prevent scheme.

It was so easy. He'd simply told the chap on the other end of the hotline that Hamid was 'hanging out' with these lads. And 'filling their heads with nonsense'.

And that was that. Job done. Words can be as sharp and as deadly as spears sometimes.

'Thank you sir for being such a good and concerned citizen,' the voice on the hotline had said, briskly.

'Well, it's the least I can do. It's *our* country, after all.'

'Ahem. Indeed, sir. Thank you sir.'

You may be interested to learn that the former pupils at Westwood High named by Benjamin – who knew nothing of Hamid of course - were also arrested and detained by officers from the Counter-Terrorism Branch. And although they were all released without charge, they are also now on the Watch List. The fact that no evidence was found will not be considered as proof of innocence by the British authorities. These days, one well-placed smear is all it takes.

Nice work Benjamin Bradshaw; a well executed revenge. You have won both my attention and my admiration.

And as for Shona – ah, you poor girl. It seems you have been bested at your own game.

Snitching.

Chapter 21

'Welcome to the Westwood Tavern, my name's Shona and we're gonna play some rock and roll,' says Shona nervously.

The crowd at the Tavern look at her sceptically. A drummer, a bassist and a singer with a violin? That's not their idea of a rock and roll line up.

'Two three four,'says Vishaal on the drums and Priya kicks off with a bass riff.

The bass riff continues. Shona looks unsure about what should happen next.

The bass riff continues.

The crowd starts to murmur and that's when Shona leans forward and starts the song.

'There's a lady, who's sure,' she sings, and pauses, until she has total silence from the crowd. Then she continues: 'All that glitters is gold.' Her voice is emphatic, and lilting. More like a folk singer than a rock singer; but her voice has extraordinary power and range. 'And she's building a stairway to heaven.'

She sings the rest of the verse, hauntingly. Then she goes into a violin riff; dazzlingly fast and heart sweepingly eloquent.

The bass riff continues, boom boom boom-boom. The hi-hats are caressed: ta-TISH, ta-TISH. The bass drum beats a slow tread to prepare the way for the coming sprint. The violin tells a story of hope and redemption to complement the obscurity of the lyrics.

When she comes to the 'oh' of the chorus she hits the note and holds the note and she sustains the note until the heartbeats of everyone in the bar are frozen, waiting for the next syllable to beat again.

'Ooh...........................

It makes me wonder.

Ooooooooooooooooooooooooooooooooooohhhhhhhhh hhhhhhhhhhhhhhhhhhhhhhhh

It makes me wonder.'

When they get to the fast bit of the song the bassist is playing both the melody and the bass riff and the drummer is smashing it. And the violin takes Jimmy Page's virtuoso riff and embellishes it into a rock cadenza of dazzling majesty, mashing up fast bowing with sharp pizzicato and soulful held notes. Sometimes Shona stamps her feet as she plays and sometimes the violin hits notes so high only the under-thirties can hear them; before soaring downwards and repeating, and repeating, and repeating a single riff, to get the jig going again.

Later some of the drinkers claimed they could see the stairway, there, right there, in the pub with them. Stretching all the way up to heaven. A white shimmering staircase that burst through the roof of the pub and reached up through the clouds; a surreal image like the cover of a 1970s concept album. And perhaps that's true. Or maybe it's just the drink, and the heavy skunk that was circulating that night, talking.

Bass, violin, vocals, drums. You'd never think they could pull it off without Hamid and his devilish guitar licks. But Shona and the Other Two, as their band will come to be called, ace the Zeppelin song and at the end the crowd are thunderstruck.

One man claps louder and longer than anyone. A man with brown skin wearing a muddy tweed suit.

The Bogman.

When Shona has packed away her instrument the Bogman approaches her, bearing a bottle of champagne and four glasses.

'The band don't drink,' she explains. They are Muslims, like Hamid, and devout.

'Then join me?' suggests the Bogman.

'I have to get home,' Shona says.

'Have you eaten? The pub do a good spread, I'm told,' the Bogman says.

'Nah,' says Vishaal, the band's bassist. 'Kitchen is closed, we're doing a Morley's.'

'The kitchen have agreed to stay open,' says the Bogman. 'They're serving dinner for you and the band in the back room.'

'How did you manage that?' Shona asks.

'Money,' says the Bogman.

'We'll do Morley's,' says Priya, the band's drummer.

And that's how Shona came to have dinner with the Bogman.

She knew he was rich, of course. He had that air of confidence, the confidence that allows you to bribe the kitchen staff to stay on late. She wondered if he wanted to Sugar Daddy her and she wasn't up for that. But she was skint, the money from the gig would barely pay their bus fare, and she liked the idea of champagne.

'What's your name?' she asks the Bogman and he tells her.

'Try that again.'

He tells her again.

'What is that? Indian? Malaysian?'

'It's an English name,' he tells her, sounding offended. Though it isn't, in fact, an English name at all; the Angles hadn't invaded this island when the Bogman was named.

'I'll call you Jimmy,' she tells him.

'Jimmy it is.'

'Are you local?'

He was once king of all this land, as far as the coast to the east and the south, as far as Watford Gap to the north, and as far as what would later become Stonehenge to the west. 'Oh very much so.'

She sips her champagne and likes it so much she gulps it and he pours her another glass. He doesn't drink himself, he just takes a tiny sip, every now and then. He has bright blue eyes and they are firmly focused on Shona, on her face, on what she has to say.

'How long has the band been going?' the Bogman asks.

'A while. It's not my band, in fact. I – inherited it. We had a lead guitarist, he, well.'

'What happened to him?' the Bogman asks.

'He had to go back to Morocco.'

'That's Africa, isn't it?' the Bogman says.

'Yeah, sort of.'

'Why didn't you go with him?'

That penetrates her. 'I don't know.'

The blue eyes bore into her, knowing all her secrets. 'He was your lover, yes?'

'How could you possibly know that?'

'The way you talk. About him. There are – signs. If you know how to. Read people. And I do.' His English is good, his rhythms are strange; he *must* be foreign. But she doesn't like to challenge him on that..

'We had a thing going, yeah,' she admits. 'But then our thing got fucked up with other things.'

'He left you, or you left him?' the Bogman asks.

'He had to do a runner,' Shona says.

'I'm sorry, I'm prying,' says the Bogman, which skilfully stops her from being annoyed that he is prying. 'You don't need to tell me more.'

'No I don't,' Shona says.

'But you want to. So. Tell me more.'

So she tells him the story of her music teacher and how she grassed him up for abusing the trust of an impressionable schoolgirl. But then, surprise surprise, the Anti-Terror police were after Hamid on terror charges!

'Is he a terrorist?' the Bogman asks.

'Of course not. He's a musician.'

'The two are not.' The Bogman frowns. There are several words he could use to say what he means but he doesn't know any of them. So he does a workaround. 'He could be the one thing as well as being the other thing.'

'Musicians are too selfish to kill people,' Shona says. 'Hamid was – passionate. But only about music. I asked him once who the Prime Minister is, and he thought it was Winston Churchill.'

'It's not Winston Churchill? the Bogman asks.

'Har fucking har.'

But then she realises, he actually hadn't known.

'You did a brave thing,' he tells her.

'I think I did the right thing,' Shona says.

'Grassing up your enemy, that takes courage.'

'Ben isn't my enemy. He's just – he shouldn't have done what he did.'

'Why not?' the Bogman asks.

'Well what do you mean, why not?' Shona says.

'You've told me his story. He deflowered you. He deflowered this other girl. Why is that a problem? Was he not good in bed?' the Bogman says.

'No, he was. I thought so. At the time.' A dreamy smile comes over her. 'Then I fucked Hamid.'

'Did he rape you? This music teacher?' the Bogman asks.

She shakes her head. 'No. No! I wasn't raped. That wasn't it, at all.'

The Bogman has raped many girls and women over the years. But he has learned discretion, and he chooses not to admit that fact at this present moment.

'Then what did he do wrong?' the Bogman asks.

'You just don't get it, do you?' says Shona angrily.

'No I don't get it. That's why I'm asking you.'

'He was my teacher. I trusted him.'

'But you enjoyed what he did to you, so why do you mind?'

And so Shona explains.

It's harder than she realised but she gives it a good go.. She explains about duty of care and about how children don't always know what's good for them and she explains how only an evil cold-hearted bastard of a teacher would seduce his own pupil. Someone he was supposed to be protecting, and educating.

It all washes over the Bogman's head. He deals in simple rights and wrongs: though mainly wrongs.

'He hurt you, this man? This cold-hearted bastard?' the Bogman asks.

'Yes. Of course he did. He broke my heart then he lied about my boyfriend and got him arrested and made him run away, and that way, he broke my heart all over again. He's a nasty conniving piece of shit and I hope one day he gets what's coming to him,' Shona says.

'If I ever meet him,' the Bogman says calmly. 'I shall bear your words in mind.'

The Bogman stands. He moves in a single flowing movement; then is motionless again.

'I will leave you now,' he says. 'Before you become bored of me. Keep the bottle, there's plenty left.   There's another bottle behind the bar, why don't you take it home with you?

'You're going already?' Shona asks.

'Yes. May I come and listen to you again?'

'Course you can. We have a website - '

'I will find it. '

'You can stay a bit longer if you like. You haven't told me anything about yourself, Jimmy.'

'What is there to tell?' the Bogman says.

'Like, who you are, what you do for a living?'

'I am just a man who lives in the woods,' says the Bogman. And he walks away with brisk strides, and a few moments later, he is gone.

'Are you sure this is not too ambitious?' says Don.

It'll be lovely.

'I've never cooked anything as, you know, complicated as this,' Don says.

Presentation. That's the key to it.

'And I wrap the Parma ham around the grissini for starters?'

That bit's the easy bit.

'I could always buy something in from Cook, I guess. If it all goes tits-up.'

Oh Don. What am I going to do with you?

Don chuckles. He is making sea bass in puff pastry in the shape of a giant fish, stuffed with prawns, served with a side dish of potato rösti. The pastry bit wasn't as bad as he'd feared and Don does have a good eye so the puff pastry fish sculpture looks quite plausible, just a bit creepy. But grating potatoes is doing his head in, he keeps cutting his fingers, and Marie keeps telling him he should have squeezed the water out of the potato more vigorously at the start.

And you shouldn't have used that dirty tea towel, that's how infections spread, she'd told him.

'It wasn't dirty it was cleaned yesterday!'

Filthy.

'Ingrained dirt doesn't count that's just like, wrinkles on a woman's face, a sign of age,' Don says.

What a disgusting metaphor, no wonder you haven't had your leg over since I passed on, you sick and twisted old man.

'Sorry love.'

When Megan arrives Don serves champagne cocktails and fresh oysters. But Megan won't touch the oysters because she's heard they are poisonous. Don has heard the same but he slurps a few anyway, and the texture in his mouth is horrible. Megan chooses to open the bottle of plonk she brought herself and by the time they are two bottles in, the rösti has burned but the sea bass looks a treat. It looks almost professional.

'You should be on Bake Off,' Megan says.

'Well it's not a cake it's a pie,' Don says.

'It's not a pie it's a work of art, and they do do savoury stuff sometimes.'

'They did have profiteroles with raw beef once,' Don says.

'Rare not raw,' Megan says.

'Ah yes.'

'It's filling, this stuff. I'm full as an egg,' Megan says.

'We had too much wine,' Don says.

Yes you did.

'You're looking very nice in that, um, top,' says Don.

Oh really Don is that the best you can do?

'Sainsbury's finest,' says Megan.

'You're kidding? You bought that in your own store?'

'Staff discount,' Megan says.

'Well it's nice,' Don says.

'Flatterer,' Megan says.

Don smiles gently. He does have a lovely smile.

'Not really,' Don says. 'That was it, that's all I've got, in terms of buttering you up. Marie always said - '

Don't talk about me you idiot.

'What did Marie always say?' Megan says.

'She always said, I had a solid lead tongue. Not silver, see, lead.'

'Ah.'

'Well it was funny at the time,' Don says.

'What was she like? Marie?' Megan asks.

Don't talk about me don't talk about me.

'She was a bit sharp. Clever woman but she had a bit of a tongue on her,' Don says.

And if you do talk about me don't belittle me.

'But we were happy. Nearly fifty years we were together, we met at college you know,' Don says.

'What was it, cancer?' Megan asks.

'It was.'

'And you don't have children?'

'Never had time,' Don lies.

Oh Don.

'I've got three,' Megan says.

'So you said.'

'They'd kill me if they knew I was out with a bloke.'

So what's the game plan, Don? Cock out next?

'Is that what you are? Out with a bloke?' Don says.

'I assume so, this is a date isn't it?' says Megan.

She's too much woman for you Don, bail now, you know you'll never manage to get it up.

'I reckon it is,' Don tells her.

'Well that's a relief. I'm sorry, I can't eat any more,' Megan says.

'You've done pretty well.'

Tell her you're tired. Tell her to piss off. Put an end to this pathetic evening and fall asleep in front of the telly like you always do.

'I can make some coffee if you like?' Don says.

'Is there no pudding?' Megan says.

'Well there is but you said you were full.'

'I can always find room for pudding,' Megan says.

'Me too,' says Don.

'But I don't want to spoil my appetite.'

'Don't you?' Don asks.

Don is baffled but plays along.

'So maybe pudding later? After?' Megan says.

'After what?'

Oh for fuck's sake Don she's asking you to fuck her.

'Well, you know.' She gives him a little wink.

'Ah,' says Don.

That's disgusting. You're not doing it. Tell her no, Don. Tell her thank you very much but no thank you tell her fuck off you harlot with your too much make up and your red lips and your big tits and your cheap top that doesn't fit you because you've been eating too many fucking –

'Shut up!' says Don loudly.

Megan is offended. 'Well I beg your pardon.'

'Not you, love. Not you. I wasn't saying - '

'Who then? I'm the only one here!' Megan says.

Don't you tell me about her you treacherous bastard don't you fucking dare.

'You're not. You're not the only one here,' says Don, sadly. And he explains carefully, to a puzzled, then intrigued, then deeply fascinated Megan, about his ghosts.

No one knows how old it is, the Oldest Tree in Old Park. Even I can't properly recall a time when there was not an oak tree there. It was there when the woods were entirely wild. It was there when the woodland was coppiced and harvested in a strict rhythm, with hacked down tree stumps being grown into trees as if they were prize heifers. And as it grew older the main trunk of the Oldest Tree split and became a hiding place and cubby hole. Cavaliers hid inside its trunk during the English Civil War, when sought after by Roundheads. Many children since then have hidden inside the Oldest Tree during games of Hide and Seek. When the Old Park was created a fence was put around the Oldest Tree and metal buttresses were put in place to support its still-living branches; and its offshoots have turned the Oldest Tree into a family of trees, clones of the parent plant, forming a dense copse at the heart of the Old Park.

There are bigger and better looking trees in the Old Park and indeed in Westwood. There are pine trees that are higher than the television transmitter over in Crystal Palace. There is a Redwood that is at least 6,000 years old and has a trunk broader than a blue whale. There are stands of mature maples that can turn an English Autumn into a New England Fall. But the Oldest Tree is the oldest and the most physically contorted and has the most history.

When the men in the Hi-Vis jackets paint an X on the trunk of the Oldest Tree I assume it's some kind of joke. The Oldest Tree is a sacred thing, it's protected by all sorts of laws, it cannot be cut down. And yes, it is diseased and warped and partially dead but I am not ready to let it be exterminated It is the only thing in my world that is almost as old as I am. I rely upon it for companionship.

But the next day the lumberjacks arrives in the park. The land designated for the new housing development is marked out by men with clipboards and theodolites. A small group of protestors with banners (SAVE OUR PARK! TREES BEFORE HOUSES!) gather to protest. Which they do in a rather lacklustre way, waving their banners while thinking about nipping back to the pub. I am shocked at how little revolt there is. In the past, attempts to hack away bits of the Old Park for corporate gain have been greeted with mass protests and sit ins. This time, no one seems to care.

I do my best to resist this outrage. I send squirrels scampering towards the Oldest Tree, to rip with their claws at its trunk in order to rub out the X. But they don't succeed and in any case, it doesn't matter. The ground has been marked out by now and the Tree is, to say the least, easy to spot. It's clear that The Oldest Tree has been doomed to die.

Men with chain saws first of all attack the stand of ash trees that border the park. The saplings are cut down, then the full size trees, and a mechanical forestry tool is used to lift each trunk and strip off its branches. When the lumberjacks tire, the machine takes over the whole job, pulling out each tree by its root then stripping it and dumping it into a nest of logs. Tipper trucks pull up and the trees are cut up into smaller chunks and thrown into the backs of the trucks.

All this takes several days and by the end of day four, when the Oldest Tree feels the bite of chain saw in its trunk, it hurts me like a knife in my heart. This tree is too large to be pulled out by any mechanical device but the chain saws make short work of it. They carve through its rotting wood like a Viking sword edge through a Saxon warrior. It's methodical, and professional, and remarkably quick. They are good at their job, these lumberjacks. Some of them have taken down entire forests in Canada and they have transformed the murder of trees into an art form.

And so the Oldest Tree is hacked down and hewn into chunks and before long all the remains is the vast tree stump and then the stump grinder goes to work.

I want to weep but I cannot.

So instead I pour with rain.

The rain lasts for seven days and seven nights.

In the South London Intensive Care Unit in Beckenham Kane is fading fast.

Most days Tanya spends two or even three hours at his bedside, in between her childminding commitments. Her boyfriend Danny has left her because he can't bear how melancholy she has become. But she has a good network of neighbours and the older kids look after the younger kids and that leaves Tanya with enough time to visit Kane and regret, bitterly, what she did to him.

It's every mother's nightmare: to be forced to choose. The Mortons made it clear that one of her children would die, so she had to decide which of them it would be. Would it be her lovely, happy smiling baby Ray? Or would it be Kane, that selfish little shit, who carries a gun and steals cars for a living?

Tanya made what she thought was the right choice and now she can't forgive herself.

It seems to me that there was no right choice. Either way, she was screwed.

Up till now Tanya has always had a flair for life. She was one of those people who never take things to heart. She doesn't brood. She doesn't fester. If one thing doesn't work out, she moves on to the next thing.

Not this time Ever since she allowed herself to be the bait on the hook that skewered her gangster son, she has reproached herself. She doesn't sleep. She is cranky. She weeps all the time. And day after day she sits beside Kane's bedside and reads him stories. Fairy stories, children's stories, all the stories she used to read to him when he was a kid including the Jolly Christmas Postman and Each Peach Pear Plum. She has been told that even when they are in a vegetative state, patients can be aware of and affected by someone reading to them. But mainly she reads the stories for herself. Because every time she reads a story, she can remember the look on Kane's face when she read it to him when he was a child. She can remember the delight in his eyes at that moment, that amazing moment, when the duck turns into a swan! When the mum turns her council flat into a fairy palace! When Meg's spells go wrong yet again!

She can remember Kane smiling, laughing, giggling. 'That's daft,' he would say, when she did all the voices of all the animals in the crocodile by the river story. 'You're daft.'

'No you're daft.'

'I'm not daft you're daft!'

'If I'm daft, you're even daftier!'

Happy memories, as she sits by the bed of a young man connected to a ventilator with a cabbage for a brain.

Then one day, while she is at home, pegging out her laundry on the balcony. Tanya gets the call from the hospital that she was told she might be getting.. She leaves her three youngest kids with the older kids, telling them where the sweets are hidden, and makes the bus journey to the ICU.

She follows a trail of colour symbols around the hospital without looking at them; her feet know the way by now. Then she is ushered through into the ICU ward.

Her other son Billy is there, at Kane's bedside, sitting on the chair they put out for visitors. When he hears her coming he gets up. He is wearing a black bomber jacket, but for him that's his work clothes. He's lost a bit of weight, Tanya notices.

'Come to gloat?' Tanya asks.

'He's my brother, Tanya,' Billy says.

'All you want to do is put him in jail.'

'He's dead, I don't need to put him in jail.'

'He's not dead yet.'

Billy says nothing. He has spoken to the doctors already.

Before long Tanya is having 'the conversation' with the consultant. Which is really more of a monologue than a conversation. And she is told that despite their very best efforts, Kane cannot be saved. So the most humane thing to do now is switch off the life support and let nature take its course.

Tanya agrees, poker faced, and when Billy tries to hug her she rebuffs him with a single raised hand: stay back.

Later she will grieve.

Or so she hopes.

There's no ceremony but Tanya and Billy are both there when the machine is switched off. The machine that makes Kane breathe stops, and he stops breathing. The tube in his throat that had been pumping air into his lungs is pulled out of his throat. Tanya is convinced that when the tube is completely out Kane will jump up and come back to life. But he doesn't.

'Let me take you home,' Billy says to Tanya.

The body is zipped into a bag and put on a gurney. A nurse wheels the gurney to the lift and the lift takes the body down to the mortuary. Kane's body is transferred on to a mortuary table where he will be collected by the Cartwright family, father and son, who run the local funeral parlour. There is no need for a postmortem because the cause of death is already known: Kane died of gunshot injuries sustained seven months before. Switching off the life support was just a way of acknowledging the inevitable.

The Cartwrights arrive promptly and decant the body into a temporary coffin made of cheap wood, not from any of my forests. And then it is wheeled through the mortuary and slid into the hearse and the hearse drives away through the streets of Westwood at a fair old lick, because today it is just a meat wagon.

It is still raining: this is Day Seven of the flood. No work has commenced on the new housing development because all the land in Old Park is waterlogged and water has got into the engines of the brush clearing machines. The restaurants and pubs are all quiet because no one wants to walk through torrential rain in order to have a night out. Water mains have burst all around Westwood and a cataract is pouring down Treacherous Avenue, a many-bodied sea snake of turbulent water that surges out of the drains in thick torrents.

Lightning flashes flash across the sky, dazzling and forked.

Wild animals hide in shelters or dig themselves into deep holes; afraid of being battered by rain as powerful as God's fists.

When the hearse reaches the funeral parlour the funeral director Carl Cartwright and his son Desmond clamber out, their well dressed bodies shielded under large umbrellas. Carl is bald, his son soon will be. They both have the physique of prop forwards gone to seed. The Cartwrights leave the corpse in the car; they can't be arsed to shift it in this rain. It will survive a couple of hours in the hearse they feel.

When the rain stops the winds begin.

Much of Westwood is completely flooded by now, cars cannot drive along the roads. Houses and restaurants and pubs have been swamped by the rising waters and their interiors are drenched. Ground floor furniture has been destroyed, lives and businesses have been ruined. Rescuers in canoers are taking away the elderly and the vulnerable. The winds whip at the rivers which used to be streets and turn them into tidal surges. The trees in Old Park are shaken by the wind and billowing clouds of pollen are swept up into the air, dampened by the rain, angry as mosquitoes.

And then, at my command, the pollen swarm narrows to the shape of an arrow and it takes flight across the sky. Forming a black contrail against the dark grey clouds.

The pollen swarm is airborne once more.

Outside the funeral parlour the hearse is rattled by gales of wind and the windows of the vehicle shatter and break.

Soon after, a haze of sodden and agitated pollen particles arrives in the sky above the funeral parlour and there it hovers. A living thundercloud.

And then the pollen drizzles downwards, and the pollen particles bounce off the roof of the hearse, and pour through its smashed-open windows. The billowing embrace of pollen covers the coffin that holds Kane Armstrong, and its tiny particles seep through the grain of the wood.

Inside the coffin, Kane wakes as if from a long dreamless sleep and wonders what the fuck is going on.

Chapter 22

Grandpa Maybe has a house guest.

It's a long time since Hilary lived with him, after she ran away from home at the age of sixteen, back in the 1990s. Those days had been the happiest days of her life.

Now she's back in the spare bedroom of Grandpa Maybe's, and it's still damp and cold in there. Grandpa's housekeeping leaves a lot to be desired; she even finds a bottle of elderflower cordial, empty admittedly, which she had left behind in her bedroom when she went off to marry George McBride, twenty five years ago.

Now Hilary has left George and she's back with her aged granddad.

'He's not such a bad man,' Grandpa Maybe tells her, after they have dined on shop-bought Jamaican patties washed down with rum. 'Not compared to some as I have known.'

'I didn't say he was,' Hilary says.

'But he's treated you bad.'

'I should have known better.'

'Well that's true. You should have known, a man like George, well, he'll always be a man like George,' says Grandpa Maybe..

'You knew he was having affairs?' Hilary says.

Grandpa laughs for a good while. 'Is that what you call it? When a man fools around upon a woman who is not his wife? All men do that, honey. It is part of being a man.'

'I knew he was having affairs,' says Hilary.

'How's that boy of yours?' asks Grandpa Maybe shrewdly.

Hilary begins to weep. Grandpa doesn't console her. He just sips his rum. They are small sips but it is strong rum, and he stays with her until she has wept herself dry. And then he gets up and totters over to her and envelops her in a skinny-armed hug.

The next day Grandpa takes Hilary to Brixton Market, next to the railway bridge. It is one of the great London markets, up there with Greenwich and Portobello Road. And the first place they visit is a vinyl record stall run by an older Rasta-haired black man with scars on his face. This is Juice, he was one of Shona Mirabelle's lovers back in the day; and so it is quite possible he is Hilary's grandfather by blood. Juice was a gangsta in those days, it's a miracle he wasn't murdered years ago. Grandpa Maybe greets him with a hand slap.

'You're looking bad, man,' Grandpa Maybe says.

'You're looking worse, my brother,' Juice says.

Hilary grins, amused and happy to be there. But she refuses to buy a vinyl album, because she threw away her record player many years before.

After this they visit a stall where a huge skillet of Caribbean stew is bubbling and they savour the smells then they move on to a retro stall run by a hippie white woman with huge dangling earrings and scores of gold bracelets on her wrists. She greets Grandpa by his name, which is Bobby, and offers to buy his jacket, which is an antique apparently. Grandpa likes to dress well, he has a whole room of suits he bought in the 1960s still in their cellophane from the dry cleaners and he alternates them carefully. Though none of them fit him properly any more. He was once a fine figure of a man with broad shoulders and muscular thighs, but no longer.

There are cake stalls and artisan bread stalls and cheese stalls and Grandpa buys Hilary a scarf from the scarf stall. And then he buys one for himself, a rich blue floral shawl, and drapes it around his neck even though he is wearing a tie. And it looks good.

They eat a Caribbean lunch at Grandpa's favourite café and she realises that he may be ninety-something years old with a gammy pair of legs and a bad cough and no flesh to speak of, but this man is *alive*.

George calls her the next day.
'When are you coming home, love?'
She hangs up.

Shona comes to Brixton for dinner and she takes over the old man's kitchen and cooks a rich and spicy chilli con carne with succulent kidney beans. And afterwards, while Grandpa Maybe snoozes in his armchair, she quizzes her mother on the state of the McBride marriage.

'You're just testing him right? You are coming back?' Shona says.

Hilary gives her daughter a calming 'mother knows best' stare but her reply is evasive.

'Maybe, maybe not.'

'What did he do? Is he like, screwing around?' Shona asks.

'This is your dad you're talking about,' Hilary says.

'So? Has he been having affairs?'

George is a man who can't pass a mirror without stopping to admire his own good looks and stylish silver waistcoats; they all know that.

'Of course he's been having affairs,' Hilary says.

'Dad? My dad? Having affairs?' says Shona.

'He always was a womaniser, your dad. Well in fairness, that's why I went for him,' Hilary says.

'Dad?'

'Sweet heaven girl, do you know nothing about your own father?'

'And what about you?' Shona asks.

'What?'

'Are you having an affair? Is there "someone else"?' Shona asks.

Hilary sighs. Her gentleness is curdled by vexation.

'Look at me Shona. Look at me. I'm a worn out old woman. Would I be having affairs?' Hilary says.

'You're not worn out. You're not old,' Shona says.

'You're trying to persuade me to fool around with some buck?'

'No I'm just saying, it you wanted to, you could,' Shona says.

'Life is not all about sexual intercourse, Shona,' Hilary says reprovingly.

Shona is exasperated. She'd thought she would crack this mystery but she hasn't.

'So why leave Dad?' Shona asks.

Hilary sighs again.

I was there. I was watching at the moment when it happened. When Hilary fell out of love with George.

'You thought I'd forget, didn't you?' George asks.

George is grinning. His trademark roguish grin.

'You never do,' Hilary says.

'Silver this is. Twenty-five years hard labour, ha ha. That's why I got you the silver necklace,' says George.

'It's lovely,' Hilary says.

George has pulled out all the stops for this special anniversary. He has booked a posh hotel out in the country, in Suffolk, with a four poster bed in their room and champagne on ice for when they arrive. A silver necklace from Cartier, or at least, with Cartier stamped all over the box, was awaiting her as her main anniversary gift. Great sex before dinner was next on the agenda, and George really is very good at sex,. And although Hilary tells herself she's not bothered one way or the other, she is in fact, when aroused, an animal.

And now they are having a posh dinner and George is wearing a new suit and Hilary did in the end manage to find her best frock. And when she laughs she is nineteen again.

She was nineteen when she met Montrose and he always made her laugh.

She was twenty-four when he died, two and a half years after she met and married George.

Hilary is full of memories of her dead gay friend Montrose today. Which is strange, since it is her wedding anniversary.

'I found your book,' Hilary tells George calmly.

'Which book?' George asks.

Normally even when she is happy Hilary feels nervous. As if something terrible is about to happen. Maybe the sky will fall down and crush her to death. Maybe her next meal will choke her. Or maybe all her friends will suddenly decide to hate her. It's crazy but she can't help herself.

But today, facing the final showdown with the man who never was the love of her life, though he doesn't know that, she doesn't feel nervous at all.

She's a bit drunk which helps.

'Your book. Your notebook. Your diary thing.' Hilary says.

'Which diary thing?' George asks.

She gives him a weary and withering look. 'The book where you write down all the birthdays, of course. Me, the kids, your parents, your mistresses, all of them. Otherwise how could you keep track? I mean, nothing pisses a woman off more than a man who forgets her birthday, or their anniversary, but you never get it wrong. Never. Not in twenty-five years and I'll be honest, I thought it was twenty-four this year, you could have knocked me over with a feather when you started giving me silver stuff. That's not like you, George. You're not a man who remembers things. So I realised, you must have it all written down in a book. Our anniversary, my birthday, and all the birthdays and anniversaries of all the other women you've been fucking for the last twenty five years.'

There is a terrible silence. At an adjoining table conversation becomes stilted as the woman, a lady in her fifties with thick horn rims, tries to listen in. while her portly husband keeps jabbering away about some problem at work.

Hilary holds George in a steely glance.

George looks defensive. Then angry. Then guilty. But eventually he gets a grip.

'I don't have a fucking book,' he says, truthfully.

'Yes but you have mistresses, don't you?' Hilary says slyly.

He can't get out of that.

'A man has needs,' George says lamely.

'Who?' Hilary asks.

'You don't need to know.'

'Who?'

'Helen. In Hackney.'

'Who else?'

'What? What do you mean who else?' George has his courtroom manner back now: what, m'lud, me, m'lud?

'Who else?' Hilary asks.

'Just stop this, Hilary,' George says.

'Who else?' Hilary asks.

'I'm not saying.'

'How many then?'

'Ever, or at the moment?'

That does it for her.

'I don't mind,' she tells him.

'What?' George says.

'I don't mind.'

'What do you mean, you don't mind?' George says.

'I mean, I don't mind. The women. I don't.'

'How the hell can you not mind?' George's tone is almost aggrieved; how dare she!

The portly husband realises he no longer has his wife's full attention; he starts listening in too.

'I mean, I know what you're like. When you're not getting it anywhere else. And it's a pain in the backside, to be honest. When you're in one of your randy moods,' Hilary says.

The couple at the nearby table are barely pretending now, they are leaning over their table as they earwig the George and Hilary showdown.

'It wears me out,' Hilary says. 'Once a week, lovely, but not the way you go at it. You have needs, I have needs. I need time to read books and be – alone with me.'

Hilary had never said any of this before and it comes as a shock to her.

I have known all this for a long time and I feel a deepened respect for this woman.

'Look, I'll turn over a new leaf, I swear,' George says.

'No you won't,' Hilary says.

'I will. I swear. I love you Hilary.'

'You're not listening. I said, I don't mind. That. I don't mind *that*. What I mind is - ' She gestures at where they are, what they are wearing. 'This. This I mind.'

'What, being somewhere nice?' George says.

'Yes,' Hilary says.

'You'd rather be at home?'

'Yes.'

'Well you could have told me that before I wasted all my bloody - '

'Jack was coming home,' Hilary says. 'From Southampton. He'd booked the train, he was on his way. Shona cancelled a gig to be with me on my anniversary, so she could share it with me. I slipped Uncle Mickey fifty quid to fuck off out of it with his mates down the pub so I wouldn't have to put up with his endless bloody prattle. And then you pull a trick like this. Train booked, hotel booked, champagne on ice, and I'm supposed to go along with it all. Being dragged away for sex in Suffolk, so you can show off how much of a catch you are. Not on, George. You should have asked me. You should have spoken to Shona, and to Jack. They're your children too you know.'

George hasn't the faintest idea what she's banging on about but that doesn't stop him from looking concerned and understanding.

'I know they are.' His tone of reproach is so subtle, you could almost miss it.

'But you never talk to them. When was the last time you phoned Jack?' Hilary says.

'Well it's not my bloody fault he's in Southampton, is it,' George says.

'When did you last phone him?' Hilary says.

'I do phone sometimes.'

'When?'

'Never?' George says.

'And you've never gone to see Shona sing. And you didn't say anything when her boyfriend had to do a runner,' Hilary says.

'I picked him up at the nick didn't I!'

'But afterwards, I mean. When she was crying her eyes out. Where were you then?' Hilary says.

'I didn't want to – pester her,' says George.

'She's your little girl!'

'Never liked the little bugger anyway.'

'Oh George.'

Hilary wrestles down rage.

'Do you love me, George?' Hilary asks.

'Course I do.'

'Would you do anything to protect me?'

'Course I would, my love!' George says.

'But if you had to choose, between me and them, I mean. What would you do? Would you throw me off a bus if you had to? To save the lives of your two children?' Hilary asks.

'Course I wouldn't,' says George, stunned she would ask such a thing.

'Okay then. Try this: would you kill *yourself*, or let yourself be killed, to save Shona's life? Or Jack's life?'

Trick question: he knows the correct answer is yes.

'Yes,' says George.

But he doesn't mean it. And she knows he doesn't mean it.

'Really? Would you really lay down your life, for your little boy, or your little girl? Would you really do that?' Hilary says.

'No,' he says.

'In that case,' says Hilary, carefully. And bear in mind that this is the Hilary who never swears, not ever; not even that time when George almost cut her toe off with an angle-grinder: 'you can fuck off.'

St John misses Hilary. He has asked George several times for Hilary's phone number but George won't give it to him. Which is annoying.

He has been busy though. Mary Runnymede, the previous owner of this house, has (so Hilary informed him, just before she left for Brixton) met a man. And so she no longer has time to travel to London every other weekend to maintain and prune and weed the garden she used to own. St John was startled to find she had been doing that ever since he had moved in. As someone new to house-owning, he hadn't realised that gardens don't look after themselves.

But now it's up to him. The weeding, the pruning, the repotting. He has some of his own ideas too and so he digs up the bottom of the garden and builds a rockery. Then he knocks himself out and builds a small pond with coy carp and a pergola.

It turns out he has a knack for such work; and it builds him up too. He is developing a tan, and musculature.

Every week he buys a Lottery ticket or a scratch card and he wins every time. Before long he is able to pay off his mortgage and clear his credit card debts. He decides it would be useful to have a new car so he wins one in a competition. HMRC decide to audit his accounts; and they find a massive discrepancy in his favour and he gets a tax refund.

And one day in London Heights the police launch a raid on the shotters working in the waste ground area, and one of them makes a run for it, legs it up the stairs; and dumps his drugs and all his money off the roof of the London Heights complex. The coke tumbles to the ground like snow and will eventually do strange things to the cherry trees whose leaves it falls upon. While the money, about two hundred k in twenties and fifties, is caught up by the wind, and is swept across Westwood as a billowing cloud of lucre; flies high above St Peregrine's church tower; flies like a flock of birds above and across Treacherous Avenue until it is a flickering shadow above Westwood Street; loses momentum in the air above St John's house; and there it falls.

St John was reading in his garden when it started raining money. It was a delightful and amusing moment. He gave half of it to the charity shop; the remainder he hid behind the books on his newly acquired bookcase, which has been filled with newly acquired books.

Even though money comes so easily to him, he is keen to keep busy. So after completing all the possible jobs to be done in his own   garden,   St John goes wandering around Westwood looking for gardens which need doing up and driveways which need paving and other odd jobs. He quickly gets a job as a tree surgeon, despite having no experience. And after boning up on Wikipedia and buying a harness and a saw, he becomes a dab hand at lopping off branches.

On a whim one day he goes for a walk on the part of the Boulevard where the road racers go, the bit of dual carriageway which leads nowhere. And with a pick and shovel he hacks away at the tarmac until he exposes the soil below.

He clears a large expanse of soil this way then he plants grass seeds and soon they begin to grow, and a meadow is birthed. Then he build a children's playground on what used to be the hard shoulder of the carriageway. The playground is much needed, and greatly appreciated by the kids who live nearby, who need a safe space where they can play.

 He isn't paid for this job but then he really doesn't need the money. Every time he goes for a walk he finds a tenner on the pavement. Every time he plays a slot machine he wins the jackpot. Everything, absolutely everything, comes easily for St John now. But he doesn't take it for granted. He cherishes each day.

During this time, he has grown his hair long and has had one ear pierced. He is thinking of having a tattoo done. He has built up his biceps to such a degree that at a first glance he could pass for a hairy-arsed working class labourer type; until he speaks.

When George McBride bodges a rendering job on the house at 598 Westwood Street St John takes over the same project. He casts his own scaffolding poles in a local foundry, he mixes the render himself; then he renders the chimney and the parapets of this entire five storey house. He charges £500 for all this work, a nominal amount, and gives it in cash to the charity shop.

The charity shop is thriving by the way.

Occasionally his parents visit and they are stunned at the transformation in their son. Mr Featherstone tries to get St John a job at a rival investment bank, which has been flourishing ever since St John brought his own firm to the point of near-bankruptcy. But St John says no. He's happy as he is.

One day while up a ladder he meets a girl who is walking on the roof of the opposite house. They build a scaffolding bridge and he walks across to join her. Her name is Daniela. She is a roofer too; and it is, without a doubt, another instance of love at first sight.

That night Hilary calls him on his house phone. She explains that she is coming back to Westwood for the evening, and she asks him to join her for a night out.

'This is for my mum' says Shona.

She takes the microphone and begins to softly sing a love song.

Hilary is there in the audience at the Saxon Arms music night with St John Featherstone and Daniela and Grandpa Maybe. St John and Grandpa are getting on like a house on fire; they bond over a shared love of Wilson Pickett and Ella Fitzgerald, especially in her Louis Armstrong duets. And when St John spots a twenty pound note on the floor beside his chair, he pretends not to see it – so that Grandpa can, delightedly, make the find.

The love song is beautiful; and Shona sings it beautifully. Hilary doesn't know the melody but to her astonishment, she recognises the words. They are from a poem about a rapper who went to hell and came back as a cheesy soul singer; one of Montrose's finest creations, but never published.

She remembers Montrose in his pomp. His purple and red zoot suits, straight out of 40s Harlem, with insanely padded shoulders and a watch chain dangling from his belt to his knee, and a pork pie hat, that made him look like a time traveller. His flights of fantasy; sometimes he would just talk, and talk, and make up lies and stories about his family and his childhood. How Bob Marley was his godfather, and how he used to swim with sharks off the coast of Jamaica as a boy, and how he came to London in a rowing boat. And other times he'd be serious, and talk about the AIDs plague, and what it was like being a gay black boy in the orphanage he lived in, after he had rowed his rowing boat down the Thames, against the tide. And Hilary never knew what was true and what was lies.

Montrose's poetry classes in the Brixton community hall weren't really classes, they were festivals of storytelling. All the would-be poets who were there had to share tales. They had to tell stories about themselves, or about their children, or about their parents or grandparents. And these were the stories that would become their poems. And Hilary attended most of the workshops, though she was too shy to write anything herself.

And in one of those sessions her Grandpa Maybe told a story about his own grandfather who had been a slave on a sugar plantation. It was a harrowing tale with a tragic finale, when Grandpa's grandfather was accused of fornicating with his owner's nineteen-year-old daughter, which indeed he had. Though not by choice, but because he had been obliged to do so. And Grandpa Maybe had all the details because he had inherited his Caribbean mother's journal, her day to day account of growing up as the child of a slave who had been hanged for being raped.

And then, a few weeks later, Grandpa Maybe wrote a poem about his ancestral story. It wasn't one of his best poems, in my opinion; the scansion left quite a bit to be desired and his final stanza was more bathos than pathos. But even so it made Hilary cry.

Shona's song continues.

Her rich voice caresses each and every heart in the room.

Vishaal dusts his cymbals with a brush; Priya pumps out a bass line that anticipates Shona's every improvised riff and scat. The audience are rapt. Even I am transfixed.

As Shona sings and as the band play, Hilary's memories mash up with the melody.

Montrose's lyrics with their pitter-patter rhythms and their haunting images take her back in time, until she can smell the ganja in the pubs they used to frequent, and she can hear Montrose's loud booming laugh as he was caught out in yet another ridiculous lie.

Hilary can only recall the aftermath of Montrose's murder, she was not present at the event itself. She was at home with Grandpa Maybe the night when Montrose in the Hamilton Arms and pissed off a group of undercover feds by calling them Babylon. And then bolted out of the pub and ran down the street laughing; before being brought to a halt by a bullet that could run faster than any black man.

Hilary couldn't believe it when she was told the news, that Montrose was dead.

She assumed it was another one of his absurd fabrications, which everyone else was sharing on his behalf as a gag. But she waited and she waited and a day went by and he carried on being dead. And that's when it became real for her.

Was that really it? One random bullet and it all ends?

And now her daughter Shona is singing one of Montrose's poems, about having a best friend who knows you better than you know yourself. My Always There Woman is the name and the refrain of the song.

As she listens, Hilary remembers it all. Visiting Brixton as a child, living there as a young woman. Being with Granny Shona and Grandpa Maybe in their big cold damp house. Being with Montrose. His goatee beard. His stupid hat. His hilarious suits. His smile that was always trembling on his lips. The soul in his eyes. The kindness in his hands, when he stroked her tears away. Dead too young. Hilary remembers it all.

And as Shona sings, Hilary is thinking: *You think I don't love you as much as I love your brother. I know you think that, don't deny it. And maybe it was true once. Maybe it was. But oh Shona, it's not true any more. I love you more than Jack. More than anyone. More than myself. You are who I always wanted to be.*

The song ends. Applause ripples through the bar.

As her dying note fades, Shona looks across at the slim young black woman who is sitting in the seat where until a few seconds ago, her mother had been sat   A shy young woman, looking scared, yet beautiful in her own way, and sexy too. And flamboyantly dressed like Queen Latifah in a black jacket with a map of Jamaica badge pinned to the lapel, looking right at her.

Then the girl becomes the middle-aged woman again and Shona starts the next song.

Chapter 23

Benjamin Bradshaw is cycling home from work.

He has a job as an insurance clerk these days, in an office on Woody Hill. It's a pretty good job, the pay is more than he was earning as a teacher, and fortunately for him the forged references he provided from the headteacher of his last school were never checked.

Bradshaw is a fast cyclist and he is cycling downhill and is travelling at about fifty miles an hour, even though the speed limit on this road is 20 mph.

He does not hear a man running behind him . He does not hear the stamp of naked feet upon tarmac. He does not hear the even-paced breathing of a man who is used to running a hundred miles in a day. And he does not anticipate that he might be being pursued by a runner, because who would pursue *him*? And how? No runner could ever run as fast as a speeding bicycle.

But the Bogman can.

The Bogman is naked, as he often was in his glory days when he went hunting in the woods. His balls are sucked up tight into his body and his peaty cock swings as he runs but it does not bother him. He runs with bare feet upon the rough tarmac but it does not hurt him. And his lungs do not burn from the effort because he does not need to breathe; he only does so to keep his rhythm going.

Bradshaw cycles into the streets of Catford and still the Bogman still pursues him. He runs so fast you have to be looking right at him to realise he is there. He is like a streak of mud across your vision. He is the glimpse of something out of the corner of your eye that gives you nightmares.

The Bogman starts closing the gap. Benjamin Bradshaw is cycling in heavy traffic now, he has to slow down to the speed limit, which is 30mph on the main road through Catford. And now the Bogman is zigzagging, and leaping over cars, and a few people see him now and some of them call the police but by the time the police get to the scene it will be too late.

Benjamin Bradshaw is two streets away from his house when the Bogman's foot strikes the back wheel of his bike and he loses control and goes spinning through the air. He lands badly and feels bones break. He assumes he has been hit by a car, and he is alert enough to open his eyes and look up, ready to memorise the registration number of the vehicle if it drives away without stopping.

Instead he sees a pair of pitiless blue eyes then a fist punches his mouth and shatters his teeth and his nose.

He can see the knife that is held in front of his face, and is still conscious when the knife cuts his clothes off. And he remains conscious when the knife slips under his skin and swiftly hacks away until the flesh is pulled off in a single tough sheet. By the time the area car reaches the scene the silently howling body of Benjamin Bradshaw has been stripped of its skin and its damp red ligaments are bared to the wind.

Benjamin is still alive at this point; most human beings can survive being flayed, which is why it was once favoured as a method of torture. He is rushed to intensive care but the prognosis was never good. He dies later that night.

The Bogman carries the skin of Benjamin Bradshaw to the woods where he has made his home. And he stakes the skin on to a tree, so it will cure in the sun. Years later a child will find this and wonder what it is.

'He's back,' Camilla tells Alice.

The door pings as the man from the Council, the one with the angular head and the taste for Chateau Rothschild, steps inside and takes a seat at one of the empty tables. He glances around, approvingly, at the lack of other customers. Dulcimer and Miguel have been laid off. There are signs on the walls saying: *We are not licenced to serve alcohol, please do not ask* and *The Purchase and Consumption of Narcotics in this Establishment is Strictly Forbidden.*

'Can I help you sir,' Camilla asks, sweetly.

'A glass of wine would be nice,' he says. Smiling at her, the way an aristocrat might smile at the fox his hounds have just caught.

'We don't serve wine, sir,' Camilla says.

He hides a smirk, but not successfully.

'Or some of your finest skunk,' the man suggests.

'We don't sell narcotics, sir,' Alice says.

My bad, Alice is thinking: *what the hell, it was only a joint!*

'Or a stolen motorbike,' the man suggests.

This is clearly highly amusing for him; for Camilla and Alice, it is not.

'We don't deal in motorbikes sir, you must have misunderstood that previous – occurrence. This is a café,' says Alice.

'Not any more it's not,' the man asserts.

The look of satisfaction on his face has become almost irresistibly slappable. Or so Camilla and Alice both feel.

Alice sighs.

'What do you mean, sir?' Alice asks.

'Eviction proceedings are proceeding apace,' the man from the Council says.

'You can't do that,' says Camilla dully.

'It's done. This rogue café is being closed down.'

This man's name is Morecambe. Like the town and the comedian. On his business card it merely says R. Morecambe and so I do not know his first name.

'Why are you doing this?' Alice asks.

'Because it's my job,' Mr Morecambe says.

He is the food safety inspector for this district and his powers are surprisingly wide-ranging.

'There's nothing wrong with our hygiene,' Camilla says.

'You have rats, cockroaches, and other creatures I did not recognise,' he says.

It's true, sometimes things do appear in the café. A severed hand was once found resting on table eight. Not to mention human entrails underneath table seven, being gnawed by rats and a carrion crow. But these are momentary phenomena. They rarely last more than a few minutes at a time.

'You're putting us out of business,' Alice says.

'Plus serving alcohol without a liquor licence. Preparing hot food with inadequate kitchen facilities. And storing cars and motorbikes in premises intended for the serving of food.'

Camilla and Alice both regret serving that forlorn Hell's Angel whose arthritis made it hard for him to ride his chopper any more. When he had finished his meal they presented him with him a brand-new silver Harley Davidson that was self-balancing and uncrashable and he left happy, and at high speed, smashing through their front windows in a most spectacular manner.

'Please, I'm begging you, reverse your decision,' Alice says.

I have known stone walls less obdurate.

'This will be your last week,' Mr Morecambe says.

'You haven't completed your final inspection,' Camilla says carefully.

Mr Morecambe blinks. She has him on the back foot now; this is not a man who likes to leave a stone unturned; especially if there may be insanitary conditions beneath it. 'What's that?' Mr Morecambe asks.

'The basement stock room, you haven't inspected the basement stock room,' Camilla says.'

'You don't have a basement stock room.'

Camilla gestures at a door opposite his table.

'Ah.' He frowns, puzzled he hadn't noticed that before.

'You may as well complete the job you've started,' Camilla says cheerfully.

Mr Morecambe finishes his toast. He finishes his tea. He gets up and strides across the cafe and opens the door.

'The light switch is on the right,' Alice calls out.

'The smell in here is awful,' he says, stepping in. Then Alice slams the door shut behind him. She turns the key that is now in the lock.

A moment passes and then there is a terrible banging on the door, loud enough to wake the dead. There is a great deal of shouting too. Very loud shouting. Very loud sweary threatening shouting.

Alice is pale; she fears that this isn't going to work.

Camilla goes behind the counter and comes back with a carving knife. Left behind from the time when they served Mr Morecambe his sirloin steak.

'You can't be serious,' says Alice.

More banging. More shouting. Then the banging stops.

'He's about to use his phone, open the door,' says Camilla, holding the knife two-handed in front of her like someone who has never before used a knife to kill a man. Alice takes a step towards the door.

The door vanishes.

Camilla and Alice share a look.

In 58 Westwood Street Don is going mad.

You're too good for her. She's just a fat old tart.

Are you listening to me?

Listen to me. Don. It's rude not to listen, did you know that? So don't ignore me you cunt.

You're a worthless piece of shit. She's worth ten of you.

I love you, Don.

I never loved you, Don..

Go on, take her, with my blessing, take her to bed and fuck her fat ugly body and stick your tiny warty cock up her loose fanny. Why don't you? Why don't you do that Don?

What kind of man are you?

You were never any good in bed!

Oh I love you Don I miss you you have no idea how terrible it is for me the way I am the state I am in the way I am the state I am in the way I am the state I am in it never ends the state I am in always and forever how can you bear leaving me in all this

Just ignore me. I'm bitter. It's what happens to

What have you done with our garden Don? What have you done? My beautiful lawn? My flowers, my herb beds, my shrubs. Look at it now, just look at it. A glass tree on top of a glass lake and every night the wind makes it tinkle and I can't sleep if I could sleep before I couldn't sleep now with that infernal bloody racket you're not going out in that jacket are you tuck your shirt in you need a haircut you

Oh Don. I'm in pain. I think this is hell.

Did you hear me? I'm in hell.

I'm in hell.

I'm in hell.

Why don't you say anything? Don't you care that I'm in hell? You say you love me, you pretended for all those years you loved me but that was all lies and piss and wind and lies and flurry and slurry and deceit and

I always fancied your brother more than I fancied you I think I married the wrong brother

PAY ATTENTION!

Don't pretend to be asleep you bastard I know you're not.

That's right, make yourself a cup of tea, have some toast, there's some rat poison in the shed why don't you put that in your tea Don that would serve you

What's wrong Don, why are you red in the face, can't you shit? I did warn you those big meals are not good for you maybe you should eat some bran oh god you look ridiculous puffing and straining away it's not going to come out you know you stupid you think this is hard you should have had a fucking baby like I did if you think shitting out a great big stool through your shrunken arse is painful you should have felt what it was like when I puffed and strained and my labia ripped and the midwife pulled out my beautiful lovely baby and he was dead, dead, dead, how do you think that felt, and don't tell me it was hard for you too, I don't believe you, it's never hard for men, men like you, you just drift though life, my baby was dead, our baby was dead, and I've looked for it, I've looked for its soul, our baby's soul, out there in the morass and the shit of what we call the spirit world, and there are many of us, souls and spirits and left behind remnants and I looked for my baby I thought how hard could it be to find a baby in the great something of a something that we call a spirit world even though it's not a world it's just a something something and a something, how hard can it be to find a baby Don, well let me tell you because you're too stupid to work it out, I can tell you, it's not hard at all because I looked and I listened for the sound of a baby and then I found it and do you know what I found? I found a baby, not our baby, but a baby, the spirit of a baby, the soul of a baby, not fully formed and not able to think as we do, as we grown up spirits do, but there it was and do you know what it was, Don, it was sad, and do you know what else Don, it wasn't alone, it wasn't a baby, it wasn't our baby, it wasn't several babies, it wasn't many babies it was MILLIONS OF FUCKING BABIES ALL OF THEM DEAD AND ALL OF THEM SAD!

She's after your money Don don't trust her

That shirt doesn't go with that jacket Don how can you not know that? How stupid are you?

I love you Don and I want you to cherish my memory and I want you to remember all the good times like that time we went driving in Scotland and got lost and started laughing and couldn't stop laughing and a Scottish man had to give us directions but we couldn't understand a word he was saying so we drove on then we had to stop in a lay-by and started laughing again, do you remember that Don? Do you remember? You don't remember do you? You don't remember because you don't think about me any more? Is that it? You've forgotten me. All you can think about is your fancy woman and you're not really planning to take your clothes off when you go to bed with that slut, are you, not with your fat tummy and your varicose veins and the hairs in your nostrils and those blotches on your bald head? Take pity on the poor woman she doesn't deserve THAT

But don't forget, I love you Don

Please don't abandon me

Please don't forget me.

And don't fall asleep when I am talking to you. Don? Don? Don?

WAKE UP!

'I don't understand, love,' says Megan. 'I thought we were, you know, getting on so well.'

'We are,' Don says.

Don is wearing a shirt that goes perfectly well with his jacket and his new shoes that pinch his toes but aren't muddy and worn like his old shoes.

'Surely we can still - ' Megan says.

'No,' says Don.

'For a chat and -'

'No.'

'Are you angry with me, Don?'

'No.'

'What then?'

She reaches out a hand. He doesn't flinch so she carries on the gesture, and she touches his arm. Her hand on his arm sends shudders of pleasure through his body.

'It's me, not you,' Don says bluffly.

'That's bullshit. That's what a teenager says when he dumps his dimwit girlfriend. Don't give me that, Don. I'm a grown woman. I've grown two grown up children from seed, that's how grown up I am. What have I done wrong?' Megan says.

'No it is me,' Don says. 'I'm haunted you see. I told you about the ghosts. The voices. The voice of – my wife. Marie. I hear her all the time now, and I miss her so much. I owe it to her memory to - '

'Don't give me that, Don. I know about Marie. You've told me all about Marie. She was a wonderful woman and I know she would want you to be happy, now that she's gone. Happy with someone else. With me.'

Smooth talking bitch, murmurs the ghost of Don's dead wife.

'Let's just call it a day, eh? It's been champion, like. But now it's over,' Don says.

'I've been "champion" have I? Well that's good to hear,' says Megan bitterly.

Leave him alone you toxic old cow.

'I'm fond of you. I will always think of you fondly. Let's leave it at that,' Don says.

'Well,' says Megan. 'If you say so, Don.'

'I do.'

Megan looks ahead to a life without Don; and decides she can endure it.

'Well, I'll be seeing you then,' she says.

When she has gone Don's house is eerily quiet. Even the other ghosts, the railways navvies and the servant women and the family who lived here all through the Second World War, even they are silent. And Don listens for the voice of Marie but he hears nothing.

He goes to make a cup of tea.

It's for the best, a voice whispers, as if from another universe.

Don doesn't reply.

Isn't it, Don?

It's just the two of us now, Don.

Together at last.

We can be happy now, Don.

Don?

Don?

Don?

He's back, the brown-skinned man is back, and he only has eyes for Shona. He's creeping her out to be honest. But she has a taste for good champagne now, so when the set is over, she joins him for a drink or two.

'That was good,' he says.

'No one liked the bhangra,' Shona says.

'That was the Indian song?' the Bogman asks.

'It was.'

'I liked it.'

He liked it because she sang it.

'You could go far,' he says.

'We're hoping to get a record deal,' Shona says. 'Maybe do a tour.'

'I could help with that,' the Bogman says.

'You're a big shot music promoter?' Shona says, sceptically.

'No.' The Bogman laughs, the first time she has ever heard him laugh. 'I am not. I am a man who lives in the woods, I live in a shed. I am a big shot nothing. Not any more. But I can help you.'

'How?'

He shrugs. The way of the world never changes.

'Money. For the tour. For a manager. For a publicist. Every band needs a publicist, I've done my research,' the Bogman says.

Sugar daddy. There it is.

'How much money?' Shona asks.

'As much as you need.'

'It takes millions to launch a new band.' Total bullshit but she's winging it.

'I have millions,' the Bogman says. As well as the cash in the woods and in his private bank account, he has access to the offshore accounts he set up in his heyday as a gangster. The money is there, but he has no need of it because he is a pagan man who lives in the woods. He doesn't, he has realised, need anything else.

'And what's the in return?' Shona asks.

'Sorry?' the Bogman says.

'You give me money, what do I do in return?'

'Nothing,' he says gently.

'Nothing at all?'

He takes her hand and puts it on his crotch. She is shocked but doesn't resist.

'What do you feel?' the Bogman asks.

'Nothing much,' she admits.

He lets go of her hand. 'I have no desires left,' he tells her. 'No lust. No rage. Once I was a great man. I owned the casino in Westwood, did you know that? In theory I still do. I owned the pizza restaurant in Treacherous Avenue. I own a row of listed houses in Despond Lane. I have a Swiss bank account. I had enemies. I had everything a man like me should have, money, status, and people he hates, and once I would have counted that as wealth. But no more.   All I want is to help you. And listen to you sing. I don't want sex. I don't want flattery. You're not my whore. I'm not your pimp. All those things you fear, you do not need to fear them. But I will make all your dreams come true whatever they are and in return all I ask is for you to sing as you do because that is the only thing that makes my heart beat faster. Because you are an angel, you are an inspiration, you are the greatest singer I have ever heard and I have heard songs sung by the greatest singers in the land at solstice dawn at Avebury and you are better by far than they.   That's the deal. Do you accept?

Shona is a pragmatist.   Fame, fortune, flattery, and she doesn't even have to fuck the ugly bastard - what's not to like?

But then her phone starts buzzing in that annoying way they do when the ringtone is turned off. And as she considers the Bogman's officer, she lifts her phone and checks the message with a swift glance. She utters a small gasp, and puts the phone face down on the table. And then she meets the Bogman's gaze. She stares deep into his blank and soulless blue eyes.

'No,' she says.

'You're reaching,' says Detective Inspector MacAlister. 'This killing didn't even take place in Westwood.' He gives DC Billy Armstrong his strongest sceptical gaze. But Billy digs in.

'Even so, there are connections, guv. Bradshaw used to teach in Westwood, he worked in an office there, he went to pubs there. The circs in both cases are well weird. I'm thinking, same perp,' Billy says, and then he looks around the room to gather some moral support for his argument..

Billy has been seconded from Streatham CID to join the Murder Squad investigating the death of Benjamin Bradshaw, a former music teacher. Witnesses reported a naked brown man pursuing the ex-teacher as he cycled home and the body was heavily mutilated. If it weren't for the wallet left at the scene, identifying the corpse would have been a major challenge.

'The killing in the park was a mugging, this was different,' MacAlister says.

'Even so, what Billy is saying makes sense to me, I'd go for that,' says DS Arnold.

They are in the temporary incident room in the Anerley Church Hall. None of them have the balls to go back to the Westwood nick, which gave them nightmares.

'One body was flayed, the other had his clothes stolen,' MacAlister says, persisting.

'Both brutal killings though, committed by someone who is extraordinarily strong,' Billy says.

'One in the woods, one in the street,' says MacAlister. But he is just playing devil's advocate by now. He too is favouring the serial killer hypothesis.

'Are we really looking for an Asian killer?' asks DC Patel.

'Brown skinned is what we were told. Naked. Muscular. The neighbour got a good look, I asked again and again if he was Pakistani, or Indian, and all she would say is brown-skinned,' says DS Arnold.

'Lots of people are brown skinned. He could be from Mauritius, Burma, anywhere where there's sun,' says DC Tanqueray.

'One witness estimates the bike was doing fifty miles an hour down the hill and the brown-skinned man was running after it and keeping up,' says DC Patel.

'Westwood magic,' says DI MacAlister. He doesn't like that there is such a thing, but he knows there is.

'Pixie, goblin, dryad?' says DC Marilyn Blaine, who is a reader of fantasy novels.

'Fuck off,' says DI MacAlister.

'Who can tell in this godforsaken place?' says Billy. 'But, back in the real world, there's another possible lead.'

He hesitates.

'Go on lad,' says DI MacAlister.

'The Mortons killed my brother, you all know that,' Billy says.

'We don't know it for certain but go on,' DI MacAlister says.

'There are stories – rumours – legends if you like – that my brother was working with a brown-skinned man. And it was the brown-skinned man who financed my brother's casino.'

'We've investigated all that,' says DI MacAlister, who led the enquiry into the London Heights massacre. 'We've identified no such man, it was Kane who signed the casino deeds, it's all just hearsay and bullshit. We deal with facts, not legends, son.'

'But what if - ' Billy begins to say, then stops.

'What if what?' DI MacAlister says.

There's a silence. Billy is nervous. He is convinced he has cracked the case but he doesn't want to make a fool of himself in front of his colleagues.

'What if there's a link to a previous MisPer case?' Billy says.

'Which MisPer case?' asks DI MacAlister.

'Spring last year a man called George McBride found a body in a house in Sylvan Way. It was taken to the mortuary and there it vanished. It was the body of a brown-skinned man,' Billy says.

'What are you suggesting, Billy? That the body came to life?' DI McAlister says.

'Stranger things have happened,' says Billy, 'in Westwood.'

DI MacAlister frowns.

'No one can deny that,' he says, reluctantly.

'Do you have a photo?' DC Patel asks.

Billy does. He takes out the mortuary photograph of the Bogman that he had sourced the day before and he passes it around. He also emails the scanned version to all his colleagues on his smartphone.

'This is not a person, this is a fucking mummy,' says DC Blaine.

'Technically yes,' says Billy. 'Mummified in a peat bog, buried for millennia, dug up by a dodgy builder called McBride. My brother,' Billy takes a nervous gulp but he's in too far now, he can't go back: 'told my mother once, about the man he was working with. A man who was a scary murderous killer and who had astonishing powers and super-strength. He called him the Bogman.'

Chapter 24

Kane is searching the Horniman Woods for the third time that day.

He has also searched the woodland areas of the Old Park and the New Park and the several smaller woodlands scattered around Westwood. He has broken into the casino and checked the rooms on the top floor which used to be the Bogman's apartment, but they are now used as a lap dancing space with benefits, including a bed and a jacuzzi. He has walked along South Norwood Lakes and through the Country Park and now he has returned to Horniman Woods. And he has finally discovered a pocket of land that can only be reached via an overgrown path, but which seems to extend for miles. This is the remotest and least used woodland area in Westwood and Kane is confident this is where the Bogman will be hiding.

You bastard, where are you? he thinks.

Kane feels alone and frightened. He has no friends. He is a dead man walking and the only person he can turn to is another dead man walking.

He soon gets lost. It's very easy to lose your sense of direction in a wood with such a dense canopy. Howler monkeys inhabit the top branches of the trees; these are another of the creatures which materialised one day here in Westwood, together with the anacondas, the cheetahs and the white Bengal tiger, and they make a ferocious racket. There are palm trees too in this part of the Great West Wood. There is a baobab tree with a absurdly large trunk. And there is sawdust. Little specks of it, but it's all the clue he needs.

And so Kane follows the trail left by trees that have been sawn into planks by the Bogman. And that is how he finds the shed in the woods where the Bogman now lives.

It is a remarkable construction. Impressive, without a doubt, but far from elegant. There is not a single level line. It is wonky to the side, wonky upwards, and there are no windows. But it's built on two storeys and there is a rope ladder on the outside leading to the higher level. You could see all this and not see it because the wooden planks blend with the wood of the surrounding forest. But once seen it cannot be forgotten.

Kane stands at a safe distance and calls the Bogman's name. His true name, his pagan name, which I know but cannot spell. And he waits.

After a while he feels a movement of air beside him and when he looks, a naked brown-skinned man is there. Muscular. Taut. Powerful. Kane can smell his flesh. It is like the smell of old compost. In his previous incarnation the Bogman had no aroma, he was desiccated and bone dry. Now he is a moist mummy with visible genitals. It is weird. Even Kane, who has just risen from the dead, is psyched out by it.

'Be my guest,' says the Bogman, beckoning, and Kane nods.

I must be desperate, thinks Kane. And he is.

Kane is led inside the shed and invited to sit on a bench carved out of an oak stump. Once Kane is sitting the Bogman leaves the shed and when he returns he is carrying a dead deer. He starts a fire and cooks it in front of Kane and the two of them eat meat off skewers, washed down with wine from Aldi.

The Bogman cannot taste any of this and he will have to shit his mouthfuls of deer out in their entirety later on. But he likes to observe the proprieties.

'I am sorry you were killed,' the Bogman says.

He is not sorry that Kane was killed. But he says it anyway.

'Me too,' says Kane.

That exchange lasts them nearly two hours.

'How are you alive?' the Bogman asks.

'Don't know. You?'

'I don't know.'

That is all there is to be said on that matter.

'I went to see my mother,' Kane says. 'It didn't go well.'

'Why?' the Bogman asks.

It's true, it didn't go well.

'How could you how could you how COULD you?' Kane had shouted and Tanya had wept. She didn't say a word, she just wept.

'Why do you think? ' Kane says. 'What happened that day, it was a trap. An ambush.'

'I know,' the Bogman says.

'And she was in on it. She betrayed me.

'That makes sense.'

'I'm guessing they threatened her. Or maybe not her, her children. Probably Ray. That's the baby, the newest one. They would have said something like, we'll kill your baby if you don't bring us your son. So she betrayed me,' Kane says.

'Mothers have to make such choices,' the Bogman says.

Kane's face is full of rage.

'No they don't! That's just – that's just - she betrayed me,' Kane says, bitterly.

'You betrayed her first,' the Bogman says.

'How!' says Kane.

The Bogman says nothing.

Kane thinks about his life of crime. His murders. His sins. His neglect of his family, and his open scorn for his mother's way of life.

'I gave her money. Every week, and a bonus payment on Mother's Day,' Kane says.

The Bogman grunts, unimpressed.

'My mother was murdered,' the Bogman says. 'By my father and brothers and sisters.'

'Yes you told me. That must have been – upsetting,' Kane says.

'It was.'

Another silence descends.

Kane wonders about the life this man has lived; so many aeons ago.

'Why are you here?' the Bogman asks.

Kane is remembering the day when he became one of Man Dem.

He remembers a twelve-year-old thug holding a gun to his head, and telling him his life as a civilian was over, he was one of them now. Kane didn't know if the gun was loaded but he was still shitting himself .

'I ain't doing it,' Kane had said that day. 'I ain't working with you cunts.'

'You're doing it,' the twelve-year-old had said. 'You'll do it, or we'll do your sister.'

'You fucking dare!'

'You have to do as you're told, cunt. Those are the rules.'

'Fuck off.'

'Your sister. Your sister. Your fucking sister! Are you stupid or what?'

'You wouldn't!'

'You'll do what you tell you to do because you're nothing, right?'

Kane had never felt so pathetic.

'I'm nothing, right,' Kane had sobbed. 'I'm nothing.'

So Kane had joined Man Dem and the shotters still did his sister and Kane was powerless to do anything about it.

*I'm **not** nothing*, Kane is thinking now, as he sits there with the Bogman, trying to make sense of his life. *I'm something. I'm something! I **can't** be nothing!*

The Bogman waits.

He can't read minds in the way that I can but he knows exactly what is going through Kane's mind.

Hate is going through Kane's mind.

But Kane chooses his words carefully. He takes it a step at a time. 'I wanted to see you.'

'Yes but why?' the Bogman asks.

'Because you're my friend,' Kane says.

'I'm not, so why?' the Bogman says.

'We've been through so much together.'

'Again, why?'

'I want to take revenge.'

'And I do not.'

The Bogman drains his glass of wine. Then he steps outside the shed. He walks until he finds a tree far from his shed. He shits and pisses, until his stomach and bladder are no longer uncomfortably full. He wipes himself with a leaf and returns.

Half an hour has elapsed. Kane has finished eating. He knows better than to leave.

'Look what they did to you,' Kane says. 'The Mortons. They kicked your arse, peat man.'

'Yes indeed. They bested me,' the Bogman says calmly.

Kane tries to stir the Bogman's rage. 'They trashed you,' he says. 'They ate you up and shat you out and made you eat the pieces!'

The Bogman remains impassive.

'Not so. They merely severed my body into many small parts,' the Bogman says.

'Don't you want to get back at them? Make them eat *your* shit?' Kane says.

'No,' says the Bogman.

Kane sighs. He tries the direct approach.

'I want the casino,' says Kane. 'It's all I've ever had, I want it back.'

'Who has it?' the Bogman asks.

'They do. The Mortons.'

'The deeds are in your name,' says the Bogman. 'Legally it's yours.'

'The law won't help me,' Kane says.

'Then what will you do?' the Bogman asks.

'I want you to help me,' Kane says.

'Why should I do that?' the Bogman asks.

Kane can't think of a reason.

'Why not?' he says, eventually.

That's a good enough for the Bogman.

Jack is on the train from Southampton.

His body aches but he is used to that. He misses Shak. He is not used to that.

For many months now he has been sharing a house with Shakil in Southampton. Shak went go to college every day while Jack worked as a chef in a café. He has a knack for making paninis and homemade baguettes. He also does a good line in Jamaican patties and other Caribbean meals. Jack is a careful and skilful cook and he doesn't need his cane to walk around the kitchen. At the end of every shift he is exhausted and has to be poured into an Uber but that's a small price to pay.

And in the evening he cooks dinner for everyone in the house. Shak and all his mates love it. There's a lot of Uni talk, a lot of in jokes, but Jack fits right in.

On the weekends Jack and Shak walk along the beach and look at the sea. For Jack the sea is grey and the clouds are grey; and Shak is not brown-skinned, he is just a darker shade of grey than his white mates. But at least Jack can see him now, at least most of the time.

But occasionally when Shak has said something really cute, or hilarious, he vanishes. And Jack has to figure out where he is from the sound of his voice and his breathing.

Shak has bought a car, a less flashy car than his London Porsche, and he's put Jack on his insurance so Jack can be the designated driver when they go to pubs. Shak's tee-totalism didn't survive Freshers Week and he likes a drink now. And it's handy to have someone who can drive them back from remote country pubs.

When Shak brings lovers home Jack can hear the noise of lovemaking through the walls. But it doesn't bother him. He's pleased for his mate. Sometimes he rates Shak's conquests on a scale of 1 to 10 and posts the results on the fridge. Shak thinks that is hilarious.

But now Jack is going home to save his parents' marriage.

The Bogman thinks hard about what he will do next.

Kane's plight has not in any way touched his heart. But he admires the fact that Kane knows what he wants and will stop at nothing to achieve it. The Bogman respects that, the clarity of purpose, the depth of desire. He himself has no clarity and no desire. And Kane's mission will he hopes give him a momentary sense of purpose.

The Bogman has forsworn violence but now he thinks about it, he does not know why.

And so the Bogman goes to work.

First he catches a train into town and purchases new clothes. There's so much you can buy locally but for really good threads Saville Row and Selfridges in Oxford Street are the places to go. So the Bogman has a makeover. Three new suits, new shoes, a Rolex watch, a gold ring, and a gold bracelet. Many men these days shy away from wearing bracelets but in his day, all men wore them.

He also checks into his private bank and withdraws a large sum in cash in a lockable metal briefcase, which the bank provides. He is given the usual warnings about taking care on his homeward journey. But it's unlikely that anyone would try to mug the Bogman and if they did, they are liable to lose one or both of their hands.

That evening the Bogman puts on one of his new suits and goes to the casino as a whale - which is casino jargon for a big spender. And he loses it all, nearly a hundred grand on the roulette table. And once he is sure he has the attention of everyone watching him on the CCTV, he approaches Cynthia, the pit boss.

'Is it really you?' she whispers.

'I've put on a bit of weight,' he says.

'Kane is dead,' she says.

He shrugs, not bothering to contradict her.

'Tell your bosses I want to meet,' the Bogman says.

The Bogman leaves. He is pursued covertly by three of the bouncers from the casino. They are well trained too, he almost doesn't notice them. He gets on a bus and they follow him by car. He gets off the bus at the Glade pub and he walks towards the entrance to the Horniman Woods. That's when they make their move.

When he has killed them, without spilling any blood, he takes off his shoes and his trousers and his jacket and packs them carefully in his metal briefcase, the case that used to be full of money. Then he makes his way through the woods to his shed and spends the night there.

In the morning more killers come for him. The Bogman had lured his followers the night before almost to the entrance to the Woods, and they would have phoned in that location before making a move. So to guess where he is living now is not that much of a reach.

Soon after dawn the Bogman hears the sound of drones above the treeline and that's how his enemies find his shed.

There are twelve of them in all, six gunmen, six samurai swordsmen as before. But the Bogman is not caught off guard this time. He watches them from his tree canopy when they arrive. He observes them calmly when they machine gun his shed and set fire to it. He watches the billowing smoke with something close to regret but he bides his time. And when they give up and start walking back home, he leaps out of the trees like a sinner's guilt and kills them all.

Later he goes into town again and goes to his private bank again and takes out a case of money, again. Then that evening he goes to the casino again and loses it all on the roulette table. Again. Effectively he is paying the Mortons to meet him, and he knows that sooner or later they will.

It's Cynthia who makes the move. She gives him a note with a time and a Zoom code. A virtual meeting.

'I don't have a computer,' the Bogman says.

So on Cynthia's orders the lap dancers are moved out of the top floor apartment and the Bogman returns home. He has two computers and full video conferencing facilities up there, together with a wardrobe full of suits that no longer fit, because they date from the days when he had no flesh on his bones. But the Bogman makes some calls and more suits are delivered. After which the Bogman has a bubble bath. Then, in his towelling robe, he watches daytime TV.

At the designated time he has the video conference with Dave and Gruff and Daisy Morton and he explains his terms. Set out in Gallery View on his computer screen the three Mortons smile politely as the Bogman talks. Then they mute him for a while and discuss the deal animatedly.

'Fucking bastard,' says Dave.

'Let's kill him,' says Gruff.

'Are you joking?' says Daisy. 'I mean, seriously, are you -

'

'We can't let this cunt outcunt us!' says Dave.

'Too cunting right!' says Gruff.

The Bogman can lipread; he is trying not to smile.

'Jesus! Let's face facts, boys,' says Daisy. 'This bastard is Vlad the fucking Impaler and he cannot be killed. Let's deal.' And her uncles shout and swear for a while and then they give in.

And so they unmute the Bogman and they agree to his terms.

The terms are these:

The Bogman will live in the casino.

Kane will have sole control of the casino but will give the Mortons a sizeable share of the profits.

And regardless of customer feedback there will be a new floorshow every night, Las Vegas style. And the headline act will be Shona and the Two Others.

In return for this deal, the Bogman agrees not to kill the Mortons, their children, their spouses or (in Daisy's case) lovers, their friends, their acquaintances, and their neighbours.

'We never wanted any trouble,' lies Dave Morton.

'All the money from the brothels, the drugs, all your other businesses, we want no share of that,' the Bogman says.

'We can agree to those terms,' says Dave.

'Yes, agreed,' says Gruff.

'I'm in,' says Daisy and that reminds the Bogman of how his business partner had once lost his heart to this conniving bitch.

'Kane bears no hard feelings,' the Bogman says.

'I feel bad about what I did,' Daisy Morton says. But her pretty smiling face belies her words.

Jack has called for a family meeting to discuss the state of the McBride marriage.

Grandpa Maybe is there and so is Uncle Mickey, sat in matching armchairs in the living room of the McBride family home in 44 Westwood Street. Hilary is on the sofa next to Shona, and Jack and George McBride are standing up, facing them all. Jack is leaning lightly on his stick, the ringmaster of this event.

'Thank you all for coming to this, well, emergency family meeting,' says Jack.

His tone is calm and authoritative. Six months ago he was a total fuck up. Now he's head of the family.

'Dad has something to say to us all,' Jack says.

'Not to everyone,' says George firmly. 'Just to Hilary. Can the rest of you just bugger off?'

'Anything you have to say to me,' says Hilary, 'you can say to everyone.'

George is stumped by that. He is surrounded by all his nearest and dearest, and clearly is not relishing the experience.

'I thought it would be cathartic to do it this way,' says Jack. 'Like family therapy.'

I suspect that if you had punched George in the solar plexus, it would have hurt less.

'Do you want to sit down, Jack?' Shona asks.

'I'm good.'

'Because if you want a chair, Uncle Mickey could get off his fucking arse.'

'Hey, I'm not a well man,' Mickey says. He has developed mild pneumonia after a night sleeping in the park after a Wild Man event, when he was unable to find his way home.

I want to fucking die, Mickey is thinking.

'Jack and I have had a little chat,' George says.

Not so fucking loud, Mickey is thinking.

'Tell everyone what you told me,' Jack says.

'Your mum and I are going through a rough patch,' George says.

'No I'm not,' says Hilary. 'I've never been happier. We love being together, don't we, Bobby?' And she pats her granddad on the arm.

'I have never known you to be so devil-may-care,' Grandpa Maybe says, smiling.

Shona, you remind me so much of Shona, Grandpa Maybe is thinking. *My lovely Shona Mirabelle.*

'Your place is home, here, with me,' George says firmly.

'That's not what we rehearsed,' Jack tells him.

I can do this I can do this I can do this! Jack is thinking.

George steels himself. 'Hilary, I've been a selfish fool, please forgive me.'

'Try it again with a bit less I'm a fucking liar in your tone,' Jack says.

'Hilary, I've been a selfish fool, please forgive me,' George says.

Jack shrugs; no difference.

'No,' says Hilary.

'Ah come on,' says George.

'I'm tired of forgiving,' says Hilary.

'But I love you,' says George slyly.

'No more forgiving. No more bullshit. No more lies,' says Hilary.

'That doesn't leave much to hold a marriage together,' Shona says, cattily.

I try to read Hilary's thoughts; but she is not thinking anything, she is just remembering an intimate encounter with a naked man.

'I had a one night stand last week,' says Hilary. 'I went home with a man and we had sex. His name was Glenroy.'

All eyes are on Hilary. Even Jack is shocked at this candour, though candour was the purpose of the exercise.

'Ah then we're even,' says George, quick as a flash.

'No we're not even,' Hilary says.

'I had an affair, you had an affair, we're even.' He stands proud. This is bloke logic and to him it seems irrefutable

'You told a lie, I didn't tell a lie, game set and match to me,' Hilary says.

'You slept with another man!' George shouts, in case rage will work better for him.

'No I didn't,' Hilary says.

'You just said you did,' George says.

'This is really embarrassing,' says Shona, smiling.

Uncle Mickey is drifting, shamefully, off to sleep.

'Family therapy can be painful, sometimes. It has to be, in order to work,' says Jack. 'I learned a lot about therapy when I was, ah, in therapy.'

'I did not,' Hilary says. 'Sleep with a man. I made love to a man, I sucked his cock, he did nice things to me, down there, though I don't like saying that word, and when he couldn't do it any more I got up and went home.'

That wakes Mickey up; though not for long.

'She was indeed very cheery, that night,' Grandpa Maybe says.

'You did what?' George is aghast.

'Missionary, then me on top, plus two sorts of oral,' Hilary says, as if she is quoting a cake recipe.

'Too much information,' says Jack.

Jack and Shona share a young people grin.

'You said we should tell the truth,' says Hilary. And Hilary fixes her son with a hard stare.

Then she looks back at George. 'You can stay, if you want.'

'What? I can stay? Here? In this house? With you?' he says, somewhat aggressively.

'Yes,' says Hilary.

'How do you make that out? It's my house, don't forget,' says George.

The mood abruptly turns toxic.

Grandpa Maybe shakes his head at George's blunder, more in pity than in sorrow.

'No you're wrong there. It's my house,' Hilary says.

'It's bloody not!' George say, sternly. He is a man who knows how to flatter, but also how to intimidate. In short, he knows how to get his way.

'It is or you're out on your ear.' She looks at her husband, fearlessly. Seeing him, seeing right through him, in a way that chills his blood.

Grandpa Maybe studies his grandson-in-law George carefully. If Hilary asked him to, he would stab this man to death.

But there's no need. George does a swift U-turn.

'It is, of course it is.' He smiles at her insincerely. 'And it's generous of you to let me stay in the house which I, um, bought and paid for.'

'I think so too,' says Hilary, sharply.

Shona is unhappy. She casts a sad look at her mother. What happened to true love? her eyes are saying.

And at the same time, her thoughts are saying: *Ditch him! Ditch the bastard!*

But the words she speaks are gentle: 'Do you love him, mum?' Shona asks.

Hilary has to think hard about that.

Do I love him? she thinks.

What the hell does 'love' mean? she thinks.

I want more than this for my daughter, and for Jack, she thinks. *Much more than I have ever had.*

George is increasingly unhappy. He feels he has been put on the spot. This is no way for a man to be treated, he feels. But he knows enough to keep his anger in check.

Tread carefully, you cunt, he tells himself. *Don't fuck this one up.*

'Look, my love, I did things I shouldn't have done,' George says slowly. 'I shouldn't have done that. Done those things I shouldn't have done, I mean. And I hope you can find it in your heart to forgive me.'

'Well I can't,' Hilary says.

'Well then. If you can't forgive me, I don't know what to say,' George says.

'Say you'll stop telling me lies,' Hilary says.

'I can't do that,' says George.

That mightily amuses Grandpa Maybe.

Jack feels that they are getting somewhere; he just doesn't know where.

Shona is looking at Jack, and thinking; he looks so *happy.*

'You can't stop telling lies?' says Hilary, incredulously.

George backtracks. 'Well obviously I can. And I will. Trust me, have me back, and I'll never lie to you again,' he lies.

Hilary sighs.

She looks around this room, at her favourite things, the furniture she chose and arranged, her family. And she decides, she likes it here. No matter what, this is her home; that's what she is thinking.

She also remembers the young George dancing with his shirt off to the radio, in Grandpa Maybe's cold damp house. She remembers his trick of jumping off the bed after sex and singing Sex Bomb to her when they are both naked. She remembers him doing his Smitty from Gavin and Stacey routine in an Indian restaurant that time, when they were out with the Madisons and the Browns, shouting it all so loudly that the staff were wetting themselves laughing: 'Pete have you thought about my bhunas? They're my bhunas, you want a bhuna order a bhuna, that's why I've ordered two bhunas!'

Comedy gold; or so she and I both felt.

And she remembers George being there, just being there, when she was reading one of her thrillers in the living room. Or when she was doing the garden, huffing and puffing on her knees weeding while he was smoking his fags offering praise and advice. She remembers him telling her filthy jokes, really filthy jokes, when she was doing the ironing. Jokes which amused her so much she burned his shirts but he never minded.

'So?' asks George. 'Are you staying?'

Hilary says nothing.

She hasn't decided yet.

She just can't decide.

Suddenly George takes charge.

'Get out,' George says to Shona. 'And you, get out,' he says to Grandpa Maybe. 'And you, leave us alone,' he says to Jack. 'And you, fuck off,' he says to Uncle Mickey. 'I don't know what you're even doing here. I need to talk to my wife, we got some catching up to do.'

When the room is cleared George is alone and defenceless.

'That was weird,' he says.

'I enjoyed it,' Hilary says.

'I don't want to lose you,' says George. 'I'd be lonely and I'd drink too much without you. That's why I don't want you to leave me.'

Hilary considers the feebleness of those words.

'Fair enough,' she says, eventually. 'And the fact is, I'm used to you, George. You're decent company and you make me laugh.'

They've spent a lifetime together these two. And I know from experience, for I am a very ancient god, how much habit matters.

'And I'll settle for that,' Hilary says. 'I'm used to you, and that'll do for me.'

She gives him a look; your turn.

'And I'll settle for you,' George says.

'No you'll be lucky to have me, you dolt,' Hilary scolds him.

'That's what I meant, I'd be lucky to have you,' George says hastily.

And Hilary nods; job done.

'What'll we tell the kids?' Hilary asks, pragmatically.

George gives that a moment's thought.

'Tell them you broke down and cried,' says George, with a dawning smile. 'You sobbed in my arms, and I sobbed too. And then I came to my senses, like the damn fool I am. And then we kissed and it was happy ever after. That's what happens in the movies. They'll understand that. They won't understand this.'

He means, the *this* that they are doing. Settling for second best, because it's familiar.

'You want me to lie to our children?' Hilary asks.

'Or I'll do it if you like?' George says, cheerfully.

Outside the room, in the hall, Jack is listening at the door. He has heard every word of this exchange. His heart is like a stone.

This is not what he wanted.

This is not what he wanted at all.

That night Shona sings in Kane's casino and the Bogman pays for drinks on the house for everyone there.

When the barman announces the round there is a raucous cheer and the Bogman gives a gracious wave to all his gamblers.   His kingly wave. He is beautifully dressed in a white Saville Row suit that is the perfect counterpoint to his dogturd-coloured skin.

They're a tough crowd, this lot; obsessed with their bets and seduced by the seedy glamour of the place. And for four or five songs in a row Shona can barely hear the hi-hats through the chatter and the sound of the roll of the roulette wheel and the clatter of dice. But by the time Shona sings 'Cry Me a River,' with high notes that shake the beard of the plaster Noah on the cornice of the Casino Hall, she has them all under her spell.

'I'll cry,' she sings, 'a river over you.'

Two days later the Mortons make their move.

Daisy as always is the mastermind; her uncles do the legwork. Deals are done.   Hitmen with a background in special forces combat are hired. A new generation of middle class samurai warriors with jobs in the City and fantasies of being Jet Li are given the word; their sacrifice is needed.

And so twelve assassins are despatched to the Casino where they break in at the dead of night. They all wear body armour and night vision helmets, and all carry rifles loaded with armour-piercing shells though some also carry samurai swords. They are confident of success. They begin to tread silently up the stairs, to the Bogman's quarters.

But the Bogman isn't there. He is downstairs in the lobby, watching them. A shadow hiding in shadows, lying in wait as he has done every night since he took over the casino.

While half the cohort of killers are busy yomping up the stairs, he kills the ones who are still in the lobby. And when the ones who were climbing the stairs hear the death rattles of their comrades and come racing down to kill him, he clambers up a service shaft and attacks them from *above*.

As always, the Bogman slays his foes so quickly that even Homer could not write the battle scene.

Cynthia the pit boss is given the job of disposing of the bodies. She takes this assignment, like all her jobs, in her stride.

Then Kane drives the Bogman to the house in North London where Dave Morton lives. The security is formidable but the Bogman has a plan.

'If I'm not back in ten days,' the Bogman tells Kane. 'Run.'

'I didn't want it to come to this,' says Kane bleakly.

The Bogman's mood darkens.

'Don't be so pathetic,' says the Bogman to Kane. 'This is war. This is what we are about.'

Kane nods.

'Yeah I guess,' Kane says.

The Bogman grunts.

'If I'm not back in ten days, run. Or stay and die. I don't give a fuck,' the Bogman says.

'Yes, boss,' says Kane.

Kane drives home alone. His conscience is troubling him, like a cancer eating away at his body from the inside. He knows that both of the Morton brothers will die soon, as the Bogman takes his revenge; and he fears their children and wives and their friends will also die. It seems certain that Daisy will die too and though he hates her, he doesn't want her to die.

He knows, in short, that once unleashed the Bogman cannot be re-leashed. And he loathes himself, his own arrogance and malice, for being the cause of all this. This *horror*.

But what can he do? He wanted to be somebody. And now he is.

For a week the Bogman vanishes from view. He's not in the casino, he's not in the woods. The Mortons' spies can't find him anywhere.

Kane closes down the casino for the duration of this war, claiming there is a problem with the plumbing. Then he books into a B&B and lies low.

In a Zoom conference with his brother Gruff and his sister Daisy, Dave Morton speculates that perhaps the Bogman died of injuries sustained during his mercenaries' attack on him. They were all equipped with guns with explosive bullets; even if the Bogman killed them, he might have been so badly hurt he could not recover. So maybe it's all over now; and they are safe?

'That's really not very fucking likely,' says Daisy, hopelessly. 'Stop clutching at straws Dave.'

'Or he's given up and run away,' suggests Dave.

'Dream on,' says Daisy; bitterly regretting every decision she has ever made.

The Mortons have hired another team of mercenaries, who are on standby; ready to

attack the Bogman when he reappears. And all three Mortons have armed bodyguards and state-of the-art security systems around and in their homes; and they resolve to stay put behind the walls of their respective fortresses. They will go nowhere; and they will see no-one in person except for their bodyguards and the people they share their homes with.

And then they wait.

Meanwhile the Bogman is digging a tunnel underneath Dave Morton's mansion. Under the fence, below the patrolling security guards, well away from the close circuit TV cameras and the infrared sensors. There are seven levels of security around this house; and the guards are well able to deal with any kind of attack from any direction or from above if need be, with a range of portable surface to air missiles available in easy reach.

But the Bogman is *below.*

Like a worm, he burrows his way through a narrow hole without pit props, his body comprised more of London clay than it is of peat.

And after a week of digging he emerges into the inner courtyard of Dave Morton's Romanesque mansion. He breaks through a paving slab with his hard fists and pulls himself up through the hole. It is night. The moon is a crescent. The stars are drowned by the wall lights but still they twinkle. And the Bogman lies on the ground for a few moments, like a mound of sensate soil.

There are no bodyguards stationed here but there are CCTV cameras positioned on all four walls . But when the Bogman moves, he crawls; inching along on the ground so slowly that his movements do not register with the guards who are watching, and the motion sensors are not triggered.

Once he has reached a patch of wall that is below and to one side of a camera, he climbs up the wall using his fingertips as suckers.

Then he breaks into a first floor window with a punch so fast it makes no noise; and he catches all the shards of glass before they can fall and tinkle on the ground.

And once he is inside the house he stands very still and he listens until he hears Dave's distinctive laugh and he follows that sound, through a maze of corridors.

One of Dave's children spots him in a corridor lined with portraits and she runs in fear of him but the Bogman continues on past her at a brisk jog. He runs into the library, and there he sees Dave, who is entertaining two attractive female guests, who it seems have been sharing this house with his wife and kids, and who are currently drinking champagne poured from a giant bottle on the table.

'I am here to kill you,' the Bogman says and the girls laugh, thinking it's a gag.

Dave throws a wine glass at him and it misses and shatters on the wall. The Bogman remains motionless and surveys the room, registering the lavishness of the décor, the value of the paintings on the walls, and the beauty of Dave's two lovers.

While the Bogman is mentally calculating the value of all he sees, Dave moves swiftly and he dashes into his study which is in fact a safe room, with a metal door and unbreakable locks. He slams the door shut behind him and the bolts slide into position. And once he is safe in his fortified safe place, he trips the alarm that will summon his bodyguards and he takes a gun out of a drawer and waits.

After a few minutes he puts down the gun. Because he knows very well this room is impregnable. He knows he is just being paranoid. No one can get to him *here*.

A few moments later the Bogman enters through the wall, punching holes in the reinforced concrete and scattering debris everywhere. Through the haze Dave is able to aim his gun and shoot, sixteen times, at the Bogman's defenceless body.

The bullets penetrate and rip through the Bogman's flesh. But then the Bogman takes five steps forward and catches Dave by the throat and kills him.

The next day the Bogman meets Kane in the lobby of the casino. He is carrying a cardboard box.

Kane has been pacing up and down for some time; almost wearing a pathway into the pattern on the carpet. He is so tense and anxious he looks as if he might explode.

The Bogman places the cardboard box on a table and stands calmly waiting for questions.

'It's done?' asks Kane.

'It's done,' the Bogman says.

'Did you kill them all?' says Kane, his voice shaking.

That was the deal. The irrevocable pledge. The Bogman had promised to kill the Mortons and everyone who was close to them if they dared to defy him. Utter carnage was to ensue. It was a technique the Bogman had perfected many thousands of years ago; you don't just kill the chieftain; you kill the chieftain and then the entire village.

For seven days and nights Kane has not slept because of his waking dreams of multiple murders of mostly innocent people for which he must bear the blame.

'Just one,' says the Bogman.

'Just one?' says Kane.

'Just the main one. The boss. Dave Morton. Just him. No one else'

Despite his supposedly irrevocable pledge, on the night that he killed Dave Morton the Bogman had chosen *not* to kill Dave Morton's wife or his children or his lovers, though he could easily have done so. He did not even kill Dave Morton's bodyguards, not even when they shot bullets into his body; he simply fled the house, running down the stairs and out the front door and leaping over the fence.

He showed mercy, in other words, which is another indication of how much he has changed.

'What's in the box?' says Kane.

'A message,' says the Bogman. And he opens up the box.

Inside the box is Dave Morton's heart.

Later that day, following the Bogman's precise instructions, Kane cuts the heart in two and then he packages both halves of the heart up and he posts the left ventricle to Daisy and the right ventricle to Gruff.

In the box for Daisy, the box which contains the left ventricle of her Uncle Dave's heart, Kane has left a note which says: 'A little reminder of how you broke my heart, Your darling, Kane.' Cheesy but potent.

The message is enough. The Bogman has won. The Mortons are a spent force. And Westwood is his.

Chapter 25

A week later the casino reopens; and Shona is once again being paid five hundred pounds a night by the Bogman to sing at Kane's casino.

It's not an established or prestigious music venue, she knows that being here does not advance her credibility as an artist. But it's good money and the Bogman is a hard man to say no to. She did it once – when she turned down his offer to help her launch her music career. She doesn't dare do it a second time.

Shona knows that the Bogman is a bad man. And she also knows that he murdered Benjamin Bradshaw. That was the message she got on her phone after his offer to help her with her career. It was from Marielle, and it read: *someone just killed your paedo teacher ha*

That's what made her realise she had to get this foul creature out of her life. That's why she had said no to him.

It was a principled and honourable decision; and as is the way of these things, she immediately regretted it. Because after a few weeks without the Bogman in her life, things started getting tough. Money was tight. The record deal didn't happen. Local gigs were drying up. Vishaal and Priya began talking about splitting up the band; or maybe moving to Morocco to be with Hamid again. So when the offer of the job at the Casino came along, Shona didn't think she could afford to turn it down.

And so here she is, every night, singing her heart out to the sound of faites vos jeux.

It's not Vegas but at least she's getting paid.

Cecil has died. It was sudden, and perhaps a blessing. But now he has gone and Don has filled a bin bag with unused dog food and untaken pills and barely chewed dog toys, and dumped it all in the outside wheelie bin.

For a while Don continues to walk around Westwood alone, nagged by the voice of his wife. But eventually he loses heart and now he stays home most of the time.

Hilary has moved back in with George, on a trial basis. And Jack has been acclaimed as the hero of the hour. His Jeremy Kyle stunt was, the family all agree, the coup de théatre that forced George to swallow his pride and beg Hilary to return.

Shona was touched when Hilary told the tale of how she and George had become reconciled. How she had been firm with him and angry with him but then finally she had remembered all the good times and she had wept. And how George had been stubborn and unyielding until she cried and then he remembered how much he loved her. At which point he too broke down and cried, before vowing to be a better person and never to hurt her ever again.

It was all total bollocks but it played well and Shona was delighted that her parents were back together.

Soon after that, Hilary asked Jack if he was planning to go back to Southampton, to be with his pal Shakil.

She said it nicely, making it clear she was happy for him, not judge-y in any way. She didn't even ask him what was really going on, if he is gay, or not gay. Because she genuinely doesn't mind either way, and she didn't want to put him on the spot.

And Jack said yes, he was indeed thinking about going back in a while to be with Shak. And of course they're in touch every day, and every hour sometimes, via their WhatsApp chat. So they're still best mates, and always will be.

But even so, Jack suggested, maybe he'll stay on here for a bit, if that's all right with her?

'That's fine with me!' Hilary said.

And they smiled at each other. But as they smiled I could hear their thoughts, clashing and contradicting, like runaway trains on the same track heading for a collision:

It will be so wonderful to have the family back together!

How could you? Why would you?

My little boy! Home again!

You're a liar, mum. You're lying to me, and you're lying to yourself!

And Jack had stared at his mother. For a very long time.

He stared at her for a very long time in a way that made Hilary very uncomfortable.

Is he angry with me? Why is he looking at me like that? Have I done something wrong?

Finally Jack looked away.

'Is something wrong, Jack?' Hilary asked.

Oh Mum, Do you really have no self respect?

'I don't know, you tell me,' Jack said to her, in his familiar sarcastic tone. A tone Hilary

had not heard for some months. A tone which sent a shudder of disgust through her body.

Not this again.

'You're upset with me,' Hilary said.

'No I'm not,' Jack said.

Yes I am.

'Don't lie Jack, you are,' said Hilary. 'You're cross with me about something. Come on, spit it out, what is it?'

'You don't love him do you?' Jack said, accusingly.

'What?'

'You know what I mean. Dad. Dad! You don't love him, do you?'

'Love isn't everything in a marriage, my sweet,' Hilary said.

'Yes it fucking well is!' said Jack.

Hilary smiled at that. And she stroked his hand, gently, as if he were still a baby who needed to be touched to know he is alive.

'You worry too much, darling,' Hilary said to her son. 'George is a good dad. A decent husband. A good provider. Great at dinner parties and down the pub. I don't need more.'

'That's crap. You deserve more. Much much more,' Jack told her, savagely.

'Do I?' said Hilary.

'Yes!' said Jack.

And then Hilary had beckoned to him. And he bowed his head downwards, to bridge the height gap. And she kissed his cheek.

'Jack listen to me, please,' she said. 'All that matters is, I love you. I love Shona, I love the fact we are a family. That's all I need to be happy and I am happy. So very happy. So you should be happy *for* me.'

'Bollocks!' said Jack; whilst thinking an even darker word..

But there is a core of steel inside Hilary. Her children rarely see it; but she showed it then.

'No it's the truth,' Hilary said calmly. 'My family is everything to me. You, Shona. You are my family and I love you both more than life itself. George, well. George is just there to keep me company.'

I could tell that Jack wanted to explode in fury. His body was tense. His jaw was clenched. His eyes flashed with rage.

But then, slowly, like a sluggish dawn, Jack realised that she was telling the truth.

Hilary really is happy and content with what she has. And her two children, both of whom she loves, really do mean everything to her.

That was Jack's thunderbolt moment.

It was at that moment that he realised what he should have realised a long time ago. That this woman, his mother, who once was Hilary Fagon and now is Hilary McBride, is the heart and soul and daily inspiration of the family in which he, Jack McBride, will always be cherished for who he is, not for what he might one day achieve.

It was a discovery which unhinged him.

And so Jack suddenly waved his arms in the air. He looked wildly all around him, eyes darting this way and that.

And Hilary looked at her son, her stomach lurching. She was terrified he was having some kind of relapse. Or a stroke even. And she was even more alarmed when he stared anxiously, not at her, but at the wall behind her.

'Where the fuck *are* you, mum?' Jack had asked.

She was utterly bewildered by these words; but I was not.

Outside in Westwood Street, but nowhere else in Westwood, a soft and gentle rain began to fall.

'The devil went down to Georgia,' sings Shona, 'looking for a soul to steal.'

The casino is packed. Some of the punters are listening to her; others are lost in adrenalin rushes as bets are made and cards are dealt and the roulette wheel spins and the ball lands.

Shona looks like a million dollars in a tightly fitting black dress and Priya and Vishaal look like the Blues Brothers in their matching black suits.

The violin dazzles; and once again, the Devil is out-bowed.

The Bogman sits and watches her and broods.

He has achieved an epic victory against his enemies, he is back in the casino, and Shona now sings for him every night. But to my eyes, he does not seem happy. He looks like a man who has lost a kingdom, not gained one.

As the band plays he stares intensely at Shona but her music does not seem to bring him any joy. Not even when Johnny tells the Devil he is a son of a gun and Shona starts to stomp around the stage with a final fiery cadenza; not even then.

Then the Bogman smiles. And his head starts to nod in time with the music. And his eyes caress Shona as she dances and fiddles and sings all at the same time.

And I wonder what is going on in that dark and cruel mind of his.

A few evenings later, when the punters have all gone, the Bogman invites Shona to his top floor apartment for a glass of champagne.

He pours out two glasses of champagne though he cannot actually savour it himself and will soon piss it away as alcoholic urine.

He passes a glass to Shona. She sip her champagne, wearing her happy face.

He sips his own glass of champagne, his sharp blue eyes do not blink, his face is devoid of emotion.

'You were great tonight,' the Bogman says. And then he smiles. His smile is almost credible, now that he has lips.

She takes another sip. She has developed a taste for it; and this is a particularly fine vintage.

I have to quit this fucking place. I'm better than this, Shona thinks.

'Thank you, you're so kind, ' Shona says merrily.

'Your dress looks – wonderful,' the Bogman says.

'Thank you!' Shona says.

'Will you marry me?' the Bogman asks.

Shona laughs.

A moment later she regrets the laugh and the mocking and contemptuous tone that lay embedded within the laugh; but it's too late by then.

'You find that idea absurd?' asks the Bogman coldly.

Yes. You're grotesque. You're a monster!

'Of course not,' she says, smiling as nicely as she can. 'You were kidding, right? You didn't really just ask me to marry me?'

'Yes, you're right, I was kidding,' the Bogman says. 'A funny joke, wasn't it? I have a highly developed sense of humour you know.'

'Yes I know!' she says. And she grins and chuckles, to help him prove his point.

'I still feel guilty, to be honest,' she says. 'About turning down your generous offer, to support my career. To be my promoter. Is there any chance - '

'No.'

'Good. Fine. Because I'm happy here. This place really suits me. I don't want – those other things. Singing in this casino, well, it's my dream comes true,' Shona says, in a voice bubbling with warmth.

'That's good to hear. I was not in fact kidding. Will you marry me?' the Bogman says again.

Shona looks frightened. 'I'm flattered,' she says, carefully. 'And you are, it can't be denied, a very desirable – person. A catch some might say. So I'm very flattered indeed. But no - sorry, no. I can't.'

'Why not?' the Bogman asks; in full interrogator mode.

'Because, although I really like you, I really do, and I think you're kind and talented, I don't – actually - love you?' Shona says, tentatively.

There's a long and very frightening pause. Then the Bogman speaks again.

'Good answer,' he says, warmly. And he smiles at her again. 'Very good answer . But you can't blame a guy for trying, can you?'

And he laughs. He doesn't laugh often but his laugh is resonant and full of mischief.

Shona relaxes. She'd thought the old bastard was going to throw a wobbly but apparently not.

'No you can't,' she says. 'You really are a nice guy and a great boss. We can still be friends, can't we?'

'Of course we can,' the Bogman says.

His eyes explore her face and body, as if assessing her beauty; she pretends she doesn't mind.

I can tell this must be hard for the Bogman. Once he was a handsome man; a sought-after man; a man who women fell in love with at first sight. It must pain him to know that he has become a creature who no woman would willingly caress.

'You're so sweet,' Shona says. 'You really are.'

'Thank you. No one has ever called me sweet before,' the Bogman says.

'Well you are.' And she bathes him in a radiant smile.

What a wanker, she thinks. *What a sad ugly fucking wanker you are.*

'Drink up,' he says.

She drains her glass, and puts it down. 'I was wondering -' she says.

But she never gets to say what she was wondering for the Bogman takes her throat in one hand and strangles her.

He strangles her until she passes out; he does not kill her. Then when she is unconscious he picks her up in his arms and goes down in the lift and puts her body in the boot of his car.

Then he drives to the Glade pub with the now-awake Shona in his boot, pounding at it in the hope of attracting police attention. But no one hears her.

This can't be happening.

I'm so stupid.

Oh fuck!

The Bogman parks near the entrance to the woods. He opens the boot, and throws Shona over his shoulder and carries her wriggling and screaming through the woods until he reaches the site of the shed, his former home. It is barren ground now. The only remnants of his former dwelling are the charred timbers left after the petrol bombing set it aflame. Then he dumps her on the ground and raised a warning finger: do not move.

And Shona stops screaming. She sits up, and looks around at the wilderness around her. She thinks about running away but immediately realises that won't work. So instead, she pretends not to realise she has been abducted, and starts to sweet-talk her captor:

'I'm glad you brought me here. And I realise now, I was a such a fool to turn you down,' Shona says to the Bogman, warmly.

The Bogman says nothing.

'I was an idiot, I was selfish, I was blind, I know that now!' Shona says to the Bogman, humbly.

The Bogman still says nothing.

'You are so – powerful,' Shona says to the Bogman, adoringly. 'And I like that. I really do! I love powerful men!'

It is plausibly done and you have to give her credit for her brave attempt at bullshitting him. But it is too late for all of that.

'Please, I want you to - ' she starts to say. But the Bogman raises a finger again, to silence her.

Then he explains to her calmly, in a dry monotone, what is going to happen.

'Listen carefully,' he says.

And she listens carefully.

Soon it will be dawn, he tells her. A summer solstice dawn.

And dawn is a magical time.

And her body is fertile with magic.

And many maidens have sought this honour; and she should be proud to be offered it.

'Oh fuck *off*,' says Shona, when she has understood what he is planning to do.

'It will be painless,' he says, as if she should be glad about that.

Then he hands her the clothes he had purchased for her to wear at the wedding; which now will never happen. This beautiful and expensive dress will now, he explains, have to serve as a sacrificial gown; the equivalent of the garment worn by the virgin daughters of his people when committing their lives to the gods. And he tactfully averts his eyes so allow her to clothe herself in its splendour..

She immediately makes a run for it; but he catches up with her swiftly, fast as a fox. He grabs her wrist, and drags her along the ground and drops her back on the patch of ground she started from. He shakes his head reprovingly.

Then he punches a tree with one fist.

The tree trembles, then the trunk cracks, and it falls.

Shona takes the point.

He averts his eyes once more; and Shona strips and puts on the clothes he has given her.

And now some time has passed and she is tightly bound and garbed in a gorgeous long white body-hugging gown. And her heart is pounding and her cheeks are damp with tears and she knows no one is going to come and save her. And she is furious for herself for ever trusting this evil fuck who is about to slay her. And she thinks: *Not fair. Not fair. Not fair!*

And it's not. Not fair at all.

Back at the casino, Kane and Cynthia are locking up.

The money is safely stashed in the safe. The chips are in a different safe. The cleaners have been and gone. The roulette tables and baccarat tables and craps table and blackjack tables and poker tables have been cleared.

Kane loves this time. It is the time when he savours his power over, his ownership, of this *thing*.

Cynthia is dressed all in black – black shirt, black trousers, black jacket, no tie. But she has taken the jacket off and rolled up her sleeves to bare her slim tattooed lower arms.

'Great set tonight,' Kane says, as he always says. He is looking at the roulette wheel, aching to spin it one more time.

'It was,' Cynthia says.

'It always is,' says Kane.

'Yeah', Cynthia says.

Kane hears a 'but'.

'But?' he asks.

Cynthia is a tough woman with a soft smile that she rarely reveals. She reveals it now.

'But nothing,' Cynthia says.

'You think we need fresh blood? Different acts?' Kane asks. It is a question that troubles him; even though the audiences never seem to tire of Shona and her band.

'Nope.'

'You think Shona is enough?'

'Yeah. I do.'

'Good.'

'Yeah.'

'But?'

'The way you look at her,' says Cynthia.

Kane is thrown by this.

'What about the way I look at her?' Kane asks.

'You look at her. You do. Don't deny it,' Cynthia says.

'Of course I do. When she sings, yeah. Shona is a great singer,' Kane says.

Cynthia looks at Kane. Her expression says: 'You never look at me like that.'

'Ah,' says Kane.

'Yeah,' says Cynthia.

'I guess we should call it a night,' says Kane.

'Yeah,' says Cynthia.

'Are you implying something?' asks Kane. 'Should I be – are you - '

'What?'

She is looking at him with eyes full of sex.

'Ah,' says Kane.

'Yeah,' says Cynthia.

Finally, he gets it.

'What do I do now?' Kane asks. For he's still a child, when all is said and done.

'You really are a fucking numpty,' says Cynthia.

Kane is remembering when he taught that word to the Bogman. It was on the same occasion when he taught him the word 'statue'.

'I am,' Kane says.

'You are,' Cynthia says.

She has to make the first move. It's not much of a move. She just steps a little bit closer to him. Even he gets the hint. He reaches out and holds her in his arms, as if she were fragile porcelain rather than hard-ass bitch. And they tilt their heads towards each other. And they kiss.

And there I leave them.

And I return to the Horniman Woods, where Shona is about to be murdered.

The aspen leaves shiver. The oak leaves shiver. The birch leaves shiver. The ground trembles.

This is all me.

Shona is about to be murdered and I have known her since she was a tiny girl and I have followed her life through all her challenging insecure years until the day she found her voice and her gift and now she is happy and now she is brilliant and now she is a radiant star with the power to light up the world; and now she will die .

And all this excites me.

This will be a ritual murder of a kind that has not been seen in my woods for many millennia. This soul fasting ceremony will, so the Bogman has explained to her, bond the two of them closer together than any man and wife. And her subsequent execution will give him even greater power. Divine power, in fact, or so he believes.

In fact his faith is rank superstition. Ritual murder does nothing to enhance magic and never has. But the Bogman doesn't know that; and his folly amuses me.

He has set the scene well, though, I'll grant him that.

Shona has been tethered with a rope on each of her wrists, and the Bogman has fastened the two ropes to two neighbouring trees, making her into a human crucifix. Her white gown is made of the finest silk and was hand made by a bridal gown maker working through the night. Shona wears sandals and has a necklace of red rubies around her neck and a white headband to keep her hair off her face and she has been made up expertly by the Bogman himself. It is all in all a masterly tableau. She looks sublime.

I slip into Shona's mind and I pry, shamelessly, as her thoughts rage.

Don't look at me like that, you ugly bastard! she is thinking, with wild intensity.

Please, do what you like to me, just don't – don't look at me!

Don't look at me like – Don't - that's how Ben looked at me! As if I was just – an object. His object. Don't look at me like that! Don't look at me at all!

But the Bogman continues to look at her; at his sacred artefact.

And all this while she is wrestling with her bonds, her arms thick-veined with effort. And from her lips she spews forth a torrent of offensive and angry comments:

'You useless fucking cunt!' she screams.

'You small-dicked turd-stained piece of shit!' she yells.

'You can kill me but you can't crush my soul, you ugly fucking fuckwit!' she rasps. For by now she is starting to lose her voice.

But he is set on his course. Crazy and cruel as it is.

I observe all this with considerable pleasure. *This* is why I resurrected the Bogman. Not to watch him doing DIY in the middle of an obscure glade, but to be the monster that he is. To warm my cold soul with horrors. For otherwise, my endless life will be drab and unbearable.

Oh it's spring again!

Hmm, that summer sun is so bright; just as it always is, each and every summer!

Ah I see the squirrels are gathering their autumn nuts once more!

And now it's winter again.

And now winter has passed and it is once more Spring.

Oho, the cherry trees are starting to bud again!

I DO NOT FUCKING CARE.

And yes, I do feel sorry for Shona, that lovely pretty girl who is about to be brutally murdered by a madman in the woods.

And that pang of sorrow is also, for me, a source of intense delight.

Thank you Shona. For gifting me with your pain.

Just before dawn the Bogman strips naked again and sits down on his haunches, and calmly offers Shona a deal.

'Fuck off,' she says.

She looks truly magnificent, it must be said. Standing between two giant trees; her bare arms outstretched, her body straining against her bonds, her eyes blazing with rage.

'Please. Be sensible. Listen to me,' the Bogman says patiently.

As if she has a choice.

'What is the deal?' She stares into his blue eyes which are bottomless and she dares to hope.

He makes her wait and her hope starts to wither and diminish.

And then he offers her his deal.

The deal is this: He wants her to sing.

And if she willingly assents to be sacrificed by him and if she sings for him with joy in her voice as she is about to be sacrificed, and if she continues singing as he starts to butcher her; then he will leave her family alive.

But, he explains carefully and brutally, if she continues to resist, and if she continues to swear like a drunken trooper – then he will slay her brother and her mother and her father and all the rest of her family in terrible ways.

When she hears the Bogman's deal Shona considers it for a little while. Then she nods. And she smiles. And she does not weep. For she is well beyond weeping by now.

Deal done! Her life is over! She will sing. So let the sacrifice commence.

So she conveys, with her silent nod.

But all this while her thoughts are in turmoil.

If only Hamid were here to rescue me, she is thinking.

If only I had blanked this ugly fucking creature from the start.

If only I had refused to sing at the casino!

If only I had agreed to marry this bastard!

Maybe someone has heard me screaming? Maybe the cops are on the way?

Maybe I'll be saved in the nick of time?

Maybe I can break free of my bonds and escape?

Maybe – maybe – maybe -

But there is no maybe. There is no nick of time. No one will rescue her. She will die, tragically and beautifully, in my woods.

The sun rises and Shona begins to sing.

She sings a Roberta Flack classic, 'Killing Me Softly With Your Song'. Her voice is lovelier and richer than ever. It is going to be a lovely warm day today, I can tell. The dawn sky slowly reddens. A thrush starts singing. A robin joins in. The Bogman stands with a knife by his side, his brown naked body dappled by the rosy light. The sun tips up over the horizon. The white flowers of a mountain ash tree burn like beacons.

Then the Bogman howls, like an animal.

Shona stops singing. Her throat is blocked with fear. The notes won't come out. But then she tries again, and she sings the next verse; with a cracked voice and duff notes, but still she sings:

Strumming my pain with his fingers
Singing my life with his words
Killing me softly with his song
Killing me softly with his song
Telling my whole life with his words
Killing me softly - with his song!

I feel proud of her. Very proud indeed.

And so I decide to encourage her a little, on this day of her death.

The two trees to which she are tethered are crab apple trees, which burst forth with purple blossoms throughout the spring but are now no longer in flower. But at my bidding, new buds start to bud.

A few moments later, and fresh stalks emerge from the buds like licking tongues; and from thence, a host of richly coloured amaranthine flowers emerge and swiftly bloom.

Then more flowers blossom forth until they cover the bark of each of the two trees, the green petioles elongating their way along the rope strands as they hunt the source of the song; for Shona's melody has become their sun.

And when they reach her, the flower stalks creep their way along her arms and around her neck until her face is nestled in flowers. And the blossoming flowers weep nectar upon her cheeks..

And as the flowers caress her, her voice becomes still richer and even more beautiful. Killing us softly with her song. Her slim and lovely body illumined by the dark red light of dawn.

Her beautiful face enwrapped in purple flowers.

My Shona!

And at that moment the ropes which bind her arms are suddenly doused in acidic sap; a toxic juice which just a few moments ago was spat out by the machineel tree that grows by the nearby marshland, and was wafted on the wind until it reached this glade, where it now drizzles down upon her bonds. Corroding the twine and making it steam but leaving her hands and arms untouched.

And she tugs. And tugs. And the brittle ropes break, and she is free. Though she is still cradled from face to feet in blooms as richly coloured as a cardinal's robe.

The Bogman is disconcerted by this unexpected turn of events. But he knows she cannot run away from him. So he takes a step towards her, holding his ritual murder knife. And he curses the infernal and capricious gods for their fickleness, and tells them he will not be cowed.

He curses *me*, in other words!

'Fuck the gods!' he screams.

No. No.

'FUCK THE FUCKING GODS!' he screams.

How dare you!

And a voice inside me keeps screaming this one word: No!

And some small and hitherto neglected part of me tells me: I *do* care. I do!

And I remember all the years I have watched Shona and seen her grow and change and become the person she is today; and it feels too soon. Too soon for her to die.

But above all else, I am enraged that this ignorant peaty corpse thinks he can challenge the pagan gods. The great gods of nature, amongst whom I am the least, a sapling in a forest of giant oaks.

Fuck you back, Bogman!

And the ground below him shifts, and the Bogman almost loses his balance. He looks around warily. He is standing on firm soil, he can see there is no one near him. But the ground shifts again, and he sways, like a mariner on a ship in a storm.

Beneath the soil are roots. Deep roots, encased by a dense layer of fungus that runs under the soil all the way from here to the New Forest in one direction, and to the orchards of Kent in the other direction; and all the way north to the outskirts of Sherwood Forest.

The ground beneath him is a single living organism in other words. And it does not like the Bogman because I do not like the Bogman.

And so, before he can move, long-buried roots shoot up out of the ground and capture his body in a gnarly embrace; and he becomes trapped by the giant roots of living and long-dead trees.

And then the roots wrap themselves around and around him like bandages upon an Egyptian mummy. And the roots that now hold him fast spawn layers of xylem that encircle him and crush him.

And the xylem in turn becomes garbed in a cloak of phloem which encircles the xylem, creating a further cage for the Bogman.

And the phloem births a thick sheath of bark that encircles *it*.

And so a tree grows. Inching upwards. Then soaring upwards, upwards towards the sky in this sun-drenched clearing, growing and thickening fast; until it is as high as the highest pine in the Old Park.

But this is not a pine, it is not an oak; it is a tree that has never existed before. A tree I have created. It is a tree which grows and flourishes and spawns myriad branches but which will never bud and never turn green and never flower and never drop seeds and never spill pollen into the air or into the mouths of hungry insects.

It is the Dead Tree of Westwood.

And deep in its heartwood is the Bogman; howling in silent rage.

And there he will stay for all of time. The bastard!

That's when Shona screams.

And I realise that my rage has overwhelmed me and I force myself to be calm. I do not want to cause another Great Storm.

Shona screams again. She is hysterical, turning around on the spot, purple flowers falling from her white-garbed body, looking for the unknown assailant of the monster who had been about to kill her. Terrified beyond all measure but also utterly confused.

It slowly dawns on her: A miracle has happened. She has survived certain death. Her heart is pounding like the drum solo on one of the rock tracks she so beautifully performs.

'What the fuck, what the fuck,' she is shouting.

And *now* what do I do? I wonder.

She is still staring all around, looking for her impossible saviour. 'Show yourself, whoever you are, whoever did this. Show yourself!' she shouts.

I say nothing.

'Who are you?' she screams.

I say nothing.

'Where are you?' she screams.

I say nothing.

'Are you going to kill me too?' she weeps.

No, I decide, and she flinches.

'No?' Shona says.

I am startled. No human has ever before heard my thoughts.

No, I think.

She weeps with relief.

I will let you go, I think.

Thank you, she thinks.

She is smart; she knows I can hear her thoughts as well as her words.

But you must never speak of what has happened today, I think at her, sternly. *Otherwise, I shall – I shall – well, I shall have to kill you.*

I am naught but a sapling; and I am fearful of the wrath of the great pagan gods who never would have spared a sweet damsel from her doom, as I just did.

I won't ever speak of what has happened today, she thinks.

Her face is full of tentative joy. I try to harden my heart; I do not succeed.

What is your name? she thinks.

I do not answer her. Because I do not know. I have never had a name, nor any need for one.

Please, tell me? she thinks.

Go, before I change my mind, I think.

What is your name?

'I am,' I say out loud, and I have never spoken out loud before, and the sound makes the leaves in the trees tremble and shiver: 'I am what I am.' But that answer doesn't satisfy her, or me. So I try again: 'I am the Great West Wood.'

She nods. And she smiles at me.

Then Shona carefully strips off her robe of flowers and her white gown and changes back into her gig clothes. She slips on a pair of trainers, then turns towards the clearing.

'Goodbye,' she says, out loud.

Wait, I think.

She pauses. Afraid, no doubt, that I have changed my mind and that I will now kill her.

Finish your song, I tell her.

'Not now,' she tells me, her lips dry. 'Later.'

When?

'When I am ready. But I promise, I will come to you. I will return.'

I think about it. It is a good answer. *Go now.*

And she walks back to the centre of Westwood which takes her a good while and by the time she gets to the bus depot she is famished so she goes into the French café and buys a baguette and chips.

She is trembling so badly she cannot use a fork so she eats her chips with her bare hands. She orders a glass of wine and downs it in one. Then she eats the baguette. Once she has some food inside her, she starts to return to something resembling normality.

I am all around her still of course. I am in the trees outside the café. I am in the soil beneath the floor upon which her table rests. I am with her, and in her thoughts, and I am glad she is alive. It won't be for long, I know that. In a blink of my eye, if I had an eye, she will be old and soon after that, she will be dead. But at least she will live just a little longer and that pleases me.

And I know that she will honour her promise. Not today, not this month, but soon. She will return to the Great West Wood and she will stand among my trees and she will sing to me. Just for me.

I look forward, Shona, to your song.

Chapter 26

This week it has been glorious dawn all day and every day in Westwood.

Some time has passed since that other dawn, the summer solstice dawn, when Shona sang and the Bogman raised a knife to slay her. And when I trapped him inside a tree, a huge leafless and budless tree which shakes even when there is no wind because of the howling of the monster trapped within.

The first dawn of this week of dawns came on Sunday at about six am. Fingers of red fire lit up the sky and if you were awake early enough to witness it you would have marvelled at the richness of the colours and the way the world rippled with the touch of the sun's rays. It was a dazzling orange dawn casting a golden glow upon the clouds as if a great fire beneath the horizon was billowing up flames.

And as the dawn progressed the sky darkened, and became purple in hue, and the streaks of yellow became broader, like the rings of a giant tree.

Then just as the purple sky started turning into a blue sky, why! a rich scarlet radiance was cast upon the scene once more. And the blue sky was darkened once again. And a red dawn spat pale pink herring bones upon the clouds, like brush strokes; until eventually the pink ribs slowly vanished and the sky began to turn blue again -

And then the blueness turned to blackness and red coals glowed on the horizon and an impasto of fiery paint was smudged upon the cloudy sky. And then the colours faded; and it all started over.

And over.

For seven days the sky has been a kaleidoscope of colours. The streets lights are on anyway 24/7 but the multi-coloured hues of the dawn light are disconcerting on a prolonged basis and most people wear sunglasses now. The view across London from Westwood is glorious as the sun repeatedly rises over the City skyscape. And the view of the dawn over the Old Park from the Sculpture Park is also glorious. And the view of the sunrise over Eastern England from the top of the forest canopies in Old Park is even more glorious. Indeed, wherever you go in Westwood, the views are glorious; and if the incessant sublimity of it all doesn't cease soon there is going to be a fucking riot.

Jack used to love walking around the park in the early morning light but now he is obliged to walk at dawn. He is using his stick less and less. The pain in his hips is becoming bearable and he is in daily contact with Shakil. There is vague talk about him going back to Southampton but Jack is feeling settled in Westwood now; he has a role here. He is the one who holds the family together. From this moment on it will be his job to remember all the birthdays and the anniversaries and to make a fuss whenever there is good news.

One day at the fishing lake he meets a young woman who is walking her dog at dawn before going to work as a barmaid for the lunchtime shift in the Saxon Arms. Her name is Melissa and although Jack doesn't like this particular dog he pretends to love it so he can get to know her. They chat and she learns all about his accident and his time in Southampton hanging out with students and the fact he has been accepted for a university place at Goldsmiths on a Foundation Degree.

Melissa thinks Jack is charming and very funny and she admires how he bears his disability with such good cheer. So when he invites her for a drink that evening she is happy to say yes. And when they emerge from the pub later that night the dawn light dapples on the pavement and the drizzle creates tall rainbows that they walk through on their way to her house. And one thing leads to another, and they end up in bed together.

In the morning it is still dawn; and that's fine because Jack has never felt so happy and Melissa is feeling pretty good too. There are many things badly wrong with Jack's body; but it is still a thing of beauty, and I think she is falling in love with him.

And as for Jack; he never tires of the beauty of the dawn light, because he can now see each and every colour. His black and white days are over; and the people he loves are all visible to him.

Shona meanwhile has moved to a flat in Central, in the area called Fitzrovia. She has a record deal now and often sings in a place called Ronnie Scott's, which I have learned is a small and fashionable jazz venue. Audiences are small and the pay is not great; all of which suggests to me she is never going to be a big rock star playing stadium gigs like Beyoncé. She will merely be a great musician, and an inspiration to all who hear her. And perhaps for her that will be enough.

But when she heard about the miraculous week of dawns Shona returned to Westwood, and moved back into her box room. And last night she came to me and she sang. She sang a capella, in the quietest part of my woods, from dawn till dawn; in other words, for about twelve hours. Some jazz, some soul, and her newest song which she has just composed, called Spirit of the Woods, which has no lyrics yet, but has a marvellous melody. And she promised she will come again – maybe next Spring?

And now, twelve hours later, Shona is having her breakfast in 44 Westwood Street and Grandpa Maybe is on a bus travelling into Westwood to visit his family but the bus driver has to stop because the dawn light is giving him a migraine. So Grandpa Maybe gets off the bus and shrugs his shoulders and starts to walk.

Grandpa Maybe's son Malcolm and Malcolm's wife Malaika are also there at the breakfast table in the McBride house, chatting with their granddaughter Shona. They have conquered their aversion to Westwood and are regular visitors now. But when the day is done they will be staying over at the Travelodge in Anerley, out of range of any toadstorms.

Hilary and George are getting on well. He still has affairs but truth to tell, his heart isn't in it any more. He is slowly realising he prefers being with Hilary to being with all these other women. He is also slowly realising that he is not God's gift to womankind after all.

Don't fuck it up this time, he often tells himself. *You've landed on your feet here, pal, just don't fuck it up.*

And Hilary is happy. She just is. She's a naturally happy person, both her children are happy, her adopted son St John Featherstone is happy; and she has George just where she wants him. And each year, a new group of small children appears in her classroom and even when they are being incredibly bloody annoying, they bring joy into her life.

The Oldest Tree is just a memory, but after the week of rain that I inflicted on the area, the new development was cancelled. And though the Tree itself is gone there are stirrings upon the woodchip that was scattered when it was so brutally cut down. A seed is growing there, on a bed of its own flesh. And one day as the dawn light warms it, the seed trembles and sprouts and a sapling emerges and within hours the sapling has grown into a small shrub and the shrub turns into a tiny tree and the tree spreads its foliage and the leaves and branches grow and the trunk thickens and nudges ever upwards.

And within seven days, on the day when the week of dawns ends, the Youngest Tree in Westwood is taller than the McBride's house; and it is growing still.

Don has died; his heart gave out, poor man. And Megan was astonished to find he had bequeathed her all his savings, in the region of sixty thousand pounds, and his house. She chose to move in there, to a place where she is surrounded by memories, and the almost inaudible voice of Don's ghost.

Put your feet up love, you deserve it.

'Thank you, Don.'

Mickey is still on the run from the police, but the chances of them coming to Westwood are even slimmer these days; the stories of floods and hurricanes and endless dawns have persuaded New Scotland Yard to turn a blind eye to anything but the most extreme cases of criminality in Westwood. But that doesn't mean it has become a lawless and violent place to live; far from it.

In Westwood, these days, you see, *I* am the law.

Meanwhile Billy Armstrong has moved to North London where he is now a Detective Sergeant; and the case files on the various murder investigations he worked on in Westwood have been closed. The prime suspect for the London Heights massacre, the murder of Duncan Colthorpe, the murders of the two Morton brothers, Psycho and Dave, the murders of three freelance security guards found buried in the gardens of the Glade public house, and fifteen other unsolved homicides in which only body parts have been recovered, has slipped through their fingers and cannot be found. An Interpol arrest for a serial killer who has been nicknamed 'the Bogman' has been circulated; but there is no active investigation in progress.

Billy's mother Tanya is pregnant, even though she is in her forties, and she is over the moon. Bless her; she's a good mum.

Her son Kane still runs the casino in Westwood with Cynthia acting as both his manager and his lover; and he and Tanya have been reconciled. He joins her at her flat in London Heights for the birthday parties for all her kids, his half-brothers and half-sisters; and he always brings chocolate and tells stupid jokes which the kids all love. And every now and then Tanya goes to see Kane at the casino and has a flutter on the roulette table, with chips Cynthia gives her.

Toby, the floating boy, is growing up; he is nine years old now. That's him up there, high up in the sky; magically turned into a firework by the dazzling orange light of dawn.

The teashop in Fairyhill Road is a roaring success and all talk of eviction and fines has been forgotten, ever since Mr Morecambe vanished from this world. The shop now has a back garden area, built on what used to be a patch of ground between the teashop and the library that was formerly the size of a shoebox. But with a bit of TLC and a dash of fairy magic the shoebox of land has become a spacious tea garden, with a dozen tables and a fountain. Camilla and Alice hired St John Featherstone to create the garden from scratch, which he did for no fee. And he is often there at teatime with his girlfriend Daniela, who is a labourer working for the building firm that is George McBride's nemesis.

Daniela, who initially assumed that Camilla and Alice were sisters - how adorable! - has become a favourite customer at the teashop, and she has wholly won St John's heart. There are notions of wedding bells in both their minds, but St John takes care never to ask Daniela to marry him when they are in the café. Because that would spoil it really.

And the arboreal grave of the Bogman is untended and much feared because of the way The Dead Tree shakes and trembles even on the stillest of days. And if you look among the charred cinders of what used to be his shed you will see, glittering in the dawn light, the Bogman's abandoned golden crown.

Welcome to Westwood.

THE END

Copyright

Published by Hellbooks in 2025

HELLBOOKS

Printed in Dunstable, United Kingdom